Providence, VA

Michael Abraham

Providence, VA

A novel

Pocahontas Press
Blacksburg, Virginia

Also by Michael Abraham

The Spine of the Virginias,
Journeys along the border of Virginia and West Virginia

Harmonic Highways,
Exploring Virginia's Crooked Road

Union, WV
A novel of loss, healing, and redemption in
contemporary Appalachia

War, WV
A fight for justice in the Appalachian coalfields

For updates and ordering information on the author's books,
excerpts, and sample chapters, please visit his website at:
http://www.bikemike.name/

The author can be reached by email at:
<bikemike@nrvunwired.net>

Providence, VA

Copyright © 2012 by Michael Abraham

These songs Copyright © 2011 by Martha Spencer, used by permission:
Home is Where the Fiddle Rings
Blown Back with the Breeze
A Lonely Old Man
Tree of Heaven
Rest for the Wicked

ISBN 0-926487-63-9

Cover photograph by Hal Brainerd
Author photograph by Tracy Roberts
Book design by Michael Abraham

Printed in the United States of America

Pocahontas Press
www.pocahontaspress.com

To Jane and Whitney Abraham,
the two most important people in my life.

Acknowledgements

I am deeply indebted to many people who supported my effort. My editors worked countless hours to help me make my book readable, relevant, and grammatically correct.

Jane Abraham, Blacksburg, Virginia
Mary Ann Johnson, Blacksburg, Virginia
Sally Shupe, Newport, Virginia
Bill Smith, Big Stone Gap, Virginia

I am also indebted to the people who helped me understand classical and Appalachian music, midwifery, Christianity and Judaism, trauma psychology, the history and culture of Grayson County, Virginia, Electromagnetic Pulse, and other technical aspects of the book. I thank them.

Richard Alvarez, Blacksburg, Virginia
Jerry Beasley, Christiansburg, Virginia
Bud Bennett, Blacksburg, Virginia
Kristi Blake, Blacksburg, Virginia
Claire Cannon, Blacksburg, Virginia
Katherine Chantal, Floyd, Virginia
Floyd Childress III, Christiansburg, Virginia
June Collier, Elk Creek, Virginia
Richard Cook, Roanoke, Virginia
C. Y. Davis, Blacksburg, Virginia
David Ehrlich, Blacksburg, Virginia
Teresa Ehrlich, Blacksburg, Virginia
Mark Fendig, Mouth of Wilson, Virginia
Laura George, Independence, Virginia
Jerry Gilmore, Roanoke, Virginia
Ibby Taylor Greer, Rocky Mount, Virginia
Don Hodges, Fries, Virginia
John Paul Houston, Floyd, Virginia
Russell Jones, Blacksburg, Virginia
Eddie Kendall, Pembroke, Virginia

Frank Levering, Cana, Virginia
Renzo Loza, La Paz, Bolivia
Jerry Moles, Independence, Virginia
Bob Pearsall, Christiansburg, Virginia
Benjamin Sax, Blacksburg, Virginia
Glenn Skutt, Blacksburg, Virginia
Martha Spencer, Whitetop, Virginia
Bailey Steele, Blacksburg, Virginia
Sam Steffens, Floyd, Virginia
Susan E. Stevens, Blacksburg, Virginia
Joanne Sutton, Milford, Massachusetts
Fred Swedberg, Orange, Massachusetts
Hope Taylor, Fries, Virginia
Charles Thomas, Fries, Virginia
Jim Thorp, Blacksburg, Virginia
Barbara Trammell, Galax, Virginia
Wanda Vest, Check, Virginia
Micah Winefeld, Boones Mill, Virginia
Nicolás Zalles, Santa Cruz, Bolivia

I give special thanks to Hal Brainerd who provided the cover
photograph, Martha Spencer who provided the song lyrics, and Bob
Pearsall who provided the maps.

Southwest Virginia and the environs of Providence, VA

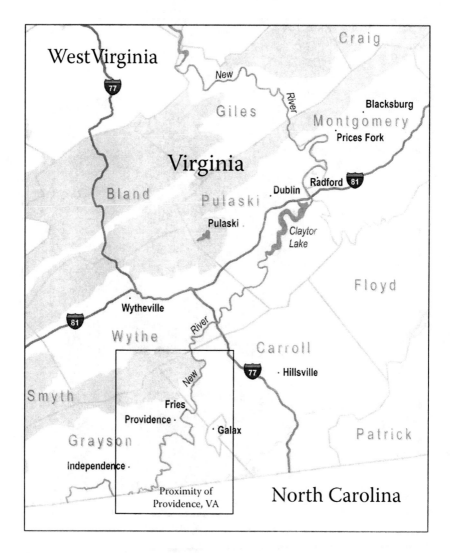

Proximity of
Providence, VA

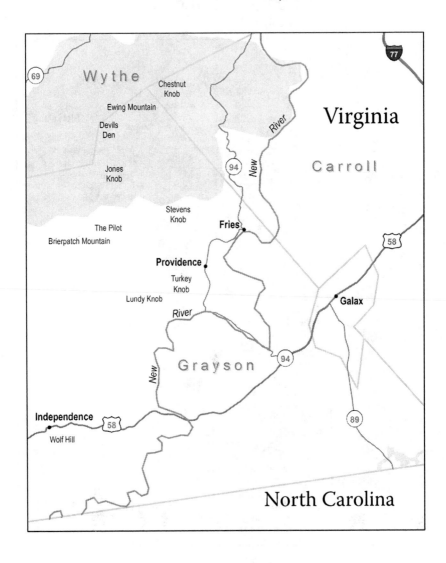

Providence, VA

Prelude: Galax

Monday, August 13

SAMANTHA FELT HER EYES rolling gently around the inside of her eye sockets as her brain waves made the every-morning transition from dreams to waking conscious thought. This morning, her dreams of Mozart fugues gave way to the cheerful expectation of a day she had looked forward to for months.

She opened her eyes to a sky of red, the inside ceiling of her tent being illuminated by the warming rays of a rising summer sun. She gave a gentle nudge to Ella O'Connor, still dozing peacefully beside her and said, "Are you awake yet?"

"I wasn't until now," said the drowsy woman, whose auburn hair contrasted with her blue sleeping bag.

"I'm sorry," Sammy confessed. "I'm just eager to get up and rock 'n roll!"

"You go ahead. I'd like to sleep for another 15 or 20 minutes."

Sammy emerged from her sleeping bag. She unzipped her travel bag and grabbed her toilet kit and a fresh change of clothes. She unzipped the tent and emerged into the moisture-laden summer day.

"Good morning, Miss Sammy," said a man she had met the night before, who at that point was sitting in a lawn chair nearby, under an expansive canopy. "How are you?"

"I am so sorry," she replied. "I'm just fine, but I apologize for not remembering your name. It was so late when we arrived last night and I certainly remember you, but not your name."

"No worries. Jamaal Hurt Winston, at your service. Please sit down and let's get better acquainted."

"I'd love to," she giggled. "But let me make a potty stop first."

"There's a row of plastic outhouses over there," he said, pointing across the way.

As she walked over and then back, several people nodded at her courteously. Upon her return, Jamaal invited to her to sit in a maroon mesh chair with a "VT" logo that still had an empty beer can in the holster of one of the armrests. She attempted to start where she left off. "I guess you remember my name is Sammy – Samantha Reisinger."

"Didn't you say you live in New Jersey?"

"Yes, I'm almost 18 years old. I just graduated from high school, and I'll be attending music school in Winston-Salem, North Carolina, next month. How about yourself?"

"I'm from Washington, DC. I'm an economics professor at Georgetown University. I come from a long line of musicians. Economics is my profession, but music is my hobby. What brings you here?"

"Three years ago, I was vacationing in Florida with my parents. We went to a music festival. One band was playing some music that was foreign to me. I talked to the violinist after the show and he said, 'I'm not a violinist. I'm a fiddler.' His genre was traditional Appalachian music. I really liked it," she smiled.

"I've been going to traditional music conventions for years," he admitted. "I like it, too."

"So," she continued, "last year, mom and dad took me to a small fiddler's convention in Pennsylvania. I met Terry and Alice Mullins and they told me that the mountaintop experience for traditional Appalachian music was this convention, the Galax Old Fiddlers Convention. They invited me to come this year. I decided that instant that I wanted to go."

"Are your parents here? I don't recall meeting them."

"No. Mom and dad promised to bring me here for a graduation present from high school, but a couple of weeks ago, dad got called out of the country for his job and mom decided to go with him. So they hired Ella to drive me here and be my chaperone. She is still in the tent sleeping."

"Oh yes, I remember meeting her last night," he sipped his coffee.

"Are you here alone?"

"Yes. My wife dropped me off here yesterday and she is on her way to spend some time with her niece in Jackson, Mississippi. She will pick me up on Sunday on her way home. I am a friend of Pike McConnell's. Did you meet him?"

"I think so. I met several people last night. But it was dark and I was tired…" she admitted, settling deep into the folding chair and crossing her legs.

"I guess he is still asleep, too. He and I met at a banjo exhibit a few years ago in Washington, DC. He is a professor as well. He teaches engineering. He's my connection to this little group."

"Pardon me for this, but I can't help but notice that you are, well…"

"Black. Yup, it seems like a permanent thing."

"Forgive me; I didn't mean it like that. It's not that I haven't seen black people before, but I doubt there are many blacks here in Galax." She looked at his long, dreadlock hair, streaming around his face. He was of average height, thin but well muscled, with a kindly face that she found appealing. His eyes were of such a deep brown that his irises melded with his pupils.

"I'm sure you're right. But I don't mind being a minority. I am a man of peace and faith. I make a point of treating everyone I meet with respect and friendship."

"So what brought you here to Galax?" she inquired.

"As I said, Pike suggested it. But I'd heard of this Fiddlers Convention before and already had an interest. Many of my relatives are musicians. I grew up in Memphis which has a vibrant music scene. My grandfather, John Hurt, was a sharecropper in Mississippi but he became relatively famous in his later years as he began to be discovered in the early 1960s by a new generation of folk musicians. I got a degree in business from American University and then got my doctorate in economics at Northwestern. I have been teaching now in Washington, DC for 15 years. Each summer, I spend a week or two on the road on musical heritage journeys.

"I can't help but notice that belong to a minority group as well," he said while looking at the Star of David pendant hanging from her necklace.

"Oy gevalt! Yeah, I guess so. More so down here than back home in New Jersey, I suspect."

He laughed at her use of Yiddish.

"Good morning, campers!" exclaimed a tall, athletic, handsome man as he emerged from his tent and walked to join Sammy and Jamaal. "How did you sleep?"

"Good morning back at-cha!" said Jamaal to Terry.

Sammy brushed her long, curly, jet black hair from the edges of her face, "Last night was such a blur. I was so tired on the long drive here that by the time we said our quick hellos and got our tent set up, the Sandman visited me very quickly. I'm sure I won't remember anyone I met last night. Please re-introduce me to everyone, would you?"

"Sure!" said Terry cheerfully.

"Is Alice awake yet?" Sammy inquired.

"No," said Terry about his wife. "She said she wanted to sleep for just a few more minutes. How about Ella?"

"She said the same thing. She'll probably be up soon," said Sammy.

"Did you sleep okay, Jamaal?"

"I slept great, thanks. Sammy and I have been getting acquainted and talking about her interest in traditional Appalachian music. She said that you and Alice invited her here."

"Yup, Alice and I were in Pennsylvania attending her nephew's wedding. We stayed a few extra days and attended a fiddlers' convention up there. Sammy was in the audience next to me. At intermission, we struck up a conversation. Don't let Alice hear me say this, but I think I fell in love that very moment."

Sammy smiled and blushed a bit.

Jamaal said, "I have been enchanted myself. It was good of you to drag her down here."

"Hello, everyone," said Alice Mullins as she joined the growing conversation. She wore a maroon shirt that said, "Roanoke College" on it. "I hope everyone got some sleep last night. They don't turn off these high street lamps and so it never really feels quite like night time around here."

Sammy said, "I get the impression that few people get their full eight hours of sleep here."

Alice said, combing her long auburn hair with a heavy black brush, "You got that right!"

Terry poured himself some coffee and said, "Now that you're here, Sammy, you'll need to understand the routine. You have a jam session with friends in the morning, the morning being about noon. You nap from two o'clock until four o'clock in the afternoon, if it's not too hot. Then you get up and jam some more. We all throw together some dinner sometime between six and eight o'clock. Then you go on stage and perform. Then you come back to camp and jam some more until the wee hours of the morning. Then you stumble to your tent and try to get some sleep. Then repeat."

Alice concurred. "This happens every day for a week and some people have been coming here for 30, 40, and in some cases 50 years."

Jamaal laughed, "How long have you been coming?"

Terry thought for a moment. "Close to 30 years. I came with my folks when I was a kid growing up in Christiansburg."

Alice smiled. "When Terry and I met, he dragged me here for the first time. In those days, we could bring our car here into Felts Park on Monday or Tuesday or sometimes even Wednesday and still find a place to camp. It has gotten so crowded over the years that people are lined up out on Main Street for two or three days prior to the official opening of the gates on Sunday morning. It looks like the Oklahoma Land Rush as people scurry inside to find their favorite spot to camp. Electrical hookups are a prized commodity. People bring long extension cords to power to their camp area from the limited number of distribution poles."

Terry nodded. "I love it here. It is a 100-percent authentic, genuine American experience. For some local people, this is the only vacation they ever do. They come here every year."

"Good morning, all!" exclaimed Ella as she emerged from her tent. "How is everyone this morning?"

"Couldn't be better," said Terry. "Come and join us. Would you like some coffee?"

"Thanks, but what I would really like is a bathroom and shower.

Where are the bathrooms?" she asked Alice.

"The portable outhouses are all over the place. But there is only one bathroom with running water. It is over that way," Alice stood and pointed to the southwest.

"Well," Ella said, "nature is calling and so I must answer. Come along with me, Sammy."

The two New Jerseyans gathered their towels and clean clothes and then walked together down the designated aisle separating the various camping areas. The convention site was a large open, mostly grassy field, the grass being interrupted at the infield dirt of two baseball diamonds. Everyone they walked past had a friendly greeting for them.

The bathroom building was large with two entrances each for men and women. There was a bench outside where people could wait. Inside, there were two sinks and several commodes, but only two showers per gender. Another woman was just leaving as they arrived and Ella took her shower first. Outside, Sammy sat on the bench and looked over the field of campers. Several people had brought tall poles from which various flags – state, Confederate, and the United States – along with an assortment of windsocks, hung lazily in the gentle breeze. A large woman carrying a towel and a change of clothes sat beside Sammy. "Where you from, sweetheart?"

"I'm from New Jersey," Sammy replied, taken aback by the woman's overtness. "How about yourself?"

"Oh, I live just over the border in Mount Airy. It's supposed to be the town that inspired Andy Griffith's town of Mayberry in his show. He's from Mount Airy and lots of folks know him." She crossed her legs and Sammy noticed that much of her body was covered in tattoos. "You're too young to even know what I'm talking about." She was quiet for a moment, and then said, "It is amazing to me how far people will come to attend this event. For years and years, it seemed like it was just us locals. Somehow, in recent years, we've gotten trendy. What do you play?"

"Violin."

The woman chuckled a little bit under her breath and Sammy

wished she had said, "fiddle."

"Okay, Sammy," exclaimed Ella, emerging from the bathhouse. She wore a T-shirt that said, "New York Giants" and a pair of jeans. She had a white and blue checkered towel around her hair. "You're next. I'll meet you back in camp."

Sammy said goodbye to the tattooed woman and entered the dimly lit room. She disrobed, entered the austere cinder-block shower stall and pulled the plastic curtain shut. She was shocked as a stream of cold water emerged from the single spout with no provisions for warm water. As her skin prickled, she was irritated by the primitive facilities. She washed quickly.

By the time Sammy arrived back in camp, Terry and Alice's group had gathered. Several vehicles rimmed the area, the largest being a small, aged bus looking like something once used at a military base to shuttle troops around. It was painted in jungle camouflage. Interspersed with the vehicles were several tents and pop-up campers. In the center were kitchen and dining areas, covered by canopies. Folding chairs of every description were strewn about, as were banjos and guitars. An upright bass lay sideways in the grass.

A heavy man had his back to the group as he tended a gas-powered camping stove. Everyone was having French toast, link sausages, and coffee for breakfast. Terry, thoughtful as always, greeted her re-arrival by saying, "Come sit down, Sammy, and let me reintroduce you to everyone."

Pointing to a tall, balding man holding a banjo, Terry said, "This is Quint Thompson. He is a pharmacist over in Fries. That is a little community on the New River about eight miles from here. Most of the folks we're camping with are from over there."

She looked at him and nodded her head.

"He's a preacher, too. Ain't that right, Quint?"

"Yup," said the man with a baritone voice. "I've got a little congregation near Fries in a place called Providence. It isn't even on the state map."

"This fellow with his back to you is Keene Campbell. He runs an auto shop in Fries." The man turned and touched his right index finger to his baseball-style cap that said, "3rd Marine Division, Vietnam Veteran" on it.

"Mornin' young lady. Want some French toast?"

"Yes, please."

"One more for me, too," said Ella, who sat comfortably nearby.

Terry continued, now teasing Keene, "He's got a singing voice you won't believe. If he weren't such a hick, he'd be an opera star."

He was above average height, in his sixties, Sammy guessed. He had a belly as round as a pregnant woman. An unlit but partially burned cigar hung from his mouth. His camouflage T-shirt matched the paint of the bus, which she assumed to be his.

"Watch yourself, buster. If you don't mind your manners when talking to old folks, I may just knock you into next Thursday," the sexagenarian quipped.

Terry shrugged off the threat and pointed at the next person in the circle, "This is Shane Wilkins. Shane goes to VMI. How far along are you?"

"I'll be starting my junior year in a few weeks," the young man said, tweaking the tuning of his banjo. "I'm studying military science and history." He had blue eyes and the reddest hair that Sammy had ever seen, short cropped, and had a face filled with freckles. He was broad-shouldered and handsome. She smiled at him and he smiled back briefly but with indifference. She thought he was cute.

"This is Ortie Shelor. And these are his kids, Rhonda and Dowell."

Ortie said, plucking the strings of his upright bass, "I am a seventh generation farmer over in Providence. My family can trace its original land grant back to the King of England in the 1700s." Like Keene, Ortie was overweight. He had unsightly boils on his face. He wore a green baseball-style cap that said "John Deere" on it and a red flannel shirt with the sleeves cut off short.

Rhonda said, "I guess that makes me the eighth generation, don't it? I turned 16 last month." She was overweight, too. She had brown eyes, long strawberry-blonde hair, and pale skin. She was working on a huge stack of French toast.

Dowell, the boy, was playing with a puzzle. He never looked up.

Ella said, "Sammy and I are from New Jersey. Sammy plays violin like nobody's business. I teach high school French. Sammy's parents sent me here as her chaperone. I'm not much with music myself, but I sure like to listen."

Sammy said, "I've been playing violin most of my life. But I'm really here to learn all I can about traditional Appalachian fiddling."

A bookish looking man with Harry Potter style eyeglasses and a receding hairline said, "My name is Pihk McConnell."

His pronunciation of his given name was with such a long, flat *i* sound that Sammy didn't understand him. Jamaal saw her confusion and said, "He always talks like that, Sammy. Took me weeks to start understanding him."

Pike elaborated, enunciating clearly, "'Pike.' You know, like the fish."

Everybody laughed.

"Ih am a professor of electrical engineering at Virginia Tech and Ih live near Blacksburg, which is just over an hour from here. Ih play the banjo but Ih never seem to have enough time to practice."

"That's evident," Terry joked, ribbing him.

Ignoring the comment, Pike continued, "Ih'm originally from Bristol, Tennessee," accenting the last syllable, "over in the western part of the state. We all talk funny over there."

"Don't let his silly accent fool you, Sammy. He's one of the smartest people I ever met," Jamaal asserted.

Pike stayed on track, "My grandparents always lived in Providence, near Quint's place." Speaking mostly to Sammy and Ella, he said, "Ih have been coming here and working on their farm most summers all myh life. That's how Ih got to know and started to play with all these nuckleheads. Myh grandpa died a few years ago and myh grandma died just last year. So the old place in Providence is vacant. Ih've been going there two or three days every week all summer trying to put the place back in shape so that we can put it on the market."

"I am enjoying this little scene from Oprah," Quint said with a scowl. "But are we ever going to play nothing?" He started to pluck away on his banjo and the melody of *Sweet Georgia Brown* began to emerge. Ortie chimed in with his upright bass and pretty soon everyone was jamming. Sammy went inside her tent and retrieved her violin case. She unzipped the Cordura top and fixed the chin-rest and shoulder-rest of her violin against her, where she could hold it firm without her hands touching it. She affixed a tiny electronic tuning meter on the far tip and quietly began to tune her instrument as the others played on. Pretty soon, she emerged and was jamming along with them.

Most of her musical training had been geared towards reading from printed music. But during the last two years, she had become more accustomed to playing by ear. Terry showed her how to do the fingering on a particularly difficult portion of *Flop Eared Mule*. Everybody did a lot of smiling and laughing and good-natured teasing.

Well over an hour had passed when Ortie excused himself, presumably to use the bathroom. As others began to drift away, Rhonda said to Sammy, "Wanna walk around and explore with me?"

Sammy looked over the heavy-set girl with some contempt, but convinced herself that if she wanted to understand the music, she needed to understand the culture of the people who played it. Putting on a happy face, she said, "Sure." She put her instrument back in its case and had Ella lock it in her trunk.

Sammy and Rhonda walked away from the campsite area of their group and towards the area of the main stage. Sammy said to the local girl, "Tell me more about yourself."

"Nuthin' much to tell," Rhonda said. "I have one brother, Dowell. You met him. He's a good boy but he's slow.

"I'm a junior over at Grayson County High. I got no idea what I'm a-gonna do afters I graduate. I might take a cosmetology class, but I dunno if I wanna cut hair for the rest of my life. I live on a farm but I hate cows. I like to garden. Momma taught me how before she left daddy eight years ago and moved to Indiana with another man. She never liked Daddy. I 'spect raising Dowell was too much for her. Or maybe it was me."

She kicked a discarded Coke can and continued, "I don't really like my daddy much either, and he don't like me. But we is stuck with each other. I do like boys but I don't have anybody steady right now. Look at me. When you look like this, it is hard to get their attention. Somehow, I think they are probably all assholes just like my daddy."

Sammy hardly knew what to make of Rhonda's quip.

Rhonda continued, "You look like you have had a pretty good life."

Sammy nodded. Initially taciturn, her impulse was to deflect the question. But she convinced herself that if she was in Galax to appreciate the music, she'd best open up to the local people as well. She said, "My parents have been good to me. Both of them have advanced degrees from good colleges. My dad works for Goldman Sachs. They're an investment bank. He is a bit high-strung and impatient, but I think he loves me. He travels all over the world, so I don't get to see him very much. My mother is a clinical psychologist. So she has a busy life, too. I am an only child."

The two girls peeked under another canopy where several people were jamming.

Continuing their walk, Sammy said, "I spend a lot of time on my own, most of it riding my horse, Wilbur, or practicing my violin. I love the stage. It is the place that I am happiest in the whole world."

"You seem really into your music," Rhonda observed.

"Yes, it's always been important to me. I inherited my violin from my grandfather. It is my best friend and my worst enemy. It is my comfort when I'm lonesome, but it knows all of my flaws and weaknesses. I feel so blessed to own it, and I thank God for giving me the gift of music."

They walked past a huge RV with a bumper sticker that said, "My Grass is Blue."

"Are you still in school?" Rhonda asked.

"I just graduated from high school in May. I'm enrolled at the North Carolina School for the Arts in Winston-Salem. When the Fiddlers Convention is over, Ella and I are going there for a few days to explore. After I was accepted, I visited there for one day. But I'd like to get to know the school and the city better. It's only a couple of hours from here, isn't it?"

"Less than that, I think," said Rhonda. "It's just down off the mountain. I've done been to Winston-Salem twice. We don't travel much. We ain't got much money."

They walked past two young men who smiled at them and said hello. Rhonda changed the subject and asked, "How about boys? You got a boyfriend?"

Sammy was again surprised at the personal nature of Rhonda's questions, but replied honestly, "No. There was one boy I liked from school last year. We kissed a few times. But whenever we were together he talked about other girls. A girl from the volleyball team started paying attention to him and she was prettier and more athletic than me. I don't think he ever looked at me again. How about you?"

"Like I said, I've had a boyfriend or two, but not for very long. Usually they don't pay me much mind. But I want a boyfriend real bad. My best friend from school had a baby last year. Girls around here have babies real young. Her boyfriend went into the Marines and got shipped off to Parris Island in South Carolina, so she moved down there to be with him. Holdin' her baby was somethin' special. Nobody loves you like your baby."

They passed an elaborate campsite where an entire living room suite with two sofas, a living room table, and a television sat underneath a canopy. The kitchen area had a full size gas range with a gas tank sitting next to it. As they looked into the camp area, the residents smiled at them and said hello. They continued walking. There were all manner of vehicles, from old pickup trucks with campers on the back to huge, opulent RVs. They passed one of the power poles that supplied electricity to the campers and held a bank of lights above. There was a jumble of extension cords draped from the outlets that reminded Sammy of strands of spaghetti on a fork.

Rhonda said, "It sure must be nice to have both your parents still around. My mama up and left me without ever saying goodbye. Daddy'll probably leave me, too. Being abandoned'll be the story of my life."

"Are you religious?" Sammy asked, thinking about the overtones of what Rhonda had said.

"I do believe in the Lord Jesus Christ. I think just about every-body around here does. Even the nonreligious people around here are religious. But I don't think Jesus will be there for me when I need him. I've known lots of totally devout people who Jesus abandoned when they needed him. How about you?"

"My family is Jewish; we attend a synagogue," Sammy said.

"Jewish, eh? I ain't never met a Jewish person before. Being a Jew sounds like an awful thing. Is being a Jew and being Jewish the same thing?"

"Yes. I don't know why Jew and Jewish seem to sound so differ-ent to most people, but it's the same thing. Lots of Jews live in New Jersey. But I think Jews are minorities everywhere in the world except Israel."

Sammy continued, "Lots of famous people live in my town. Chris Rock, Britney Spears, Stevie Wonder, and Wesley Snipes all live near-by."

"I only dream of places like that," Rhonda said, wistfully. "Shit, pretty much everybody here has always been poor. The way the econ-omy is these days, that damn sure ain't never gonna change. My great-est dream is that someday, some Prince Charmin' will come along and swoop me outta here."

Sammy let that thought sink deep into her head. Her greatest dreams had always been about personal achievement, about learning philosophy, politics and economics, and of course music. She had been to many of the great cities of Europe and Asia already and dreamed of seeing more of them. She was about to share this with Rhonda and then she changed her mind and stayed quiet.

They walked past a red Hyundai sedan with a silver shade in the windshield. The front bumper had a sticker that said, "Driver under the influence of Bluegrass."

Back in camp, Sammy decided to take a nap. She found Ella al-ready inside her tent, reading a Spanish novel. Ella asked, "Are you enjoying yourself?"

Sammy said, "This is really an incredible place. Rhonda and I have been wandering around the park and there are jam sessions going on everywhere, all the time. It seems like almost nobody's had any formal musical training. Everybody here seems to have come upon their skills through the practice of listening to and watching everyone else."

Around dinner time, Sammy's cell phone rang and the caller ID said it was her mother. "Hi, mom."

"Hi, sweetheart. How is everything going?"

"We're doing fine. Ella and I have met several interesting people in Terry and Alice's little group. Everybody treats us like we are long lost friends. There is a black man named Jamaal from Washington, DC. I really like him. His wife dropped him off on her way further south to see relatives. He has a fascinating family history in music. There is a girl here in our little group who is 15 years old and she seems very nice. I can't wait to tell you all about them when I get home next week. How are you doing?"

"Travel is hectic," her mom sighed. "Right now we are in Belgrade. We're here for one more day and then we will go to Sofia. After that, we will fly to Zagreb and then Paris. We should be on our way home by Friday."

"How's daddy?"

"He's fine. He's in a meeting right now."

Before wrapping up they talked for a few more minutes about plans for Sammy's move to school in September. "I love you, mom."

"I love you too, Sammy. I am glad you are having a good time and I am eager to hear all about it."

"Please tell daddy that I love him too. Bye-bye."

That evening, the group jammed some more, joined by a couple of Terry and Alice's friends from Roanoke. Afterwards, Terry said to Sammy, "I have been assuming all along that you intend to compete while you are here."

Sammy said, "To tell you the honest truth, I never really thought about it. But I do love to perform. What do I need to do?"

"You simply need to register with the folks in charge of the competition. You need to tell them what category you want to be in. It would be a good idea to get someone to accompany you while you play and I would be happy to do that for you. And then all you need to do is pick a song and be ready to play at the designated time. It is only Monday and the competitions do not start until Wednesday night. So you still have some time to practice."

"Great!" said Sammy. "I'll sign up tomorrow."

Tuesday, August 14

The morning came and Sammy and Ella did the same routine with their showers. This time, Sammy found herself in conversation with a woman from Alabama who said, "I graduated from college a few years ago with a degree in fine arts. I am trying to make a go of it as a professional photographer. I travel to music festivals all across the mid-Atlantic and the South." She wore a tie-died shirt and jeans, and she had a dozen or more earrings in each ear. "The money isn't very good, but it is an interesting life," the woman continued.

Back in camp, Samantha stumbled into a conversation between Pike and Keene about the price of gasoline. Ella was listening, and she said to Sammy, "Now that I think about it, we did arrive here on fumes Sunday night. I suspect there will be a run on gasoline stations here in Galax next Sunday as people get ready to head home. I think I'm going to go into town and fill up right now. Do you want to go with me?"

"If it's all the same to you," Sammy said, "I think I'll stay here and catch up on some of my reading."

That evening, Shane approached Sammy for the first time, saying, "Wanna go watch some of the performers on the main stage?" So they took a short walk together to the main stage area. Shane showed her where to register for her own competition, which was scheduled for Friday evening. She wondered if he was interested in her.

In front of the stage, they found a sea of lawn chairs. When Sammy asked about them, Shane said, "Many of the people who come to the convention put their chairs in place and then they wander through the campground. There are always plenty of spare chairs. If somebody comes along and tells you that you are sitting in their seat, you simply apologize and find another."

Many younger musicians were performing. Sammy was delighted watching the children handling instruments that in some cases looked bigger than they were, and seeing the enthusiastic reaction from the crowd. Once during the evening, Sammy felt Shane's hand rest atop hers, only to move away to applaud the musicians. He never placed it back.

Wednesday, August 15

The next morning Sammy was awoken at dawn by the sound of sirens, emanating from an emergency vehicle. The sound grew louder as the vehicle evidently entered the park. The sound abruptly died. She didn't think much more about it, until she returned from the bathroom and Quint was talking about it. "Two boys from Greensboro were killed here this morning. They were eight and ten."

"What happened?" asked Jamaal.

"They were sleeping in their tent when an RV backed into a light pole and knocked it over. It fell into their tent and killed them. They were dead before the rescue squad car arrived."

"Tragic," said Pike.

"How awful!" Alice added.

"Sure enough," Quint continued. "It's the will of the Lord. Sad. Somebody said there was a fist-fight afterwards. The kid's father 'bout killed the RV driver for what he'd done, even though it was an accident."

Ortie said, "It caused a blackout throughout the park, too. But the power company had it back on quickly. It's scary, though, the randomness of death. Ya never know when disaster can strike."

During the jam session that morning, Ella walked away from the group to take an incoming call on her cell phone. When she returned, she wore a sad expression and shook her head back and forth. She mouthed silently to Sammy, "Come here," motioning with her index finger.

Sammy put her violin gently on her chair and walked over. "What's up?"

"Bad news. That was a call from the hospital back home. My mom fell earlier this morning and broke her hip. She's stable now, but she needs me to come home and take care of her. We will need to go home. Say goodbye to everyone, pack your things, and let's go."

Sammy was dumbstruck. What should she think? It was obvious that Ella's need to leave was real and valid. She returned to the group, still in the midst of playing the same tune, and looked at each person for a moment. She put her violin back in its case and she zipped it shut. Terry and Alice looked at her as if to ask, what's wrong? She smiled a wan smile and walked over to her tent. Terry followed her. "What's wrong?"

Ella, already wrapping up her sleeping bag, said, "Mom has broken her hip and I need to head home. I am really terribly sorry. Sammy needs to go with me."

Terry said, "You can leave Sammy with us. We can take care of her. Can someone come later and pick her up?"

"That's really not up to me. Her parents are paying me to bring her here and take her home. So if there is to be another plan, it will have to be cleared with them."

Sammy said, "Let me call my mom." She hit the speed dial code on her cell phone and waited anxiously as the international call was connected.

"Hi, sweetheart," said her mom. "How are you doing?"

"Mom, we have a problem. Ella just got a call. Her mother broke her hip and Ella needs to head home. Mom, I really don't want to leave. Please let me stay."

"No, I think you'd better go home with her. Your dad and I aren't comfortable with you being there alone."

"Please, mom! I'll be 18 in a few weeks. I am surrounded by people who I like. I am sure they will take care of me. Can you come and get me when you get home?"

"Hold on for a moment. Your dad is right here. Let me put him on."

"Hi, honey," he said. "Your mom tells me you have a bit of a dilemma."

"Dad, I really want to stay. I am almost 18. I'll be fine here."

"Let me talk with mom for a minute, sweetheart."

The phone was quiet for several seconds.

"We'd like to know there is someone with children there looking after you."

"Terry and Alice are here and they'll look after me."

"Are you sure? Are they close by now?" her father asked.

"Yes." She put Terry on the phone with her father.

"Hello, Mr. Reisinger. This is Terry Mullins. Yes, sir. Yes, we live in Roanoke. It's 90 minutes from here but we'll be here all week. Yes. I have kids myself, so I understand. Yes, it is no problem. Okay."

Terry handed the phone back to Sammy.

"Dad?"

"Okay, you can stay. Your mom and I are flying home on Friday from Paris. On Saturday morning we will get up early and drive down there. We'll spend the night somewhere close by and pick you up Sunday morning. Then we can go to Winston-Salem and look around your school before we drive home."

"Thanks, dad."

"You behave yourself down there and don't get in trouble. I want you to call your mom every day until we get there; you promise?"

"Yes, I promise. Every day."

"One other thing. I'm concerned about your violin. Keep it locked in Terry's car whenever it is out of your sight. You know how valuable it is."

"I will. I promise. I love you both. Bye!"

Sammy helped Ella finish packing her things. In just a few minutes, they were exchanging hugs and Ella was in her car, ready to head northbound. Sammy put her face inside the open window and touched her cheek to Ella's. Ella said, "Enjoy yourself and call me when you get home." And then, Ella was gone.

Alice had come over and was listening in. She squeezed Sammy around her shoulders. "Don't worry about anything. You are in good hands here. Everything will be fine."

Thursday, August 16

Thursday morning was bright and clear. Upon Sammy's return from the toilet, Pike said to her, "Jamaal and I would like to break up the routine for a few hours. He and I are going to go for a drive in the countryside. Would you like to come with us?"

"Where do you plan to go?"

"The Blue Ridge Parkway. It isn't very far from here. It is one of the country's most famous scenic drives."

"I'd like to! Let me ask Terry and Alice."

Sammy found Alice inside her camper and obtained her approval. Alice locked Sammy's violin in its red case inside the rear compartment of Terry's Toyota 4-Runner.

Sammy returned to Pike and said, "I'll be ready in a sec. Let me call my mom."

Everything was going well for her parents in Europe. They still planned to travel home the following night.

Next thing she knew, Sammy was in the front seat of Pike's Nissan SUV while Pike drove and Jamaal sat in the back. They drove eastward to Pipers Gap and took the Parkway northbound. Occasionally, they spotted deer grazing alongside the road or some buzzards soaring overhead. They parked in a large parking lot at Mabry Mill. They took a short stroll around the restored water-powered grist mill that Pike said was the most photographed place on the whole Parkway.

They drove onward as the road gained elevation, topping out at 3800 feet where signs said "Rocky Knob." They stopped at an overlook with a vast view towards the southeast, with the Piedmont area of Virginia and North Carolina before them. There was a misty haze over the lowlands, something Pike said was a common occurrence that time of year. "By the fall, the air will clear out and the views here are spectacular. Plus, when October rolls around, the leaves change color and it is beautiful." A brief thunderstorm swept through on their way back. They stopped at an overlook as sheets of rain streamed down their windshield. "We get some butt-kickin' storms around here in the summer, but they typically don't last very long."

They finished their drive in time for dinner and the evening's jam session. Terry and Sammy practiced together, playing *Durang's Horn-pipe* over and over again. Jamaal sat in on the sessions even though he was not planning to accompany Sammy onstage. Sammy's competition was to be held the following evening, so they would have one more practice session the next afternoon.

Terry did some coaching for Sammy. "I know you've been schooled in the classics. Your posture and position on the violin are impeccable. But try to relax. You're used to seeing the notes on a piece of paper. But with fiddling, you'll want to improvise some and see where your fingers take you. Oh, be animated. Smile and show the audience how much you enjoy the music and how awesome you are."

Friday, August 17

The next morning was overcast as Sammy wandered the festival lot listening to musicians jam. Around mid-morning, she returned to her group. As she did, Terry approached and said, "Alice's mother is taking care of our boys at our house in Salem, near Roanoke. She called a little while ago to say that Dan, our oldest boy, was stung by a wasp this morning. She is pretty sure there is nothing to this, but she would like us to come home and take him to a clinic. We should be back in plenty of time so that I can still accompany you on stage tonight. It only takes us an hour and a half to get there. Give me your telephone number, and I'll call you with an update." They exchanged telephone numbers and within a few minutes, Terry and Alice had departed.

Sammy had a sinking feeling in her stomach, for some inexplicable reason worse than when Ella had left.

Sammy called her mom and said, "Good morning, mom! How is everything?"

"We're fine, sweetie. As you know, it's afternoon already where we are. Your dad is making good progress with his work and we look forward to being home. Our schedule has us flying back to Kennedy Airport tonight. I think we arrive around 9:20 p.m. Eastern time."

They chatted for a few moments about the weather, which had been filled with thunderstorms, and the sights of the old cities of Europe. Wrapping up the call, Sammy said, "Have a good flight, mom! Please call me when you arrive." She decided not to mention Terry's and Alice's departure, fearing it would make her worry.

"We sure will, sweetheart. We love you."

At 4:30 that afternoon, Sammy's cell phone rang. "Sammy, this is Terry. I've got bad news. Our son has had an allergic reaction to his bee sting and we need to stay here overnight. I'm sorry."

"Is he going to be okay?" she inquired, sympathetically.

"Yes, I'm sure he will be fine. But the doctor wants us to keep an eye on him and Alice's mom wants us to be here. I am sure that Jamaal won't mind accompanying you on stage tonight. I am really sorry I can't be there. You're very talented, and I really wanted to perform with you. We'll be back tomorrow morning."

"It's okay. Jamaal and I will kick some butt up there. Perhaps Pike will bring his video camera and will tape-record it so you can see it tomorrow."

After they hung up, Sammy found Jamaal reading a spy thriller. She told him about the news, and he agreed to accompany her. They rehearsed together for an hour.

At one point, Jamaal said, "You're violin looks quite old."

"Yeah, I inherited it from my grandfather. He played for the New York Philharmonic."

"Wow!"

"He was a world-class musician. When I was young, he used to play for me. Even today, whenever I am feeling troubled, I feel his presence with me, like a guardian angel. He died when I was only six years old. This violin sat inside its case on our mantle piece for four years until one day I told my mother that I wanted to learn how to play it. She said, 'That will be wonderful and we support you 100-percent. But you are not ready for an instrument like this.' It was made in Cremona, Italy, in 1740.'"

"Wow!" he exclaimed again.

"For real! A few days later, mom went to a music store and bought me an $800 violin and signed me up for lessons. She said, 'If you stay with it and show us you are devoted to learning how to play, you can have your grandfather's violin when you are 13.' I think mom could see how dedicated I was, so I was given this instrument the day I turned 11. It was made by Peitro Giovannie Guarneri, who was the son of Andrea Guarneri, who like Antonio Stradivari was an apprentice of Andrea Amati."

"What's it worth?" He sipped his Coke.

"I can't even imagine. I would die if I ever lost it. I don't even like other people to touch it."

At dinner that night, their group had thinned out to only Sammy, Jamaal, Ortie, Rhonda, Dowell, Pike, Shane, Keene, and Quint.

After he helped her wash dishes for everyone, Shane asked Sammy if she wanted to walk around the park for a few minutes prior to her appearance on stage. She said, "I need to be there in 45 minutes."

He said, "That's fine. Walk with me for a half hour and I promise to have you back here in time to get your fiddle." As they walked, he said, "I am very impressed by your fiddle playing. You're a great musician; I'm sure you'll do just fine." He reached over and put his hand on the back of her neck and he gently rubbed her hair. It felt good. She put her hand around his waist. They walked silently, on and on.

"Tell me about yourself," he asked. "You said you were from New Jersey."

"Yes. I just graduated from high school. Dad is an economist and he shuffles money around the world. Mom is a doctor, a psychologist."

"Are you going to college?"

"Yes. I'm going to the North Carolina School of the Arts in Winston-Salem in a few weeks to study music. I hope to play for one of the major symphonies someday.

"How about you?"

"I go Virginia Military Institute," the redhead said.

"I think I've heard of it."

"Yeah, it's one of the oldest military schools in the country. Stonewall Jackson was teaching there when the Civil War broke out and George Marshall, the World War II General studied there. All my life, I've been around military people. Dad was a Marine. He was abusive to mom and they split years ago. Last time I heard, he was in prison in Indiana. Mom is an assistant to the police chief in Fries."

Letting that sink in, she said, "I really must get back to camp and get my violin… oh, my fiddle."

He said, "That's fine. Let's go. But one minute. I like you a lot." He slid a hand behind her neck and gently twisted her head towards his, pulling her close. He kissed her softly and quickly. "I'll be in the audience watching. You'll be great!"

His kiss felt good. She held his hand as Shane walked her back to camp. She retrieved her violin and asked Jamaal if he was ready. They walked together to the back of the main stage. On the audience side, the bright lights were already on as the sun was sinking low in the western sky behind the grandstand. As they waited their turn, they caught some curious stares, this mid-40s black man and the black-haired, white teenage girl. There was nobody else of color in sight.

They were told back stage that they would have three minutes to perform. She closed her eyes and she visualized the music, note to note, progression to progression, and how she wanted to play it. The stagehand ushered them onstage at the appropriate time. A master of ceremonies said, "Please give a warm welcome to our next performer, Ms. Samantha Reisinger from New Jersey, playing *Durang's Hornpipe*, accompanied by Jamaal Winston from Washington, DC." The audience clapped politely.

The fiddler and the banjoist walked out onstage, she one step ahead of him. She adjusted the microphone to her diminutive height and looked at the bright lights illuminating the stage and seating area.

The sun was setting behind the grandstand but it was a warm, peaceful night.

She set her posture, took a deep breath, and looked at an expectant crowd before her. She looked again at Jamaal, nodded imperceptibly, and he started first, as they had agreed, alleviating her fear that she might start with the wrong notes. Then she began.

Within seconds, the audience began to quiet. She focused her eyes on her fingering hand and envisioned the most difficult measures in her head. In the audience, she envisioned a likeness of her grandfather, beaming with approval. She came to the most complicated part of the song and she focused all of her attention on the subtle vibration of the strings under the fingers of her left hand as she moved her hand fluidly up-and-down the neck of her precious violin. As she completed the last bar, a hush fell over the audience. In an expectant moment, applause began to build. Jamaal looked at her and smiled. Silently, he mouthed, "Bravo!"

Several people in the audience began to stand, intensifying their applause. She smiled and nodded to the crowd. And then, every light in their universe went dark.

Part 1: August

SAMANTHA'S EYES TOOK a few moments to adjust. She had turned her head away from the audience and had taken her first steps towards the short wooden stairway that led off the stage. She felt Jamaal's presence behind her as she turned once again and looked towards the direction of the grandstand. A mere sliver of a receding moon chased the sun into a darkening horizon.

She looked over her shoulder and asked him, "What has just happened?"

"Looks like we've had a power failure," he said.

She reached the bottom of the stairs and tucking her violin under her right arm, she pushed the tiny button on her digital watch to illuminate the numbers and tell her the time of day. It was completely inoperable, offering neither illumination nor digital figures. "What time is it? My watch doesn't seem to be working."

Reaching into his pocket, he retrieved an old pocket watch and said, "It's 8:55 p.m."

It was dusk; there was enough light to allow them to find their way back to their camp, nearly bumping into scores of other people scurrying around. Shane caught up with them and said jocularly, "You did a nice job, Sammy! Interesting how you made the lights go out so you'd be the last person on stage and surely the one they were most likely to remember."

Once back in their camping area, they found Ortie walking around to the back of his camper with a flashlight, looking for his lantern. "I never use my lantern here in Galax, but it's always in my camper for when we go on mountain camping trips."

Sammy fumbled around in the tent and found the *Forever-lite* forehead flashlight she'd brought but not yet used. She opened the packet of batteries and stuck three AAA cells inside. Then she flipped the switch and was surprised at the intensity of the beam. She emerged from the tent and walked to the outhouses for her nighttime testimonial. Upon her return, she scanned the rest of the group, sitting together in the near dark, chatting quietly. "Goodnight, everyone. I'm tired and I'm going to go to sleep."

"Goodnight, Sammy," the others said in unison. "Sweet dreams."

Sammy awoke in the middle of a dream about riding her horse. Her tent was being unzipped. A familiar voice she recognized as Jamaal's said, "Sam, you need to get up right now."

"What's going on?" It was pitch dark other than the flashlight he pointed at her.

"I don't know, but we appear to be having an emergency. Please get up. Now."

"Okay."

She scrambled from her bag and found her own flashlight. She flipped it on and then found her jacket and sandals. She stumbled outside the tent.

"Sammy, come here," said Quint. "Okay, we have Ortie, Dowell, and Rhonda, Sammy, Jamaal, Shane, and Keene. Pike, tell them." He pointed his flashlight at the bespectacled man.

"Things are serious. Pack all your stuff and put it in Keene's bus, and do it NOW!"

It was totally dark except for some eerie, almost phosphorescent greenish and pinkish lights that danced on the horizon. The moon had set and there were thousands of shimmering stars in the sky.

"What time is it?" Sammy asked.

"It's probably before 10:00 p.m.," Quint said. "But the only time that matters is how quickly we get out of here. Let's get!"

The friends ran to their accommodations. Sammy threw her things into her travel bag and stuffed her sleeping bag into its sack. She started to unpitch her tent, but Quint grabbed her by the shoulder of her jacket and said, "Leave it. Let's go."

"I've got to get my violin!"

"I'll get it for you."

The group shuttled aboard, first Ortie, Dowell, and Rhonda, and then Sammy and Shane. Jamaal hustled aboard ahead of Pike. Keene, already in the driver's seat, said to Jamaal, "Not you, buster."

"He's with me," insisted Pike. "You get him to Providence; that's all I ask."

"Hurry up," said Quint from the back.

"Fine," grumbled the rotund driver.

"Let's go," said Quint, clutching Sammy's violin case and clearing the doorway.

The engine to the bus cranked over and fired. Keene inched forward, moving without headlights, driving over Jamaal's tent, and pulled the bus into the aisle, working only from the flashlight Quint shone through the windshield. The bus inched to the gate as if tip-toeing. Only outside the gate did Keene flip the headlight switch, and then only one light shone.

The bus made its way down one of Galax's arterial streets where Keene had to swerve around immobile cars.

Nobody said anything until Jamaal broke the silence. "Do ya suppose somebody can tell us what's going on?" echoing what Sammy was thinking to herself.

As Keene drove on, Pike said, "We're pretty sure that what happened a few hours ago was not your routine power failure. It is even worse than a regional blackout. Anybody got a digital watch or a cell phone?"

"My wristwatch isn't working," said Shane. "Damn!"

Pike said, "Shortly after the blackout, I started putting two and two together. I tried to start the Nissan. It was dead."

"I am getting really frightened," Rhonda said, her voice quaking. "What's going on?"

Pike said, "I think we experienced what is called an EMP, or Electromagnetic Pulse. Every piece of electronic equipment is probably toast."

"Fuck!" exclaimed Shane. "Everything?"

Pike said, "Everything around here, anyway. We have no idea how widespread the damage is, but from what I've read, things like this aren't local. It could be nation-wide. It could be even worldwide. The more modern the piece of equipment, the more vulnerable it is. We're talking about phones, computers, cars, televisions…"

And airplanes, Sammy thought to herself, as a toxic wave of

shock and grief swept over her. Her head felt dizzy and her torso collapsed, sending her into a fetal position on the vinyl seat of the bus. She began to sob fitfully and vigorously. She lost track of time, but in her next conscious thought, Pike and Jamaal were by her side, supporting and comforting her. Jamaal hugged her and said, "Please, Sam, hold yourself together. We'll make it through this."

Pike spoke next, his words interrupted by Sammy's wails. "What has happened is dreadfully, frightfully serious."

A hush overtook the group as each person contemplated the impact.

Pike continued, "All the vehicles we have were destroyed except this bus. It has survived because its ignition system predates microprocessors. All the new cars' electrical systems were fried by the Pulse. Thousands of people at Felts Park will soon realize they are marooned there."

At the first intersection, they had to drive with the outside wheels on the curb in order to move around immobilized cars, which were everywhere, as if someone had simply yanked out everybody's keys at the same time. Within a mile, they took a left turn, following a sign that Sammy could see outside the windshield. It said, "Fries 8."

Ortie asked, "How about my farm equipment?"

Pike said, "This old bus was built with old ignition stuff: points, condensers, and distributors. Anything that runs with this old technology – things like chain saws, gas generators, and farm tractors – will run normally. But there won't be deliveries of gasoline, so they'll soon be crippled, too."

"Keene, Pike and I have been doing some talking," Quint announced. "Shane, you will get off first at your place. Then Keene will drop off Ortie and his kids, and then Pike at his folks' place. Sammy and Jamaal, for the time bein', you are going home with me."

The bus drove slowly down a long incline and then crossed a low bridge that seemed just a few feet over a river as wide as a football field. The road swung to the left and Sammy saw a sign outside the windshield that said cheerily, "We welcome you to Fries." The lone headlight lacked the luminous intensity for Sammy to see much of the town. But it appeared very small. At one point, the road was completely blocked by immobilized cars. The bus had to push a small car out of the way to continue.

Beyond the town on a road marked plainly, "Scenic Road," Keene stopped at the entrance to what looked like a small trailer park. Shane got up from his seat and said to Sammy, "I hope everybody is okay. I'll be seeing you." He grabbed his things and departed.

A quarter of a mile later, Keene turned right up a long driveway that ended in a poorly kept double-wide house trailer. Toys were strewn about the yard of uncut grass. There were chickens flitting around and an immobile hound dog on the wooden porch. Ortie, Dowell, and Rhonda got off the bus, barely saying goodbye to anyone.

Back on Scenic Road another smattering of houses appeared along with a sign proclaiming the hamlet to be "Providence." An Isuzu SUV sat in the road. To the rear door was affixed a spare tire with a vinyl cover that said, "Life is good!" written in a playful font.

Two hundred yards later, at the intersection with Turkey Knob Road, the bus stopped once more at the end of a long, dirt driveway. Grabbing his things, Pike said to Quint, "Ih don't think there will be any food in the house. Let me get settled in and I'll give you a call." He smiled a crooked smile, understanding his own sardonic attempt at a joke. "I appreciate your help. Take care of this young lady," nodding in Sammy's direction. He grabbed her hands for a moment, squeezed paternally, let go, and descended the stairs.

A quarter-mile later on Scenic Road, Keene took a left turn again and drove a dirt road for a half-mile to an old white-frame farmhouse. Quint turned to Sammy and Jamaal. "Okay you two. Grab your gear and let's go." After unloading everything, Quint thanked Keene and said, "Will I be seeing you in church Sunday morning?"

"If I'm there, you will," the bus driver joked, closing the door and revving his engine.

The three new friends schlepped their belongings up the stairs onto the porch, using their flashlights to find their way. Quint opened the unlocked door.

"Jamaal," the tall host said, "you'll sleep here on the living room sofa tonight. Tomorrow we're going to find a more permanent home for you. Sammy, you're staying here. Follow me upstairs."

Illuminating their way by flashlight, he led her into a bedroom with twin beds. "This'll be your room. Try to get some sleep."

"Are you married?" she asked him, realizing she hadn't asked before. "Do you have any kids?"

"It's just my wife and me now. Get some sleep and I'll tell you about it in the morning."

Saturday, August 18

Sammy awoke to new surroundings. She wandered into the hallway and found a bathroom. This, like the bedroom to which she had been assigned, was clearly the lair of the female gender. There were racks filled with scented soaps and perfumes. Two dusty toothbrushes hung in a porcelain rack with a plastic cup between them. An unopened packet of birth control pills sat on the counter. It looked to Sammy as if nobody had touched anything for years.

After she peed, she flushed the toilet, but there was no sound of water replenishing the tank, and the bowl remained empty. She turned on the faucet to wash her hands and face, but there was no water. She wiped her hands anyway on a hanging cloth towel.

She peeked inside the second of the two upstairs bedrooms. There was a bed with a Western theme bedspread. Pictures of Washington Redskins football players were thumb-tacked to the wall. A collection of plastic dinosaurs roamed the primordial plain that was the top of the chest of drawers. She wondered why Quint hadn't invited Jamaal to sleep in the unused bed, then hoped her conclusion was wrong.

She walked back to the room where she'd slept. The other bed was still made, fitted with fluffed pillows and a sheet and cover turned back as if ready for someone to occupy it, as hers had been. A white wedding dress hung on a hanger outside the closet door, draped in a clear plastic protective cover.

Sitting on the bureau was a picture of two girls who looked like twins in their teenage years, one looking more alert and more attractive than the other. Both girls had light brown hair and green eyes. The more attractive one was beautiful indeed. There was also a photo of the same pretty girl alongside a horse, her hand alongside his face. The horse had a white facial marking but otherwise was chestnut brown. There was another photo of the same girl feeding a dandelion flower to a white goat.

Sammy opened the top drawer of the bureau and inside she found several bracelets, rings, and other pieces of jewelry. There was a picture of the attractive girl in a prom dress, sitting beside a standing boy in a tuxedo. He had dark, closely cropped hair and a cheerful smile. She put everything back inside the drawer and shut it as she heard Quint ascending the stairs.

"Good morning," he said. "Did you sleep okay?"

"I don't know. I feel like I'm living in a nightmarish dream. We're in your house, right?"

"Yes."

"The national power grid is dead, right?"

"Yes, as far as we know. At least some portion of it."

"I'm an orphan, right?"

"I don't know, Samantha. Let's not go there. We don't know for sure."

"Why have you brought me here?"

"I suspect we're part of the lucky ones. With no communications and no cars running, there are going to be thousands of people trapped at Felts Park, unable to get home. At least we were close to home and had a vehicle working. We felt responsible for you since you'd become part of our group. You'll be safe here, or at least safer."

She sat on the bed and began to cry. He walked from the room saying unempathically, "It's God's will."

Some time later, Jamaal appeared by her side and he hugged her. They sat together, sobbing, immersed in their tragedies but understanding the part they, as outsiders, would need to play for each other. Jamaal confessed how spooked he was, being in the bus with some people he knew to be hostile towards him because of his race.

"Jamaal! Sammy! Please come downstairs," came Quint's voice from the stairway.

The two pulled themselves together and walked down the stairs.

Quint said, "Sammy, you'll be living here with us for the foreseeable future. Jamaal, we're going to ask the widow Ayres if you can stay with her. She's a midwife. I suspect she is going to be pretty busy and can use a man's help. Please get ready. Find some breakfast for yourselves in the kitchen. I've got a few chores to do outside."

Sammy and Jamaal began exploring the main floor. It was a simple house with a living room, a dining room, a kitchen, and what appeared to be the master bedroom in a new addition. The furniture was dusty. Sammy listened to the rhythmic ticking of the immense grandfather clock in the foyer but was startled when it struck 11 and the Westminster chime resonated through the otherwise deathly quiet house. The moon-dial showed a mere slither of an emerging moon, a facsimile of the previous night's real thing.

She and Jamaal went into the kitchen. She took a glass from the cupboard and turned on the faucet to get a drink, but no water flowed. She opened the refrigerator where she found a pitcher of water, some of which she poured into a plastic cup. But there was no electric light on the inside. Jamaal said, "Whatever is in that refrigerator won't last long."

The two new friends sat at the kitchen table contemplating their fate. As far as Sammy knew, her parents were dead. As far as Jamaal knew, his wife was marooned away from home as well. Both of them realized that their fates, at least for the time being, were tied together and tied to Providence, Virginia.

Quint re-entered the house and said, "Okay, Jamaal, let's walk over to see the widow Ayres. Sammy, do you want to come along?"

"Yes."

Jamaal grabbed his travel bag and Quint picked up Jamaal's banjo case. They walked to the road, which was devoid of traffic. They walked silently past several abandoned cars. An immobilized Dodge Magnum RT had a bumper sticker with the words "Earth First! We'll strip-mine the other planets later."

Without prompting, Quint interrupted the silence and said abruptly, "We have had our share of tragedy, my Hattie and me. We had three
children. All of them are dead. Our precious son Gary drowned in the
river. Our twin girls were three years old then. They're dead now, too."

The grief that Sammy was feeling already began to intensify again.

"The room you're staying in, Sammy, belonged to the twins, Bonnie and Ronnie. Ronnie died first. Each loss has been devastating, but
Hattie has never been quite right since Bonnie died. She rarely speaks
to anyone. She won't mind you staying here, but don't expect much
conversation from her. Our Welsh corgi, Snoopy, is by her side constantly and seems almost as distraught as Hattie. I hope he'll warm up
to you eventually. No telling how long you'll be with us."

"Where are they?" Sammy inquired.

"I don't know. Hattie is almost never around. She must have some
secret hiding places. We have lots of land that is mostly wooded. She
could have several hiding places. She tends to the garden and the goats
and she makes goat cheese. But she never associates with anybody I
know of except her bitch of a sister Marissa who comes from time
to time from Galax. I don't know how Hattie will react to you being
here, Sammy. But everybody will need to make some adjustments."

Sammy said, "I'll try to be a good guest. I appreciate you taking
me in."

Moments later, she said furtively, "I tried to wash my face this
morning. There was no water at the tap."

"We get our water from a well out back. The pump is electric."

A black crow chased by a blue jay swept over the road in front
of them.

Quint continued, "People who live in the country seldom throw
anything away. We've had an electric pump for almost 50 years, but
the old hand pump was still in the barn. While you were eating breakfast, I rigged it up and now we can have all the water we ever want; we
just need to pump it. There is a bucket in the bathroom upstairs for
you to wash with. But from now until this crisis passes, we will all be
doing our business in the outhouse."

When Sammy reacted with horror, Quint added, "Hattie and I, we are glad you are here," as if softening the blow for the out of place newcomer.

Jamaal asked about Mrs. Ayers' water supply, but Quint didn't know the answer. "We'll know soon."

A few hundred yards later, Quint said, "Okay, Jamaal. This is Mrs. Ayers' house. Let me do the talking."

The three ascended the stairs and Quint rapped the door knocker. A tiny woman that Sammy estimated to be perhaps 70 with a kindly face, pale skin, and gray braids opened the door.

"Please come in, Quint. Hello Jamaal and Sammy. I'm Emily Ayres. Come on in. Pike was here earlier and he told me about you," she said. "I'm happy to have you with me, Jamaal," she said, brightly.

The four of them discussed the situation and the arrangements necessary for everyone's well being. Quint said, "I need to walk to Fries and check on the pharmacy." He took his leave.

Emily escorted Jamaal upstairs and returned shortly without him, asking Sammy if she'd like some tea. While Emily heated the water over an old Coleman camp stove in the kitchen, Sammy scanned the room. The sheer volume of books on the bookshelves impressed her. She thought back to her grandfather's apartment in New York City and how there was virtually not a single inch of shelf space not occupied by reading material, as he had been a voracious reader. There were several musical instruments strewn about, on pegs on the wall and resting on the floor. There were metal bars on the windows, something that surprised.

As Jamaal descended the stairs, Emily returned to the living room with a steaming pot and three cups. She served her guests before herself. Sammy asked her about Quint and his family. Emily said, "Quint and his wife have been through the most dreadful thing that any parents can endure. By the time my husband and I retired back here to my place of birth, Quint had already lost his young son in that terrible drowning accident. The two girls have died since I have been back. Have you met Quint's wife, Hattie?"

"No."

"She is in a terrible way. With the passing of each child, she has become increasingly more withdrawn, seemingly embracing grief as a lifestyle. I have no idea how she will react to your presence in her house. I'm not saying she is right or wrong, but after my husband died, I spent almost a year in a fetal position on my sofa. Through the help of some friends and a terrific counselor, I decided it was time to regain my life and move on. I was a nurse early in my career and I decided to study to become a licensed midwife. So this is my new calling."

"Do you think Hattie has sought any professional psychiatric care?" Jamaal asked.

"I doubt it. I don't think Quint sees her condition as being treatable. No, I take that back. I think he probably believes his religious convictions prevent psychiatry. He rules the house over there; I'm sure you know that. He is a deeply religious man, and he preaches some radical stuff."

"I am afraid that I am just beginning to get an inkling of that," Sammy shrugged wryly. "I didn't know midwives still existed. I thought everybody gave birth in hospitals these days."

"I have only a handful of clients right now. Most are dedicated back-to-the-landers or deeply devout people like the Mennonites and the Quakers. I suspect that most of them are too far away for me to help now, given that my car doesn't work. On the other hand, I'm guessing that I'll soon be hearing from a whole other group of expectant mothers who had planned to give birth at the hospital in Galax who now won't be able to get there. Or if they could, they might find that the hospital is no better than being home.

"Before my husband died, a widow of a farmer gave me a horse named Maggie. My husband and I collected old farm relics for years. We have an old wagon. It might come in handy if it is in working condition.

"But the first thing you can do is help me work the garden this afternoon. Pike tells me that you met Rhonda at the Fiddlers Convention. She has been helping me, Hattie, and several other people along the road here with their gardens. Within a day or two, food is going to stop showing up at the grocery store in town and we will need to start fending for ourselves. Fortunately, we've had a pretty good summer with lots of rain, but fending off the stinkbugs and other insects is always a challenge. And the deer will eat anything that we will, seemingly always the day before I plan to pick it!"

Emily took Jamaal and Sammy around her property, which was expansive. She showed them her horse, Maggie. She showed them the old wagon. Jamaal saw several broken parts, but was sure he could fix it.

Emily said, "That would be great. Perhaps we'll have some mobility."

The three picked some fresh carrots and potatoes from the garden, which Emily boiled for their lunch.

Afterwards, Sammy became fatigued and it occurred to her that she had not changed her clothes for two days. So she departed and walked back to her new home.

She stopped outside to pump some water for herself, which she carried inside in a bucket. Finding the house unoccupied, she climbed the stairs back to her new bedroom. She opened the drawers in the bureau. She laid out several T-shirts, shorts, bras, and panties of the dead daughter, planning to try them on. The thought of wearing a dead girl's clothing revolted her.

As she removed her dirty shirt and bra, her eyes were drawn back to the picture of the pretty young girl with her horse. Her eyes felt suddenly droopy and her head began to swim. She felt dizzy and nauseous. She grabbed the back of the painted wire rim chair with the pink seat upholstery and she sat and looked at herself in the mirror. Her eyes darted from place to place on her own visage, moving from her dark eyebrows to her full lips and down to her shoulders and breasts, with the Star of David suspended between them. She again looked to her own face and for an instant saw the image of her grandfather staring at her, before her own likeness reemerged. A teardrop formed in her right eye, which spilled down her cheek and dropped to her lap.

Gathering herself, she went to the bathroom and found a washcloth. She spilled some cold water from her glass onto it and wiped her face and eyes. She combed her curly, black hair. She put on her own clean bra, panties, and shorts, the last clean clothes she had. She removed a t-shirt from the girl's dresser that in dark blue lettering had the words, "Grayson County High School, Home of the Blue Devils," and a cartoon devil character holding a three-pronged spear.

She pushed the reflective striping away and unzipped the long zipper of her violin case. She removed the bow and the Guarneri. She tightened the bow and drew several long notes. Her mind couldn't fashion a tune or song, but she let the long notes resonate with vibrations in her head.

Upstroke. A.

Downstroke. G.

Upstroke. D.

Over and over her bow moved, back and forth, to and fro. Her eyes closed and time passed.

The grandfather clock struck again, this time 4:00 p.m., waking her with her violin beside her on the bed. She shook grief-stricken doldrums from her head and took a sip of water. She stood and walked to the closet where several dresses hung. All were her size, but unfashionable. Church was in the morning, she remembered Quint saying. Would he want her to go? Would she go?

She fell into another uneasy nap.

When she awoke towards evening, she entered the kitchen ate some left-over cooked beef and noodles she found in the refrigerator, along with some fresh tomato slices. She washed her dishes in the sink.

As the sun reached towards the horizon of distant hills, she took her violin to the front porch and played some of her favorite classical pieces. Her mind, swimming in sorrow, found comfort in the music. She was lost in thought when Quint arrived, walking back from Fries.

"Did you find something to eat?" he asked.

"Yes."

"We only have another hour or so of daylight," Quint said. "Go on upstairs and arrange your things. We need to leave for church earlier tomorrow morning given that we will need to walk there."

"I'm Jewish. I'm not much on attending church."

"You'll be going to church with me in the morning, young lady. Even if you aren't there for the preachin', there will be folks from the community that you should meet. There's gonna be a picnic afterwards. People will be bringing the food that is thawing in their freezers. I suspect that for the next few days, we will be gorging ourselves on food that would ultimately spoil."

Not wanting to go to church but not wanting to create any tension either, she decided that she would do what she was told, at least for now. Besides, she would need to eat and it appeared her attendance at the afternoon meal would be predicated on her attendance.

Momentarily maintaining her composure, Sammy said, "Thank you for taking me in." She turned and walked away towards the stairs, thinking about what her life would have quickly become if these people had been less generous and what her life was to become now.

Inside her new bedroom, she flipped the switch on the wall instinctively. When the darkness stayed on uninterrupted, she shook her head, felt her heart sink, and began to sob once again. "This sucks!" she thought to herself. "I don't deserve this crap. Dammit, dammit, dammit! I just want it to be over." She pounded her fist hard against the door jam, angrily. She became more angry as she realized how much she'd hurt herself. She plopped face-first onto her bed and cried herself to sleep.

Sunday, August 19

"Rise and shine," said Quint, rapping at Sammy's door. "It's the day of the Lord and we must go offer our blessings." She got out of bed and walked to the closet where she found a bathrobe and a pair of fluffy pink slippers. She walked down the stairs, through the kitchen, and down the back steps and used the outhouse. As revolted as she was from the stench, she was pleased that it seemed amply supplied with toilet paper. She realized that her period was soon in coming and wondered what situation she might find herself in having not brought any tampons with her.

She walked back inside and ascended the stairs. She brushed her teeth and splashed some water on her face. She found a box of tampons in the closet. Then she found a suitable dress hanging in the closet and she put it on. It had a floral pattern that was dowdy by her standards. She went to the mirror and she brushed her hair. She put on her necklace with the Star of David on it, hiding it beneath the décolletage, reasoning that it was not a subject of conversation she wanted to entertain at Quint's church.

She took the time to inventory all her possessions. She had her soft suitcase, filled with six bras, seven panties, six shirts, and four shorts, all now dirty. She had two long pairs of pants, two belts, two pair of shoes, and a jacket. She had a toothbrush, hairbrush, make-up, and some jewelry. She had a *Forever-lite* flashlight and two romance books. And she had her Guarneri inside its case, along with a photograph of her grandfather and some sheet music.

Once ready, she decided to play her violin for a few moments by herself rather than walking downstairs. Soon, Quint came upstairs looking for her. "Are you ready to go?"

"Yes."

"Let me put my violin away."

"Please bring it with you. It may come in handy this afternoon."

The country preacher and the Jewish girl began their stroll to his church, nearly a half-hour away by foot. The subject came up about his various vehicles. He told her that he had tried to start each machine that had an internal combustion engine. What he found was exactly as Pike had said: new things didn't work. But all the old stuff, like tractors and garden tillers, still worked. But he had no working vehicles that would take him much of anywhere.

They walked up the stairs to the front door of Ortie, Dowell, and Rhonda's house. The portly man and his daughter emerged from the house. Ortie and his son were wearing button-up shirts and blue jeans. Rhonda was wearing a low-cut dress that seemed one or two sizes too small, revealing her ample bust-line. She had her hair in a bun with a silver comb.

As the quintet continued their walk, Rhonda said to Sammy, "We don't go to church much. Papa said that under the circumstances we'd best attend today."

At Sammy's insistence, they stopped at Emily's house, where Sammy ran to the door and knocked.

"Good morning, young lady," said Emily. "Thanks again for your visit and your help yesterday."

"You're welcome. We're on our way to church and I stopped to see if you and Jamaal would come with me."

Jamaal appeared beside his host, arranging his dreadlocks around a shirt that had been owned by his hostess' late husband.

"Jamaal, you must come to church with me," said the Jewish girl, hoping he would understand her urgency.

"Okay," he said understandingly. He yelled towards the others, "Quint, I'll be ready in a few minutes. Why don't you and the others go ahead and Sammy and I will follow shortly?"

"Don't be long!" came the retort.

Within fifteen minutes, the two new friends were strolling side by side towards the church.

"How are you hanging in there?" Jamaal asked.

"I feel like I've arrived in hell."

"At times, I do too," he admitted.

They walked in silence for a mile before Sammy asked him about Emily. He said, "She's the widow of a history teacher from the University of Virginia. He was a real Renaissance man. He seemed to have interest in lots of things, including music. He was not a great musician, apparently. But he had several nice instruments.

"Also, he was Jewish, so she knows a lot about Judaism. She is being treated for cancer. I suspect that Quint and Pike wanted me to stay with her because they felt I might be as helpful to her given this new crisis as she would be to me. Please don't say anything to her about her disease; I suspect she told me about it in confidence."

They talked more about their situation. Sammy admitted her fears in being there.

Jamaal shrugged, "You're not alone. Frankly, I'm scared shitless.

When black folks are surrounded by whites, we always look for an escape route. There aren't any. It's anybody's guess how long we'll need to stay here. We need to stick together, you and me."

They reached the church where on a sign-board was written, "Running low on Faith? Stop by for a fill-up." Everyone was already inside. They walked inside as quietly as possible, but when Quint's eyes met them, he hesitated for a moment and everyone looked their way. Jamaal was the only black in the room. The two visitors took a seat on the back pew, and Quint continued.

"Today I'm goin' to talk about how to be saved. People say to me, Preacher Thompson, I would like to be saved but I don't know how.

"Let us start with a prayer. Please bow your head.

"Our most gracious heavenly Father, in Jesus' precious name, I humbly and thankfully bow my head this beautiful day of the Lord. It is a blessing to pray for salvation in the good grace of God. We ask that you help us spread the Gospel of the Good Word of Jesus Christ. May we think or say nothing contrary to the divine and perfect word of God. I pray that you reach everybody with your good and divine word that you care for and love everybody."

His voice rose and fell in volume and exhortation. His enunciation was pronounced and forceful, almost trance-like.

"We pray that those who are hurting through the catastrophe we have suffered, those that are brokenhearted and discouraged, will find strength in the truth of your Word. We pray that you are speaking to the sinner today. We pray that you can reach every sinner and tell him that we're praying for him. We hope you will bless those that are hurt and suffering, and those that are brokenhearted and discouraged. We pray for peace in Jerusalem. We thank you Lord for the privilege of prayer. We ask this in Jesus' name. Amen.

"Now then, how can we be saved? Nobody should perish but all should come to repentance. There is a doctrine across the land that only a select crowd can get to heaven; if you're elected you get to go but if you're not elected, you're not. That's contrary to the word of God. The great heavenly Father loves us all equally. Don't die without Jesus! The only way you can die and have peace with God is through

Jesus. The Father's love has been demonstrated through the ages of the past.

"There is simplicity in salvation. The simple plan of salvation is that whosoever doth believeth and confesseth shall be saved. All of us sin and come short of the Glory of God. People look at drunkards and harlots and say they are sinners. But we have all sinned! You might be peaceful in your heart and devoted to goodwill or you might be an adulterer. But all of us have sinned and come short in the glory of God. But those who have accepted Jesus are included; none are excluded."

Several heads in the congregation bobbed up and down in agreement.

"You might be living a righteous life in comparison to your neighbor, but no! You are not living a righteous life beside the Lord. The soul that sinneth shall die! The wages of sin is death. I tell you, No! But unless you repent, you too will all perish. The reward of God is eternal life! Amen!"

"Amen!" someone shouted.

"Christ died for us! Before you were born, Christ died for you. Christ bore all our sins in His own body for us as He died in agony on the cross. Because of the heavenly generosity of Jesus, we sinners can live in righteousness, praise God!

"Those who have died in sin are not ready to meet God. Their eternal destiny is sealed. Hell is nothing to laugh about. Hell is a horrible place, of burning eternal torture. It is God's will that nobody goes to Hell. God wants all of us to reach repentance.

"The simple plan of salvation is simple indeed. For God so loved the world that he gave his only begotten son that whosoever believeth in him will not perish but will find eternal life. If thou believeth in thy heart that Jesus died for your sins and raiseth from the dead, thou shall be saved!

"Let us sing together,"

O Day of wrath…
Day of wrath! O day of mourning!

See fulfilled the prophets' warning,
Heaven and earth in ashes burning!
Oh, what fear man's bosom rendeth,
When from heav'n the Judge descendeth,
Wondrous sound the trumpet flingeth;
Through earth's sepulchers it ringeth;
All before the throne it bringeth.
Death is struck, and nature quaking,
All creation is awaking,
To its Judge an answer making.
Lo! the book, exactly worded,
Wherein all hath been recorded:
Thence shall judgment be awarded.

Concluding the service, Quint announced that the authorities in town had called everyone to come together the next morning at the town hall for an update to the crisis and a coping strategy. Then they sang their concluding hymn, with Rhonda's clear voice echoing above the others.

Just A Closer Walk With Thee
I am weak, but Thou art strong;
Jesus, keep me from all wrong;
I'll be satisfied as long
As I walk, let me walk close to Thee.

After church, the congregation met outside where a huge spread of food materialized under a pavilion. Sammy and Jamaal met several members of the congregation. Nobody was outwardly rude, but their homeliness and stares at her gave her the creeps.

Both Sammy and Jamaal played their instruments with everyone else, but a deathly pall permeated the air. Sammy departed with Jamaal and walked the rest of the way home alone.

Monday, August 20

Quint woke Sammy for the hour-long walk into Fries for the town meeting. There was some milk in a pitcher on the table along with some peaches. She helped herself and ate alone. The milk tasted good. It was lukewarm and sweeter than she expected.

The sun was bright and the day was rapidly warming on their eastbound journey. They stopped at Emily's house as they had done the day before to gather these friends with them. During most of the walk, Quint and Emily walked together ahead and Sammy walked with Jamaal several steps behind.

Jamaal said, "We're about to learn more about where we stand. I don't expect any good news."

They arrived at the dark brown building marked with a semi-circular green sign with yellow characters, "Fries Theater". A colorful sign indicating "The Crooked Road, Virginia's Heritage Music Trail" hung beside the double-door entrance. A large, anxious crowd gathered outside. Quint was immediately engaged by some townspeople. Several people stared for a moment at the young dark-haired girl and the black man, recognizing them as strangers.

Sammy saw Shane talking with a small, uniformed woman. As Sammy approached, he said, "Samantha, I'd like you to meet my mother, Annie."

"Hi, I'm Samantha Reisinger."

"It's nice to meet you. I don't mean to be rude, but I gotta go inside and help Chief set things up."

The woman took her leave and Shane said, "Mom is an assistant to Chief Cunningham. In fact, he and she are the only police we have in Fries."

A large, uniformed man appeared in the doorway and said, "Y'all come in and let's get started." His belly was so large that his belt went under rather than around it. Varicose veins gave his nose and cheeks a ruddy appearance.

The small theater-like room was packed. Pike was up front, as was the large man and Shane's mother. Sammy, Jamaal, and Emily stood near the back. Sammy nodded to Keene Campbell. Rhonda, Dowell, and Ortie Shelor sat towards the front but appeared not to see Sammy.

"Y'all settle down," Chief Cunningham said briskly. "We've got lots to cover today. Mayor Lester and his family are on vacation in Florida, so I'll conduct the meeting. Looks like we have no way of telling when they'll be back.

"My job is to keep the peace and see that as many community needs are met as possible. I've been to more emergency training sessions than I can count. But nobody done been trained for this. The basic stuff we're all going to need is water, human waste disposal, food, and shelter. Plus, we'll need to find a way to communicate with each other and with surrounding communities. Professor Pike McConnell from Tech and Woody Dalton from the Rescue Squad have been working with me overnight to discuss this stuff. They'll be helping me with the meeting."

Pike and the other man nodded to the audience, while Cunningham continued, "We're fortunate in some regards in that we have plenty of water. Those of you on the municipal water system know there's already nothing coming out of your tap. For the time being, Willy over at the water purification plant will be funneling water from Stevens Creek through some of his filters. If anybody has a large water tank that we can put on a cart, let me know after the meeting. Otherwise, y'all will have to go to the water plant on foot and carry jugs with you. Those of you outside the town limits are welcome to use the water if you don't have access to a spring. We all have access to the River, but be sure to purify the water if you're going to drink it. You'll need to boil it or use water purification tablets.

"I have instructed Wayman from the sewage treatment plant to work with Pike to retro-fit the school's locker rooms to be the town's latrine."

Pike said, "Until we can get water back into your houses, we're all going to have to crap there. If you can fashion a chamber pot, you can use that and empty it at the latrine. Otherwise, if you have your own outhouse, particularly you folks outside the town limits, you can use that. But anybody caught dumping human waste on the ground will be arrested, because it will spread germs and nothing will destroy all of us faster than widespread illness."

Cunningham took over, "For those of you who ain't stored up some food, I suspect you're going to start having problems pretty soon. Keep your refrigerators and freezers closed as much as you can. The food inside should last a few days if not a week or two. Food deliveries from outside are not going to happen. I've already told Dale over at the grocery store to shoot looters on sight. Any questions?"

"Yeah, I got one," said a man wearing bib overalls and a hostile expression. "What the hell happened?"

"Sorry. I guess we should have started there. Pike, you want to explain?"

"Thanks Chief Cunningham. We all know the power is off. Our best guess is that we've suffered what scientists call an EMP, which stands for Electromagnetic Pulse. Nothing else would have done as much damage to the electrical systems. They can be natural or man-made. The man-made variety comes from nuclear explosions set off high in the sky, anything over 40 miles. The natural cause is typically solar flares or what is called coronal mass ejections. With things being as they are, we don't have any way of knowing.

"We do know that solar EMP blasts have occurred before. One was before the Civil War, in 1859. The other was in 1921. The first was before electricity and the second was weaker and when electricity was only beginning to be distributed. So neither did much damage.

"Ih won't go into a lot of detail, but electricity moves from generating plants, whether they are coal, nuclear, or hydroelectric, to us via what's called the grid. The grid, to a solar flare, looks like a giant antenna. In the same way that lightning rods attract lighting bolts and channel the energy to the ground, the grid attracts space weather bolts. The weakest points are the transformers, which convert the power for use. Ih'm guessing thousands of transformers are destroyed and they are not easily replaced. So it looks like we'll be without electricity for months, perhaps even years, depending upon how widespread the damage is."

A groan of shock came over the crowd. "This sucks," a younger man screamed. Several heads nodded in agreement.

"How come my car don't work?" said a woman, angrily.

"Basically anything that is microprocessor-based is vulnerable. That's why your digital watch and phone don't work either. Cars are filled with computerized things these days, the controls and most significantly the ignitions. The parts under the hood have accentuated the effects of the Pulse."

Ortie said, "But we got a dam right here in Fries. Don't it work?"

Cunningham said, "Its generator hasn't been run in years. Professor McConnell and I are pulling together a team to look into that. Even if we don't have transformers, we may still be able to generate some power for the town. Pike?"

"We're going to do the best we can," Pike replied. "Ih'd also like to talk about communication. Right now, we have none. We have six or eight ham radio operators in town, but most of the equipment is ruined. Frankly, Ih'm not sure we really want to know what's going on elsewhere, but Ih daresay most places will be much worse off than we are. The cities and suburbs will be in turmoil within days, if they aren't already. Still, if anybody here has skills or equipment for radio communication, raise your hand."

The man near him said, "I'm Woody Dalton. I'm the new head of the rescue squad. I'll be coordinating that effort."

To Sammy's surprise, Jamaal raised his hand. When Pike recognized him, he said, "I have some radio skills. After the meeting, I can tell you what I know."

"This is dreadful. When's this going to blow over?" yelled a professional looking woman from the back row of chairs, as if in denial.

"When is somebody going to fix this?" another woman screamed.

Pike said, "May Ih take this, Chief? With all due respect, ma'am, this isn't going to blow over. This is a frightfully serious matter. We only have an inkling of what we're up against. Anybody who was on life support over at the hospital in Galax is surely dead already. Anybody who relies on regular doses of medicine for survival, particularly those medicines that require refrigeration, will probably die soon. Is anybody here diabetic and on insulin?"

A few hands went up.

"If your insulin doses need refrigeration to keep from spoiling, you may die. We won't be getting more doses from anywhere else either. We're going to have trouble keeping diseases from spreading and providing relief to those who get sick. Most of us will at some point soon begin going hungry. As I said a moment ago, we should fare better than some places, but only if we work together and avoid internecine strife."

"Inter-what?" yelled someone.

"We need to keep from killing each other," replied Pike, matter-of-factly.

A hush fell over the audience. Sammy looked at the stylish woman, whose eyes nearly popped from her sockets.

"Let's go about our business," said the police chief. "Let's meet here again in a week and re-assess our situation."

Walking to the door, Jamaal said to Emily and Sammy, "I'm going to stay behind and meet the rescue squad guy and see how I can help with the communications."

Emily said to Sammy, "Why don't you come home with me and let's have another look at the garden? I think we're going to need it more this year than ever."

Sammy waved at Shane and then departed with Emily.

On their way home, Sammy said, "The faces in that room really scared me. There was so much fear and anger."

"It's to be expected," Emily said sagaciously. "They're in shock, facing mortal grief. People cope with it in predictable ways."

"What do you mean?"

"Back in 1969, a psychologist named Elisabeth Kübler-Ross described five discrete stages that people typically go through when facing a catastrophic loss. First is denial, arguing that it can't really be happening. Then they express anger, displaying rage that they are victims and others might not be afflicted. Then they bargain, asking for mitigated circumstances. The fourth stage is depression, with crying and grieving. Finally, if they live long enough, they accept their fate and deal with it the best they can. Each face in that meeting displayed where each person was in that process."

"I think I'm still in denial," Sammy offered. "I can't believe this has really happened, that my parents are dead and I'm stuck here."

"I don't know you very well yet, but spending as little time in stages two, three, and four and moving right to acceptance will help you sustain yourself and be more successful."

"Thanks. Knowing the stages will help me, I'm sure."

"Speaking of which, Jamaal has told me a bit about you, but I'd like to know more. Please tell me about yourself."

"I live in Alpine, New Jersey. Dad works for Goldman Sachs in international finance. I think I told you, Mom is a clinical psychologist. I never thought of us as rich because all our neighbors have money, too, but I guess we are. We have a second home an hour from Alpine and a vacation home in Aruba."

"Are you in school?"

"Yes, ma'am. I just graduated from a private school called The Hudson School. I'm enrolled at the North Carolina School of the Arts in Winston-Salem in the fall. With what's happened, I have no idea whether I'll be able to go. My parents have always been good to me but my dad doesn't have much tolerance for people who are less fortunate than we are."

"What do you do for fun?" Emily asked.

"I love playing my violin. I inherited it from my grandfather who played on the New York Philharmonic. It was made in Italy in the 1700s. My grandfather died when I was six, but we were very close.

"Also, I have a horse named Wilbur. She's a Leopard Appaloosa mare, black and white in color. She's a little thing, only 13-hands. How about yourself?"

Emily deflected her question, "Tell me more about you. How did you end up here?"

Three black vultures flew in the lazy breeze overhead, evidently looking for some carrion. Sammy wondered whether these birds would have a more difficult time with fewer cars running over small animals. Perhaps all creatures were due to suffer.

Sammy told Emily about her earlier experiences at fiddlers' conventions and learning about Galax. "My parents were in Europe last week and they were scheduled to be on an airplane when the Pulse hit. I assume that their airplane probably crashed. Every time I think about them and all of the other passengers in that airplane at the time, flying high over the Atlantic Ocean and having everything go dark and the engines quit and the plane plunging into the frigid water, it makes me sick to my stomach. I assume I'm now an orphan." She could feel her eyes moisten.

"I am really sorry," Emily said. She patted Sammy on the shoulder. "I don't know what else to say."

A brown groundhog sat alongside the road munching grass. Sammy thought what it might be like to resort to eating such a creature. Looking to change the subject, she said, "You said earlier that you were a midwife. What does that entail?"

"There are several different levels of midwifery. Virginia requires a license. It is called a CPM. A direct entry midwife follows from the old tradition of granny midwives. As I mentioned, I was a nurse. When I decided to become a midwife, I went to a special school in Florida. Then I had to take an exam for my license.

"Helping a woman give birth is a heady responsibility. It takes time for a midwife to build her skills and confidence level. The skills that a midwife must master are things like drawing blood, stitch and suture, taking blood pressure, doing an internal exam, assessing if any medical conditions are arising in the mother or fetus and making appropriate assessments of the fetus. It's interesting, rewarding work."

Sammy thought she might volunteer as a helper, but wanted to think about it more.

Sammy and Emily arrived back at Emily's house and Emily invited Sammy to join her for a cup of tea. Again, while Emily heated some water over a small camp stove, Sammy looked around the living room. It was filled with books and artifacts from what appeared to be a world of travel. There was an entire bookcase filled with books on religion.

Returning from the kitchen with two cups, Emily said, "I am truly sorry for you. I know what it is like to lose loved ones. My mother died when I was 18 and my father when I was 30. It's never easy."

The two new friends were silent for a moment, sipping their tea.

Emily continued, "I don't know if Jamaal told you, but I have cancer. Anal cancer. For obvious reasons, it's not a topic of polite conversation," she smiled wanly. "It is most effectively treated with surgery, but the sphincter is removed, the sufferer is left incontinent. I refuse to live that way. So I'm having it treated with radiation and chemotherapy. This has been effective for the last six months, but with the situation as it is, I don't expect I'll survive it. Several women have become dependent upon me as their midwife and I will do everything I can not to let them down. But if you have any interest, having you along will be very helpful to me."

The women worked in Emily's garden for a couple of hours in the afternoon, bringing in tomatoes, summer squash, and broccoli. Sammy took some home with her for Quint and Hattie.

Tuesday, August 21

With all her underclothing now dirty and in a pile, Sammy finally donned a bra and a pair of the dead girl's panties. She took an old pair of shorts and a worn T-shirt from the dresser.

Sammy spent much of the morning working again in Emily's garden, digging weeds, and gathering vegetables before the sun got too hot. It was a warming, muggy day, and the bonnet she'd found in the closet kept the sweat from trickling from her forehead, although she thought she looked silly in it, like a character from a long-ago English movie. Rhonda arrived within an hour, quickly assessing the needs and devoting her prodigious energies to the garden. Sammy was impressed that her new friend was agile and active in spite of her girth.

The garden yielded a bounty of vegetables, including several varieties of tomatoes, radishes, beets, potatoes, summer squash, and peppers.

As the girls were finishing their work, a long-haired woman appeared at the fence. She yelled winsomely, "Hello, girls!" They walked over to greet her.

The woman said, "Hi Rhonda. Who's your helper?"

"This is Sammy. She's stuck here. She's from New Jersey."

"Hi Sammy. I'm Marissa, Hattie's sister," smiled the new arrival.

"Hi! Quint mentioned you," Sammy rested on her rake. "It's nice to meet you."

"It's a long walk from Galax!"

"You walked here?" Rhonda exclaimed.

"Yup. My car is dead like everybody else's. I live about eight miles away, and I left early to avoid the heat. According to my old wind-up watch, it took me almost three hours to walk here." She wound it reflexively.

The two girls and the woman walked back to the house together and stopped in the shade of one of the two large maple trees in the yard. Sammy guessed her to be in her late thirties. Marissa asked Sammy about her circumstance, which Sammy relayed again.

"I sympathize," the woman said. "My family's had more than its share of heartache," Marissa admitted.

She had a pleasant way about her. Sammy liked her and wondered about Quint's disparaging comment about her.

"Thank you," Sammy said. "I feel like I'm having some sort of awful nightmare. I don't even know how to cry. I feel like I'm in a catatonic state and somebody is going to come along and snap their fingers and I'll awake and find that everything is fine again."

"It's the Lord's will, I'm afraid. I'm sure your parents are prepared for the afterlife."

"What do you mean?"

"We are all meant to suffer and to die, where if we're saved, we'll spend eternity close to Jesus."

"I'm Jewish," Sammy asserted.

"I don't know much about Jews," Marissa said, chuckling. "But we are religious people. We understand suffering. Hattie and I married brothers, Quint and Rupert Thompson. So we're double-kin. This happens a lot around here, more in the past than now, but it is still common. Rupert got me pregnant with Tommy when I was only 18. I was eight months pregnant when we married. He left me a couple of years later. Last I heard, he was living in some hollow in Kentucky. He was a good man when he was sober, but he wasn't sober very often. I always figured it was good that he left us when he did."

Marissa took a sip of water from a plastic bottle she'd carried, and then continued, "I finished an associate's degree from Wytheville Community College and now I work at the library in Galax. Tommy is in the infantry and right now he's in Afghanistan. So I come over here a lot to help Hattie. She milks the goats and makes cheese. She is too traumatized to do much socializing, so I take the milk and cheese and sell them for her. She had two main customers, the nursing home here in Providence and the health food store in Galax. Without any refrigeration or vehicle, I won't be able to take anything to Galax, but I suspect she'll have plenty of demand for her products here in Providence."

"Quint told me he and Hattie lost their children."

"Yes, all three of their children are dead. Danny was the oldest. Danny was seven or eight, I can't remember. He and his uncle Hank had taken a canoe on the river. The current was too strong for them. They were swept towards a snag in the river and the canoe capsized. Hank was able to swim to shore. Danny was still in the river, so Hank swam back out to catch him, but he wasn't able to reach him. Hank almost died, too.

"The twin girls were four years younger. Ronnie got a right tearful start in life. From a young age, she had leukemia. Her condition deteriorated until she was fourteen, when she passed. Bonnie carried all the family's best hopes on her shoulders and when she got engaged two years ago, everyone was mighty happy. We were sure she would produce the grandchildren Quint and Hattie longed for. Hattie was devastated when the first two deaths came, but Bonnie's death was the last straw. I'm not sure she'll ever recover. She'll occasionally mutter a few words to me, but she's withdrawn herself completely from everybody else."

"What happened?" Sammy asked, with sincere interest.

"Hattie and Bonnie went to Roanoke to shop for a wedding dress. On the way home, Bonnie was driving her new car. There was fog on Bent Mountain. The driver of a truck carrying logs down the mountain misjudged a curve and slammed into them. Their car was thrown over an embankment. Hattie had a broken arm, but she was still conscious. Bonnie got the worst of it. Her skull was fractured and she lost consciousness and died as Hattie held her with the unbroken arm.

"Quint isn't much help. They have a tragic relationship. They basically live separate lives in the same house. They rarely converse with one another and I'm sure they don't sleep together."

"Seems to me Hattie blames the Lord," said Rhonda.

"I think you're right," Marissa brushing gnats from her eyes. "Quint is fixated on his religion, at least what he thinks it is. He believes that God has a reason for everything and everything happens for a reason. Hattie believes that God has forsaken her, taking the three most precious things in the world. When their son died, Hattie and Quint were in the church and a state policeman arrived with the news. Hattie hasn't been in the church again since. The church has become what psychologists call a 'traumatic trigger.' For her, uniformed men and cars are triggers, too. Quint picked her up from the hospital in Roanoke where they treated her for her broken arm, but I don't think she's ridden in a car since."

"My mom is a psychologist," Sammy said. "But we never talk much about her work. She won't tell me anything about her clients. You seem to know a lot about trauma."

"Well, I work in a library. We have some slow times and when we do, I like to read to pass the time and learn as much as I can. My job doesn't pay much but it's steady. I've always figured that I might find myself needing a new situation, so I'd best be as prepared and educated as possible."

"What do you think religion says about misery?" asked Rhonda, curiously.

"I am a Christian woman. I accept Jesus Christ as my Lord and Savior. I have sin in my life; all of us live sinful lives from birth. But I try my hardest to live a life pleasing to the Lord. It is my responsibility to take care of Hattie; she really needs me."

"How do you feel about her rejection of the Lord?" Rhonda continued her inquiry.

"I understand where she's coming from. Lots of my friends believe that through the belief in Christ is the only way to salvation. I used to believe it, too. Now I'm not so sure. There are seven billion people on earth. About two billion consider themselves Christian. I'm not sure anybody can realistically say that the Christian way is the only way."

Sammy noticed a female figure and a small dog cresting the horizon at the pasture beyond the picket fence row at the end of the garden. Marissa said, "That is Hattie and Snoopy, the dog. I'm assuming you have been introduced by now."

"No," said Sammy. "I've been here for a couple of days now. I was beginning to question whether she really existed."

"Well, let's walk that way and perhaps she will walk towards us." They dropped their garden tools and walked to the end of the row and then towards the fence. The woman in the field stood immobile for several moments and then she began walking towards them. A tricolor Welsh corgi trotted along beside her.

Reaching the fence, Marissa said to her sister, "Hattie, I would like you to meet Samantha Reisinger. You may be aware that she is staying in Bonnie and Ronnie's bedroom."

Sammy approached her new host. Placing her left hand on a fence post, she presented her right hand for a handshake. "It is nice to meet you," Sammy said.

The woman on the other side of the fence had a pleasant face but her blue eyes conveyed a vacancy that prickled the skin on the back of Sammy's arms. Hattie wore a thin, dirty pink scarf over her strawberry blond hair. Her light-weight blouse was mis-buttoned. She stared for a moment at Sammy's outstretched hand but did not present her own to reciprocate.

"Sammm. Mannnn. Thaaa," muttered the woman. The corgi at her feet growled at Sammy for a moment, and then found a gap in the wire fence and rushed over to her feet, smelled her for a moment, and then jumped excitedly towards her waist. Sammy bent down on her knees and the dog briskly licked her face. Sammy smiled, soaking in the affection.

"Sammy is going to be living with you and Quint for the time being. I'm sure you know by now there has been a serious power failure. Sammy may stay here until power is restored and she can go home to New Jersey."

Marissa continued, "There is another member of the family that I want you to meet. Are you aware that Bonnie had a horse named Jackson?"

"No, nobody has mentioned him to me. I love riding horses and I have one of my own back home. Do you think it will be okay if I ride him?"

"I doubt he'll let you. I'm told that Jackson hasn't been ridden since Bonnie died. I'm not even sure he'll let you near him. But on the other hand, if Jackson reacts to you the same way Snoopy has, maybe I'm wrong. Please come with us, Hattie."

Marissa, Sammy, and Rhonda began walking southward, but Hattie and the corgi stayed immobile. They walked towards, then around a large barn, with wooden plank walls and a rusting metal gambrel roof. It appeared to have never been painted, and was a lovely, rustic sight. As they passed a tree laden with yellow apples, each of them picked one for themselves. Knowing horses' love for apples, Sammy picked two extra for Jackson.

They approached a metal gate to a sweeping pasture, where there was a great view towards the mountains of the west. Buzzards soared in the moist, cloudy sky. A fine horse, dark, with a large dapple on his flank, grazed peacefully. Marissa yelled, "Jackson!" but the horse was unmoved.

Sammy said, "Let me try it." She whistled as she always did for Wilbur, and held an apple high over her head. Jackson looked their way and came trotting over. He was a large, muscular chestnut brown, warmblood gelding, with a large head and wide feet below black lower legs. His mane and tail appeared to have not been brushed for awhile. He stopped a dozen feet short of the gate, gave them a second look, and then ambled over to take the apple from Sammy's outstretched hand. He drooled profusely as he chomped the fruit. Then he nuzzled Sammy's shoulder.

"Well look at that," said Rhonda. "He's never let me close to him. I think he likes you."

"Maybe he sees something of Bonnie in you," smiled Marissa.

"I think he just wants the other apple," joked Sammy, modestly. "Here you go, big guy." He stood about 17 hands. "You and I are going to be friends, aren't we?"

"Like I said, I'm sure he hasn't been ridden since Bonnie died," Marissa said.

Sammy stroked his chin and said, "Horses need to be ridden and worked. He looks a bit overweight. Maybe I can work with him and maybe he'll let me ride him."

"All his tack is still in the barn. Let's go inside the house and see what we can find for lunch. If you want, maybe you can come back to the barn this afternoon and find some brushes for him."

Sammy smiled, "Yes, I'd like to do that."

"May I stay for lunch?" asked Rhonda. "Afterwards I'm going over to Emily's house to help her with the garden. Don't forget there is a jam session tonight in town."

"What's that?" Sammy asked.

"It's been going on for years, perhaps decades as far as I know. Daddy says the Tuesday jam sessions were goin' on even when he was a child. I don't know how many people will attend, what with the power failure. Dad says we've had crises before and the jam never stopped happening. Why don't I come by after dinnertime and we can walk into town together?"

"You girls go ahead and go. I'll stay at the house and see if I can help Hattie. Maybe she'll talk with me about how she feels about having you here, Sammy. Sometimes she talks a little bit to me and sometimes not."

The three grilled some hot dogs, along with fresh tomatoes and lettuce. At the insistence of the others, Sammy talked about her family and life. They seemed amazed at her travels and cultural experiences, from seeing the Metropolitan Opera to watching the New York Yankees baseball games.

After lunch, Rhonda departed and Sammy returned to the barn where she enticed Jackson inside. She spent the better part of the afternoon brushing him, pulling burrs from his tail and mane, and trimming his hair. His gentle approach surprised her. He nuzzled against her ear several times. She was happy for the first time since the Pulse. She thought he was happy, too.

She returned to the house and had supper with Marissa. "I'm going to stay overnight tonight. It's too far for me to walk back to Galax tonight. Do you mind if I take Ronnie's bed in your bedroom?"

"I'm hardly thinking of it as 'my bedroom,'" Sammy admitted. "It will be good to have some company. How did your afternoon go with Hattie?"

"Some visits she's good and some not. She was not communicative with me today. I'm not sure what she makes of you."

"With all due respect, I'm not sure what I make of her, either. I hope to make myself a good visitor and I will treat her as nicely as I can."

"That's all anyone might ask or expect."

That moment, Rhonda arrived. "Ready to go?"

"Let me wash my face and grab my violin. I'll get my flashlight, too."

"Bring a jacket with you. Up here in the mountains it can get chilly any night, even in the summer."

During their hour-long walk into town, Sammy asked Rhonda about her song-writing.

"My life has had a lot of pain. Mom left me and my little brother, Dowell, when he was young. He is developmentally disabled. He's 11 now. Dad tries hard, but he drowns his sorrows in working the farm. I guess it's better than drowning in alcohol, but still, he has no idea what to do with Dowell."

They stopped at Emily's house to ask Jamaal if he wanted to go, but he said, "I'm not really in the mood for music just yet. You go on without me."

The girls arrived at the jam session venue in Fries the same time as Shane. "How're y'all doing?" he asked boisterously.

"Makin' do," said Rhonda. "You?"

"Insane and angry! Mom is stressed out to the max. So is Chief Cunningham. Folks are coming to them looking for answers that they don't have. There is no radio communication around here, maybe anywhere. People are already reporting larcenies. Old man Bates died yesterday when his breathing apparatus failed. Word has it that two old people died up on Hilltown, but I didn't know them. I imagine Viller Boyd over at the Funeral Home is going to run a brisk business for awhile."

Sammy saw Quint arrive, presumably walking from the drug store and she said hello to him. Keene and Pike were talking to each other, along with a third man Sammy didn't recognize. Pike said hello to Sammy and Jamaal. Then he introduced them to Woody Dalton from the Rescue Squad. Woody said, "I understand you are marooned here." He was a kindly man, tall, with wild grey hair and a salt-and-pepper beard. He spoke with a scratchy voice.

"That's not a way I would have phrased it, but that looks to be the case. How about you?" Sammy asked.

"I live on a farm near here with my wife, Caroline, over west of Providence. Do you know where that is?"

"Yes, right now I'm staying with Quint and Hattie Thompson."

Woody continued as if old friends, "Our farm has been in the family for years. My real name is Forrest, but everybody calls me Woody. Get it?"

He walked inside with Sammy and Rhonda and they found seats together. He had a viola that he removed from its case. "Anyway, we were living near Durham, North Carolina until a few years ago. I was in pharmaceuticals and Caroline was a nurse. About seven years ago, my parents were in declining health and Caroline decided that we needed to move to the farm." He began drawing the bow back and forth, tuning the instrument. Once satisfied, he continued, "By the time we moved there, papa was in a coma and mom had dementia and was getting worse. There was an old elementary school in Providence that the county had abandoned the prior year. So we bought it and turned it into a nursing home that Caroline runs. Papa died within weeks of moving in and Mom died two years later. So now I run the farm and Caroline runs the nursing home. She's spent just about every minute since the Pulse over there. They've already lost seven or eight of their twenty-four residents. I was helping out but I needed a break from all the death. Besides, there's way more work on the farm than I can do."

Sammy realized that Caroline's nursing home was the one Marissa had mentioned as being one of Hattie's customers. It surprised her how forthcoming people were about their lives.

Pike started to strum a song he called *Betty Liken* on his banjo, interrupting the various conversations going on. Seven musicians attended and eleven people sat in lawn chairs in the audience section of the old theater. During the song, Rhonda's dad, Ortie, arrived and began playing an upright bass that somebody had left there.

They played several tunes, some that Sammy recognized and some not. Woody helped Sammy with the fingering on a couple of songs she didn't know. They played several traditional Appalachian tunes. Rhonda said, "I've been working on a new song. Y'all mind if I sing it?"

"Please!"

"It's called, *Home is Where the Fiddle Rings.*"

When people ask me where I come from
There's only one place I think of
It's where I hear them old timey songs
It's where I know I'll always belong
Home is where the fiddle rings
Home is where my momma sings
Home is where the mountains are high
And home is where my heart is

Only a few tunes later, Rhonda said to Sammy, "Dad ain't feeling good. We're leavin'. You can come, or you'll need to walk alone later."

Quint said, "I'm going home now, too, to check on some things at the house. Sammy, you need to come with us."

Shane, overhearing the conversation said, "If it's all right with you, Quint, I'll walk Sammy home," neither man asking Sammy for her desires or input.

"You all go ahead," Sammy insisted. "If Shane will walk me home, I'll be fine."

Ortie Shelor stashed the bass in the back room and he and Rhonda waved to everyone. "Are we going to keep doing this each week?"

"This power outage be damned," said Keene defiantly, striking his lighter to light an oil lamp someone had brought. "As long as I'm livin' and breathin' I'm comin' here to play music. Folks were coming here to play music before we had electricity and I'll be damned if I'm going to stop coming now."

Heads around the room nodded in agreement as Rhonda, Ortie, and Quint departed.

They played a few more tunes before everyone decided to call it quits. Sammy and Shane stashed their instruments in their cases and emerged from the dimly lit room into the night. A sliver of a moon cast just enough light to see their way on the dark road.

"You played really well tonight," said Shane.

"Thanks, although I'm not really sure I deserve the compliment. I have been taking violin lessons since I was eight years old, but everything that has been taught to me has been from the perspective of written music. I'm really not accustomed to improvisation. My musicianship is much more mechanical. I mean I look at what is on the sheet of music in front of me and I play that."

"I see what you mean," he said. "I have never learned to read music at all. When I was in elementary school, I took lessons in tablature, which is a simplified way of reading music. I think most people who learn in tablature use that merely as a transition to playing by ear. My guess is that just about everybody in the room, with the exception of Woody Dalton plays by ear."

"By the way, music jams are informal, but there is an unspoken protocol that you might want to know about."

"Yes, please," Sammy said, eager to learn how to better fit in.

"There is usually a leader. It's typically Quint when he comes. He gives a nod to each person to take a break. A break is jam-speak for a solo. When he nods at you, go ahead and take your lead. If you don't want to, give a negative shake of your head and he'll pass you by. Generally, the songs to be done are selected in sequence around the circle, clockwise. This person selects the key and announces it to everyone else. When there are vocals, usually you'll only want to contribute during the chorus, and then you'll want to harmonize. If you have to re-tune your instrument or want to learn a new lick from someone, step outside the jam and work on it separately."

"Thanks," Sammy said. "These are good things to know. It is certainly a much more joyous music than what I am used to. I have a feeling that the time will come when we will need as much of that joy as we can find."

Beyond the outskirts of town, the road banked sharply and turned away from the river. Deep woods surrounded the road on both sides and the darkness was pervasive. The meager light emanating from the moon was blocked by the branches of trees, overhanging the road. Sammy was startled when she thought she saw something move in the road. Shane said, "It is probably nothing more than a garter snake. No harm done."

They walked in silence for a few moments but Sammy found herself uncomfortable in the enveloping quiet. All she could hear was the chirping of crickets or frogs, she wasn't sure which, on the creek beside the road.

Making conversation, she said, "Fries is an unusual name for a town."

"It is not pronounced as 'fries,' but as 'freeze,'" he said, correcting her. "It got its name from the town's founder, whose name was Col. Francis H. Fries. The Fries family was in the textile business in North Carolina and his father was treasurer of the first cotton mill built in Winston-Salem before the Civil War.

"Fries left the textile business in his 20s and got a job with the Roanoke and Southern Railway between Roanoke and Winston-Salem. He also got involved in banking."

"How do you know all this stuff?" she asked.

"I told you I am working on a degree in military history at VMI. But I have always been interested in Virginia history, particularly history of my town. I think everybody who grows up in Virginia is interested in history. We're infested with it.

"Anyway, nearing the end of the 19th century, Fries rejoined the textile business and became president of a mill in North Carolina. In 1901, he was convinced that this area would be a good place to build a mill because they could get cheap power from the New River. For some reason that I can't remember, it required an act of Congress to build a dam on the river. But when this was done in 1902, the town of Fries, which was soon named for him, exploded in population."

"Did your relatives work there?"

"Yup. Both grandpas did and one grandma. Almost everybody around here did. It was a typical mill town. Everything was tightly controlled by the company. The company built streets, boarding houses, a bank, a post office, a commissary, and almost 300 houses. The mill began operation in early 1903, the same year the Wright brothers successfully flew for the first time on the coast of North Carolina. Fries is an older community than Galax, which was founded a few years later.

"When word spread throughout the South that people could find work, soon, whole families migrated here. Even though the wages were low, the hours were long, and the conditions were difficult, people preferred working a cash job rather than working in the fields. Grandpa Wilkins talked about it all the time before he died.

"Like so many other manufacturing concerns in this country, the tide began to turn in the 1970s and 1980s as foreign competitors began to rob jobs from Americans. Ironically, when the plant closed in 1989, it was actually at its peak in employment.

"The town has been in decline since then, although things have turned around in the last few years, as these old houses have begun to find new owners. Even today, the New River is largely unspoiled, likely the longest stretch of un-industrialized river left in the eastern United States. Nowadays, fishermen, hunters, canoeists, and bicycle riders come to Fries. Or at least they did until last Friday."

"It's certainly a beautiful setting," Sammy observed.

"True, but there has never been much money or much in the way of income for most people who live in Southwest Virginia. The great economic boom that this country has seen since the Second World War has largely bypassed Southwest Virginia. Grandpa used to joke that even during the Great Depression, things didn't change much here because the area had always been depressed. The Civil War left this area largely in ruins, with fractured lives and fractured communities. We have really never fully recovered. We have had to rely on ourselves, on our culture, and on our music to build successful and happy lives."

Green, red, and pink lights danced across the night sky, looking like what Sammy thought the Northern Lights looked like. She had never seen the Northern Lights before and wondered if it was an effect from the Pulse.

Shane kicked a small rock ahead of their path. "I've heard it said many times that it is hard to go past three consecutive houses in Southwest Virginia and not find a musician. But Fries in particular has had a tremendous history in traditional Appalachian music. I know that being here in this tragedy is tremendously stressful for you. Nobody knows how long this crisis will last. But we all need to do what we can to make the best of it. If you're as interested in music as I think you are, you will find much to learn here in Fries.

"Fries is a tiny town, but its contribution to music has been considerable. When better music is made, it will be made in Fries." He boasted.

Nearing Quint and Hattie's house, Shane said, "Is it okay with you if I do not walk you to the door? Quint and I have never really cared much for each other. I don't want him to think there is anything going on between us."

"That's fine," she said holding out her hand to thank him, wondering what he thought was going on between them. Setting down his banjo case on the edge of the pavement, he took her hand and he pulled her close. He reached behind her neck and pulled her cheek towards his. Then, he pulled her lips together with his. She closed her eyes and felt his tongue parting her lips and brushing alongside her teeth. He pulled his body close to hers. He reached behind her and rested his hand on her rump and pulled her hips close to his. Her pulse quickened and she felt her hips brushing against the bulge in his trousers. She closed her eyes and felt moisture forming in her groin, silently scolding herself and her new suitor for experiencing sexual pleasure at a time of grief and mourning.

She took a deep sigh and thought how good it felt to be held. But she pushed herself away. "I must be going," she said. "Thanks again for walking me home." She turned and walked briskly towards the dimly lit farmhouse.

Wednesday, August 22

The next morning, the eastern sky was bright when Sammy was awoken by a knock at her door, interrupting a dream. In it, she was in a big house, like a mansion, but there were shelves of toys, stretching higher than she could reach. There were fantastic things everywhere, models of mechanization and modernity. When she wanted to reach something on the shelf, the slab of floor she stood on would raise up for her to get it. But it would knock something off and break other toys. The lights were bright but they threw off sparks, frightening her. She went to the Ladies Room, where instead of toilet paper there was a spray from below, but it fouled her clothes. She was angry that nothing worked as it should and she awoke shaken.

"Sammy," said Quint, "Wake up. You need to do something for me this morning. There is a meeting going to happen at the Providence General Store to talk about provisions. I want you to go and see what's going on. I would go myself but I really need to tend to the pharmacy. Hattie has left some goat's milk cheese. See if anybody needs it."

Sammy went to the outhouse for her morning constitutional, and then to the pump to collect water for her sponge-bath. She almost forgot about Marissa, but saw that the bed beside her had been neatly made and assumed that Marissa had already departed. She found some yoghurt in the refrigerator, which by now was barely cooler than room temperature. Leaving the house on foot, she went out of her way to go by the apple tree where she took an apple for herself and fed another to Jackson.

She walked to Emily's house to tell her and Jamaal about the meeting. Jamaal met her at the door. "Emily has left this morning to attend to one of her clients who's expecting in the next week or so. But I already know about the meeting. I've been talking to Carlene who runs the place. We're going to present a new way to do business."

Sammy gave Jamaal some cheese that he put in the kitchen.

Descending the front porch stairs together, Jamaal asked, "How are you doing, Sammy?"

"My stomach is in a knot," she confessed. "Sometimes I think I want to die. Sometimes I think I already have. My heart feels like it's been ripped from my chest and thrown into a toilet – or an outhouse," she joked, nevertheless appreciating his kind paternalism. "But I'm still alive. How about yourself?"

"Right now, I'm more worried about my wife than myself," Jamaal admitted, ruefully. "I'm sorry about what may have happened to your family and terrified for my own. We often use the expression, 'What's the worst that can happen?' This seems to be it. We're going to have to make the most of it; we're not given any other choices, are we?"

The General Store was only a quarter-mile from Emily's house. Among a crowd of perhaps three dozen people, Sammy saw Pike, Ortie, Dowell, and Rhonda, and recognized Woody Dalton. Everyone wore faces of concern and shock. The owner, Carlene Bartlett, was on hand. Bartlett was a stocky, well-muscled woman, clearly no stranger to hard work. She wore a cotton T-shirt under a store clerk's apron. She had short, uncombed hair and piercing blue eyes.

Carlene spoke first. "Hello everyone. As you all know, I've been running this store almost singlehandedly since dad died 28 years ago, and he ran it for 37 years before me. My grandfather ran it before that. Our business has been brought down to just about nothing by all the big boxes over in Galax. Looks like trips to Galax to buy toilet paper and coffee filters are a thing of the past. With practically nobody working at a job that pays in currency, the money we're accustomed to using to buy things is essentially worthless. I've been talking with Jamaal Winston, who many of you know, about starting a new way of trading. He's staying with Emily Ayres. He is an economics expert."

Jamaal took a step forward and said, "As I'm sure is obvious to everyone here, life as you have known it has changed forever as of late last week. Carlene and I have been working on a system for exchange that we think will work.

"For decades, our economy has been about large, distant, and impersonal corporations. Now, with limited transport, communications, and money, our new normal is a return to an economy that is smaller, more localized, and more commodity-based.

"Many of you are creating food and other necessities in a way that most people throughout America are not. The problem is, if you have 30 chickens, you probably have way more meat and eggs than you need. Your neighbor may have more fruits and vegetables. You are certainly welcome to barter these items with one another, as you've likely been doing for years or even decades. We're proposing a new kind of money."

Carlene spoke again, "This is going to sound funny, but my daddy gave me some advice that I never forgot. He said, 'There are two things that people around here will need if a calamity ever occurs, and they are cigarettes and canning jar lids.' I have always kept several times as many cigarettes on hand as any other store this size. And I have always kept 20 times as many lids as anybody would consider appropriate. In my storeroom right now there are 48,000 canning jar lids and 12,000 jars. The lids normally sell for fifty cents apiece. As of right now, I am setting a price of one dollar per lid and I will trade them for anything of value. I will also buy them back from you, assuming they're usable, for ninety-five cents each, netting us a five percent commission. Of course, you are always welcome to put them to their intended use. But now your medium of exchange, unlike traditional dollars, is actually worth something to you and to everyone else.

"As a good-faith gesture, I am prepared today to give 50 canning jar lids to any household who has done business with us before and who will pledge to continue to trade them locally."

"This sounds to me like the old scrip system that the mill used when I worked there years ago," said an older woman in the back.

"It's true," said Jamaal. "It is a system that has been working and will continue to work around the world as long as there are people who wish to trade something. I think it can work again here. Nobody knows how long this crisis will last and what will emerge from it. I think it is our best bet right now."

Carlene said, "Maybe this system of trading will work for all trading. It seems likely that the clinic will accept lids for payment. Anything you can bring to the store that is of value to other people, I will pay you for it with lids. Anything you see on my shelves that you need, I will accept lids for payment. So in a way, this store will not only be your commissary but your bank. I have no idea how this might work, but I'm willing to give it a try."

"Will this work with services, too?" asked Ortie.

"What do you have in mind?" asked Jamaal.

"I do some plumbin' and well-drillin'. And I can construct outhouses."

"I'd say if anyone wants to pay you in lids and you're willing to accept them, then sure."

Jamaal continued, "As much as 30-percent of the world's trade is still in barter and 65-percent of Fortune 500 companies engage in some form of barter. Barter has always seen a spike in activity during weak economic times. Throughout ancient times, bartering was the standard way of trading. Bartering of goods and services became popular again in this country during the Great Depression and once again in the 1970s.

"I'm not your tax accountant, but if you make a profit from bartering, the IRS still considers that taxable income. Somehow I doubt many of us will be too worried about that right now."

Several people emitted nervous chuckles.

Sammy, feeling brave, said, "I suggest we call them Providence

Lids." The crowd responded with their approval by applauding.

As the meeting ended, Carlene handed out lid allocations. Sammy approached Carlene with the goat's milk cheese and Carlene agreed to give her eight jar lids for it. Plus, she gave her fifty lids for her allocation, of which she spent one on a candy bar from a rapidly depleting shelf. Carlene gave Jamaal fifty lids for Emily and thanked him for his help.

As he and Sammy left the store, Jamaal implored, "Come on back to Emily's house with me and let's see what we can scrounge up for lunch."

On the way, Sammy asked him to explain the monetary system in more detail. He said, "I spoke about the internationalization of commerce. Our televisions, washers, air conditioners, and cars can be made anywhere in the world. Corporations have globalized everything. They constantly look to make things in the cheapest ways. Manufacturing facilities in distant countries came to dominate our own, primarily because with large peasant classes, workers are willing to work for ridiculously low wages.

"Also, our food supply became increasingly available only from distant farms and processing facilities. Most beef cattle growers across the country send their cows hundreds of miles to feedlots in the Midwest where they are slaughtered and the meat distributed around the nation."

"Do you mean a farmer here might send his cows to Iowa and then the meat will come back here?" she asked. "Why don't they just butcher them here?"

"They could butcher them here, but our laws make distant production more profitable. The main thing that made the global economy possible is the explosion of transportation options, facilitated by seemingly unlimited supplies of cheap energy, almost solely in the form of fossil fuels, primarily oil. This is the trend that doomed the Washington Mill in Fries.

"The medium of trade in this nation has almost solely become money, delineated in dollars. In 1913 the U.S. Congress created the Federal Reserve System. This is neither federal nor does it have much in the way of reserves."

"You're kidding!"

"Nope, it's true. The Federal Reserve System is actually a consortium of our major national banks and they make decisions outside of the control of the Congress or the people. When the Federal Reserve System was created, the money in this country was redeemable in gold. It said as much right on the piece of paper currency. In an agreement made at Bretton Woods in 1946, a system of exchange rates was established that allowed individuals or other governments to sell their gold to the United States treasury for $35 per ounce. That system ended in 1971 when President Richard Nixon ended the trading of gold for currency or vice versa. At that time, any link between the world's current currencies and a fixed, valuable commodity was broken.

"Our current system is what is called a fiat currency. This means that money has no intrinsic worth and only has value because the government says it does."

"Does that mean the government doesn't have any gold?" she asked incredulously.

"Certainly not enough to cover the money in circulation. When most of us think of money, we think of actual bills and coins. Actually, these physical things represent a small fraction of monetary exchange. Almost nobody who is employed in a conventional job gets paid in cash. Nobody makes car payments or mortgage payments in cash. Most monetary exchanges these days are made through computerized systems where actual currency is never materialized or traded.

"If you think about it, you'll realize that our current system – that is the system we had before the Pulse – was close to international implosion. Many European Union countries are teetering on default. The Federal Government of the United States is deeply in debt.

"The Federal Reserve has made a habit of working with the biggest financial institutions in the world to systematically wreck economy after economy, manipulating them through wild swings in interest rates."

Sammy thought about her dad's work with Goldman Sachs. She wondered about his future and the future of the company with its nerve center in New York likely destroyed.

"Consider that during the olden days, our federal government minted money and there was no such thing as electronic money transfers. That money was created out of a valuable mineral such as nickel or gold. When paper money came into being, that money still needed to be backed by gold. Now, or until the Pulse, the government had abdicated that responsibility to the Federal Reserve and they created money, or more accurately credit, out of thin air. Then they loaned that money into circulation at an interest rate that was favorable to the richest and most powerful people on the earth.

"In the post-Pulse world where we now live, that system is now inoperable. Nobody knows how long this crisis will last and what will emerge from it. I hope we'll establish a new normal and we won't return to such an unfair and undemocratic monetary system. We'll see, I suppose."

Emily wasn't home when they arrived. Jamaal had picked some apples from one of four trees they had in the side yard, an area that once appeared to have been part of a much larger orchard. There were some crackers in the pantry. He set this and Hattie's cheese on a tray in front of them and they ate, picking from it.

Ruefully, he said, "I've been thinking a lot about you and me, stuck here. I think the people will treat us well. But you probably noticed, we don't 'blend.' If push comes to shove, we'll need to take care of each other and ourselves."

"What do you think we need to do?" she asked, inquisitively.

"First, take care of our own health. Watch what you eat. Keep yourself as clean as you can. Keep practicing your music; it's good for your soul. Do you know how to defend yourself?"

"I've never really had to think about it. I've never used a weapon."

"For now, I don't think that will be necessary," he said optimistically. "But it would be good to know some personal defense. I've taken karate classes for years, and once studied to be a teacher. We should get together from time to time and I'll show you a few simple moves."

She agreed. "I'd like that," she said, trying to feel empowered.

Sammy excused herself after lunch, thanking Jamaal for the invitation, explaining to him that she needed to get home to work on the garden. She walked back along the paved highway, still eerily silent but with most of the cars now pushed out of the way, opening up the road to occasional horses and horse-drawn carts. One man rode by on an old motorcycle, waving at her. The sun was bright in the midday sky and the air was humid and fragrant with the smell of honeysuckle.

Arriving home, she found Hattie working in the springhouse, churning some butter. Sammy sat with her reticent hostess and took turns pushing the plunger up and down, humming to herself but not saying anything.

Thursday, August 23

The next morning, Sammy awoke to a gorgeous day, with clear skies illuminating wispy clouds. She looked longingly for any sign of jet contrails painting white brushstrokes across the blue sky. But of course there were none.

She decided to try working with Jackson, so she dressed and had breakfast, and approached his pasture again. She again picked several apples from the tree to offer to him. He came trotting over to the fence line to greet her. "Okay, big boy. Will you let me put a bridle on you today?" The big horse's head bobbed up and down, a sign that she took as a positive acknowledgment. She lifted herself onto the fence and sat where her knees could brush against his head. She stroked his ears. She sat for some time, allowing him to become more familiar with her. Finally, she let herself to the ground inside the fence. Patting him on the cheek, she walked towards the barn.

Inside, she saw two saddles, and several halters and leather bridles, along with several other pieces of tack. There were blankets and saddle pads lying in a pile. The barn had the usual redolence of hay and other organic matter. Barn swallows flitted to and fro, escaping through the open door and an upstairs portal. "Let's start off with a halter and see how you do with that, Jack-Jack."

She picked up a halter with blue nylon straps and placed it over his head and behind his ears. "Let's just go for a little walk, shall we?" They walked outside the barn together and she took him to the tree where she had just picked his apple and let him pick a couple more for himself. She picked still another one and stuck it in her pocket for later. She walked him back into the barn.

"Good boy! Let's try a bridle on you." She picked up a leather bridle and used a rag to remove some of the dust. She wiped the bit several times until it was shiny again. In a quick, practiced motion, she removed the halter and replaced it with the bridle, inserting the bit into his mouth. "Good boy, Jackson!" The horse seemed to her to be contented, happy to have a human touch. Again, she walked him outside, and marched him a few hundred yards up the gravel driveway. He was prancy, as if he had had a massive weight taken off his shoulders. His exuberance reminded her of the racehorses she had seen as their handlers took them towards the starting gate.

"Are you ready for a saddle, big boy?" They returned to the barn and she found a clean saddle pad in the stack. She threw it over his back. Throwing the reins over his neck, she removed a pretty English style saddle from a large peg on the wall. She found a rag and she brushed it down. The big gelding watched her every movement. She clicked her mouth and she showed him the apple. He walked over beside her. She picked up the saddle and hoisted it high atop the horse's back. She reached underneath and cinched the girth underneath his midsection. She took him outside again for another walk, this one longer. Taking him back inside to untack him, she said, "Tomorrow, you and I are going to go for a ride." She gave him a big hug around his neck and said aloud, "Someday Jack-Jack, I think you are going to save my life."

Friday, August 24

The next morning, she bounded out of bed, eager to see if Jackson would let her ride him. Quint was in the kitchen when she walked through towards the outhouse. Upon her return, she told him about the bartering system that Carlene had worked out at the store. He was attentive and inquisitive, and said he was thinking about how to establish a similar system at the pharmacy. "People are coming in with all kinds of herbs and natural medicines, wanting me to buy them. But what's money these days? I need to have some mechanism for dispensing the pharmaceuticals we still have left."

She decided not to tell him yet about Jackson, thinking he might forbid her from riding him. Sometimes it's better to ask forgiveness than permission, she thought, something her grandfather had once counseled her, much to her parents' consternation.

Quint mentioned that he had found an old bicycle in the barn that belonged to his late daughter, Bonnie. "It is pink. It has a wicker basket on the front that makes me feel silly. But I can get to Fries in half the time it takes me to walk." He departed and Sammy saw him ride away. It reminded her of the scene in The Wizard of Oz as the villainess Almira Gulch rode away with Dorothy's dog Toto in the rear bag. She giggled quietly and then felt embarrassed.

Taking a carrot from the kitchen, she bounded with alacrity to the pasture to find Jackson. Again, much to her delight, he came trotting to her eagerly. She walked into the barn where she found a helmet. After cleaning it the best she could, she strapped it on. She tacked him up and placed a portable two-step platform beside him from which she hoisted herself onto his back. "Easy, big boy. Easy, Jackson!" She decided to stay in his pasture awhile, until they became more accustomed to each other. They walked the entire perimeter of the pasture. The morning sun rising in the east presaged another warm, fragrant day. She looked at the pervasive green vista before her, amazed at the fecundity of the Appalachian summer. Goldfinches darted in and out of the posts of the plank fence. In the near distance, she could see the New River, glistening in the sun.

The bay seemed eager for more movement, so she loosened the reins and he began trotting. Her cares succumbed to the exhilaration of the moment. She felt a giddiness sweep over her, and she felt the hairs on her neck bristle.

Samantha and Jackson, girl and gelding, played together for the better part of an hour. "Let's see how you do on the outside," she said. She dismounted and opened the metal gate to the gravel driveway. Holding his reins in one hand, she looped the gate's chain on a stake so the gate would stay open for their return. She positioned him near the fence so she could climb the wooden slats to hoist herself back aboard again. She turned him towards Providence.

As she rode the shoulder of the asphalt highway, she felt that her entire perspective had changed. She passed a couple of people walking the road and they smiled at her, smiles she thought were all too rare since the Pulse. She alternated walking and trotting him until they arrived at Emily's house where she tied his reins to her front fence.

Meeting Sammy at the door, Emily said, "Please come in. Looks like you and the horse have made friends."

"I'm so excited Jackson let me ride him. Where's Jamaal?"

"He walked to town. He found an old radio in the attic and he's trying to scrounge some parts to make it work."

Walking inside, Sammy saw another woman. Emily said, "Sammy, I'd like you to meet my friend Avalon Parker. Avalon, this is Samantha Reisinger. Sammy is a musician from New Jersey."

"My pleasure," said the new woman, smiling while warmly taking Sammy's hand in hers.

Sammy beheld the radiant beauty of the woman who stood before her. She had long, blonde hair intertwined with beads and feathers and had clear, tight skin. She wore a long, off-white canvas dress, a blue butterfly necklace, and several earrings.

"It's a pleasure to meet you, too."

"Avalon is an herbalist. She brings me some of the tinctures, teas, and salves I use in my midwifery practice. She also brings me eggs."

"Tell me about yourself, Sammy," the pretty woman asked.

Sammy told her about her home in New Jersey, her education in the violin, and her interest in Appalachian music. She told her in detail about her attendance in Galax and the abandonment of Ella and Terry and Alice Mullins. She spoke about her parents' death.

"I'm so sorry for your loss. Does anyone know why the power failed?"

Emily said, "The consensus seems to be some sort of Electromagnetic Pulse. Scientists understand these can occur from nuclear blasts high in the atmosphere. They can also be caused by solar flares. Goodness knows, I hope we've not been attacked."

"Me, too," Avalon concurred. "A solar flare would be no less damaging, but at least it's a natural thing."

Emily added, "If we've been attacked, I wonder what's next."

Avalon waved her hand through her hair. "The power grid was destined to fail. The way it was configured and maintained was unsustainable. 'Sustainability' is the most disrespected word in the English language. Few people take sustainability seriously."

"What do you mean?" asked Sammy.

"I'm really in a rush today and I can't take the time to discuss this now. I have some boys helping me with garden chores and I need to get back to the mountain. Please come by and visit with me any time and I'll be happy to talk more about it with you."

"Do you live nearby?"

"Yes, on the other side of the road that circles Turkey Knob. Beside my driveway are metal sculptures of little dancing devils. Barkus my dog will announce your arrival, but he's all 'bark-us' and no 'bite-us'. The door is always open; don't bother knocking."

The women bid adieus and the blonde woman left through the back door and rode away on a mountain bicycle. Sammy envisioned a nation-wide revival of the bicycle.

As Avalon rode away, Emily said, "Tell me more about Jackson."

Sammy told her about working with him, getting him into the bridle and saddle, and exercising him. "He's a good horse. I'm sure he's had lots of training already. He just hasn't been ridden for awhile. I think he's as happy to have me riding him as I am to be riding him." She talked about how beautiful and happy she felt with him, trotting across his pasture. They talked for twenty minutes about the horse, about Avalon, herbs, and midwifery.

They ate some lunch together, mostly fresh tomatoes from the garden that Jamaal had picked the day before. They were delicious, dripping with juice. They seemed to Sammy to be an entirely different food than the bright red but tasteless store-bought tomatoes she was used to.

As they were cleaning up the kitchen, Emily said, "I want you to know how sorry I am about your parents."

"Thanks."

"Jamaal and I talked about whether we should try to piece together some sort of ceremony or mourner's Kaddish. We decided that if we did, we'd be sealing their fate as being dead. We want to do what's right for you and provide comfort in any way we can. But somehow, we felt that keeping a glimmer of hope alive was the best thing to do. My husband was Jewish so I thought I could find an appropriate prayer if you thought it best. I have a book of Jewish cultural traditions that I was reading last night. Let me go upstairs and get it."

Emily walked up the stairs leaving Sammy to look around. There were several musical instruments in the room, with two banjos and a guitar hanging from the wall and a viola on a stand in a corner. There was a piano with a clarinet case on it. She was still surprised by the bars on the windows. There were books everywhere. She glanced at several titles which were about childbirth and midwifery.

Emily returned with the book but before she had a chance to speak, Sammy said, "I'm curious about the bars you have on your windows."

"When we first moved here, we were gone for weeks at a time. Once, we had a break-in and some of my jewelry was stolen. My husband had the bars installed. We never got around to taking them down.

"Now then," Emily continued, "Would you like to have a look at this?"

"Perhaps later. Let me think about it."

"I think that's best. Say, would you be interested in going with me to call on a pregnant client? She's in Riverside. That's a couple of miles south of here alongside the New River. I need to walk there. If you'd like to go, I'll give you a head start. You can ride home, put Jackson back in his pasture, and then walk back to the road. If we time this right, we'll meet at the junction and walk the rest of the way together. It's another mile from the junction."

Following the plan, Sammy rode Jackson home, untacked him, and gave him the carrot in her pocket she'd almost forgotten about. She filled a plastic bottle with water and walked back to the road. She waited a few minutes before Emily came into sight. They walked together south downhill on Scenic Road towards the New River. At the junction to Riverside Drive, they turned left and walked a hundred yards and turned left again on a gravel driveway. They stopped at a mobile home where Emily knocked on the door. A woman came to the door wearing a dirty white T-shirt that said, "Independence Chamber of Commerce, In God We Will Grow" and green sweat pants. "Hi, Thelma. Are you doing okay?"

Letting Emily and Sammy inside, Thelma said, "Yes, ma'am. Of course, everything hurts. I have indigestion and I'm constipated. My legs and ankles are swollen. I'm okay.

"But I'm scared. We don't have any money and not much food," she said, forcing a smile. There were four other children darting about the house. Emily introduced Thelma and Sammy to each other.

Sammy looked around the small trailer. There was an orange shag carpet on the floor, well worn near the entrance door. All the windows were open, but it was still hot inside. A mounted deer head with eight points on the antlers lorded over the small Formica dining table, strewn with papers and cigarette butts.

"Where's your husband?" Emily queried. "I thought he'd be home by now."

"His last furlough was eight months ago," Thelma said, patting her distended belly. "His current tour was supposed to be over in July. But his unit got waylaid. Their last orders was for August 14th. With the power failure, he never made it."

"You should have told me sooner."

"Yes, ma'am, but I figured you had your hands full with the first-time mothers."

"You're a saint, Thelma. But I would have been here for you if you needed me."

"Well, you're here now."

"Thelma, Sammy is learning to be my helper. If you're comfortable with her, I'm going to let her become more involved." When Thelma nodded her approval, Emily withdrew her stethoscope and fetoscope from her bag.

Sammy said, "How old are you, Thelma?"

"Twenty-eight."

"When are you due?"

"September 15th."

"But we all know that this baby could pop at any time," said Emily, moving her stethoscope from place to place on the woman's abdomen, as plump as a watermelon. "He sounds good in there." She handed the stethoscope to Sammy to let her listen. Emily patted Thelma on the shoulder and said, "Keep this baby inside until your due date, would you?"

Thelma smiled a hopeful smile. "I hope we have enough to eat by the time he's born."

"Sammy and I will be back in two weeks. Send your eldest over to my house to get me if this baby wants to see the world before then."

"Yes, ma'am."

As she put her tools back into her bag, Emily withdrew from it six large potatoes. "I hope these will help for a few days. Potatoes are very nutritious."

The midwife and her new helper said goodbye to Thelma, who offered 20 jar lids in payment to Emily. Emily accepted five instead, and she and Sammy walked back to the road. Sammy said, "She sure seems poor. I suppose there are lots of people like her around here. Do you think she'll be all right?"

"I don't know. I don't think anybody knows. Are you going to be all right?"

"I don't know, either. I'm not sure what that means," Sammy admitted. "What am I supposed to be thinking or feeling or doing? What if my parents are really dead? I can't let myself believe they are dead. I miss them so much. What would they want me to be doing? I keep thinking about them being here with me when the Pulse hit. If they were here, what would they be doing? I feel so much grief."

"I don't have any answers for you, dear," Emily replied. "An awful thing has happened and many people are suffering and will suffer. I'm thinking I need to go on with the time I have left serving people. And I'm doing what you and I have just done, helping expectant mothers bring healthy babies into this world, as damaged as it now is."

"One minute I want to be strong and the next minute I want to melt away," Sammy vented.

"I hope this doesn't sound heartless, but you must grieve in the best way you know how and then you must move on," Emily said, maternally. "You will find an inner strength you never knew you had."

Sammy began crying. They continued walking but Emily took her hand. Moments later, Sammy composed herself and spoke again. "It was nice of you to take such a small payment from Thelma."

"I hated accepting anything at all, but I know that doing anything professionally implies some sort of payment. Even before the Pulse, sometimes I bartered my services for food or anything of value the family offered. I want you to take these lids as payment for some of Hattie's cheese that I'd like you to give Thelma next time you're passing this way.

"Poor people are everywhere around here. The central Appalachians have always been poor, but since the jobs started being sent overseas in the '80s and '90s, things have gotten much worse. Outsourcing and free trade agreements have shut down almost all the manufacturing around here. I assume you know about the mill in Fries."

"Yes, a friend I met at the Convention told me about it," she said, reticent to mention Shane by name.

A doe and two fawns ambled into the road 50 yards ahead of them. The doe looked at them quizzically, shook her ears, and then trotted into the woods, white tail and fawns following her. "I suspect somebody will have that doe for dinner sometime soon," said Emily with resignation. "I hope the fawns are old enough to fend for themselves when it happens."

A few seconds later, she added, "I hope we're not so desperate that we shoot the fawns, too."

"You said something at Thelma's house about potatoes. Weren't they the cause of a famine in Ireland?"

"It's a long story. Where do I start? The Irish Potato Famine, or in their own legend, The Great Hunger, persisted from 1845 until 1852. This period of mass starvation and emigration was a tragic confluence of bad governance and bad agriculture. I'll tell you about the governance first.

"From early history, Ireland was dominated by the heavy and exploitive influence of its neighbor, Britain. Ireland had a tiny aristocracy. The rest of the people were laborers, often unemployed, living in appalling conditions with among the lowest standards of living in the world at the time. They were forbidden to receive an education, at least the Catholics who made up 80 percent of the population, and they were forbidden to own land.

"Most people don't know that potatoes were not native to Ireland. The potato is a New World crop. Even today, hundreds of varieties grow in the Andes Mountains of South America. After Columbus opened the Americas to vast exploitation by Europeans, the explorers not only took precious minerals from the Americas, they took plants and animals, too. A hundred years before the blight, there were perhaps three million people living in all of Ireland, living largely on beef products, including meat, butter, and milk. When the potato began to make inroads as a food, this new food source was ideally suited to the poor soils and growing conditions of that misty, windswept island. The population increased to around eight million, largely because of this single crop.

"Then the blight struck. The potato blight is a fungus-like microorganism, but it is not a fungus. The potatoes that contracted it are shrunken, corky, and rotted. They stink awful, and they cannot be eaten.

"Here's the part about bad agriculture. It is thought that the blight that arrived in Ireland originated in Peru and was brought to Ireland on ships carrying guano, which is bird crap. You can imagine what it says about Europe in those days that bird shit was valuable enough for sailing ships to carry it across the Atlantic Ocean. Because Ireland has essentially a consistent climate and soils, almost the entire crop was one particular kind of potato, the lumber. So when the blight struck it, this particular strain was devastated.

"Meanwhile, back in South America, there are thousands of different climates, elevations, and soils and hundreds of types of potatoes, most of which weren't affected. So the blight was largely a footnote in its history, whereas Ireland was crippled."

A red cardinal flashed across the road. A boy rode his bicycle past and he waved at them.

Emily continued, "Within a few years, a million people starved to death and another million fled Ireland. Many of these people landed in America into an underclass here."

"It sounds like a typical case of too many eggs in one basket," Sammy suggested.

"To the extreme! But we don't learn. Do you know that 99-percent of Iowa is under cultivation and 80-percent of that is in one strain of corn? Can you imagine the impact of that being struck with blight? But we think crop failures are only from the history books.

"Of course, nobody around here knows whether the Midwest was impacted by the Pulse. If they don't have electricity, they won't be able to get the fuel to power the tractors that harvest, process, and deliver the corn to markets anyway. Imagine a whole state sitting on a worthless crop of corn they can't harvest while millions of cows in feed lots in neighboring states starve to death because the corn can't get delivered."

"Wow. I suppose the message is a need for diversity."

"Yes, and localization. Diversity means resilience. We put a lot of our 'eggs' into the power grid and our electronic systems. Now that they've failed, we'll see what happens. Avalon, who you met at the house, is more prepared than anybody I know. I hope you take her up on her offer to visit. She has much to share with you."

"I will. I like her."

As they approached the junction to Sammy's new home, it began to sprinkle with rain. Clouds swirled overhead and the wind picked up. Before parting from her new mentor, Sammy said, "Let's put off the Kaddish for awhile. I'm trying to believe that somehow my parents are still alive."

"Very well."

By the time Sammy arrived on the front porch, it was pouring and she was soaking wet. Listening to the rain and hail pound the tin roof, she realized that it had been a week since she and Jamaal walked off the stage together in Galax, and how the world had changed.

Saturday, August 25

While getting dressed in Bonnie's clothes, Sammy took notice of the growing pile of dirty clothes overflowing her hamper. She'd never washed clothes before and resigned herself to the fact that she'd need to learn how sometime soon.

She also became conscious of the fact that she hadn't played her violin for several days. As she thought about it, she decided that it had probably been several years since she had spent three consecutive days without playing at all. She remembered the old saw her grandfather had repeated so often, "When I don't practice for a day, I know it. When I don't practice for two days, my wife and friends know. When I don't practice for three days, my audience knows."

So she unzipped the new case and removed the old instrument. Reflexively, she switched on her electronic tuning device and just as quickly realized that it was not going to work. So she did the best she could, tuning her instrument by ear.

Knowing that she was going to be away, weeks earlier her tutor had given her an assignment, to practice Mendelssohn's *Concerto for Violin in E Minor*. Placing the sheet music on the bureau in front of the mirror and beginning to work, she realized that even a modest few days away from her instrument negatively impacted her practiced touch. As the hours passed she began to regain her acuity.

Finally tiring, she decided that she would enjoy visiting with Emily and Jamaal, so she tacked up Jackson and walked him outside his enclosure and toward Scenic Highway. It was an overcast day, muggy, with limited visibility.

When she arrived, Emily met her at the door and told her that Jamaal was in town. She expected him back soon.

Sammy said, "I appreciate what you're doing as a midwife."

"I really love doing it."

"I'd like to learn more myself. Do you think I could become a midwife?"

"Maybe, but it takes real dedication," Emily insisted.

"I've always been a focused person."

"I thought your passion was music."

"It is. But who knows what part of our lives music will play now?"

"You're right to have concerns about the 'new normal'. But people have always played and enjoyed music, in the best and worst of times in the most primitive and advanced societies."

"I sure hope that's true. But if I'm going to be here for awhile, I want to contribute in a grander way."

"Okay, that's fine. If you're serious, here's what you can expect. There is a huge amount of counseling that goes into the craft. I care for a woman at perhaps the most pivotal moments of her life. Much of the mother's history comes up. Issues like sexual abuse, incest, and relationship issues with the baby's father and the mother's mother all enter into the equation. If these issues exist, it is certainly best to learn about them during the prenatal visits. If I am not made aware of these things prior, they often certainly arise during delivery."

Emily led Sammy towards comfortable chairs in the living room and then continued. "The baby needs space in the mother's life. The mother needs to prepare herself emotionally, physically, and financially, to take on this new family member. Things can be a great deal more challenging if the baby's father is not supportive or is not even present. Families are constructed this way more and more frequently, unfortunately. In better circumstances, the baby's father has the opportunity to step forward and be a solid source of emotional security that he should be.

"I assume you have tools like any doctor?" Sammy asked.

"Yes, the case that I carry with me contains many things. One of my mentors once said that there are few problems that may arise during birth that cannot be solved with your hands and some herbs. I carry tinctures, decoctions, and compresses. I carry various vitamins. I carry various homeopathic medicines that are typically pills. Some of these are to help the mother relax.

"I have seen a situation where the baby emerges white and limp as if the spirit is not yet in the body. I need to get the baby's spirit into its body and get it to wake up and to be alive. I administer this by putting the homeopathic medicine into a little bit of water and then dabbing it on the baby's lips with an eye dropper or a tiny syringe without the needle.

"In some cases, the baby is blue and lifeless and is not breathing. Time stands still when a baby doesn't capture life right away. Babies appear to shrink and they feel boneless when they're not breathing. There are homeopathic medicines specifically for that constitution. Homeopathic remedies are developed for specific acute situations. I carry about 15 different herbs. I carry skullcap and St. John's wort. I carry blue cohosh and black cohosh. I carry Motherwort to strengthen the mother's heart and Angelica, cottonroot bark or the blue and black cohoshes for bleeding situations. Getting a mother to talk to her baby and to let the baby know it is loved and wanted and is safe can be key in getting a baby's spirit to fully come into its body.

"A recipe I use to help a mom rest and relax might be 20 drops of St. Johns wort and 20 drops of motherwort with a tablespoon of liquid calcium and magnesium. If a mom is bleeding with the placenta still inside of her, I often try 50 drops of ground ivy or angelica with or without 10 drops of the blue and black cohoshes which cause rapid emptying of the uterus. In cases where that didn't work, I've even had to do a manual extraction of the placenta."

"Does that mean what I think it means?" Sammy asked, with mild revulsion.

"Yes. I reach inside the birth canal and I yank it out."

Sammy winced.

"A preventive for post-partum bleeding is 10 drops of mother-wort and 8 drops of ground ivy after the birth. Mothers with lots of emotional baggage tend to bleed a bit more than others do.

"The first solution I try for most problems is to do nothing. Nature has a way of making things work out. The next step is for me to use massage and to help the mother with visualization and relaxation techniques. The next step beyond that is using herbs or teas or a warm bath. Then, I may choose to use homeopathics, which can be stronger. Some situations require you to act swiftly with herbs or body maneuvers. But often the best solution is to do nothing.

"In 95-percent of the cases, all I really need to do is to be present. I am there for emotional support. My primary responsibility is to hold the circle together for the family to do their work and for the mother to find her inner strength that has been there since the day she was born. At childbirth, women are so receptive to the energetic influences around them that simply being a witness at the gates of life and death for this family as their baby comes through is the number one job of a midwife.

"Childbirth is a natural process and usually it goes smoothly. And of the 5-percent of cases when things don't go smoothly, perhaps 75-percent of them simply need a little support in terms of an herb or a homeopathic remedy. Most women just need you to be there and hold her hand and walk with them around in circles, sometimes for hours.

"I always try to attend births with an assistant. Most of the time, one or the other of us gets to take a break and perhaps get a little nap. I have been in or have heard of enough life-and-death situations where two people were needed and so I always prefer to be accompanied by a helper."

"Maybe for awhile that can be me," Sammy said.

"I'd like that."

As she spoke, Jamaal burst inside and exclaimed, "I got a crystal!"

"What's it for?" asked Sammy.

"I found an old crystal radio in the attic. I had one when I was in Boy Scouts. This one was missing the crystal itself. The owner of a rummage store in town suggested I visit an elderly woman named Mrs. Taylor on Lee Drive whose late husband was into radios. So I went there and found a crystal. Hopefully I can get the radio going soon."

Sunday, August 26

Sammy and Quint walked to church together, Sammy wearing another of Bonnie's dresses. Quint said nothing, evidently envisioning the sermon he was soon to present.

Inside, he began the service with the Lord's Prayer. Then, as he did each week, he welcomed Sammy, Pike, and the other guests in attendance. Then he began his sermon, again speaking in his rich, mellifluous voice.

"Last week, I spoke about finding salvation and eternal life. It is becoming increasingly clear that the timing of that sermon was appropriate, as a great tragedy has befallen us. The Bible warns of such impending tragedies. The Bible is voluminous. Thirty percent of it is prophetic, meaning it deals with the future.

"Writers of the Old Testament predicted 1000 years before Jesus' birth where he would be born, where he would be raised, and that he would die by crucifixion. Psalm 22 would have been written by King David around 1000 BC. Isaiah also predicted the suffering of the coming Messiah, writing around 700 B.C.

"Most of the prophecies deal with what we Christians call the End of Days. The Bible refers to the last days as the 2000 years or more since the time of Christ's death until the second coming. Ladies and gentlemen, that time is likely upon us!

"Jesus Christ is the Lord, He is our Savior, and He is the Messiah. God is not physical. He is a spiritual being. When God reveals Himself to us, He works mysteriously. We are finite and He is infinite and therefore we cannot accurately envision Him. As He reveals Himself, He speaks to us in terms we can understand. We should think of God, the Son, and Holy Spirit as three distinct persons but they all share the same character, the same nature, and the same power. They are all omniscient. Where they differ is in function. In creation, the Father designed it, Jesus created it, and the Holy Spirit was present. We see this in Genesis chapter 1. The Trinity is a very important part of our Christian faith.

"According to the Scriptures, the End Times look very gruesome. The Scripture says that believing Christians will be supernaturally removed from earth.

"Near the end of His life, Jesus brought His disciples into Jerusalem. They got together over the Passover meal. Passover is a Jewish holiday."

He glanced at Sammy, as if for approval.

"All of them were in attendance except for Judas, the betrayer. In the Bible, John discusses the conversation between Jesus and the disciples. Jesus knows that His death is nigh. He knows that those who hate Him and are pursuing Him will soon catch Him and put Him to death. Jesus has been in the ministry for only three-and-a-half years. He has said some things that many of the Jews do not like. The Gentiles hated Jesus just as much as the Jews did.

"Jesus said that nobody was taking His life from Him, but that He instead was giving it freely. He told his disciples that He was going to a place where they could not follow but that He would be preparing a place for them. And in John 14:1-3, He told them that He would come again.

"The disciples did not know what He meant. As the apostles began to write about it and as God began to give them revelations, they believed that when the end would come – and they believed that He would come again in their day – He would supernaturally snatch them away from this mortal world. When this actually happens, the true believers will be literally snatched away in an instant with their clothing left in a heap.

"Our ancestors of every generation since then have been actively looking for Jesus to arrive again during their lives to take them to heaven. Until the Pulse struck, what we have here in our nation, in our state, and in our region is pretty good and most people are happy with it. We should have loved and enjoyed the life that we had. The Bible teaches that. But what we may have in heaven is better.

"Did the disciples feel cheated? No!" Quint screamed. "Did other good Christians feel cheated if they were not alive during the Second Coming? No! All of us are submissive to the inexplicable will of God." More quietly, "We Christians are people of faith. Faith is not a blind leap into the dark. When you have a personal relationship with God – and that relationship is available to anybody – you have the best of both worlds: this world and the world to come!

"God is not some sort of cosmic king who pushes little buttons and we as robots respond unknowingly without our own will. He created us to have our own will. However, God is in control of nature. When the End Times come – and this may be nigh – true believers, the people who have fully accepted Jesus Christ and they are living for Jesus Christ, will simply disappear off the face of the earth. If this were to happen this very second, I would literally be in the middle of a sentence, speaking to you, and a split-second later I would be gone with my clothing draped over the chair or fallen to the floor. This is the 'Rapture.'

"The Bible says that a short time after that, a new figure will emerge: the Antichrist. The Bible says that there are many antichrists and we have seen some of them already. It is a general characterization of people who act like and have similar characteristics to the real Antichrist. What will identify him as the true Antichrist is that he will force a covenant upon Israel.

"Next week, I will talk more about Israel and her fate. But now, let's please sing the hymn, *A Mighty Fortress Is My God*, found on page 81 in your hymnal."

The congregation found the page and began singing.

A mighty fortress is our God,
A bulwark never failing;

Our helper He amid the flood
Of mortal ills prevailing.
For still our ancient foe
Doth seek to work us woe –
His craft and pow'r are great,
And armed with cruel hate,
On earth is not his equal.

As lyrics continued to flow from the mouths of the parishioners, Sammy's mind drifted to her parents. She began weeping.

Quint continued, "Now then, before we conclude, many of you may have heard, Chief Cunningham is dead. He committed suicide yesterday. Killed his wife and two kids, too. Apparently the load of responsibility on his shoulders was too much for him to bear. We mourn their loss and hope the Lord is with them. My guess is that Annie Wilkins will be running the weekly community meeting tomorrow. I suspect that she'll be the new chief, at least for now.

"Ladies and gentlemen, we have suffered a great tragedy. Many people here have lost a loved one since the Pulse hit, just ten days ago. May those who grieve be comforted. The Lord is close to the broken-hearted; He rescues those who are crushed in spirit."

Sammy's wails intensified. People filed from their seats and walked slowly outside, with several patting her gently on the shoulder, sympathetically.

Eventually, Sammy regained her composure and she walked home with Quint. Along the way, she asked him about his church. He said, "Mine is a Pentecostal church. The word Pentecost means the 50th day. It was a Jewish feast that was celebrated 50 days after Passover. In Acts, Chapter 2, is this passage: *When the day of Pentecost came, they were all together in one place. Suddenly a sound like the blowing of a violent wind came from heaven and filled the whole house where they were sitting. They saw what seemed to be tongues of fire that separated and came to rest on each of them. All of them were filled with the Holy Spirit and began to speak in other tongues as the Spirit enabled them.*

"Fifty days after Passover was the Pentecost, or the feast of booths or the Feast of the Tabernacle. Jews lived outside of their house in thatched roof structures for seven days to remind them of the time when they lived in tents as they wandered through the wilderness. Before Jesus ascended to heaven, he told his disciples to wait in Jerusalem until they could be endued from on high. So they waited for 10 days. The Christian church began on that day when the Holy Spirit arrived.

"Christmas was originally the pagan holiday of the solstice. Nobody knew the day when Jesus was born. So they just decided to take December 25, associate that with the winter solstice, and proclaim it to be the birthday of the Savior. The Druids were celebrating the return of the sun. So pagan holidays were simply Christianized. Non-Christians want to criticize us because we've adapted pagan holidays for our own, but I have no problem with that.

"Through the decades and centuries there have been frequent movements to become more apostolic, meaning a closer tie to the roots, to the beginning. Various churches like the Church of the Nazarene have sought a closer relationship with God through a more disciplined and holy life."

Sammy said, "You talked about something you called the rapture. Pardon me for saying so, but it sounds crazy."

"Not at all, child! I believe it! The End Times are not far away. The bad news I hear encourages me that Christ will soon be coming back. When Christians read what other people consider bad news, we consider it good news. I will escape. Christ is going to rapture us up. The Scriptures teach us that Christ will come like lightning from east to west. In the twinkle of an eye, Jesus will gather His people from here. Even people who are already dead and buried in the grave will be like new, like Jesus' body after the resurrection. If you are walking here talking to me, I would literally vanish. Almost all Protestant churches believe in the rapture. In Christ, people pray that they will be worthy enough to escape the bad things that will happen on the earth.

"What makes us evangelical is that there will be people we care about who have not yet accepted Christ and they will be left behind. That is what makes me ask everyone to repent and get right with God.

It is God's will that everyone can go. I hope you will realize that and accept Jesus Christ as your personal Lord and Savior. I pray for you!

"There will be 1000-year reign on earth when peace and justice are restored and everything will be as it is supposed to be. There will be no devil. This event is something we look forward to. Jesus said that when we see all of these things happening, look up for your redemption draws nigh. What I am watching now is an economic war in the world. All the gentile world powers are portrayed as beasts of prey. These are the Babylonian empire, the Greek empire, the Roman Empire, and all the tributaries that have come from them. They are all depicted in the book of Daniel and of Revelation as beasts of prey.

"Nebuchadnezzar was the conqueror of Jerusalem and destroyer of the First Temple. In Daniel, he has a vivid vision of the world powers. He saw it as a huge statue with a head of gold. The arms and upper torso were made of silver. The belly and thighs were made of bronze, its legs of iron, and its feet were made of clay and rock. The statue was rich with symbolism, with each part representing a part of the world, from the top down was increasing strength as iron is stronger than bronze, stronger than silver, stronger than gold. The feet were Christ, the strongest. The legs were the Roman Empire and Europe. The belly was Greece, the chest Medo-Persia, and the head Babylon.

"The break-up of the Roman Empire is symbolized by the ten toes, made of clay and iron, which never adhere well to each other."

Sammy's head spun with the implications and complications of all she had heard. It all sounded nonsensical, but scary. Arriving home, she spent the rest of the afternoon practicing her violin, better understanding its meaning in her life and finding solace in its sounds.

Monday, August 27

"Sammy, I'm headed into town," yelled Quint after rapping on her door. "Are you coming to the meeting?"

"Yes," she said, wiping sleep from her eyes. "I'll get up now."

"I'm riding the bicycle into town now to do some work at the pharmacy. I'll see you there."

Sammy dressed and ate a peach and a slice from the loaf of bread that Marissa had left. She tacked up Jackson and rode him to Emily's house where she put him in a fenced field. She and Jamaal walked into town together.

Sammy saw Rhonda and Ortie Shelor standing beside Carleton Skinner. Woody was there with a woman Sammy assumed was his wife, Caroline. Quint walked in and nodded to her.

"Hello everyone. I was about to say, 'Good mornin', but it just ain't," said Annie Wilkins, sarcastically. "Chief Cunningham kilt hisself and his family. I talked with Viller Boyd over at his funeral home. There's done been 18 deaths this week where we'd usually have one or two. I assume the mayor is still in Florida, we ain't heard 'boo' from him. So it looks like I'm now in charge. We've heard lots of rumors about mayhem all over the place. I hear tell that much of downtown Greensboro has been burned to the ground. There's a rumor that Roanoke has had massive riots. I can't even imagine what's happened in DC or New York."

Sammy looked over the faces in the crowd, which were decidedly ashen.

Wilkins continued, "Fortunately everybody appears to be behavin' for the most part here in Fries, at least so far. So let's keep it that way. Mr. Dalton, what's your status over at the Rescue Squad?"

"We still don't have anything in the way of communication," he admitted sadly. "We were able to help two people this week. One was having a mild heart attack and the other was having an epileptic seizure. Our people were only able to help because they lived right in town and we got word early. I'm aware of seven deaths that would have been prevented if the victims had their medications and if we'd been able to get there sooner. It's still pretty desperate."

"Mister Skinner, what's going on with the water?" asked the new chief.

"I have one purification tank going. But I literally need to lift buckets of water and pour through it. I've given water to anybody in town who has come by for it. I spoke with Wayman over at sewage treatment. He's got some chemicals he's using on the wastes accumulating at the high school gym. So far, we're not dumping any excrement into the River. But no telling what other communities upstream are doing. Nobody should drink from the River. If sewage gets in it, nobody should eat the fish either. Far as I know, we have no way to monitor that."

"Professor McConnell?"

"Yes, ma'am."

"When are we going to get some power?"

"Ma'am, as you know, Fries was founded on this spot because of the potential for water power. Ih've been working with Keene Campbell to turn that water into power again."

"Ma'am," said Keene, "When the mill shut down, they decommissioned the power plant and tore down the building. The dam is still there but it ain't generatin' no power. Old man Thornton let me into his warehouse on Saturday and we found an old industrial dynamo that must have come from the power plant. It is stamped '1939' and it obviously ain't worked in a coon's age."

"It's in rough shape," concurred the engineering professor. "The main shaft is seized so the rotor won't turn. There are several missing brushes. Several elements of the field coils are gone. And we're not quite sure how we'll be able to excite the coils to energize them, something that needs to happen before we can get any power from it."

Keene continued, "I got an old lathe in my garage that I can turn parts, but we need to scrounge the metal. Oh, and we need some way to turn the parts on the lathe."

"And after that," continued his new partner, "we need to fashion a water wheel, a main shaft, and a building to house everything. We're still scrounging around for a regulator or some way to regulate the power."

"Bottom line, gentlemen?" said the new chief, impatiently.

"Several weeks," they said in unison.

A collective groan emanated from the crowd.

"After that, our community faces still another problem," said the professor. "We will only generate a fraction of what we once used. We need to decide who gets the power and what it's used for. It sure as hell will be too valuable to power anybody's air conditioner."

Several people chuckled sardonically.

"Anybody have anything to report as far as communications?"

"I do," said Jamaal. Everyone stared hard at the newcomer. "I'm trying to get an old crystal radio I found to work. These things have been around for a long time. American prisoners of war used them during World War II to learn what was going on outside. One advantage is they don't need any power to work. One disadvantage is that they only receive; they can't transmit. Another disadvantage is that without amplification, the incoming broadcast can only be heard by one person, listening to earphones."

"Is anybody broadcasting at all?" Wilkins asked.

"The signals I'm getting are weak and largely unintelligible. There are people transmitting somewhere, but not close by. The Pulse's effect is widespread."

"Mr. Dalton, does the Rescue Squad have any ham radio operators?"

"Yes, ma'am, but everybody with modern equipment lost everything. We've yet to track down a working system with old technology."

"Okay, please keep trying. I'm not going to ask if everyone has enough to eat. I suspect things will get way worse before they get better. Questions?"

"How are you handling law enforcement?" asked a Hispanic woman.

"We're sending anybody caught breaking the law to the jail in Independence. We have a man in custody caught stealing from Quint Thompson's pharmacy. I don't want to give too many details, for obvious reasons. Let's just say I'm doing the best I can. Again, I suspect once we start hearin' from the rest of the nation, we'll find things a lot worse elsewhere."

Sammy looked at Jamaal's dark face, which looked more ashen than usual. She could see his face contort as the muscles clenched. "Let's go," he said.

They walked towards the exit as the meeting began to conclude. Sammy brushed by Rhonda and said, "Do you know where Shane is?"

"Who wants to know?" Rhonda said briskly.

"You don't need to be so snotty," Sammy said, taken aback.

"Let's go," said Jamaal, again, tugging Sammy's arm before she got an answer from Rhonda.

Outside in the warm summer air, Sammy said, "I wonder what's gotten into her. You and I are the victims here. Anyway, why are you in such a hurry?"

"I didn't like the way a couple of people in there were looking at me, Keene Campbell and his sidekick, whatever his name is."

"You're being paranoid. I'm different, too."

"You're a Jew. I'm black. The people who know you know you're Jewish. But other people don't. Everybody knows I'm black. I know what 'the look' looks like. I'm too busy to be worried; I've got work to do on the radio."

They walked back to Emily's house in silence, each ruminating on their fates.

Emily was fixing lunch as they arrived. "Sammy, I've got another client I want to call on this afternoon. Would you like to go with me?"

They walked to Hilltown where they met with a woman in her thirties who already had two children, one 13 and one 10. The house was tidy and well kept. The woman's name was Estella. She said she was six months pregnant and had just started maternity leave as a secretary to a lawyer in Galax. "Thank you for checking up on me, Emily."

"You're welcome. I thought it would be a good idea to see how you were doing."

"Emilio and I never expected to get pregnant again. This was an accident," she said, patting her belly. "We considered aborting it, but my conscience wouldn't let me do it. I've always tried to be a good Christian." She smiled at Sammy, knowingly. "I was on maternity leave anyway, but will there ever be a job to go back to?"

"Maybe not, but we need to stay optimistic," asserted Emily, with all the conviction she could muster.

"I was planning to have this baby at Twin County. A friend of my husband was in Galax three days ago and he said the hospital was nearly in ruins. Will you be able to help me deliver my baby?"

"Of course."

"Both my prior births were difficult. I'm scared."

"We're all scared," the older woman confessed. "We're going to have to do the best we can. When's your due date?"

"November 10."

"Don't worry. Worry never helped anybody. We'll be here for you."

The midwife and her assistant walked outside and began the hour-long trek back to Providence. Sammy said, "What you told me the other day about Ireland was fascinating. Quint and Hattie have a set of Encyclopedias that were printed in 1969. I looked up the potato blight."

"What did you learn?" Emily asked pedagogically.

"The spores traveled in the air. It struck the harvest of 1845 and then again in '46 and '48. They arrived literally overnight and turned productive patches of potatoes into a fetid, stinking rotting mess. The leaves got black spots first. The poison traveled down the roots like gangrene. The potatoes themselves turned into black, mushy slime. Damn, it must have been awful!"

"You're right," Emily agreed. "It was the smell of impending death. I think I mentioned that the population had grown to eight million people, largely on the bounty of this new food source. When the potato brought more nourishment to Ireland, the population increased. But then, unemployment grew and wages fell. The potato was a mixed blessing. People's fortunes became tied to it.

"What's also interesting is that the potato seemed to be a good metaphor for the Irish people themselves. Wheat, corn, and other grains only grew on good land in cultivated rows, stretching to the sky. They had to be carefully sown, harvested, milled, mixed, and baked before they could be eaten. They were dignified and in a way, regal. Bread became a medium of trade.

"On the other hand, the potato grew in the ground below haphazard plants, strewn in every-which-way directions. Potatoes could grow perfectly well in a pile of manure. Its consumption required only that it be dug from the ground and placed in boiling water. If that was too much trouble, it could simply be thrown into a fire. It was considered a primitive food, unmentioned in the Bible, suitable for animals and heathens. To the gentry of the day, the potato made humans animal-like all over again. The Irish were literally dirt poor, living in huts without windows, floors, or chimneys. Everybody thought they were uncouth and uncivilized.

"The famine was the worst disaster since the Black Death, 500 years earlier. One of every eight Irishmen died of starvation or another cause related to malnutrition. Cholera, typhus, and other communicable diseases swept through villages. People went blind. Others went crazy. Some particularly hard-hit towns didn't have enough able-bodied people to bury all the dead. People ate weeds, pets, and even their deceased neighbors."

"How horrible!" Sammy exclaimed. Continuing to think about it, she said, "Worldwide populations seem to keep increasing."

"That's because we're eating crude oil."

"We're what?" Sammy asked, incredulously.

"We're almost to my house. I'll tell you next time we're on the road together. I'll also tell you a story about reindeer. Remind me."

"Okay, I will. Thank you for letting me tag along. I'm learning a lot."

"It's great to have you."

Tuesday, August 28

Sammy awoke to find several plastic containers filled with goat's cheese in the kitchen. She remembered Marissa saying that Hattie often made cheese to sell to the nursing home in Providence. Not knowing when she'd see Marissa again, Sammy decided to do the delivery herself.

She rode Jackson into Providence, and then west on Spring Valley Road to the old elementary school turned nursing home, which she'd recognized from passing by the prior week. She hitched Jackson to a tree outside and walked in. A woman scurrying down a hallway said, "Hello, may I help you?"

"I'm Sammy Reisinger."

"Oh yes. Woody has mentioned you. I'm his wife, Caroline. Welcome to hell." She was tall with an elegant demeanor.

"I, I," Sammy stammered, dumbstruck.

"Pardon my manners. It's just that things have been tense here since the Pulse. I'm guessing you've brought Hattie's cheese."

"Yes, ma'am."

"Follow me to the kitchen, what there is of it. I'll tell you what's going on."

They walked down a hallway together. There was a tile floor and tile walls. It was dark, but a window at the end of the hall allowed them enough light to see their way. It smelled awful. Caroline introduced Sammy to Martha Allen and her son Frank. Martha appeared to be in her fifties, a black woman. Her son was in his twenties. "They're the only reliable help I have. They've pretty much moved in since the Pulse."

Martha declined to shake Sammy's hand, saying, "There's no telling what germs are on my hands. Nice to meet you." Martha asked Caroline for some instructions in the kitchen, and then she and Frank continued down the hallway.

Caroline continued, "Martha does kitchen work, takes care of the residents we have left, and tries to keep this place clean. Frank does maintenance and all the heavy lifting, which these days generally means digging graves and burying people out in the ball field."

As they continued walking, Caroline said, "We never worked with the worst. Our residents were either independent or they needed some assistance with two or three aspects of living, things like dressing or toilet. But just about everybody here is on medications.

"When the Pulse hit, we lost three of our 24 residents that first night. We had four people on staff. They carried out the corpses into the baseball field. In the next week, we lost six more."

"Oh my gosh!" Sammy sighed.

"You know, I'm a Christian woman. I believe in the afterlife and I have committed my life to Jesus, my Lord and Savior. But I never thought I'd go through something like this. Wait for me a moment. I've got to go change Mrs. Linkous' diaper." She vanished into one of the rooms.

Sammy heard some piano playing down the hall, so she went to investigate. She found an old woman, sitting at an upright piano in what had been the former all-purpose room, playing Gershwin. The piano was badly out of tune. The pianist had unruly grey hair, flowing like a waterfall from her head, and thick, dirty glasses. She saw Sammy enter and said, "Hello, young lady. Who are you?"

"I'm Samantha Reisinger."

"New Jersey or New York? I recognize the accent. What are you doing here?"

She told her about the Convention and being marooned by the Pulse. "I'm sorry, ma'am. I didn't catch your name."

"Dyson. Professor Margaret Dyson, at your service. I'm 89 years old. I'm not long for this earth, but I'm going to keep playing this piano as long as the good Lord will let me. Come take a seat!"

Dyson explained that she had retired decades earlier from teaching at Dartmouth. When her husband died and her daughter moved to Galax to take a job as the superintendent of Galax City Schools, she moved in with her. The daughter was twenty five years younger than she, but still predeceased her. When she couldn't take care of herself at their house in Galax, Caroline was opening this nursing home and Dyson was an original resident.

Sammy asked about life there since the Pulse.

"Miserable. Awful, as you might have imagined. We inmates were in every state of decay already, some of us physically incapacitated and some mentally incapacitated. There are only six of us left that are still cognizant. We understand what Caroline has had to do. Nobody envies her position."

"What did you teach?"

"Biology and ecology."

"I'd be interested in hearing about it, but I bet Caroline probably wondered where I went. I'd best find her."

"Well, come by again and I'll tell you more about it. I'll be here, I hope. I feel like I'm the pianist in the dance band on the Titanic. I'll keep playing as long as my fingers still keep moving."

Sammy stepped back into the hallway and almost literally ran into Caroline, who began in mid-sentence where she had left off. "When the meds started running out, we had four residents who had dementia, and they became delusional. Our staff, those that were here and couldn't get home, stayed to help. But only three others, plus me, ever came in after that. Family members came for three residents and took them home, two in horse-drawn carts and one walking.

"Even though we were already rationing, we started running low on food. The community has always donated food, but less so now. So even our healthiest residents became increasingly hungry. One of my favorites was an old English professor who was in pretty good shape. He slit his wrists leaving behind a whimsical suicide note, written in rhyme.

"I'm sorry to lay all this on you. You seem like a nice girl. But if I don't vent, I'll die.

"So anyway, day before yesterday, Mr. Britt, who is on meds for dementia, got increasingly anxious and was screaming for hours. I met with the two other staff members still here. Now mind you, even under the best of circumstances, none of our residents ever leave here other than in death. We decided that to preserve our limited food and the sanity of other residents, Mr. Britt needed to die."

"So you killed him?" She asked incredulously, realizing what Dr. Dyson was really talking about.

"Jesus as my witness, yes. I had the other two staff members hold him to his bed and I held his pillow over his face until he suffocated. And it's not over. We have several residents who are incontinent. We have only a week's worth of incontinence products left. Once we're out, we won't be able to keep these people clean and they will die in their own infections. We can't let that happen. We'll have to kill more of them if necessary."

"Do you still have staff people here, other than Martha and Frank?"

"They come when they can and go when they must. I haven't had a day off since the Pulse. My husband has been working the farm and I barely remember what he looks like. Sometime soon I'll need to go home for a day and change my clothes."

Sammy left for home where she ate some dinner, then rode Jackson to Emily's house to retrieve Jamaal for the weekly Tuesday jam session in Fries. Jamaal said he wanted to remain at home but added, "Tomorrow morning why don't you stop by? I have a surprise for you."

Sammy continued on. At that evening's session, much of the regular crowd was there. Rhonda sang another new song, accompanied by her father.

Momma, please stand by my bedside
Hold my hand, please stay
For the darkness is growing, time is so short
And life is fading away
For I must travel alone, And leave this old home
But the mountains are closer to heaven, they say
So, I won't be goin' so far away
Momma, please call for daddy
Tell him it's time for goodbye
It breaks my heart, I'll miss you both
But momma please don't cry

Wednesday, August 29

Only imagining what Jamaal had in mind, Sammy quickly brushed her teeth and hair and put on one of the last clean pairs of Bonnie's jeans and a t-shirt. She put Jackson's bridle on him but decided she was comfortable enough with him to ride bareback. She rode over to Emily's house where Jamaal met her at the door. "What's the surprise?"

"Come on in. Pike is here, too."

"Good morning, young lady," said the professor.

"Hi. What's going on?"

"I've been working on the radio, all the live long days," sang Jamaal, cheerily. "Take a listen," he said, handing Sammy a set of headphones. She put them over her ears but she heard mostly static. "I can't make out anything."

"I've gotten this crystal radio to work," Jamaal said proudly. "It picks up A.M. signals. They're much clearer in the evening."

"Last night I listened as long as I could stay awake. I heard a station in Salt Lake City, Utah and another in Phoenix, Arizona. They still have power in the west."

"What did they talk about?" asked Pike.

"Things are pretty grim. The federal government is inoperable. Many divisions of all our armed forces have been instructed to return home as quickly as possible. Most of our navy that was overseas is still operational. But with the Pentagon being inoperable, getting messages to them has been problematic. There are fears about coups with governors and senators from the Western States who were home at the time making bold statements like, 'I'm in charge now.'

"They are getting some information from ham radio operators throughout the east coast who have older vacuum tube radios and some means to generate enough electricity to broadcast, but there is understandably much confusion. Anyway, what they're reporting is horrific: riots in the cities, ransacking of the suburbs, and roving bands of people scouring the countryside near the cities in search of food."

Sammy thought about what this might mean for her town in New Jersey. She looked at Pike who was deep in thought as well. She said, "I feel like we're living in a bubble here. Dad used to have three televisions going on at the same time, keeping up with international news and the markets. I didn't think I paid any attention, but not knowing what's going on is killing me."

Jamaal said, "Most of what I'm hearing, I wish I hadn't. As miserable as it's been here, it's worse most other places. I think it's best for rural America to keep a low profile."

Pike said, "Ih keep thinking Ih should go back to Blacksburg. But Ih'm guessing Blacksburg is worse off than here."

"There are problems everywhere, as far as I can tell. I have no way to contact my wife in Mississippi," added Jamaal.

Sammy thought about her home in New Jersey, now unattended and without power. Would looters come? Would it be ransacked? She thought about the fate of Wilbur, her horse, kept at their country house an hour west of Alpine, near Sussex.

The two men looked at each other, searching for an answer that wouldn't make things worse. Neither could say a word.

Finally Jamaal said, "Everybody has lost somebody or something near and dear. But we have to focus on what we still have. Right now, we have each other. We are still alive and we need to plan to stay that way. A person every day has to choose between living and dying. Right now, I'm choosing to keep living. I need you two with me."

"Well said, my friend," said the engineering professor, walking towards the door. "So Ih'd best be getting back to Fries so Ih can help get that generator working. Ih'll see y'all later."

After his friend departed, Jamaal said to Sammy, "Let's you and I practice some karate. This seems like as good a time as any to teach you some self-defense."

Jamaal carried an old green packing quilt discarded from Mayflower Moving Company outside and placed it under the large maple tree. "The first thing I want you to know is that karate is as much mental as physical. *Mushin no shin* means being 'in the moment'. It is supreme focus. It is what karate is all about. In an attack, it is the movement of the other person. The *tori*, the attacker, has a goal of hurting you. The *uke* is you, the defender. The *uke* takes the energy of the *tori* coming at you and uses it to make the *tori* unsuccessful.

"Being 'in the moment' is finding your place. The *karate-ka*, the practitioner, wants to find his or her place both in self-defense and in life in general.

"If you are confronted by someone bigger, you can do serious harm by gouging an eye or punching two fingers into a neck. If you are attacked by a man, you can incapacitate or kill him by ripping off a testicle. Rape is not a sexual act; it is an act of aggression. Rapists take power by removing it from their victims. But if you are threatened, you must outfox him, gaining access to his eyes or his testicles. The rapist will not be thinking. He will only be acting from lust and power.

"You must find your 'center' and determine what you have to do. If you kick a man, you will likely fail because he will overpower you physically. It's physics. He has more physical power. The bigger athlete has the advantage over the smaller. You must outthink him. A front-kick to the stomach will drive him back, but will not likely overwhelm him.

"I'm going to teach you a few basic stances. First, we'll do the Ready Stance. I haven't officially earned the title *sensei*, which means instructor, but it will have to do. You are the *kohai*, the student. First, we stand facing each other. Then we bow to each other, recognizing our worth to each other and to humanity. Like this," he bowed from his waist. She returned the bow.

"Now then, when the *sensei* says, 'Ready!' you will close your hands, bend your elbows, and place your hands a few inches from your chest while simultaneously moving your right leg outward and placing it back on the ground at about the width of your shoulders, bending your knees slightly. Ready!"

Teacher and student assumed the Ready Position.

"Now then, let's do a Forward Stance. You can do this from either side. Are you right-handed?"

"Yes."

"Okay, let's do the right foot first. Move your right foot forward about one-and-a-half times the length of your foot. Like so. My right foot is still pointed forward. My right knee is bent while my back leg is straight. My shoulders are still straight. You can tell you have put your foot forward enough if you drop your back knee to the floor and put your fist between your feet and it touches both. Try it.

"Look what you can do from this stance. Your forward arm is

your right. You can thrust it straight for a forward punch. You can thrust your back arm, your left, straight. This is called a reverse punch. You can kick from your back leg. Or you can get a front snap-kick. Let's try this. Good. Again. Good."

"Jamaal, I'm scared," Sammy admitted, dropping her arms.

"Sam."

"No, really," she quivered. "I've never hit anybody before."

"Sammy."

"And I'm scared about what might happen to me. To us."

"Focus on the task at hand. Try your kick again."

She dropped her arms and started to cry. Soon her tears became a torrent, a full-fledged, unabashed wail. Jamaal walked to her and embraced her, but she was inconsolable. Her fit of agony and despair continued. The intensity of her grief was so violent that her body shook spontaneously. She choked on her tears, but they continued to flow, dampening his shirt.

"Oh, Sam," he said, gently.

Gradually she regained her composure, but she continued to hold him. "I am so scared."

He took her by the hand and led her to a nearby bench. "I'm scared, too," he admitted. "A person would be crazy not to be scared right now. But we must be strong."

Seeing her still wavering, he said, "Sam, for whatever reason, we're being tested. We're not the first people who have ever been scared.

"I'm sure my ancestors experienced intense fear. They were scared when they were roped like wild horses on the plains of Africa and placed in chains into stinking, putrid holds in the bottom of ocean-going ships to sail to America. They were scared when as slaves they knew that at any time, their children could be sold away from them like chattel. They were scared when their daughters, younger than you, were forced to copulate with and bear the children of their masters."

She looked at him with horror, but he continued.

"They were scared when they heard the drum-beats of the Civil War. When the war was over, they were freed, but were given nothing with which to earn a living or feed themselves. As sharecroppers, they were forever bound to poverty. They marched with Martin Luther King, Jr. in Selma and were shot with water cannons and attacked by police dogs. I'm sure they were scared.

"My mother's father was named John Hurt. He was raised in north central Mississippi in the late 1800s. It was, and still is, the poorest area of one of the nation's poorest states. He was a farmer but he never owned any land. He taught himself how to play the guitar before he turned ten. He made some pocket change with his music and did some recordings but was largely unknown for his entire life until the folk revival of the 1960s. Now he is considered one of the most influential blues musicians of all time. I've spent much of my adult life chasing his legacy.

"My father's father served in Korea, fighting for a country that never considered him a full citizen. He returned with a severe back injury and never was able to work another day in his life. And my own father was killed in a drive-by shooting in Memphis.

"That my country elected a black man as its president, that I was able to earn a PhD and get a job at one of the nation's finest universities, that I married a wonderful woman, that I am now living in the home of a selfless woman who may die soon, and that at this very moment, I am in your presence, is breathtakingly astounding to me. I am humbled, I am amazed, and I am terrified. But you know what? We're going to make it. Fuck this Pulse! I'm not about to piss away a legacy of multi-generational pain and anguish because we don't have any goddamn electricity."

She hugged him greatful for him strength and defiance. A mockingbird chirped a song from the fence-post. She took a deep breath and wiped her face with her sleeve. "Your story reminded me of stories my grandfather told me about the Nazi Concentration Camps," she said.

"You said you were close to him," Jamaal recalled.

"He always seemed like an old man to me, but he loved me. Oh, did he love me! I remember from my earliest childhood sitting on his lap and kissing me with his scratchy beard. He was in his sixties when he acquired my violin. It was made in the 1700s in Italy, by a son of the patriarch Guarneri. Now that it's mine, I treasure it more than anything. Many of my friends have everything money can buy, but somehow I feel blessed, singularly blessed, because of my Guarneri. I would die if I ever lost it.

"I was only six when my grandfather died. So I'm not sure how much of what I know now I remembered from him or from what I've read since. But his experience during the Nazi occupation was the most awful thing anybody could ever imagine. He grew up in Poland, in the south near the Czech border. When the Nazis overran Poland, he was an early teen. They lived in a small village, and some of their neighbors hid them for several years as Jews from the cities, principally Warsaw, were being carted away in cattle cars to die in the gas chambers.

"First, the Nazis shot his sisters and mother. In the Nazis' minds, all the women could do was produce more Jewish babies, and that was the last thing they wanted. They kept the men and boys alive and worked them to death as slaves in the concentration camps.

"He and his father and brother were taken to Auschwitz. His brother and father died before the liberation. He said he weighed 95 pounds when he was finally set free.

"He was able to immigrate to the United States after the war and he worked for years as a tailor in New York City. But he had amazing musical talent. He scraped together the money to buy a cheap violin and began practicing classical music. He befriended a wealthy man and somehow was able to save the man's son's life. As a sign of his appreciation, when the wealthy man died he bequeathed the Guarneri to my grandfather.

"I remember something he said to me over and over again. 'Don't ever take today for granted.' To tell you the truth, I wasn't old enough to even know what it meant. When I was bat mitzvah, the rabbi spoke about it and I thought I understood it by then. But after the lights went out last week, I think it took on a whole new meaning."

"Every age has had its challenges," the *sensei* said. "My ancestors dealt with slavery, peonage – debt servitude – discrimination and illegal wars, something the black people have fought disproportionately to whites. Your grandfather dealt with the Holocaust and we have dealt with terrorism."

"Oh, my God," Sammy shrieked. "I will never forget watching the sky over New York turn black with smoke when the World Trade Center towers were attacked," she remembered.

He said, "I saw much the same thing from my home in Georgetown when the Pentagon was hit an hour later. The point is that we are part of a continuum. Each of us will be born into a family and will make friends, will pursue our dreams and passions, perhaps have a spouse and children, and then die, leaving the earth to the next generation. Our generations have been largely spared the agonies of our forefathers. Our ancestors often went through living hell to allow you and me to be healthy and free and to share this day together. Your grandfather is right; we should never take it for granted because it can vanish in a flash of lightning. It is an astounding gift we have been given. We owe it to those who have gone before us to accept our fate, however difficult it may seem right now, with grace and appreciation."

Across the fence, Jackson scratched the ground, a sign Sammy took as his approval.

"Thanks, my friend," she said to him.

"Thanks to you, too. Now shall we get back to work?"

They worked for two hours until both were too tired to continue, and Sammy left for home. When she arrived, Marissa and Hattie were sitting on the front porch, with Snoopy resting nearby. As Sammy approached, Hattie looked more peaceful and contented than ever before. Marissa was crocheting a skull-cap sized for an infant. When Sammy asked about it, she said, "I make these all the time and give them to either expectant mothers or to the hospital in Galax to anyone who might need them. Busy hands are happy hands. The peaches are ripe on two of the trees out back. Tomorrow, I thought we'd do some canning."

The two sisters and the girl fixed dinner together. Someone had given Marissa a smallmouth bass he'd caught in the New River that afternoon. They breaded and fried it, and ate it with garden vegetables.

During dinner, Marissa spoke about having visited Felts Park in Galax, the venue for the Old Fiddlers Convention. She described it as a scene from hell. Several thousand people were marooned there by immobilized cars. "The city has tried to care for them, but hundreds have died. It is good you were able to leave when you did." They played Scrabble afterwards and Hattie surprised Sammy by being quite good at it, although she said almost nothing.

Quint arrived as darkness was setting in and only a few letter tiles were left in the Scrabble game sack. His presence cast an immediate pall over the room. Hattie walked away mumbling something about having to pee, but never returned. "No dinner for me," he growled, moving into the kitchen to find something for himself in the dark room. Sammy excused herself and went upstairs to bed. "Get some rest, Sammy," said Marissa. "Tomorrow we're going to can peaches."

Thursday, August 30

Sammy and Marissa awoke at the same time in the twin beds formerly belonging to the Thompson twins. Before they got out of bed, Sammy said, "I think Hattie seems better now, more serene than when we met last week."

"It's funny. Somehow I think this tragedy has changed her. She's been living in her own world with her personal demons. She's seen other people share good times and joy. I think it has made her ever more isolated. Now, I think she senses that others are dealing with serious trauma, too, and I don't think she feels so alone. On the other hand, Quint may be worse now."

They had oatmeal with black raspberries that Marissa had picked on her way to the house the day before. They left a bowl behind for Hattie, who was nowhere to be found. Outside, the air was cooler than prior days, with Sammy thinking about the onset of fall. She always loved the fall season best of all. She loved the colorful trees around her home in New Jersey and found the briskness in the air invigorating.

They spent the next two hours picking peaches. Sammy couldn't resist eating two of them right off the tree. They were smaller than the supermarket peaches she'd been accustomed to, but were fuzzier and more delicious, dripping with juice. Marissa had instructed her to pick for canning the same ripeness she'd pick for eating – not too hard but not mushy, either.

Back in the kitchen, Marissa put extra logs on the woodstove and placed a huge pot on top. The women carried several gallon jugs of water inside from the pump and began boiling water. They assembled the tools they'd need for the canning process, including a jar grabber, a lid lifter – a magnet tied to a string – several spoons and a large ladle. Marissa retrieved a water bath canner – a large pot equipped with a lifting rack to sanitize the jars – from the basement. Sammy noticed other fruits, vegetables, and even meats in hundreds of jars marked by the month and year on the lids that were already stored from prior harvests.

To Sammy's surprise, Emily arrived and said, "Am I on time?" grinning broadly.

"How did you know we were canning today?"

"Just something women tend to know."

Within moments, Rhonda and Dowell arrived, too. Marissa asked Dowell to wash the peaches, reasoning that it was something he could do without much instruction. Emily and Sammy washed the jars and lids by putting them into the biggest pot containing boiling water for several minutes. Meanwhile, a smaller pot with sugary water heated up beside it.

Rhonda helped Marissa with peeling. Sammy watched for a moment and saw the peels coming off easily. "Peeling by hand is way too much work," said Marissa. "Watch this." She put three peaches into the boiling water and left them there for 30 seconds. She took them out with a slotted spoon and placed them into a pot of cold water. The skins practically came off themselves. She handed them to Rhonda who sliced them and removed the seeds.

Emily and Sammy took the peach slices and put them into the pot of lightly boiling syrup solution. Sammy said, "With this crisis, how much sugar do you still have?"

Marissa answered, "We still have 30 pounds or so."

"I have some at my house, too, if we need it. When we do the apples, I can get mine," offered Rhonda.

"The sugar isn't necessary to preserve anything," Marissa noted. "The air-tight sealing of the jars prevents spoilage. If you see a jar on the shelf that is rotten, it's because the seal wasn't tight."

"There seems to be a lot of food in the basement already," Sammy noted.

"It's only there because we've worked like this in the past to put it there," Marissa said. "I daresay there wasn't a house in the county fifty years ago that didn't have a year or two supply of food in the basement. These days, people have gotten lazy. They buy more from the stores. In those days, if a farmer's primary product was beef or dairy, he'd still grow a garden. Nowadays, most farmers shop for food at the grocery stores like everybody else."

"Nobody where I live grows a garden," Sammy said. "We have a huge refrigerator, but it usually doesn't have much in it because our maid goes shopping every two or three days. The only time the 'fridge was full was when we were throwing a party."

"I think this is a sign of the times, here and everywhere else," Marissa concluded. "But people here always remember the bad times. This has never been an easy place to make a living, but families never went hungry, even in the worst of times."

Sammy thought about this and how different it was from her community. Rhonda didn't have much to say to anyone, but kept her head buried in her work, occasionally humming some songs.

The work was hot but the mood was jovial, and the women worked with purpose. As the day passed, everybody ate as many fresh slices as their stomachs would hold. Marissa took off her shirt and worked in her bra and shorts, something Sammy found amusing.

"Sammy," Emily said before departing, "tomorrow I'm going to call on another client. Would you like to go with me? I'd like to leave in late morning. It will be a long walk."

"Sure."

That evening after dinner of mostly fresh vegetables, Sammy, Marissa, and Hattie sat on the front porch, Marissa and Hattie on the swing and Sammy sat on the wicker chair. A nearly full moon rose in the eastern sky, reflecting off the ripples of the New River waters a mile away and a hundred feet below. Sammy went upstairs and retrieved her violin and she played several quiet, reverential melodies. The sisters hummed along, but nobody had much to say.

Sammy was ready to retire when Quint rode his bicycle into the yard and crashed into the fencepost, sending him sprawling across the grass. Marissa giggled quietly. Quint picked himself up – nobody moved to assist him – and walked noisily onto the porch. "I don't suppose anybody has made me any dinner."

"We fixed our own and cleaned the kitchen hours ago," said Marissa assertively. "We left some tomatoes and a potato for you. Help yourself," and as he turned away at a lower volume, "if you know how."

Sammy packed her instrument. "I think I'll turn in now. Should be another busy day tomorrow."

From her room, she could hear Quint back on the porch, assailing his wife and sister-in-law for some failure to meet his expectations. It hurt her ears to listen, and she closed the window, even though the room was warm and the nighttime air was cool. Before she closed the shades, the moonlight streamed in, illuminating the photo of her grandfather she'd left by the vanity. When she looked at his image, he seemed to nod gently to her.

Friday, August 30

Sammy said goodbye to Marissa as she prepared to walk home, carrying three jars of peaches in a small backpack.

Sammy rode Jackson around his paddock for an hour in the morning. He felt like he wanted to practice his dressage training, so she put him through some paces alternating his leg yields and haunches in and out routines. There was a slight chill in the air and he was energetic and vigorous. Her shoulders and butt were sore from the previous day's karate lesson. But she realized that she and Jackson needed more time together, both at work and at play.

Rather than riding him to Emily's, she untacked him and left him to pasture. She had a bite to eat and departed. She found Emily and Jamaal waiting on the porch for her. Jamaal explained that he wanted to go as well. So the grey-haired woman, the black man, and the thin Jewish girl from New Jersey began walking the deserted Spring Valley Road to the northwest, towards the Iron Mountains. This was a longer walk than Sammy had taken since her arrival. Emily estimated it at six miles each way. They had plenty of time to chat.

Sammy started off. "You were talking to me the other day about diversity and resilience. It was interesting to me. And you told me to remind you something about reindeer."

"Yes, I sure did. Here we go.

"The earth is a fickle mistress," Emily proclaimed, flatly. "Nature doesn't care if you're having a good day or not. Species come and go on earth. As far as we know, human beings, Homo sapiens, have been the only species to ever inhabit the planet that had self-awareness and the ability to consciously alter the environment either to help or hinder its survival.

"Let me tell you a story that is illustrative of how nature works. All species have the ability to reproduce at prodigious quantities, some more than others. A queen bee can produce tens of thousands of eggs. It's been said that compounding interest is the most powerful force in the universe."

"Didn't Einstein say that?" asked Jamaal.

"Anecdotally, perhaps," said his host, "but nobody is for sure. Anyway, nature works this way. If a bee lays 1000 eggs and they live to sexual maturity and each lays 1000 more, and each of them lays 1000 more, within three generations there are a trillion bees. Obviously, this can't go on very long. What happens instead is that statistically, they all die before sexual maturity, except one. That one is able to continue the cycle. This happens with all species, on average, or soon there would be a population explosion.

"So here's my reindeer story. There is an island off the coast of Alaska called St. Matthew Island. It's in the middle of the Bering Sea, one of the most remote and inhospitable places in the world. Reindeer eat lichen. Until 1944, there were no reindeer on it, so the lichen was untouched and thus thick. A small herd was introduced there by the US Army. Because there was a ready food source in enormous quantities, the herd grew explosively, and within 20 years there were 6000 of them. By the 1960s, they had consumed almost all the lichen and in 1964, there was a severe winter. When it was over, all died except 42, and they were starving.

"Every ecosystem has a carrying capacity. That capacity can change due to changes in the environment or the way a species interacts with the environment. The same thing happens when a tornado sweeps through a dense forest, as the termite population explodes to take advantage of all the surplus food. The same thing happened to the Irish people when the potato was introduced. Biologists call this 'bloom and overshoot.'"

Jamaal contributed, asking Sammy, "Have you ever seen a chart of human population on the earth?"

"I'm not sure," Sammy replied. "Doesn't it grow quite a bit?"

The economics professor said, "It resembles a hockey stick, being flat for a long time then jumping upwards. There were never more than a billion people on earth in 1820. Now there are upwards of seven billion, growing by a billion every 25 years. Do you know how that happened?"

"Better medicine?"

"Yes," Emily took over. "But that's only part of the answer. Humans discovered and began putting to work in expanding quantities the endowment of fossil fuels that had always been buried literally under their feet. And they turned that fuel – coal, oil, natural gas, and related things – into all the trappings of modern life, including medicine. Energy is the kingpin resource, allowing access to all the others. The improvements in medicine have been a byproduct of surplus energy.

"What Jamaal and I are saying," said Emily, "is that humans are exploding in population like the reindeer on St. Matthews Island, and oil, coal, and natural gas are our lichen."

"I think I see what's wrong with that," Sammy offered. "I'm guessing some of those fuels are limited and we are nearing the point where all of them will reach an apex in availability."

"Right," said Jamaal. "Less energy means less industrialization, less mobility, less prosperity, and ultimately fewer people. That's what a lot of people are concerned about. How many people can the earth support with diminishing fossil fuels? Not seven billion like we have now, I'd guess.

"I'm sure the death toll from the Pulse is already in the millions," he said sadly. "The good news of all the bad news we've had in the last few weeks is that the United States, which consumes a greatly disproportionate share of the world's energy, is being forced to take a break for a while, until we can get the lights back on."

"If we ever do," said Emily, ruefully.

They turned from the paved road onto a gravel road, deeply rutted with rainwater drainage. Curious, Sammy said to Jamaal, "What brings you along with us today?"

"Two things. First, Emily said it was a long way and I wanted to make sure you girls were okay out here. Second, the pregnant woman is black and I'm interested in making contact with other blacks."

A white frame church came into view, so small that Sammy thought perhaps only 25 or 30 people could sit inside. There were several small homes and decrepit automobiles. Three black kids, ages perhaps five to eight, ran to see them. "Hello, kids," Emily said. "Where does Ebony Freeman live?"

"I'm Marcus Freeman," said one of the kids. "She's my mom. Are you here to see her?"

"I'm here to make sure the little baby inside her is doing okay."

He led the trio to a tiny house that badly needed a coat of paint. Inside were the expectant mother, her husband DeAngelo, and a girl Sammy thought was about three. "My name is Chastity," she said proudly.

"Mine is Sammy. Can we be friends? "

Sammy kept her ear on two conversations at once while she played with the girl. Emily examined Ebony while Jamaal spoke with DeAngelo. The black man was slight in build – all of them were. DeAngelo said, "This is a tiny enclave of us blacks. After the Civil War, my people were released from slavery off a plantation from the Williams family down the hill in Spring Valley. They had no money and nowhere to go. Old man Williams was crippled from his war wounds, but he told his former slaves that if they would help him on the farm, he would give them the going rate of pay, which was just about nothing, but when he died he would deed about 220 acres up here in the hollow to the blacks. So my people have been here ever since. Family lore is that we took the name 'Freeman' because that's what we were. My wife is from War, West Virginia, deep in the coal country. I drug her here."

"I've been mad at him ever since," she said, listening in while the midwife palpated her distended belly.

"You liked it over there?" asked Jamaal incredulously.

"I'm a West Virginia girl. My grandparents and thousands of blacks migrated there during in the 20s and 30s to work in the coal mines. It was a good place for blacks because they were paid the same as white folks for the same production. But with the mechanization of the mines, there are no jobs over there any more."

"Hush," scolded Emily, trying to listen to the fetoscope.

"I came back from the military seven years ago, after serving in Iraq," said the expectant father, more quietly. "I got some skills in mechanics, but my hand was hurt by a roadside bomb and nobody around here would hire me. I get some work from my neighbors, but I'm basically living off a government check. Nowadays, with the power out, that's not coming any more. I'm told the stores have nothing in them to buy anyway."

He asked Jamaal what brought him to the area, and Jamaal told about the Fiddlers Convention and his encounter with Sammy and their new hosts.

"You've still got the third trimester to go, so I'll try to come again in a couple of months and check on you," Emily told her client.

"Listen, brother," DeAngelo said to Jamaal, "and you, too, sister," nodding to Sammy, "we ain't got much, but whatever we have is yours, if you should ever need it."

Sammy walked out the door first, verklempt that this poor family opened their lives to her, the rich Jewish kid from New Jersey, who until mere weeks earlier had everything she ever could dream of.

On their way home, the sun reached low into the western sky, casting long shadows on the walkers. Clouds illuminated in pink and yellow pastels from the light seemingly emanating from below them. A full moon rose in the east over gentle, brilliantly lit green mountains. Sammy saw it first, "Look!"

"Beautiful!" exclaimed Emily.

"Today's the full moon," said Jamaal. "Did you know the full moon always rises at sunset? The reason we see it as full is that the sun is opposite from it in the sky. This one is a blue moon, too."

"What's that?" asked the teenager.

"It's the second full moon in the same month. The lunar cycle is 28 days long and months, except February, are 30 or 31, so if the full moon is on the first or second day, there will be another before the month's end. The second one, from folklore, is the blue moon, and we get about seven every nineteen years. It's where that expression, 'once in a blue moon,' comes from. This nineteen year time period is remarkable because it is nearly a common multiple of both the lunar and solar cycles."

"I know about the lunar cycle. The Hebrew calendar is a lunar calendar, isn't it?" Sammy recalled.

"Yes."

"It's why Hanukkah jumps around during the Christian month of December."

"That's right," said Emily, struggling to keep up the walking pace. "The Christian calendar has 365 days, with months averaging around 30 days. It adds an additional day every four years on leap year to make up for the additional quarter-day. The Hebrew calendar has 12 months, averaging 29-1/5 days, which is a lunar cycle. The calendars synchronize every nineteen years. During this time, in the 3rd, 6th, 8th,

11th, 14th, 17th and 19th years, an additional month is added to keep things close. The biggest difference on a practical level is that Hebrews consider the day to begin at sunset the prior day, holidays and regular days alike."

"In any event, the moon sure is pretty," said Sammy. "It's huge in the sky!"

Sammy walked on, thinking about what the next moon and the moon after that might bring in her life. It was so bright that the three peripatetic souls cast discernable moonshadows, and Sammy could easily see the outline of distant hillsides and trees.

Nearing Emily's home, Jamaal said, "I was scrounging around the barn yesterday and I found an old church bell. If you two like, I can mount it on a pole near the house so if Emily needs you, Sammy, she can ring it. It will be your 'bell system'." He chuckled at his own joke.

"That would be helpful," Emily said. "Thanks."

Before they split to go their separate ways, Emily said to Sammy, "I saw Caroline Dalton yesterday. She told me to tell you that she was going to take tomorrow off from the nursing home, and would enjoy seeing you at her house. Why don't you go by for a visit?"

Part 2: September

Saturday, September 1

SAMMY'S EYES FELT GLUED SHUT as she tried to shake off a persistent dream. A big-screen television hopped around her family's den. She shook the remote control at it, pointing and pushing buttons. It jumped wildly from show to show, first airing *Oprah*, then *Who's Got Talent*, then the *Nature Channel*, showing whirling planets. The television became flexible, like a rubber sheet, flowing and dancing from floor to ceiling and back. A peacock like the NBC logo took wing and flew from the screen and around the room. She was annoyed but amused at the same time. She awoke to a sunlit room, startled by how long she must have slept after the previous day's exertion.

She tacked up Jackson and led him outside through the gate, then climbed the gate to hoist herself atop him. She rode him south to Riverside, then west on Riverside Drive, where she stopped to deliver some cheese to Mrs. Thaxton, the pregnant woman she'd met a week earlier. Then she rode northwesterly on Carsonville Road until she found a mailbox saying "Dalton."

The dirt driveway ended at a white farmhouse surrounded by barns and pastures. She draped Jackson's reins over the wooden fence. As she began to let herself inside the yard, Caroline emerged from the house to meet her.

"Hello, Sammy, it's great of you to visit. I was afraid my behavior last week might have scared you away forever."

"Hi Sammy," said Woody Dalton, emerging from the largest barn. "Nice to see you."

"It's good to see you both. This looks like a real, working farm!"

"Why don't you show her around, Woody? I've got some things to do in the kitchen. Come on in when you're done and we can eat."

Woody waved his hand broadly and said, "Yes, this is the farm where I grew up. We have about 120 acres. That's about as small as a

122

farm can be these days and still survive financially. It's a good thing we put some money away before we moved back. We joke that the way to make a small fortune in farming is to start with a large one."

Sammy laughed. She said, "Caroline said you were in the pharmaceuticals business before."

"That's right. Of course, I grew up here. I went to University of Richmond for my bachelor's degree. After I got my PhD at Tulane, I worked at Merck in North Carolina. My parents were getting increasingly frail. I shouldn't admit this, but I was ready to send them to a nursing home. Instead, Caroline shamed me into moving back and taking over the farm. And then we started a nursing home. My wife – she's a saint."

Swallows darted rapidly to and fro.

Woody continued, "Anyway, we both quit our jobs and we moved back. We were going to rent a little place in town until we could build a house, but we could see quickly that mom and dad couldn't stay here much longer on their own. So we bought the school building and started the nursing home in it. We moved them there and moved ourselves here. Caroline said she already downloaded on you about what's gone on there since the Pulse."

"Yes, she did," Sammy admitted. "It is awful there. What has the Pulse meant for you on the farm?"

"Difficult, to say the least. Farming is mechanized like everything else. A hundred years ago, 30 percent of our nation's population worked on farms. Now, only 2 percent work on farms. Electricity and oil do most of the manual work for us. Since the Pulse, we have none of the former and little of the latter. We still have a reserve of diesel oil and some of our older tractors work, but we ration it like crazy, because we don't know when or if we'll ever get more.

"We grow primarily cows and corn. All the cows we've raised in recent years have been shipped by truck or rail to the Midwest to the huge processing facilities. The corn is mostly for poultry feed. There are huge chicken and turkey houses in the Shenandoah Valley that buy most of what we grow. I suspect they've killed most of their flocks by now being unable to get feed for them.

"We planted everything before the Pulse, when our tractors ran. Now, we have fields of corn that we can't harvest and a herd of cows that need to be fed. So we're back to the good ole days. We're employing lots of people around here to do farm work. The cows are doing part of the harvest for us by feeding themselves. We rope off a section of the cornfield every day and lead the cows to it. Several workers stand in the field with the cows to keep them confined, because the rope is insufficient.

"Every week, I march a steer to Ms. Bartlett's store and we butcher him on the spot. I get paid in jar lids like scrip. Then I take the lids home and pay the workers with them. Then they spend the scrip back in her store or wherever there is food.

"Obviously, like everyone else, now I wish I'd planted a bigger garden. We grow tomatoes, cucumbers, sweet corn, pinto beans, October beans, green beans, squash, beets, radishes, corn, cabbage, carrots, turnips, potatoes. Caroline has always taken most of what we've grown to the nursing home. I hate to say this, but now that there are fewer residents there is more of it for those of us still trying to eat."

Looking over a huge cornfield, he continued, "In my parents' era, the wives of farmers worked the gardens. Now, the wives typically have other jobs, often teachers, nurses, or professional jobs, in order to provide the medical insurance. Did you know that farming is one of the most dangerous industries in the nation? We don't have OSHA looking over our operations and we often employ people who are inadequately trained. When somebody gets hurt, it is more difficult to get to the hospital. Many of the nation's agricultural workers are undocumented and unprotected."

Sammy and Woody went inside the house and washed with some water from a pitcher in the kitchen. Then the three sat down to have some lunch, including green beans and tomatoes from the garden. It was a simple meal, with only salt and pepper for spicing, but Sammy was delighted by the flavors of the fresh vegetables. Woody continued his thoughts on farming.

"We're the people who grow the food that keeps our citizens alive. But farming is an increasingly difficult business. Farmers must be good weathermen, agronomists, bookkeepers, mechanics, technical directors, human resources managers, veterinarians, and brokers. And we're still likely to get creamed by the big agribusiness corporations like ADM, Cargill, DuPont and Monsanto. Sometimes you get, and sometimes you get got."

His wife chuckled.

He continued, "Every change in the environment produces winners and losers. When I say the environment, I'm not just talking about climate. I'm talking about the total scientific, climate, social, and economic environment. When Hurricane Katrina struck the Gulf Coast a few years ago, hundreds of thousands of people, perhaps even millions, were affected. Most of them were losers. But there were a handful of winners. The people doing insurance adjusting and home product salvage were winners. The Pulse has produced millions of losers. But when the dust settles, there will be a few people, who due to luck, planning, hardiness, or shrewdness, will emerge in good shape, if they can overcome the emotional toll. Maybe we'll see a new golden age of farming and people will start appreciating where their food comes from again."

"I never thought much about it," Sammy admitted. "We've always had food in the refrigerator. Our maid buys it from the store. I never spent much time thinking about how it got there. I don't recall ever having a conversation with my friends at school about where food comes from."

Caroline said, "I think that conversation will be happening much more often in the future, for those lucky enough to be survivors."

"Has anybody stolen anything from you?" Sammy asked.

"Yes," admitted Woody. "We've lost some cows. And of course crows and deer need to be shooed away from the garden."

"What happened to the cows?"

"I presume they were rustled," Woody said.

"What did you do?"

"Nothing. In fact, I almost caught some people who I think were in the process of stealing a cow. I probably could have caught them if I'd tried harder. But what then?"

Caroline said, "Woody and I have done lots of soul-searching since the Pulse. We're in a crisis and we have to look out for each other. If we have something people need, we will have to share it. There will be folks that will take advantage of the situation, but we will have to let that go. People will do anything it takes to feed their families. We think people will recognize generosity and will ultimately reward it. At the nursing home, we've already seen a situation a thousand times worse than my worst nightmare, and it's not over yet. But we will just have to deal with it, like everybody else."

Woody said, "Listen, if you don't mind, why don't you walk with me over to Carlene's Store? I'm taking a steer there to be butchered. We can talk more on the way."

"Sure!" Sammy agreed.

He rounded up the steer and she took Jackson by the reins. As they left the property, Sammy said, "You seem to have a good perspective about the culture around here."

"I do try to understand people. Because I've had the opportunity to live elsewhere, I think I see my neighbors more clearly. Here's how I see it. It is an overgeneralization, but let's say Grayson County has two types of people: old-timers and newcomers.

"There is almost no racial diversity within either type. Over 90-percent of the people in the County are Northern European white, with only a smattering of Asians, Latinos, and blacks.

"There are around 15,000 people here. The county has only three incorporated towns: Troutdale, Independence, and Fries. There were more people in this county 100 years ago than there are now. The highest population was in 1940, when it neared 22,000. So we've lost a third of our population in 70 years. When I was a kid, I and others like me that had some ambition and intelligence saw opportunities elsewhere, and we decided to leave. I'm unusual in that I came back. Like most counties in the central Appalachians, Grayson is seeing more people leaving than arriving.

"The old-timers are descendents of immigrants primarily from Scotland, Ireland, and Germany. They are almost exclusively Christian, many quite fundamental in their beliefs. The Germans were more prosperous when they arrived and became landowners. The Scots and Irish were dirt poor and became the working classes.

"Until about a generation ago, the people generally found work in three areas. Chronologically, the first was farming. The second was extractive industries like timbering and mining. The third was manufacturing.

"Farming is still going on, but it is highly mechanized and it doesn't take as many people to get the work done – at least it didn't before the Pulse.

"Timbering still goes on at a modest level and mining is a relic of the past.

"Manufacturing was huge in Fries, and Galax once had six large furniture factories. But jobs like these vanished over the last few decades as corporations found that people across the world would work for drastically less money than Americans, so they shipped the jobs overseas.

"What that left us with here in rural Appalachia is a mish-mash of occupations, most low-paying. A lot of people around here think the glory years were from the late 1940s, after the war ended, until the 1980s, when everything started shutting down. A working man, or increasingly a working woman, could make enough money to raise a family, take a summer vacation, and have their medical needs met in case somebody got sick. Those times are mostly gone, or were gone even before the Pulse. What will emerge from the ashes is yet to be determined. But I hope those that survive will treasure the efforts of rural people a bit more. We've all got to eat."

He looked at the cow, following behind, and continued his comments. "From a religious standpoint, almost all of the old-timers are Christian, almost solely Baptist and Methodist. Many of the newcomers are Christian, too, but with a sizeable number of people who identify with the New Age movement. Both groups perversely wish for the End Times to come."

"I'm learning more and more about the Christian viewpoint," Sammy said, "but what's the New Age thing?"

"The New Age movement is an alphabet soup of '-isms' drawing spiritual themes from atheism and pantheism to the sciences of ecology, astronomy, psychology and physics. It draws its name from what people call the Age of Aquarius. It is the upcoming astrological age. It was popularized in a song from a musical production called *Hair* that had a song called the *Age of Aquarius*. It included a line, 'This is the dawning of the Age of Aquarius.' It spoke about a time of peace, trust, sympathy, and harmony.

"But both groups hate now. The Christians want the second coming of Christ. The New Agers want the Age of Aquarius. The New Agers think that only a complete cleansing of what we have now will allow the new society to emerge. Part of that is a mass contraction. What's crazy is that for different reasons, both groups don't fear the End Times because they think they will somehow be reincarnated into a better place. New Agers get 'Hindu' about it, as if the suffering of the End Times is part of their karma. There is greater reason and they don't worry."

A striking black and white bird, as large as a crow, with a flowing red crest, flew in front of them and alighted in a large maple tree where it began pounding its chisel-like beak into the trunk.

Woody continued, "Anyway, everybody is fanaticizing about what things will look like on the other side of the chaos. The fundamentalists think they will get to go to heaven with Jesus. They're waiting for a physical messiah. The New Agers think the Garden of Eden starts over, here on earth. They're waiting for a metaphysical Messiah. They think we will wake up magically and everything will be rosy. Neither group sees themselves eating grass or cooking groundhogs over a campfire. The two groups are contemptuous of each other."

"That seems so crazy to me," Sammy asserted. "I don't see God as a positive or negative force. We've always been on our own and I think we'll always be on our own."

Woody said, "The thing I find most hypocritical is that while Jesus was a priest of tolerance, acceptance, and peace, fundamentalists are ethnocentric, intolerant, and militaristic. Most of the fundamentalists around here have never lived in an ethnic or religious minority. When that happens, it's easy for racism to spread."

Sammy said, "There's a woman at Quint's church that found out I was Jewish and she looked at me like I was from another planet! She was staring at me so much that I went over to her and asked her why she was staring. She said, 'I've never seen a Jew before.' I think she thought Jews have three legs! One man said, 'You don't look Jewish.' I think he thought he was paying me a compliment by telling me that I didn't look like his image of my own people."

Woody continued. "I'm sure he thought so. But many people here are insular. One of the interesting things about the local take on the End Times is that Revelation, where it is discussed, mentions a river running through the New Jerusalem. The New River is the oldest river in the Western Hemisphere, here long before the mountains, which are some of the oldest on earth. Many local people see the New River as the river running through the New Jerusalem. The New Jerusalem starts right here, right here in Fries. This is where the Second Coming will happen."

"Wow! That's something to think about," Sammy said. "You said Caroline was a follower of Christ, but how about yourself? Are you religious?"

"I'm Farmish," he chuckled.

"Come on. Seriously!"

"I'm probably best described as ambivalent agnostic. But I'm a farmer. Food is my religion. Soil and good weather are my gods. Right now, I see the future only conceptually. I don't know what it will bring. I'm just trying to produce enough food to keep my wife's nursing home residents and my neighbors alive."

They reached the store and Sammy rode Jackson home, thinking, for the first time mindful of the sacrifices of working people and the power of generosity. She had been a child of affluence, never experiencing hardship or adversity. Those days were gone.

Sunday, September 2

At Quint's insistence, Sammy got prepared for church, donning another of Bonnie's dresses.

After the usual preliminary portions of the church service, Quint quickly returned to the portion of the sermon left undone from the prior week.

"Israel is situated amidst a neighborhood of Islamic nations, all of which hate her. The Antichrist says that he will provide peace and security for Israel for seven years. While he is protecting Israel he will diplomatically and militarily desire to take over a one world government.

"Before all of this happens, some form of one world government, something similar to but more powerful than the United Nations, will emerge. The Antichrist then forces a covenant on Israel. The Bible makes clear that this seven-year period is split into equal periods of three-and-a-half years each. At the midpoint, the Antichrist turns against Israel. He goes into the Jewish Temple and demands that the entire world worship him as god.

"The rapture has happened before the beginning of this seven-year period. This seven year event is considered the tribulation. Any Christians who have not been whisked away to heaven along with everyone else will soon learn that this covenant has been forced upon Israel. There will be widespread understanding that the tribulation is underway because those left behind will obviously have seen the departure of the true believers, happening right before their eyes.

"Will you be one of them? How will you react? Will you pursue answers as to why that happened? Repent today, my children!

"In the second three-and-a-half year period, the world will fall under the rule of the Antichrist. At the end, Jesus Christ literally returns to the Mount of Olives in Jerusalem. He destroys the forces of the Antichrist in Israel and he reestablishes his dominance over the world for the next 1000 years. He will rule as a benevolent dictator, as a righteous king. It will be paradise.

"My children, today the Jewish race is three-tenths of one percent of world population. Christians are perhaps sixteen percent, but some smaller percentage is true believers. Everyone else is Muslim, Hindu, Buddhist, atheist, or some other religion.

"When the end comes, the Antichrist will be a Muslim. True Islam is a religion in place to destroy all the others. The founder of Islam was Mohammed. He preached jihad. He told his followers that they were to take over the world politically, economically, and militarily and they were to dominate and subjugate all people.

"Is the rapture nigh? Is the Pulse God's signal for the beginning of the rapture? Our society has forgotten the Ten Commandments.

"This country was founded on Judeo-Christian traditions. When the United States goes down as a superpower, there will be a new world order and a new structure. All nations then will submit to a consortium of nations like the United Nations only much more dominant and perhaps much less benevolent than what we have now.

"Was the Pulse natural? Were we attacked? Is our nation doomed? There isn't a moment to lose; now is the time to repent!"

Many heads nodded in agreement. Quint gave a final prayer and then adjourned.

After the service, Rhonda, Dowell, and Ortie walked back to the house with Quint and Sammy. Quint and Ortie carried on a long conversation about the sermon as they walked, but Rhonda spoke little to anyone, as if she was pouting. Her brother shook his right hand vigorously as he walked and hummed to himself. Ortie clearly labored under the exercise and kept everyone's progress at a snail's pace.

After lunch of lettuce and boiled potatoes, everyone sat on the front porch, chatting and singing. Sammy got her violin and some sheet music, and played Bach's Violin Concerto in A minor, stumbling on a few bars, but doing a good enough job to bring a "Wow, wow, little lady," from Ortie. "You're good as hell on that fiddle. I've never heard such a sound like that." She waited expectantly for the others to voice agreement, but none did. She did, however, see Hattie hiding behind the hedge, seemingly listening intently.

Monday, September 3

Sammy awoke to the sound of Emily's bell. Upon her arrival, she found a man she didn't know and Emily scurrying around preparing for departure. "Sammy, honey, this is Paul Wilkinson. He's here to get me. His wife is in labor. They live close by. Please come with us."

Mr. Wilkinson had actually driven his car there, an antique Chevy that still ran. "But," he said when they talked about it, "there's not much gasoline around anyway, so I really can't drive it except for emergencies, this being one."

The house was less than five minutes away by car. Wilkinson's wife Lottie was in bed in a nightgown, already in advanced labor. Emily introduced Lottie to Sammy, and then pulled a fetoscope and sphygmomanometer from her bag. She took the woman's pulse and blood pressure and listened to her heart and the baby's heart. "Blood pressure is 127/82, with 94 beats per minute. All looks good!" she said happily. A boy of three stood aside watching the proceedings. "You did a good job taking care of your mom when your dad went to pick us up," said the midwife, reassuringly. To the mother she said, "You're at 6 cm already. I don't want you to start pushing just yet. How's the pain?"

"Not bad. But I know what's coming," she smiled wanly.

Sammy began playing with the boy who said his name was Danny. He had a toy banjo. "Show me how you play it," she suggested, which he did.

"How are y'all coping with the power outage?" Emily asked.

"It's been tough for us," said Paul. "I've been trying to take care of Lottie and the boy by myself. It's a lot of work and we don't have a lot of food. But we're not complainers. I know everyone else is struggling, too. The Lord has been with us and is blessing us with this new child."

Moments later, "Whoa! Whoa! I'm getting real contractions now. Owww. Owww. This really hurts. Can you give me something for the pain?"

"Let's try to focus on the baby, not on your pain. See if you can go a bit longer."

The contractions subsided and Lottie asked to get out of bed to walk around the room a bit. She drank some water and tried to pass the time.

"What's going to happen next?" asked the boy. "When is my baby sister going to be born?"

Lottie lay back on the bed and Emily examined her vagina again. "Eight centimeters. Won't be long now. Sammy, have a look."

Sammy looked at the pregnant woman's crotch. It was the first time she could ever remember giving more than a casual glance at another woman's private areas. She was revolted but curious, steeling herself for more experiences to come. Excusing herself, she said to the boy, "Let's you and I go into the other room. I think your mother needs to be alone now."

Lottie smiled at her son and said, "Run along now with the nice lady." A fearsome contraction doubled her and she gripped Emily's sleeve.

Sammy and the boy left the room and continued playing with his toys. Within the hour, they heard a baby crying. Paul poked his head outside and said, "Y'all come on in. Danny, meet your new brother."

The baby was wrapped in a beach towel and wore a knit stocking cap. Emily showed him to Sammy and the boy. "Everything went just fine." Everyone looked at each other, hugged one another, and marveled at the new creation.

"It's a miracle, childbirth," said Paul. "Thank you so much for being here to help my Lottie."

The midwife and the midwife's apprentice helped with cleanup and departed a mere three hours after their arrival. "Don't bother giving us a lift back," said Emily. "We aren't far from my friend's house where I get my herbal remedies. We'll just walk there and then walk back to Providence."

"How can I pay you? I don't have much cash around, but I don't suppose cash means much of anything anymore, anyway."

"You raise hogs, don't you?"

"Yes, ma'am."

"How about next time you slaughter one, giving us some of the meat."

"Yes, we'll do that. Thanks again."

Emily kissed the mother on the cheek, kissed the baby, and walked towards the door. Sammy self-consciously kissed the mother and the baby as well and followed her mentor. She turned to the people who she had met only hours before and said, "Congratulations to you. I hope this baby brings you many blessings."

A mile up the road, Sammy said, "I'm so impressed by the work you did there."

"It was smooth as a granite-top table this time. People aren't always so lucky."

"Still, it was a beautiful thing," Sammy kicked a pine cone.

"Childbirth is an unbelievable experience, every time it happens."

"Next time, I want to be more involved."

"Things get pretty graphic sometimes. Will you be okay?"

"I won't know until I try," Sammy concluded.

"Good girl. I have a book at home I'd like you to study. It will help you prepare for some things we might encounter."

They walked south back to Spring Valley Road, then east towards Providence before turning right on Turkey Knob Road. Emily explained that Turkey Knob was a small, isolated mountain and the road encircled it. Reaching a driveway that had metal sculptures of little devils on each side, they turned right again on a hard-packed gravel road. A hundred yards later, Emily announced, "That's Avalon's place."

It was as charming a place as Sammy had ever seen. It had a natural wood siding and a red tin roof, with multiple gables. There was a pergola in the front and several outbuildings. Inside the pergola hung a glass wind-chime, tinkling lightly in the soft breeze. A split-rail fence encircled the house, and there were beautiful, tall trees on the sides and back. There was a bank of solar panels on a platform to the south of the house, where there was an expansive view. A stack of neatly piled wood rested alongside the driveway and there was a grape arbor on the other side. A white Akita emitted a throaty bark as they walked up the stone path. "Hello, Barkus," said Emily. "Meet Sammy."

The dog ran to her and gave her a big lick on the cheek. He was a powerful, well-proportioned dog, with a triangular shaped head, broad and blunt.

Avalon emerged from the screen door, wearing a pale green peasant dress and many of the same beads as the prior meeting. "Welcome," she shouted.

The three women exchanged pleasantries and Sammy told Avalon about the delivery, how well it had gone, and how impressed she'd been. "Emily is nothing but the best," she complimented her friend. "Let me show you around."

"You girls go on. I'm going to rest here on the porch," Emily sighed.

Avalon got Emily some water and led Sammy through the house. "My husband and I came here in 1998 and built this house. We were living in San Jose, California at the time. There was increasing talk about the computers crashing at the turn of the millennium which would cause our economy to collapse. We knew we stood a better chance of surviving it if we lived in a rural area and had some neighbors to share with. So we found this community and we moved here."

"Why here? There must be a million rural places in the country."

"We spent close to a year looking. The Rocky Mountains are wonderful, scenic and rugged. But they aren't nurturing. The Cascades in Washington and British Columbia were rugged as well, but the weather was harsh and emotionally draining. So we crossed the Great Plains and kept coming east until we arrived in the Southern Appalachians. Neither of us had ever been in this region.

"These mountains invite you to live in them and with them. Southwest Virginia quickly stood above the rest. There were some other places in Tazewell, Bland, and particularly Floyd Counties that were wonderful. But our hearts kept tugging us here. You can see how beautiful it is. The people are plain and unworldly, but they showed us no hostility. Land was cheap and we were able to spend most of our money on the house."

"Your husband?"

"He's dead. He died in 2005 from pancreatic cancer."

"Oh, I'm so sorry."

"I'm still devastated that I lost him."

They walked outside. "Here's the solar panel system. It generates all the power I need. I'm totally off the grid. He built a control system that was isolated from electromagnetic pulses by heavy blocks. I know there is some crazy stuff going on in town, and I can barely imagine what's going on in DC, Los Angeles, or New York..."

Sammy cringed.

"...but here at my house, not much has changed.

"Here's my witch's laboratory," she said, opening the door to a small outbuilding. It was filled with beakers, scales, and burners, and looked like an old chemistry lab. Several plants hung from strings strung across the room from wall to wall. It was richly fragrant. "This is where I process the herbs I sell to Emily and in town. Occasionally, even Quint will buy some ginseng from me, the coot!" She opened a tiny bottle and waved it under Sammy's nose. "Mint."

"It smells delicious."

They walked outside again and Avalon pointed to another small building. "This is my sauna. There's a small pot-bellied stove inside. I treat myself on some cold winter nights." Pointing across the well-tended garden she said, "That little building back there is the spring house. You'd be surprised how long food will stay fresh in there. I have a small refrigerator, too. Quint came over after his power failed and laid a guilt trip on me, convincing me that I needed to store some of his diabetes medicine stock, since he had no way to keep it cool. I'll have credit with his pharmacy for years, but I can't imagine he'll ever sell anything I'd ever want in my body.

"I also have a working washing machine. With the electricity the panels make, I can power a water heater and a washer. I still hang my clothes to dry, but if you ever want to wash some of your clothes, bring them on over."

As they walked back towards the house, Sammy remarked, "You seem to be dealing with this tragedy better than anybody I've met."

"Preparation certainly helps. But most of what's needed is in here," she said, tapping her temple. "This Pulse was something scientists have told us for decades was a possibility. Now that it's happened, it is up to each of us to decide how to react."

"What a wonderful place you have here," Sammy said, looking

over the beautiful lawn and garden. "It feels like paradise."

"Well, I certainly love it here. I'm sure I will spend the rest of my days here. It takes a lot of work, but all my efforts are being rewarded. My home is always open to you. Please make this your refuge whenever you wish."

Sammy thought to ask about moving in. Something deep inside told her that staying with Quint and Hattie was what she needed to do, at least for now.

"I may take you up on your offer sometime. There is lots of sadness and fear in my life right now. There are times coming when I'm sure I'll need a break."

"As I said, my door is always open. Don't bother knocking."

The warmth and kindness of this stranger took her by surprise, as it was normally something she'd only experienced from family and close friends.

They walked back inside and joined Emily, where the herbalist and midwife conducted their transaction.

"I'm tired, Sammy. We'd best be going." So the women bid farewell, and Sammy and Emily continued their journey. On the way, Emily said, "I don't think I've asked, but how old are you?"

"I'm 17. I'll be 18 next month, on October 13."

"I'm sorry you've had to deal with such horrors at such a young age. I think I mentioned that I lost my mother when I was thirteen. I remember not knowing what we were supposed to do after the funeral. Was I supposed to go back to school the next day? We were supposed to be 'in mourning' but I didn't know what that meant. I knew I loved her and I knew I missed her, but I didn't know how that was supposed to change my life. Was I supposed to live differently, and if so, how? We're not born with owners' manuals and aren't given clues how to adjust. Most of us just have to muddle through."

"Was there something that helped you?"

"I learned to sew when I was only 9, and I found it pleasurable and relaxing. So I did as much sewing as I could, making clothes for charity organizations. I had many good friends and I began to rely more and more heavily on them emotionally. They helped get me through. A friend of mine had lost her mother at about the same time and she found solace in her religion. My advice is to find comfort and support wherever you can."

A hawk swooped low across the road in front of them, startling Sammy. "It's a red-tailed," Emily said. "It's probably hunting a rabbit. Many things in our lives have changed lately, but I suspect this guy is doing the same thing he's been genetically programmed to do forever."

"I've been meaning to ask you since we left the birth today, but I saw you place the baby's body next to your head. Were you listening for something?"

"Yes, I make a point to listen to the baby's heartbeat. It's good as a diagnostic tool, just to see how the baby is doing. It seems more natural and less stressful to the baby than sticking a cold stethoscope diaphragm on him. As I began to do it more and more, I realized that it was as much for my edification as for the babies'. I have listened to the sounds of the great symphonies of the world. I have listened to the sound of ocean water crashing to a rocky shore. I have listened to an oriole sitting above her nest. But the finest sound God has ever created is the sound of the heartbeat of a newborn. Listening to it always renews me and gives me hope."

Tuesday, September 4

Sammy had a breakfast of goat's milk, peaches, and granola. She decided the day's work would be to dry some apples for storage. Emily had given her a good idea to try. Before that, however, she decided to ride Jackson for an hour, putting him through some dressage exercises. When she was done, she cleaned the grit from his hooves and brushed him down.

She went to the apple trees with a plastic bushel basket that she thought Hattie also used for the household laundry. She picked a bushel and carted them into the spring house. She washed them and carried them to the shaded back porch. She found a paring knife, a peeler, and a corer in the utensil drawer and brought them outside. She put a tablespoon of sugar in a bowl of water. Then she peeled and cut into bite-sized pieces apple after apple. Once the bowl was full, she placed the apple slices on several baking pans she found in the kitchen. Then, following Emily's suggestion, she went to Quint's Ford hatchback which she knew had been crippled by the Pulse. She found it unlocked, as she expected. She wiped away some spider webs and lowered the rear seats. Then she placed the baking pans with apples into the car.

She returned to the porch to repeat the same process again. She found Hattie sitting in her place, peeling apples. Snoopy lounged nearby, his front legs extended forward and its back legs extended back, like a cat. "Hi Hattie."

"Sammm. Mee."

"Thank you for helping me."

The woman said nothing and barely raised her eyes. Sammy pulled another chair closer to the operation and picked up the corer and began working. "We'll just do this together. No need to say anything if you don't want."

The time passed until all the apples were done. When Sammy returned from placing the last pans, she washed and put all the dishes and utensils away. She walked upstairs and retrieved her violin. Returning to the porch with it, she removed it from its case and tuned it, limbering up her fingers. She took the sheet music for Beethoven's *Violin Sonata No. 7* from her case and played it over and over until she grew tired. She carried it back upstairs and she took a nap.

After supper, Rhonda and her brother Dowell came by to go to Fries. The three of them walked to Emily's house first to retrieve Jamaal, but he met them at the door, saying, "Emily isn't feeling well tonight. I think I'll stay here with her."

So the three young people walked to town together. When they arrived, the regular crowd was there, some chatting and some tuning up. Quint was notably absent. Sammy spoke with Woody Dalton and offered to bring some dried apples to Caroline's nursing home. Sammy noticed that Rhonda had found Shane and they seemed to be arguing with one another.

After only an hour, Dowell seemed restless. Rhonda said to Sammy, "My brother is being a pest. I need to take him home."

"Don't worry about me," Sammy said. "I'm going to stick around. I'll find my own way home."

Rhonda and Dowell departed, and the group played for another hour or so. By unspoken mutual consent, the musicians and the few listeners began standing and putting their instruments away. Shane spoke from across the circle in a way Sammy could lip-read, "I'll walk you home," and she nodded back at him. He raised his eyebrow smartly.

Outside and on their way, he said, "It's great to see you again. I've been thinking a lot about you."

"I've been thinking about you, too. Last week, last time we were together… it was nice."

"Maybe tonight might be even nicer," he offered.

"How are you holding up? How's your mother doing with her new responsibilities?"

"Mom is stressed to the max. But we're military people. We deal with the mission. Me? I take what comes to me. This situation sucks, but life at VMI sucks, too. If we've been attacked, I'm sure there will be war and that will suck, 'cause I'll probably end up in it. But I ain't dead yet. And there are still some possibilities. How about you?"

"I'm emotionally comatose. For the most part, I feel like I've been kicked in the gut. But the people I've met have been great to me. I'm trying to get myself out of bed each day and hope the next day will bring me something good. I'm doing some work with Emily Ayres on her midwifery rounds. Oh, did you know Quint and Hattie's daughter, Bonnie, had a horse?"

"Yes, I knew Bonnie in school. She dated my best friend for awhile. He moved away with his family to Charlotte so his dad could get a better job. Bonnie was a sweet kid. Tragic what happened to her."

"Well, I've been riding her horse. His name is Jackson. He's my Jack-Jack. He's not warmed up to anybody since she died, I'm told.

But he's been great for me."

Reaching for her hand, he said, "When we reach your place, why don't you show him to me?"

The couple walked together, mostly with him talking about the things going on in town to get the dam producing some power again. They reached the driveway where Quint's Ford was parked. "You won't believe this, but I've been using Quint's car to dry fruit," Sammy said proudly.

"What?"

"You know how hot a car gets with the sun on it? Well, I've cored some apples and left them inside the car to dry. It's a trick Emily told me about. Quint hasn't driven the car since the Pulse killed it. So I thought I'd use it for something." She leaned over the back window and pointed inside where the trays were.

"What a great idea," he volunteered. "Let's go sit in the gazebo."

They walked over and sat on the wooden garden swing chair. Moments passed in awkward silence until he leaned towards her and wrapped his hand behind her head, bringing it to hers. He reached around and grabbed her hips and pulled himself towards her, moving up and down gently. "Hmmm." His hands moved upwards and cupped her breasts. She turned around and reached his head. She pulled his lips to hers and they kissed. He began unbuttoning her blouse. "Hmmmmmm."

"Hmmm yourself," he said. "This is too good." His tongue forced its way into her mouth and brushed against her teeth.

"Sammm Meee," said a female voice from across the hedgerow.

Startled, the two love birds jumped away from each other.

"Ma'am," said Shane.

"Hattie!" exclaimed Sammy, turning away to re-fasten her blouse.

"I'd best be going," Shane said. "Ma'am. Samantha." The redhead scurried to the road and disappeared into the night.

"And I'd best be getting upstairs," said Sammy, not knowing whether to giggle or apologize. But she was glad if she was to be caught, it was by Hattie rather than the judgmental Quint.

Wednesday, September 5

As Sammy was finishing breakfast, she heard Emily's bell ringing, summoning her. She tacked Jackson and rode him over. The morning was lovely, with white wispy clouds floating overhead. Jamaal came outside to greet her. "I'm the one who rung for you," her friend said. "I want to go to town and see what's going on with the dam and the power plant and thought you'd enjoy going along."

He walked and she rode Jackson into Fries. They walked to the dam spanning the New River. Keene looked at the pair disdainfully, but when Jamaal offered to help, he softened his stance.

Keene said, "This dam was built back a hundred years ago. It's a bit rusty," obviously joking because it was made of concrete rather than metal. "Washington mills built it to provide power to the millin' equipment."

"Does anything work now?" asked Sammy.

"The mill originally used direct shafts, turning overhead. They were connected to all the equipment by huge belts. When the belts were tensioned, they spun the flywheels on the equipment and when they were slacked, they stopped providing power. Eventually, in the 1920s, the company electrified the dam and all the equipment was then converted to being powered by electric motors. They made so much electrical power that all the houses in town were electrified, too. It is one of the first communities in all of Southwest Virginia that was electrified. The power was so cheap they didn't even bother to invoice their customers. My granny had free electricity her whole life."

"So what's the status now?"

"When the mill shut down 20 years ago, they decommissioned the power plant. The turbines haven't spun since then and the dynamos are rusty. We've gotten one of three turbines spinning again, but it's not producing any electricity yet because some of the dynamo parts are missing."

Pike walked over and exchanged greetings.

"How's the lathe coming along?" he asked Keene.

"I was just tellin' our visitors here that the power plant needs some work."

Pike told Sammy and Jamaal, "We've done an assessment of the dynamo and there are a few parts we need to either find or fabricate. We're trying to set up a lathe and find some raw steel to make some of the parts. The only lathe we could find was in an old company warehouse. It hasn't been used in 30 years. But things were made very well in the old days."

"You got that right," said the grizzled mechanic. "Back when we used to make things in America, we made the best. Nowadays, we don't make nothin' and the stuff we import is crap."

Pike listed their priorities: transfer the lathe near enough to the dam to be reached by a power shaft, build a building over it to protect the metals from rusting, build the power shaft, overhaul the lathe, and then equip it with a flywheel that the dam's shaft could turn. Then, once it was operational, they would fabricate the parts they needed for the dynamo and get it running. Then, somebody would need to climb a series of power poles to flip levers that would isolate the small area of town near the dynamo to contain the electricity they were going to generate.

The first priorities were for municipal water, municipal sewage treatment, and communications. Any excess power would go to refrigeration of pharmaceuticals and food. Private homes would be the last priority.

Jamaal told the men about the work he was doing to try to achieve a functional two-way radio. Pike assured him that as soon as he had something, it would likely be commandeered by Alice Mullins for police work.

On their way home, Jamaal said to his young friend paternally, "Sam, you're a big girl now, almost a woman. I assume you know the facts of life."

She smiled at him sheepishly. "Thanks for caring."

"Well, I'm sure you know what you're doing in certain aspects of adult life. But have you ever been a Girl Scout?"

"Seriously?" she chuckled.

"Seriously."

"No. I was in Pony Club. What did I miss?"

"From what I've found, lots of kids these days don't know any-thing about taking care of themselves in a world outside of paved streets, air-conditioned buildings, and shopping malls. There are a few things you'll need to know now that you'll be outside and on your own more of the time."

"Like what?"

"What compass direction does the sun arise from?"

"I don't know. South?" she guessed.

"Hell!"

"I assume I'm wrong. West?" she guessed again.

"We have a lot to go over. Now pay attention, please.

"The sun rises in the east and sets in the west. In our hemisphere, the northern, the sun at noon is overhead in the summertime, moving south towards winter. In mid-winter, at noon, your shadow will point north. In the morning, the sun will be in the eastern half of the sky and in the afternoon in the western.

"At this latitude, in the summer, we'll have about 14 hours of daylight. The longest day is June 21 and it's called the summer solstice. The shortest is December 21 and it's called the winter solstice, when there is about ten hours of light. The two midpoints are April 21 and September 21, the equinoxes, which have exactly 12 hours between sunrise and sunset."

"That's really interesting. Bonnie had a little sun-dial in the win-dow of the bedroom. I never thought much about it, but maybe I should start paying more attention."

"Yes, I think you'd find it useful. Now then, what do you think is your biggest concern if you ever get lost?"

"Well, I could starve to death."

"True, but not likely, at least for several days, unless you were already malnourished."

"Water?"

"Lack of water can kill you more quickly. But your biggest threat is hypothermia."

"What's that?"

"Freezing to death."

She thought about how warm and comfortable the day was, buzzing gnats notwithstanding.

He continued, "You won't starve to death for weeks and won't die of lack of water for a few days, although you'll be mighty uncomfortable. But you can freeze to death in an hour. Moisture is your worst enemy. Cold is miserable and wet is miserable, but cold and wet can be lethal. People have died in temperatures in the 40s and 50s when they've become wet."

"So I guess I need to carry an umbrella," she joked.

"Please, this is serious. Cotton clothing, particularly jean fabric, can be fatal. Wet jeans will siphon the heat right away from your skin. They're almost worse than naked. And they take forever to dry. Do you have a waterproof jacket?"

"No. I just brought a light windbreaker with me."

"See if you can find one from the house. Pour water on it. If it pools up, it's good. If it absorbs, don't use it."

"What else?"

"Always carry some water with you to drink. If you must drink from a stream, look into the mountains for small creeks rather than bigger ones; drink upstream from the herd. If you get cold, seek shelter anywhere you can. Even covering yourself with leaves will keep you warmer than being in cold air. Of course, if the leaves are wet, it won't do you much good. If you're traveling a long distance by foot or on Jackson, take a blanket and extra food. Do you have a flashlight?"

"Yes, I brought one from home. It's a headlamp that straps around my head."

"As they say in the credit card commercials, don't leave home without it."

"It's funny, isn't it?" she chuckled.

"What?"

"Commercials. Credit cards."

"Yup."

Thursday, September 6

Sammy worked alone in the garden until dark clouds began gathering overhead. A fast-moving storm sent bolts of lighting down. She had barely put the tools in the shed when rain began pelting down and she raced into the house. She had just put on dry clothes when Marissa came inside, opening the heavy wooden front door and yelling, "Sammy! Hattie!"

"Hi, Marissa. How are you doing?"

"It's such a long walk. I'm soaking wet, but it is God's will. Where's Hattie?"

"Oh, I never know. She must have some hiding place somewhere. I never go looking for her. I'm always concerned, but I think she must need her space. I really don't know how to give her the support she needs." She ran upstairs and got a towel and dry clothes for Marissa, who continued the conversation right where she left off.

"Don't feel bad; nobody else around here seems to know, either."

"Do you mean Quint?"

"Let's just say Quint hasn't been too supportive. When you and I first met, I remember telling you that Quint and Hattie see what's happened to them in completely different ways.

"Yes, I remember."

"Well," she peeled the wet shirt over her head, "it's driving them further and further apart. I'm beginning to see his anger getting the best of him. I suspect he's been abusive towards her, and if not, that he might become. I'm a woman of the Lord, but if I ever find that he's harmed her physically, I swear I'll kill the son of a bitch myself."

Uncomfortable with the notion, Sammy said cheerfully, "Hattie helped me earlier this week – I can't remember what day it is any more – to prepare some apples for drying."

"She's certainly aware of your presence and I think she really wants to like you. But she's afraid of caring about any young person again. I think she sees something of Bonnie in you – lots of us do. And it scares her."

"What do you think I should do?"

"Just be yourself. These are troubled times and people do crazy, irrational things. Watch your backside. Keep your guard up. I think most people around here are friendly, accepting people, at least when situations are normal. Right now, they're not normal. Nobody knows what to expect. So be yourself, stay alert, find comfort and friendships where you can, and try to make the best of your situation."

"My situation sucks."

"Maybe, but you need to get over it. Lots of people are suffering; lots have died already. You have your life; you have food to eat and a roof over your head. You have friends here to support you in any way they can. It may not always be this way."

"I suppose you're right," Sammy shrugged. "I can't bear to think that this is it, that I'll never see my parents again, and will be stuck in this God-forsaken place forever."

"Watch your profanity in front of me, please. This place isn't God-forsaken; it's God-blessed. Find everyday blessings. I'm not here often, but when I am, I will be here for you."

"Thanks."

Just then, a knock came to the door. Marissa answered it.

"Hello, I'm Caroline Dalton. Oh, hi Sammy."

"Hi, Mrs. Dalton."

"Caroline, please. And I don't know if we've met," she said, putting her hand towards Marissa.

"I'm Marissa, Hattie's sister. I live over near Galax. It's a pleasure to meet you."

"Likewise! I just came over to ask Sammy if you'd like to come to our home again and have dinner with Woody and me tomorrow. You're welcome to join us too, Marissa."

"Oh, no thanks. I'll leave for home tomorrow afternoon."

"I can come. Thanks for inviting me. What can I bring?"

"Just yourself. Oh, bring your violin. Maybe we can play some classical together for a change."

"I wish I could come," said Marissa. "I hope y'all have a wonderful time."

"See you tomorrow," Caroline said. "I've got to run to the nursing home and see what new tragedy awaits me."

Friday, September 7

Sammy tacked up Jackson. She strapped a small satchel containing some goat cheese and the case to her Guarneri to his saddle. She rode over to the Daltons, mostly at a trot. Jackson seemed to enjoy the workout.

Sammy assisted Woody with the cooking, most of which he said he'd been doing himself since the Pulse, what with Caroline spending so much time at the nursing home. As they ate a dinner of beef, beets, and October beans, Sammy asked Caroline to tell her more about their move from the city life back to Providence.

Caroline said, "We pictured an idyllic country life, where everybody got along. There is almost no racial diversity here. But there is a lot of diversity amongst the white folks. There is an active KKK group in the area, although they keep a low profile. I have heard that they have gatherings with cross burnings and robes and all that nonsense. As long as they don't hurt anybody, I'm sure there is nothing anybody can do about it. Nobody can control who they decide to hate."

"What we found," added Woody, "is that there are animosities and hatreds like anywhere else. There may not be the quantities of murders and hate crimes, but it's just because there aren't as many people overall.

"I'm sure nobody has told you yet, but ten miles from us in Elk Creek, a black man was murdered a few years ago. He was set on fire and then beheaded. The perpetrators were two white men who apparently knew their victim. Imagine doing such a thing!"

Caroline said, "Everybody was talking about whether it was a hate crime. What the heck does that mean? They murdered him in cold blood. They bound him with ropes, poured gasoline all over him, and set him on fire. His body was still bound and smoldering when the sheriff arrived. His head was on the ground a distance away. He was a 40-year old former Marine. The killers were doped up to the clouds on alcohol and drugs. Does it matter whether they hated him or not?"

After the meal, Sammy on her violin and Woody on his viola played several classical pieces. Caroline, who had some opera experience, sang several songs. Everyone laughed and kidded themselves for being so rusty.

By the time Sammy departed, the night was clear, moonless, and cave-dark. Sammy was barely able to see the road. After a few minutes, she gave Jackson his way and he walked directly to his barn.

Saturday, September 8

Sammy rode Jackson to Carlene Bartlett's General Store with more of Hattie's cheese. She traded for some jar lids and purchased some home-made soap and some candle wax.

She stopped to see Emily and Jamaal on her way back. The door was cracked open. She found Emily in her bedroom, dozing. She woke the older woman to ask if she was okay. "I'm not feeling well today. Do I have a fever?"

Sammy felt her forehead. "Maybe slight."

"My guess is that with the cancer, I'll be having more bad days. Bring me some water, would you?"

Sammy found a pitcher in the kitchen. She poured some water into a glass and carried it to her mentor. "Where's Jamaal?"

"I think he went into Fries. He said something about looking for a tube for his radio."

"Has he been listening? What's going on in the world?"

"I think so. Nothing good is going on, from what he's told me. I think I'd like to try to sleep again."

"I'll stay for awhile, if you don't mind."

"That would be nice."

Sammy left the room and looked at the extensive library in the living room. She found a book on midwifery and she sat with it, the pages illuminated by sunbeams streaming through the window. Sammy read with interest the history of midwifery and the transition American culture had made to having deliveries in hospitals. She learned that as a natural part of life, most deliveries go smoothly, but that when things went wrong, it was best for the health of the mother and baby to have access to surgical equipment and know-how. She was amazed to learn that in the early 1800s, the average woman had between seven and eight live births in her lifetime. Most people lived only to the age of forty in America, black people less than whites, and that mothers lost during childbirth was a substantial cause of the lower life expectancy for women than men. Childbirth was always a life or death situation. In 1850, over twenty percent of babies died at birth, with that number dropping to a third of a percent in 2000. But that was before the Pulse.

She fell asleep studying. When she awoke, the sun was low. She bid Emily farewell and she rode home to find Quint working on his sermon for the following morning. She fed herself and played her violin in the dark before bedtime.

Sunday, September 9

The next morning, she told Quint that Emily wasn't feeling well and asked if she could skip church in order to be with her. So she spent some time by Emily's bedside, studying her midwifery textbook and asking questions about many things she was learning. She rode home in mid-afternoon to find Quint had already returned. As usual, Hattie was nowhere to be seen.

After asking about Emily's condition, Quint said, "I forgot to tell you this morning, but there has been news in town. The people working on the dam have apparently gotten the dynamo to work and there is some electricity now. You and Jamaal might be interested in seeing what's going on. For the next couple of days, I'm going to work with them to get some refrigeration at the store for some of the drugs that I've been storing in your friend Avalon's refrigerator."

"Jamaal was in town yesterday so I'm sure he knows. He and I will go to town tomorrow."

Monday, September 10

Sammy awoke and did her morning chores. She saddled Jackson and walked him down the quiet highway towards Jamaal and Emily's house. Sammy noticed that some of the shrubs were starting to turn yellow and red with the coming of autumn. It was a stunning day with a cloudless sky. It seemed to her that she could see 100 miles.

Arriving at the house, she first met Jamaal. "Come with me. Emily has asked me to retrieve a vial of herbs she has stored in her cave."

"Her cave?"

"Yes, there are several caves on the property. This area is completely underlain by karst soils, meaning limestone. You may have noticed some areas that were sunken like a bowl, but not filled with water. These are sink-holes. Wherever you have sink-holes, you have caves. From what I can gather, there are thousands of miles of subterranean passages around here."

They walked across a pasture that Emily had leased to a neighbor to graze his cows. Jamaal commented on what a beautiful day it was. "Tomorrow is September 11, the anniversary of the attack on the World Trade Center and the Pentagon. The memory is seared into my brain."

"Mine, too. I was in school that morning. I was in kindergarten or first grade. The principal made an announcement on the intercom that something terrible had happened. We were sent home immediately. I was really young and I don't remember much, but everyone was so shocked and sad. My home is twenty miles or so north of lower Manhattan. Dad's office was near the Trade Center. I don't remember why, but for some reason he didn't go to work that morning. He was lucky. I remember I could see the smoke in the sky. The day was completely cloudless."

"I remember that part of it, too. I was teaching at Georgetown. Somebody came into my classroom and told us to turn on the TV. We saw the video of the second airplane hitting the second tower. We were all horrified, wondering what was next. We'd find out too soon, another jetliner was on its way to the Pentagon. I was wandering outside when it hit. The Pentagon is only three miles from Georgetown. I swear, I felt the ground shake when it hit. Lots of people's lives changed forever that day. I wanted to move back to the south, but my wife insisted we stay. 'We don't want to let the bad guys win.'

"Then, a year later, the DC area was terrorized again by a random assassin who drove around shooting people from his car. There were two gunmen, both African Americans. They killed a dozen people over a three week period. They were indiscriminate. They killed black people, white people, and Asian people. They killed both men and women. It felt like the whole metro area was being held hostage."

Sammy told her friend about the murder in Elk Creek that she'd heard from the Daltons. Jamaal asked several questions about it, few of which Sammy had answers for. He said, "I'm aware of the risks of being here, but I'm aware of the risks of moving someplace else, too. Besides, Emily needs me. So I'm going to stick around, at least for the time being. But I'll be watching my back. You should, too."

"I'm sure you're right. Never in my life have I imagined that anybody would want to hurt me. But grandfather told me so many stores about the Nazis. But that madness could never happen in America."

He said, "We all hope not. But before World War II, Germany was one of the largest, best educated, and most prosperous nations in Europe. It was stunning how quickly it was taken over by racist ideologues and its people turned into mass murderers. Hitler could never have done what he did without a willing populace."

"What do you think this crisis will bring?"

"Nobody knows. I think everyone around here is eager to learn what's going on elsewhere. But once we're able to do that and understand the breadth of the problem more fully, I think we'll wish we hadn't."

They approached a wooded area with some slope to it, where they had to climb a steep trail, using roots and branches to pull themselves upward. Below an overhanging rock, there was a hole which emitted a cooler air. Jamaal took a flashlight from his pocket and said, "I'll go inside first. Then you come along."

Sammy raised her left eyebrow.

"Are you claustrophobic?" he asked her.

"We'll know in a minute," she sighed. "I've never been in a cave before."

"The opening is about ten feet long. We'll need to scurry through it on our bellies. Then it opens into a room where we can stand up. Come on." He squirmed inside and his legs vanished into the hole. Sammy looked inside, and then looked around at the beautiful day, wondering why she'd ever want to do this. Then she followed him.

She inched along, keeping her head down to keep from bumping the low roof. The fit was apparently tight for him. Her smaller stature made it relatively easy, but she was still unnerved. She thought about some playground equipment from her childhood. She expected it to be dirty, but countless ingresses and egresses before took most of the mud away. Finally, she reached his hand where she was able to stand upright with him in a large, linear room. "Welcome to Casa Deville," he joked.

They explored the room and some adjoining rooms. The floor was uneven and slick. Sammy had difficulty walking, feeling unbalanced and tipsy. There were some impressive stalactites and stalagmites, looking slimy and wet. There were several bats hanging immobile from the roof. They reminded Sammy of furry rabbit's foot key fobs. Jamaal took her to a flat area where there were several small padlocked wooden boxes on the floor. Jamaal took a key from his pants pocket and opened the lock on one of them. Inside there were vials of tinctures and herbs. Jamaal placed a couple of them in his breast pocket. He closed and re-locked the box. His flashlight flickered off for a moment. Sammy gasped. "No worry," said her friend reassuringly. "Sometimes the bulb shakes loose." She could hear him unscrew the bulb holder and re-tighten the bulb. The only other sound was dripping water. She placed her hand six inches from her face, but she couldn't see it.

"I can't believe how dark it is in here," she said uneasily. "I've never seen dark like this. It doesn't seem to matter whether my eyes are open or not."

Jamaal concurred, "Once when I was a Boy Scout, we camped overnight in a cave. It was surreal. We slept several hours and then just about everybody woke at the same time, much like we'd all do when the sun came up. But it was still totally dark."

"I bet it was scary!"

"It's a world most people never see. But I've been more scared walking some of the streets of Washington, DC, than I ever was in a cave."

"Still, can we just get out of here, please?"

"Sure, let's go."

They made their way back to the opening and emerged into the bright sunlight again. Her eyes were blinded for a few moments as he followed her outside. She asked him how he knew about the cave and the cache. He said, "Emily took me here a couple of weeks ago, not long after I'd arrived. She said she expected her health to begin deteriorating and she wanted me to know about it. She is too frail to get inside herself. There is one Hispanic boy who lives over in Fries whom she entrusts to deliver and pick up things from inside. He was my guide. They, and now I, may be the only people alive who know about this cave. And of course, now you as well."

"The secret is good with me. It was spooky in there, but for some reason, I wouldn't mind going back inside again. But this time, I'll bring my own flashlight, too."

"Let's see about getting into Fries, shall we?"

The two returned to the house where Emily was up, although still dressed in her nightgown. She looked to be in good spirits, but tired. They pieced together some food for lunch, eating mostly vegetables. Jamaal made a quip about the food actually making him healthier.

Jamaal told Sammy that he'd finished working on repairs on the old horse-drawn wagon. So Jamaal and Sammy hitched Maggie to it and walked her towards the highway into town. Jamaal engaged Sammy in conversations about her symphony performances around her community and in New York. It was a pleasant afternoon and both exhibited signs of sangfroid. Jamaal told a story about dating the woman who would become his wife that was so comical, Sammy's gut ached as she laughed. It was the first real laugh she remembered happening since the tragedy.

Nearing town, they could see that there were more people milling about than usual, many buzzing with enthusiasm. Quint was talking with Keene and a couple of other men. Sammy launched herself from the cart and walked over as Jamaal stayed to secure the horse, wrapping her reins around a defunct parking meter. Sammy learned that electricity was flowing from the dam nearby. A man named Oscar worked for Appalachian Power, the regional electric utility. He had obtained some charts of the local grid and instructed some workers to scale utility poles and flip some switches so the power could be isolated to the town center.

As they spoke, Annie Wilkins emerged from the town hall wearing her police uniform and yelled, "Y'all please come inside. I'd like to make some announcements. Please spread the word."

The crowd gathered inside where Wilkins stood with Pike McConnell. She said, "I finally have some good news for everybody. We have a limited amount of electrical power back running."

Everyone in the crowd cheered.

"Let's not get too excited," Pike said. "The old dam has three turbines and we've only been able to get one working so far. It's not much power, but it's something."

"And we've got to be careful how we use it," Wilkins said. "As Interim Police Chief of Fries, I'm making some decisions about it. I know many of you are hungry and having some refrigeration will help, but the first thing that needs our immediate attention is sanitation. So I've ordered the sewer plant on-line first. Wayman is already working on that. Once that's back up and running, the water plant is next, and Willy is working on that. Once we can get the pump working, we can re-fill the town water tower and we can all have drinking water back in our houses."

Again, everyone applauded.

"Third on my list is communications. We have only four ham radio operators in town and only one, Newman here, with a system that wasn't destroyed in the Pulse. We're gonna get him up and broadcastin' as soon as we can. My first priority is establishing regular communication with the sheriff's office over in Independence. Then we'll try to see how broad this Pulse was and who in America still has power and who doesn't."

Pike said, "This radio won't be used to check to see how your grandma in Marion is doing. We've got lots more work to do before we can start offering personal use."

"One other thing," Chief Wilkins said. "It's a fair bet that many other communities and cities are doing far worse than we are. I urge you in any communications, whether on the radio or any other way, not to give too many clues as to how we're doing here."

"What do you mean by that?" asked a man Sammy didn't recognize.

Wilkins continued, "Part of our survival is dependent upon real and perceived distances from the population centers. And I don't mean to be selfish, but if the State Police are instructed by the Governor to commandeer any power resources for the state, we'll be right back where we started from. That's all I want to say about that."

Tuesday, September 11

Sammy spent most of the day working in the garden and harvesting corn, potatoes, peppers, carrots, and tomatoes. She and Hattie canned several jars of tomatoes. Hattie said nothing to her, as usual. But Sammy was appreciative of the help and the company.

The evening before, after she and Jamaal had returned from town, the two sat outside and practiced some bluegrass tunes they'd heard at prior jam sessions. This was the night of the weekly session and she was eager to show the others what she had learned. She walked to Emily's house to get Jamaal. He met her at the door and said, "Emily isn't well again tonight. I'm going to stay with her." So Sammy continued into town alone. "Don't be out too late, please. I don't want to worry about you."

Sammy entered the community center and found a seat opposite Shane. There was a sparse crowd, with several familiar faces, but neither Rhonda, Ortie, Pike, nor Keene was there. They played *Golden Slippers*, and when it was Sammy's turn, she took her solo, which she'd practiced with Jamaal. Everyone seemed mightily impressed.

Sammy only played for a short while, remembering Jamaal's admonishment to be home before dark. As she packed her violin, Shane said loud enough for most to hear him, "I'll walk you home," an offer met by a chorus of licentious knowing smiles amongst many of the men.

Sammy was happy to have his company. She liked him and enjoyed the attention he'd directed towards her. On their way home, he carrying his banjo case and she carrying her violin case, they talked about having electricity in town and what it might mean for the town's future. They shared some optimism and agreed that people seemed more upbeat.

They reached Jackson's paddock as the sun sank below the horizon. She showed Shane how Jackson came to the fence to eat from her hand, but Shane seemed wary of him.

"Do you have a saddle for him?"

"Yes, it's in the barn. I'll show you."

They walked inside and she showed him the saddle, bridle, and reins. He seemed not to be listening, but instead found a blanket and laid it on some hay bales. "Your lips felt pretty good on mine last week," he said with a lascivious tone. "I'll bet they'll do the same now." He grabbed her shoulders and brought them towards him. Their lips met again.

She closed her eyes and pushed her body forward into his. She put her hands on his shoulders and they felt good to her, wide and muscular. She felt his left hand reach for her right breast and it squeezed gently. His index finger rubbed around her erect nipple. It felt good.

She felt his other hand begin to unbutton her blouse. She backed away and said, "I'm not sure about this." As soon as she said it, she thought he would mock her and think her immature.

"Sure about what? What's stopping you? Listen, girl; the life you've always thought you'd have is gone. What we have is each other and we have right now. I want you bad!"

"But…"

"Hey," he interrupted, pulling off his shirt, "you're not a virgin, are you?"

"No, of course not," she lied.

She looked at his chest. There were a million freckles behind wispy reddish hair. He had a chiseled physique. She reached out to touch him. Her mind reeled with indecision. She didn't love him; wasn't love supposed to be part of it? He was cute, sexually attractive, really strapping. Someday she would have to have a first time. What he said seemed correct, these were tragic times and her old life was gone. People were dying by the millions; she could be next. If not now, when?

She felt herself acquiesce and she knew he felt it, too. He undid her jean buckle and unzipped her pants. She slid them to her ankles. He removed his pants and she saw his penis, bigger and redder than she envisioned.

"What are you looking at, girl? I know you want it." He stepped forward, removed her bra and slid her panties to the floor. She felt her pulse rate accelerate. He picked her up and placed her on the blanket. He penetrated and began to pump. It hurt her and she suppressed a cry. He pumped more, then climaxed, then lay limp on top of her.

Moments passed and he got up. "Hey, thanks. You were good. Real good." He put on his pants and shirt and pitched her clothes towards her. "Listen, I want to see you again. But I gotta run." He grabbed his banjo case and he vanished.

She sat up and brushed her hair out of her face. She put her shirt on and noticed blood-stains on the blanket. She put on her panties, pants, shirt, and shoes, and stood up, dazed. She wondered if what she was feeling was what she was supposed to be feeling, a dizzying mix of satisfaction, revulsion, and victimhood. She picked up the blanket and folded it such that the stains didn't show, and returned it to the pile where it had been before. She shoved her bra into her violin case and walked towards the house. Her mind remembered that it was September 11, thinking she'd just had one more experience which would make this date live forever in her mind.

As she climbed the stairs, liquid goo ran down the inside of her left leg. She was thankful that neither Quint nor Hattie was anywhere to be seen.

Wednesday, September 12

The next morning just after sunrise, Sammy heard Emily's bell ringing. So she hurried herself out of bed and got there as quickly as possible. Emily answered the door, saying, "Mrs. Thaxton is having contractions. Her eldest daughter who is twelve came over early today. I sent her back to be with her mom. Let's go."

By the time the two arrived at her home by the river, Mrs. Thaxton was having contractions every eight minutes. "How are you doing, Thelma?"

"I'm doing good. As you know, I'm an old hand at this," she smiled. Her four other children were darting about the house. "I just wish Dewey was here."

"I assume you haven't heard anything from him," Sammy suggested.

"Has anybody heard anything about anybody overseas?" Thelma asked. Nobody answered.

"Owww. Owww. Another contraction. I feel this baby coming. She's an eager girl. It's a crazy world I'm bringing her into, but not much choice now. Owww."

"Sammy is going to help me, Thelma. Let's start with measuring the dilation." She took a small, cloth measuring tape from her bag and handed it to Sammy.

Sammy lifted Mrs. Thaxton's nightgown. "Oh!" Sammy shrieked, feeling nauseous. "I think I'm gonna..."

Thelma laughed. "Take it easy, child."

Sammy bolted outside where she vomited. Regaining her composure, she walked back inside and found a towel to wipe her face. The pregnant woman and the midwife teased her.

"I'm not sure what I was expected," Sammy admitted.

"While you were gone," said Emily, "I measured the cervix. It was dilated to eleven centimeters."

"Owww. Owww! Contractions."

"You know as much about this game as I do," Emily suggested to Thelma.

Emily and Sammy helped Thelma from the bed where she walked around the room. "The movement might help move things along."

"I'd like to get back in bed," Thelma said.

She rested for twenty more minutes or so, and then had another contraction.

"Are you ready to start pushing, Thelma?" asked Emily.

"Yes."

"Do you want to sit up?"

"Yes, I think so."

They helped her up and she got off the bed.

"Let me just kneel here by the bed."

Sammy re-engaged and placed a folded towel under her knees. Thelma began pushing and the baby's head emerged from the birth canal. Sammy reached below and held the baby's head.

Emily said, "You are both doing good. I'm here if you need me. The baby's face is pointed to the back, perfectly! Sammy, help the baby twist her head slightly. It will help her squeeze her shoulders through."

The baby hung in place for a moment and Thelma took a deep breath.

Emily said, "We're all preparing for that final push. Sammy, you take a deep breath, too. And baby, you take one, too."

Thelma chuckled which seemed to loosen her abdominal muscles momentarily. The baby's shoulders squirted through and then the entire body in an instant, falling into Sammy's hands. "I've got her! Look, I've got her! I've got the baby!"

"Don't sound too surprised, child. That's what we're here for." Emily said with a smile as she handed Sammy a blanket. "Wrap the baby in this. Be careful not to damage the cord." She helped Thelma to her feet and swiveled her so she could lie back onto the bed.

"How's my baby?" the new mother asked.

Sammy said, "She's beautiful!" She placed the baby on Thelma's chest. The umbilical cord stretched from the birth canal to the baby.

"What do we do with the cord?" Sammy asked Emily.

"Feel it gently in your hands."

"It is pulsing," Sammy reported. The cord was a translucent white, about the diameter of a kindergartener's pencil.

"That means it is still working. Let's leave it be for a few minutes. Let's measure the baby."

Sammy took the tape measure and read the numbers to Emily. "She's 52 cm long. Her head is almost 30 cm around." Emily handed her a fish-scale with a basket. Sammy gently placed the baby into the basket, affixed it to the scale, and then lifted all three. "Eleven pounds."

Thelma gasped. "What!?"

Emily laughed. "That's the weight of the basket, too. Sammy, the basket weighs 3-1/2 pounds. So the baby weighs 7-1/2 pounds."

Emily asked Thelma if she could listen to the baby's heartbeat, for which permission was readily granted. Emily held the baby's chest to her ear as she had done during the prior delivery Sammy had attended. "Once the baby is born, I try to listen to his heart as quickly as possible. All babies have what I call a heart song. During prenatal care, I hear the baby's heart song through the fetoscope from the time the baby is about 18 weeks old. To me, it sounds like the flutter of a butterfly wing. The whisper grows louder and stronger as the fetus gets older. Listen," she said, handing the baby to Sammy.

Sammy held the baby to her ear as Emily had done. "It's beautiful! It's so fast and rhythmic. This would make a great metronome! It's allegro! I can hear the baby breathing, too. I thought we needed to spank it."

Thelma reached for her baby and held her tight.

"Not typically," said Emily. "That's only in the movies. Babies usually start breathing on their own. This baby is perfect!"

Sammy said, "The umbilical cord looks limp."

"Feel it," said her mentor.

"It's not pulsing any more."

"Then its work is done. Pull on it gently and let's see if the placenta can be expelled. Are you ready, Thelma?"

"Yes."

"Sammy, what's going to happen is that it is attached to the placenta which has now been separated from the wall of the uterus. As you pull the cord, the placenta will be born."

"How big is it?" Sammy asked.

"You'll see."

Sammy pulled gently and the placenta emerged.

"What does it look like?" Emily asked, knowingly.

"It's dark, reddish-blue."

"Take it in your hands."

"It is about eight inches long, like a disk but plumper in the middle. The cord is attached to the middle, but I don't think there is anything going through the cord any more."

The experienced midwife felt the cord. "You're right. The baby is fully born now. Let's cut the cord." She took a pair of scissors from her bag and handed it to Sammy. "Cut it about two inches from the baby."

As Sammy prepared to cut it, Emily said, "Even if the baby is breathing and living on its own for a few minutes, once you cut the cord, the baby has a reaction. I believe the baby actually realizes that it is now a separate, whole, functional human being. Until then, it was part of a connection to another body that was keeping it alive."

Sammy clenched her jaw and made the cut. Then she handed the scissors back.

"Congratulations, Thelma!" Emily said.

"Congratulations, Mrs. Thaxton," Sammy said.

"Congratulations to you, too, Sammy," Thelma said. "Thank you for being here. I only wish my husband had been here with us."

"We do, too. And we hope he's here soon."

Packing up the tools, asked Emily, "Where are your people, Thelma?"

"My parents are over in Grundy. Mom was planning on staying with me, but she never made it over. My eldest is twelve now. She'll have to take care of us for now. I suspect all our children are growing up pretty fast these days."

Sammy thought about her life and turning twelve, an eternity yet only the blink of an eye earlier. Yes, she thought, everybody was growing up pretty fast.

The two midwives stayed for a couple more hours and fixed the children something to eat. It was mid-afternoon by the time Emily said, "I'll stop by again tomorrow and see how you're doing." The midwife and her apprentice stepped down from the trailer and began the journey home.

"Sammy, you performed very well today. I'm impressed by your poise."

"Thank you. I was about to freak out a couple of times. But I knew if I lost my composure, it wouldn't help anything."

"True enough. Everything went really well today. Births are usually routine. Pregnancy and childbirth usually happen the way they're supposed to. That's nature working for us. You and I are there just to assist. Frankly, if I'm expecting a problem, I'll encourage the mother to go to the hospital. Well, I used to encourage the mother to go to the hospital. We don't have that option now. I hope you never have a problem delivery, because without surgical options, midwives are limited in what we can do."

"It was interesting to me, what you said last week about the baby's heart," Sammy recalled.

"I always listen to the baby's heart both before and after it is born, if the mother will let me. It is part of my service. But the baby belongs to the mother and I never listen without asking.

"The rhythm of every baby's heart is different. Each baby sings his or her different heart song. It almost has its own personality. During prenatal care, I always listen to this song and I let the mother use the scope to listen as well. During labor, I can listen to the song and feel an understanding of what the baby is going through. So the connection is already happening even before the baby is born. Once the baby is born, it seems to understand that it is working on its own for its own body and there is a maturity to the sound. It is now fully its own beat and it is no longer part of the mother's heart beat."

"It's really a miracle, isn't it?" Sammy commented.

"Aye, lass. A miracle it surely is."

As they approached their parting place, Emily said, "I spoke with Avalon yesterday. She asked me to mention to you that she planned to be herb hunting tomorrow. She said she'd enjoy your company if you were interested. She'll be expecting you."

"That would be great. I'll do that."

Thursday, September 13

Sammy fed herself some breakfast, then tacked up Jackson and rode to Avalon's house, nearly an hour away. Avalon greeted her at the door with a hug, looking bright and cheerful as always. She gathered a set of garden shears, a small trowel, and a wicker basket. They walked towards the nearby woods.

"I always keep my eyes open for ginseng. Folks around here call it 'sang'. It is a native plant to the central Appalachians. It is widely used medicinally. The wild sources have been vastly over-harvested and so some of it is now being grown through cultivation. Who knows what will become of anything imported or exported in our post-Pulse world.

"Anyway, ginseng is a longevity herb that is used continuously over time, presumably to increase human lifespans, through contributing to the vitality of many of our internal organs. As we age, our internal organs age. Ginseng is food for those organs.

"Many people in the country who hunt for ginseng will sell it for cash. But I've also used it as a medium for barter. It has an oval green leaf and a red berry. It grows six to eighteen inches tall, with three leaves and several smaller leaflets. It is usually near water and on hillsides facing north or east. If the sun hits a hillside in the afternoon, you won't find ginseng on it. Other plants like jack-in-the-pulpit, black cohosh, stinging nettles, and ferns often grow in the same types of areas, so I look for them as telltale signs.

"There are many other common herbs. Many of them were named for what they looked like or what they were good for treating."

They walked slowly through a deep, hardwood forest. Squirrels scampered from tree limb to tree limb. A blue jay cawed raucously.

"Another common herb is coalsfoot. It has a little yellow flower, similar to the dandelion. When I find it, I gather the leaves and dry them. This herb is gathered in the springtime, so we won't see any today. The tincture is used to treat colds.

"Mullein is gathered from long rows that grow along the country roads. It has a tall, fuzzy stalk and is rimmed by many rather large, fuzzy leaves. It has a bright yellow flower. The leaves are good for treating bronchitis and chest problems. Mullein and coalsfoot make a good combination for a tea to be given to someone who has a chest cold."

The women walked through a forest on mostly game trails, stepping over fallen trees, some thick with lichen.

"Echinacea is also a good medicine for colds and the flu. It is the purple coneflower and it grows commonly around here. It is specifically good for strep throat. This is one of many traditional medicines that can now be found in mainstream pharmacies.

"Pennyroyal is a mint. Mints grow as many shallow roots. It can be prepared with oil to be used as an insect repellent. Taken as a tea, it can prevent or cure many types of nervous headaches. It is a strong and powerful herb. For that reason, it is often not recommended for pregnant women. In fact, it may be used to abort unwanted pregnancies. I suspect the market for it will increase now with limited access to contraception."

They descended to a small stream which they crossed, skipping over some rocks. It was a dense, beautiful forest.

"Look. Here's some blue cohosh. Emily will want some of this because it is used for the regulation of menstrual cycles and to ease cramps. Emily always has this herb to help the mother in labor during delivery because it has a relaxing effect on the uterine muscles. It's also called squaw root. The leaves are bluish-green. It has a single stalk, with a large, three-branched leaf. The leaflets are shaped like tulip petals, entire at the base but serrated at the tips. The fruit is a rich, blue berry."

Avalon pulled many leaves and placed them in her basket, picking alternatively. "I always leave some behind for the next time or the next herb hunter. I never take a whole plant of anything if I can help it."

Sammy scurried along breathlessly behind her new friend, who was amazingly fit.

"Emily also carries Lobelia, a muscle relaxant and shepherds purse, which is useful to stop bleeding. Yellow dock is a great source of usable protein, iron and potassium and it acts as a kidney tonic. It is great for people who are anemic. It is good for women during or after pregnancy. The yellow dock flower is edible.

"For sources of food, people could find wild squash, wild cabbage, and the flower from yellow dock. Traditionally, people may have consumed this in extra doses during the springtime when it first came out to accommodate for the lack of vitamins during the winter. In the fall, yellow dock grows quite tall as it is preparing to go to seed. The brown seeds can be gathered and ground and added to flour or corn meal to stretch those foods.

"There are also many wild mint plants. Peppermint. Spearmint. Cat mint. For cats, it makes them crazy. But for us, it is a relaxant. It is particularly good for the stomach and the uterus. You can tell why that would be helpful for Emily to have in her bag. Mints are dried and then turned into teas."

The two took a short break, sitting on a fallen log. Avalon, however, continued her lecture. "Comfrey is wonderful for healing wounds. It is commonly found around old farmsteads. Comfrey leaves are really big. You can soak them in water and then literally wrap them around the wound like a bandage. Once, my husband cut himself chopping wood. I wrapped Comfrey leaves around the wound and it healed in just a few days without infection."

They stepped onto an unpaved road, deep in the forest. Avalon said, "Herbs are abundant around here. Many of them are found at the edges of forests, fields, and roads. You don't have to go far to find herbs."

They walked northeast on the road for a few hundred yards, then re-entered the woods. Avalon said, "Do you know that the common dandelion is edible? From the roots to the leaf to the flower, all of it is edible. The leaves are very rich in Vitamin A. If your lawn hasn't been sprayed with chemicals, you can simply go out into your front yard and pick dandelions and eat them. The root is a wonderful liver tonic. The root is dried and then roasted and then brewed like coffee. It replenishes liver cells.

"Wild foods are highly nutritious. There is more nutrition in a wild carrot than perhaps one twice the same size in the store."

They picked two dozen more, then returned to the stream and washed off the dirt. They ascended the hill and returned to the house.

"If people get hungry, there are things around here that they can eat. Of course, people are doing a lot more hunting. People eat deer and bear all the time around here. In a pinch, you could also eat squirrels, raccoons, and rabbits. But there are many food plants.

"Herbs as food and medicine are gifts. There are no herbal cures for viruses like polio or my late husband's cancer. But for most everyday ailments, nature gives us everything we need."

Sammy ate dinner with Avalon, particularly enjoying the wild carrots they'd found. She gave Avalon a hug and a kiss and rode home.

Friday, September 14

Sammy took some cheese to Carlene Bartlett's store and exchanged for some pears. She had plenty of apples and peaches, but the pears were a welcome change. She longed for an orange or anything citrus. She also bought some of Woody's beef from the steer slaughtered the day before.

She asked Carlene how the barter and scrip system was working.

"Pretty good," said the proprietress. "It's still a learning process for me and my customers. I'm having to be both a retailer and a banker. People ask me for credit, so I've got a ledger system that I can track who's borrowed what. I charge one-percent per month, so if someone takes 100 lids, I ask them to return 101 within a month. If they can't, it doesn't matter, as long as everybody gets fed. Right now, that's all I'm trying to do."

"What are the hot items, other than food?"

"Cigarettes, of course. And hygiene products. People are bringing surplus food to trade when they have it, but nobody has any hygiene stuff. I think women are using whatever they can find for sanitary napkins or tampons. We've had a few people bring in surplus napkins when the woman in the house has died, but we could sure use more. Do you have enough?"

"Yes, for now. Bonnie had several boxes, so I'm using them."

Saturday, September 15

Sammy had more cheese that Hattie had made, so she decided to call on the Nursing Home. After leaving it with Frank, Caroline's assistant, she walked down the hall to see if she could find Professor Dyson. She found the old woman sitting at the piano. "How are you doing today?"

"Hi Sammy! Well, I got out of bed another day. I always consider that a triumph. My goal is to be as self-sufficient as possible and be as little trouble to Caroline as I can. How about yourself?"

"As well as can be. I'm just trying to make it from day to day, too."

They spoke briefly about the weather. Then Sammy said, "The other day, you said you taught Biology and Ecology. Where was that?"

"I was quite something in my day. I earned my PhD from Oxford, in England. I taught my entire career at Dartmouth, in the White Mountains of New Hampshire. It is one of the oldest colleges in America, founded before our nation was formed.

"I was at the forefront of the ecological movement. I appeared at conferences with Rachel Carson, Margaret Mead, Wendell Berry,

Loren Eiseley, Dian Fossey, and Jane Goodall. I wrote and lectured extensively about mankind's impact on the planet."

"What did you conclude?"

"We're a scoundrel species. We treat the earth like a cash machine with endless resources."

Changing her own subject, the old woman said, "I love this tune." She played *Put On A Happy Face* from the musical *Bye Bye Birdie*. The woman played as if there was no problem whatsoever with the stuck keys and the poor state of tune.

When she finished, Sammy applauded politely. "I'm not sure what you mean by the cash machine."

"The earth is filled with things useful to us: resources. Most are non-renewable. Many can be recycled and used over and over again, although we do far too little recycling. But let's look at a non-renewable resource like coal. The earth once had an incredible amount of it. But our exploitation is proceeding at a frantic pace and someday it will be scarce and difficult to find and extract. What then?

"But let's look at even a renewable resource, like fish. The oceans are vast, yet not unlimited. Fishermen now have amazing technologies to find and catch the fish. Nowadays, they're catching fish more rapidly than the fish can replenish their own stocks.

"Here's an analogy. If you have money in the bank, the bank will pay you interest. You can withdraw the interest indefinitely without ever touching the principal. So theoretically, your money will last forever. But when you withdraw more than that, you compromise your future. That's what we're doing with the fish, and almost every important resource."

As Sammy processed this new knowledge, her mentor changed the subject, saying, "Here's another piece I love, it's *I Feel Pretty* from *West Side Story*."

The woman launched her fingers flying around the keyboard again. As Sammy listened, Caroline entered the room to ask for her help in the kitchen. As Sammy departed, the old professor said, "Next time you come, bring your violin and play along with me."

Sunday, September 16

"Rise and shine, Sammy," Quint yelled, while rapping at her door. "Today is the day of the Lord and it's time to get ready for church."

"Come in, please," Sammy said, already awake.

"Yes, what is it?"

"Today is Rosh Hashanah. Happy New Year to you!"

"It's what?"

"Rosh Hashanah, the Jewish New Year. I've been going to church with you almost every week. Please, let today be my day back in Judaism, the faith of my people. Emily and Jamaal are hosting a service and a meal for me tonight. You're invited to attend with us if you wish. Did you know Emily's late husband was Jewish?"

"Yes, I seem to remember that about Emily's husband. But, no thanks. I don't think I'll attend. I've got a family in the church that is having some problems. I'll spend the afternoon with them."

"Thanks for understanding. I'll see you later."

Quint left her room and shut the door. She was relieved that her church burden had been waylaid for at least a week. She didn't explain that all Jewish days, and thus all holidays, actually spanned the hours between sundown and the following sundown. So technically, Rosh Hashanah didn't start until 6:00 p.m. But without working watches, what were a few minutes one way or the other?

Sammy lounged in bed until Quint left. Then she went to the river to rest and meditate. She took her violin and played for the birds. There was nobody else around.

Later in the day, she walked to Emily and Jamaal's house. Emily looked good, more vital than in recent days.

Emily began, "Happy New Year everyone! This is the start of a ten-day period which Jews think of as the 'High Holy Days.' Sammy, help me with this."

"You're correct. The tenth day is Yom Kippur, the Day of Atonement. This is the day when Jews around the world ask forgiveness for their sins."

Emily continued, "Rosh Hashanah is on the first two days of the month of Tishrei, the seventh month on the Hebrew calendar. It's pretty confusing when you're accustomed to the Christian calendar, when New Year's Day is on the first day of the first month."

"Credit one to the Christians," said Jamaal sarcastically.

"Hush. Anyway, the literal translation of Rosh Hashanah is 'The Head of the Year.' During the week and a half to follow, Jews embark on the process of examining their lives and asking forgiveness of their sins. They are encouraged to not just ask amends from God but from anyone they have wronged.

"The two most common prayers are the *Unetaneh Tohkef* and the *Avienu Malkeinu*. The former is the most important prayer on life and death to the Jews. Part of it reads, 'On Rosh Hashanah it is written, how many will leave this world and how many will be born into it, who will live and who will die... But penitence, prayer and good deeds can annul the severity of the decree.'"

Sammy's mind swam in a turbulent sea of emotion over the life and death struggles she'd witnessed and imagined during recent weeks, and over her lost virginity.

Emily continued, "This is also the holiday in which we blow the shofar. It is made from the hollowed-out horn of a ram. Of course, because it has no keys, it resonates with only one note. The player is called the *tokea*, which in Hebrew means the 'blaster.' Because there are no notes, the blaster merely alters the duration of the blasts, like Morse Code. The playing of the shofar is a call to worship and is thought to ward off demons."

"Because we don't have a shofar," Jamaal said, "I will play this trumpet." He did an unbroken blast of three seconds. Then he did three in a row. Then he did nine rapid blasts. Finally, he blew for six, seven, eight, nine, ten, eleven, twelve seconds. His face turned red with exertion. Finally at fifteen seconds, his breath expired and he slumped forward in exaggerated effort. Emily and Sammy clapped.

Emily continued, "The blowing of the shofar is also thought to hope God will remember Abraham's devotion. Abraham was willing to bind and sacrifice his beloved son, Isaac, on Mount Moriah.

An instant before the execution, an angel of God stopped Abraham, saying the Lord now understood Abraham's commitment. Abraham released his son and caught a ram which he sacrificed. All shofars, and presumably my dear late husband's trumpet, are descendant – let's say 'inspired' – by that original ram's horn.

"All of us are blessed by your presence and your friendship, Ms. Samantha. We all expect difficult times ahead, but we wish you health and prosperity in this New Year."

"Shanah Tovah!"

"Shanah Tovah! Happy New Year!"

The three friends shared a meal of beef from Woody's farm, potatoes from the garden, and Hattie's cheese. Towards the end of the meal, Sammy said, "You know, the things I'm hearing about Revelation and the rapture are pretty strange."

"I can see why that would be so," said Emily. "What's your Jewish education?"

"I had a bat mitzvah when I was thirteen. Most of my friends did. But I'm not very knowledgeable about Jewish law, especially about the End Times."

"I learned a lot from my husband, who was really interested in it." Emily said, "The word 'heaven' in Hebrew is translated as fire and water. It is a paradox. It is only when paradoxes are reconciled emotionally and intellectually can there be heaven. But, to talk about the eschaton…"

"The what?" interrupted Jamaal.

"The eschaton. Did you skip church that day, Mr. Economics Professor? It's the End Times. Eschatology is the study of the End Times. It's when God decides everybody's fate. To talk about the End Times or to interpret events in a day-to-day life as a sign of the end would be really problematic for Jews. They just don't do it.

"It took centuries for the pyramids of Egypt to be built. The workers understood they would never see the overall awesomeness of it, as it would not be completed in their lifetimes. But as amazingly large and glorious the pyramids are, God is still beyond that. Jews took that as a metaphor of the universe.

"As we are learning more about acceleration of time, dark matter, and all these things, we can't even imagine the creation, let alone the Creator. Beyond that, we certainly cannot know the *will* of the Creator. It is beyond time, beyond imagination, and beyond our ability to know. Human beings cannot even really talk about this subject because as human beings, we are limited in our ability to understand.

"The Torah is God's word on earth, but it was written with human hands. That already means that God is one step removed from the process.

"Over centuries, Jews have been criticized for living in the present tense. It is a survival mechanism. Historically, the passage of Jews from place to place has been fraught with danger. Jews are focused solely on meeting present obligations in the present. We've all heard people around here saying this calamity is a punishment from God. Jews do not find God in the negative side of catastrophes but instead in the positive side of people coming together to assist. In these moments, people who do not agree on anything politically or socially can agree that there are people in need and they come to help.

"Christians are evangelical by nature. They want everybody to be Christian. Jews won't turn anybody away, but they do not care who joins them. The Christians are obsessed with preparation for the End Times. The Jews are not. The Jews seem equally ambivalent about heaven and hell. If there is a heaven, it is a huge yeshiva hall where everyone is studying the Torah. And they are doing that for eternity. For some of them, it is heaven. For others, it is hell."

Everybody laughed.

Jamaal said, "You won't hear me say this anywhere but in your company, but many Christians seem deeply conflicted and somewhat hypocritical."

"I agree," Emily said. "Christians in America are a huge majority, yet they have an uncanny ability and frequent willingness to express persecution. Anybody who didn't know better would get the feeling that Christians are an endangered group. Yet, they can't imagine a president who is not Christian. Nobody in America is out to do away with Christianity.

"They will vote for politicians who preach 'Family values' but are known adulterers. Jesus was an anti-materialist, yet Christmas is an orgy of consumption. Many Christians have formed a Faustian bargain with gun ownership. Jesus preached non-violence, but the incidence of gun ownership in America by Christians is huge.

"When I'm at Quint's church and people find out I'm Jewish," Sammy admitted, "they tell me they'll pray for me. Quint told me he'd pray for me. I don't want to be rude because I'm sure they mean well, but I want to say, 'Pray for yourself instead.' I know I need these people and I'm trying to earn my keep by helping them. One woman in church told me God wanted me here. My being here is part of God's way. She thought everything we are experiencing is a sign from God. As far as I can tell, the Pulse was simply an act of nature. Nobody is to blame and nobody is being punished. I just want to go home."

Emily concluded, "Christians apparently feel that their security lies with a lifetime in Christ. Jews feel that their lifetime is a template on how to live a life. Living a good life could guarantee you a place in what the Jews consider a world to come. But everybody goes there. There is no admission requirement."

Jamaal said, "I hate to show off my ignorance again, but I've always heard that Jews are God's Chosen People. I've never understood what it meant."

Emily said, "They are chosen to live out the burden of God's word, of God's law. There is a Midrash, a commentary to the Old Testament, which tells the story of God taking his laws to all of the people of the world. God asked each tribe if they wanted to live by these laws. All of the tribes of the world gave God reasons why they did not wish to abide by the law. But the Hebrews accepted and chose to live the laws of God. God didn't choose them; they chose themselves. The idea is to create an upright sense of holiness by which people can see how God's ways are. It is a way to create a light upon the nations. It is a way to create ideal communities the rest of the world can emulate.

"Jews were forced into living in small minorities virtually everywhere. The United States of America has been a unique place in the world for Jews to live and to flourish. George Washington wrote a letter to the Rhode Island synagogue in 1791, responding to a request to speak there, saying to them, 'I will not treat you as a tolerated minority but instead as equal citizens.' In the day, you can't believe how unusual that was. Here, Judaism is secondary to American citizenship. It is almost as if America is the new Israel.

"Unfortunately, since then, there has been a long history of anti-Semitism in America. As recently as the 1950s, there were country clubs that would not allow Jews.

"There are approximately 13-million Jewish people worldwide. One million of them live in New York City, and they are of the six million that live in America. Five million of them live in Israel. There are only about 2 million Jewish people everywhere else in the world. Those outside of the United States and Israel have a very different experience on what their Judaism is. In years past, anti-Semitism caused Jews to band together for mutual support and protection. When there is freedom as there is in contemporary America, Jews do not feel obligated to commit to other Jews.

"Jews have a strong sense of what is right and wrong by the law. There are a disproportionate number of lawyers and judges that are Jewish. Jews value justice more than love. Christians tell you to love your neighbors as yourself. Jews don't care whether you love them or not, only that you treat them justly."

Sammy mentioned her grandfather and his imprisonment in the Nazi Concentration Camp. Emily said, "The Holocaust is difficult for Jews to rationalize. There is nihilism that always creeps in."

"What's that?" Sammy asked.

"It's the rejection of religion. It happens when religious leanings are obliterated. The Jews understand persecution; they've lived with it for centuries. But the systematic execution and torture of people across borders by the Nazis and the complicity of everyone else, including people who were supposed to be their friends, does not lend itself to answers from theological questions. If you are going to believe in a God, how do you believe there is a God that would allow this to happen?

"Christians find God's plan in every thing. The Jews don't find God's plan in much of anything. The Jews have not seen much of anything go right for them historically. The fear of the unknown is real for everybody. For the Jews, it happens to be historically justifiable."

Monday, September 17

Sammy awoke to the sound of Emily's bell ringing. Her first thought was that it being Rosh Hashanah, at least until Sunset, perhaps a day of meditation might be in order. She quickly changed her mind, reasoning that the best way to start a new year was by helping to bring a new baby into the world.

She washed and dressed, then had a fresh peach and some goat's milk for breakfast. Then she saddled Jackson and rode over. Jamaal had hitched Maggie to the wagon and Emily was stepping on the seat. Sammy tied Jackson's reins to the back of the wagon and rode beside Emily, who told her, "We're going over to Hilltown. It's just up the hill from Fries. It's not named Hilltown because it's on the hill; it's named that because a predominant family up there was the Hills."

The expectant mother was black and the father was white. It was their first child. The father worked in a warehouse in Wytheville, a 45-minute drive back when people were driving. They appeared to not have much money. While the mother was having contractions, the father cowered in the corner of the room, looking faint. Sammy split her time in holding the mother's hand and convincing the father that everything would be all right. Both seemed impossibly young to be parents; Sammy didn't ask their ages.

The baby, a boy, emerged with no problems within three hours of their arrival. It was umber in color with coffee colored curly hair. The parents were elated. Emily and Sammy stayed until everything looked settled, then started home.

On the way, Emily said, "I've got something for you back at the house."

"What is it?"

"I took an old leather doctor's case I found in the attic and I have loaded it up with some herbs and spare tools. It will be your midwife's bag. If you're going to take this work seriously, I want you to take it with you everywhere you go."

They arrived back at Emily's house. Sammy unhitched the horse while Emily went inside and fixed them some eggs, tomatoes, and potatoes. After eating, Emily showed Sammy the bag. It was a typical doctor's bag, made of heavy black leather, similar to what Sammy had seen in one of the old Westerns her grandfather used to watch.

Emily said, "I have put in here different herbs, including skullcap and St. John's wort, blue cohosh and black cohosh. There's Motherwort, Angelica, cottonroot bark. These, plus the blue and black cohoshes are for bleeding situations. If the mom is having trouble resting, you might use 20 drops of St. Johns wort and 20 drops of motherwort with a tablespoon of liquid calcium/magnesium. If the mom is really exhausted you might use 60 drops of lobelia and 60 drops of skullcap. If you have a mom who is bleeding with the placenta still inside of her you can try 50 drops of ground ivy or angelica with or without 10 drops of the blue and black cohoshes which cause rapid empting of the uterus.

"A preventive for post partum bleeding is 10 drops motherwort and 8 drops of ground ivy after the birth. It is handy if you have a mom with lots of emotional baggage as they tend to bleed a bit more then others do."

"Thank you very much for this kit. I'll carry it with me."

"You're welcome. Thanks for helping me. By the way," said Emily, "do you know what today is?"

"No, what?"

"It's the one month anniversary of the Pulse."

"Yes, and of my parents' deaths."

"May God console you among the other mourners of Zion and Jerusalem."

"Thank you. I suppose there is some significance that this anniversary falls on New Year's Day."

"Let's not make too much of it. I'm just glad you're here and safe."

"Obviously, this isn't where I want to be. But blessings to you, Jamaal, Quint, Hattie, and everyone now around me. Without you, I'd be... I don't know where I'd be."

Emily gave her a hug, then a smile, but said nothing else.

Sammy bid Emily adieu and walked outside. She strapped her new bag to Jackson's saddle, hoisted herself on his back, and set off for home walking him. She murmured a prayer to herself, "May the words of my mouth and the meditations of my heart be acceptable in Your sight, Oh Lord, my rock and my Redeemer."

Tuesday, September 18

Sammy spent much of the day working in the garden again, with the harvest in full swing. She dried some more apples, along with peaches and pears. She placed several trays in the car to dry, spreading fruit throughout. That afternoon, a thunderstorm passed through. To pass the time, she read one of Bonnie's romance novels on the shelf in the bedroom. Before dinner, she took all the fruit trays inside, thinking it may be chilly overnight and she would return them to the car tomorrow.

After dinner, she tacked up Jackson and rode into town, carrying her violin case strapped over her shoulder. Ortie and Rhonda were there, as were Caroline and Woody Dalton. Several other "regulars" were there and Sammy realized how many of them she was starting to recognize. Rhonda was cold towards her, making her wonder what she had done to cause any riff.

Sammy had practiced a tune called *Jerusalem Ridge*, and she took the lead playing it for the group.

She rode home at a trot. Vespertine stars appeared on the northern horizon. She carried Jackson's saddle into the barn where she was startled by the silhouette of a male form. "It's nice to see you, Sammy."

"Oh, Shane. It's you. What are you doing here?"

"I couldn't make the jam, so I thought I'd come over here and see if I could 'make' you," taking her saddle from her and hanging it on the peg.

"You're such a tease," she said, grinning.

"Whatcha got for me tonight, baby?"

"What do you want?" she said, seductively. She was glad he was there.

"Mmmmm."

"Come outside. Let me show you something." She walked with him to Quint's car that earlier in the day had been her fruit dryer. She opened the hatchback. "This might be a good place to hang out."

When they had intercourse before, it hurt. But touching him didn't. She felt lust for him and she liked the way it felt. The word "sin" crossed her mind, but she didn't understand what it meant. She convinced herself that a second time might be better, more satisfying.

They jumped into the car and heavy petting ensued, soon followed by lovemaking. To her delight, Sammy found this episode more pleasurable if not any more tender. She felt no greater emotional attraction for him than before. But the act was enjoyable and she wondered whether these trysts would become regular. She chuckled to herself thinking that Yom Kippur was only a few days away, the day she'd ask forgiveness for the sins of the past year. Might as well go out with a bang, she decided, noting her double entendre.

They dressed themselves and Shane helped Sammy get vertical again outside the car before vanishing into the night.

Wednesday, September 19

Sammy decided to visit Jamaal and Emily, so after her morning chores, she walked over. Emily wasn't feeling well, resting in her bedroom. Jamaal said he'd stayed home the evening before to take care of her.

"Emily's late husband was a ham radio operator. He quit using his radios years before he died. But I've been trying to piece together a working system for the past couple of weeks. I think I have everything. I'm planning on driving the wagon downtown to see if I can talk Pike into letting me connect it to the mini-grid he's got going and see if we can begin communicating to the world again. Why don't you go with me?"

"Sure."

They hitched Maggie to the wagon again and put a cardboard box in the back, packing the radio gear carefully inside. They drove Maggie into Fries, where they went directly to the dam and the power plant. They found Pike working inside.

Pike greeted them, saying, "Hih. How's it going? Have you got that radio working, Jamaal?"

"I think so, but I haven't had any juice to run through it. Are you ready for me to plug it in and see if it works?"

"Ih'll give you everythin' she's got," the professor said, imitating Montgomery Scott, the Scottish engineer on the Star Trek's Enterprise with a mixed Tennessee and Scotland accent. "Seriously, we've been having some problems. We don't have the right equipment to properly regulate the dynamo, so the cycles are varying somewhat. This is no problem for powering pumps and electric motors, but it may fry your vacuum tubes."

"Do we have any options?" said Jamaal.

"Not now. Not if we want to give it a go. There is a small office in the upstairs of the power plant. Why don't you set up there?"

Jamaal and Sammy carried parts upstairs. They pushed some papers aside from a folding table and began attaching all the parts, including the assortment of vacuum tubes in sockets at the top. "This is an old 'Glowbug' set," explained Jamaal. "My dad was in communications in the Navy. He had one of these for his hobby set. It was missing a couple of tubes and the crystal. One of Pike's friends here in town has an old electronics repair shop. We found some tubes and we had to re-wire some sockets so they'd fit. We got a crystal from Emily's old color TV. Without power, she figured she'd never use it again.

"Okay, here goes."

The tubes atop the metal box began to glow. Jamaal put on a set of headphones and he began to listen, carefully turning the two dials on the front. His eyes widened and shut as he detected incoming signals. Pike walked inside to check their progress. Jamaal put his index finger to his lips, indicating he needed quiet. A few minutes later, he spoke to Pike and Sammy.

"I'm listening to a guy in Albuquerque. I can't figure out who he's talking to, but I think someone in Canada. From what he can tell, the blackout extended all the way across the East Coast, from New Hampshire south to Florida, and west beyond Kansas City. Apparently, South Florida's Pulse was weaker, so none of the electronic gear was ruined, but the power plants that feed that area are further north, so they lost power anyway. The Vice President was visiting troops in Afghanistan when the power went out, and he's been flown back to the states. He's set up a command center at Fort Lewis Military Base, outside of Tacoma, Washington. The president is apparently safe, but is in an undisclosed location. He made an address to the nation last week, indicating what steps were being taken to restore order, but of course millions of people couldn't see or hear it. Most military people in the hundreds of bases we have around the world have been recalled to the states, primarily to the Norfolk Naval Base and the Quantico Marine base outside of DC."

Jamaal turned his attention to the radio for a moment. He spoke again, talking like a newscaster. "There's mayhem at virtually all the major cities in the east. There have been extensive riots. Roving bands of desperate people have left the cities for the countryside, robbing and pillaging at will. The rural communities have faired somewhat better, but many adjacent to the cities have been pillaged.

"New York and Boston are reportedly the worst hit. There is way too little food for everyone. So again, marauding hoards have swept through the surrounding areas."

Sammy envisioned the worst for her beautiful community of mansions just across the Hudson from the city.

"Without fuel moving around, transportation is at a standstill. And the people who do have vehicles and fuel are being attacked and robbed. We think things are bad here, but they're much worse else-where. This is sickening to listen to."

Sammy could see that her two friends were as shaken as she was.

"Wow," said Pike, wiping his nose with his dirty handkerchief.

Jamaal continued, "The Intermountain West and West Coast were spared. They've been working hard to assist by sending supplies and food across country, primarily by rail. The problem is that when the Pulse struck, it destroyed the locomotives. So there are massive trains sitting on the tracks that must be moved. It wasn't much of a problem for the few working automobiles around here to skirt past immobilized vehicles on the roads. It was a bigger problem on the highways of the major cities. But it is a huge problem for the trains."

One of the tubes on the top of the radio glared momentarily like a light-bulb, and then popped, showering them with glass shards. Then the rest went dark.

"Damn! Back to the proverbial drawing board," sighed Jamaal.

Thursday, September 20

The next morning while she was having breakfast, Sammy found Quint's wallet on the kitchen table. She assumed he must have left it by mistake. So she decided to ride Jackson into town and return it to him.

His drugstore looked to her more like an old-fashioned bank than a store. There were heavy metal bars separating the entry room from his counter in the back. A partition kept her from seeing the stock room shelves, but what she could see looked largely empty. She could see a few normally packaged remedies like nighttime cold remedies and cough syrups, but also some Mason jars with leafy herbs. "Thank you for bringing me my wallet," he said. "Frankly, I've had so much on my mind that I haven't even missed it. There's nothing to spend money on anyway and I sure as heck don't need my drivers license to ride Bonnie's bicycle here."

Pike walked in and said hello. "Quint, you got any cold capsules?

My nose is running so fast Ih can't keep it wiped."

"We still have a few dozen pills. I'm down to selling them by the pill."

Pike handed him a small bag containing 5 Mason jar lids. Apparently the monetary system from the Providence General Store was working its way into town. "Thanks, man."

"Hey, how's the power plant going? I appreciate you getting my refrigerator running. What's next?"

"We're trying to get the other turbines operational. A couple of the guys have gone to Galax to see if they can get some of the parts we need to run them. I'll keep you posted."

Sammy walked outside the store with Pike. "The things Jamaal heard sounded really awful. It scared me."

"It scared me, too. Things are really bad, especially in the cities. But things might get much worse."

"How can anything be worse?" she asked with trepidation.

"We have a risk of some major radioactive releases from our nuclear power plants. I'm sure that when the power failed, the power plants went off-line immediately. Remember the nuclear plant in Japan that was crippled by the tsunami? I'm sure ours have trips like that to stop the nuclear reaction whenever there is a problem. But even if they tripped off, they still emit lots of heat. That heat must be removed from the fuel by circulation of water. If the water sits, it soon gets hot enough to boil. Then the fuel rods melt, releasing nuclear fuel and radiation. There can be steam build-up, which can cause massive explosions, sending the radioactive materials into the atmosphere and spreading radioactivity all over the place. Keeping the water moving is done by huge pumps that take electricity to run. If there is no power grid, there is no electricity."

"Don't they have backup generators?" Sammy inquired.

"Yes," Pike said, "but they only have enough fuel to run them for finite periods of time. Sooner or later, they run out of that fuel and they can't power the pumps. If the Pulse ruined their control systems, they won't run even if they have fuel."

"Are there power plants around here?"

"The closest is due south of here, near Charlotte, North Carolina."

"Is it safe?" she inquired.

"We don't know yet. We can only hope. This area is further from a nuclear plant than almost anywhere in the Eastern United States. Two-thirds of the people of our country are at risk. Things are bad right now, really bad. But they might get much worse. Not much for us to do except keep our fingers crossed."

"Have you told Chief Wilkins? Is she going to tell everyone in town?"

"Yes, Ih told her," he confessed. "It's her call whether to spread the word. Not much for anyone to do about it, really. So Ih'm not sure she'll say anything, at least just yet."

"Wow," she shrugged

"Yeah, double-wow."

Sammy hopped on Jackson and rode him back towards Providence. She stopped to see Emily who wasn't feeling well again.

Sitting on the sofa, Emily said, "I'm glad we haven't had much work in the midwifery business lately. Hopefully I'll feel better again in a few days. Honey, would you mind going by Avalon's house tomorrow and picking up some blue cohosh for me? I'm running low. Here are a dozen Mason jar lids to pay her."

"Sure," Sammy said. "No problem. I hope you feel better."

Friday, September 21

Sammy hopped from bed, eager to see Avalon again. In the kitchen, she found a glass of goat's milk, apparently left behind for her by Hattie. Per usual, Hattie was nowhere to be seen.

Sammy rode Jackson past the Providence store and towards the road circling Turkey Knob. She waved at several people who were attending to their small gardens. She turned on Avalon's road and found her friend peeling apples in the gazebo outside the house.

"*Hola, mi amiga,*" yelled the busy woman. She wore her typical peasant dress and beads. She had a morning glory blossom in her hair.

"Hi, Avalon," replied Sammy. "How are you?"

"I couldn't be better. *¿Qué pasa?*"

Sammy considered telling her about her recent encounters with Shane, but decided not to confide in her, at least just yet. Instead, she told her about the birthing events with Emily and Emily's need for some herbs.

"I think Emily has high hopes for your help with her work," Avalon admitted hearing.

"I am fascinated by delivering babies. Maybe it's my calling."

"I can't imagine a more wonderful occupation than helping mothers bring their babies into the world. I suspect people won't quit having babies just because there is no electricity."

Sammy told her about the horrors she'd heard from Pike. Listening attentively, Avalon said, "I think we all knew, or I should say many of us knew, something like this was coming."

"What do you mean?"

"Sit, my child," she said, handing Sammy a spare paring knife that seemed to be magically waiting for her. "Let me tell you my story.

Avalon began, "I've had an unusual life, to say the least. I was born on June 6, 1966 near San Jose, California. During my formative years, I was convinced I was the Antichrist. Everything in my life revolved around the number six. I was born with six fingers on each hand and six toes on each foot. The extra digits on my hands were removed surgically when I was a toddler. But I was aware of what was happening.

"Look at my feet," she said, removing her slippers. Sure enough, six toes on each.

"My father was an engineer who worked for most of his life at Hewlett-Packard. He was an electrical engineer, your typical propeller-head. He wore a white shirt, a dark tie, and dark glasses every day. He was not particularly religious, nor was my mother. Mom was a woman of style and fashion, a California woman of the 1950s. If they ever realized any connection with the antichrist, it was never mentioned to me. I remember rebelling constantly."

A long apple peel fell to the floor.

"From as long as I can remember, people have told me how beautiful and charismatic I was. These fit into the mystique of the image of the antichrist in the book of Revelation. I always simply wanted to fit in, but I always felt that I was somehow quite different. I never knew how I was supposed to behave if I was the antichrist.

"I was too young for the Summer of Love in San Francisco, but the hippie element was still active in the Bay Area as I came of age. I grew up with beads and weed and free love.

"During my first year at Berkeley, I met a professor of anthropology. He was married at the time, but I lusted for him. During spring break, he told his wife that he was going on a field trip but instead he drove me to Utah to do an exorcism on me. He had a Native American friend in Moab. We went to the most dramatic natural place in the world, a cliff overlooking the confluence of the Green and Colorado Rivers at a place called the Island in the Sky in Canyonlands National Park. They erected a sweat house. They lit a fire inside. We all got naked and for two days we fasted and they fed me peyote. The Indian man chanted for hours and hours. At the sunset of the second day, we emerged from the sweat house and watched the rise of the full moon.

"The spell of the antichrist was dead within me from that time. However, on the sixth day of every month, I still find myself anxious, behaving erratically and uncontrollably."

Sammy was enthralled as Avalon continued, "Within a few months, my professor left his wife. Years later, we were married on the North Pacific Sea coast of Washington state with the sun setting into the surf. I always felt pangs of regret about wrecking his marriage. But he dismissed my concerns; he said his relationship with her had run its course.

"He and I lived for many years in Olympia, Washington where he taught at Evergreen State University, one of the most liberal schools in America. I roamed the Olympic Mountains looking for herbs and mushrooms. It was an idyllic life, but I never became pregnant. It is just as well because I would have had serious reservations about bringing a child into the world.

"We became deeply concerned about what might happen to society at the turn of the millennium. I think we talked about this last time you were here. There was great fear throughout the country that the computer systems which dominated our lives were not properly programmed to move from the last day of 1999 until 2000."

"I remember that!" Sammy shouted. "Daddy works in the financial industry and I remember how concerned he was about it. Didn't all the old computers need to be thrown away?"

"No. Many older computers simply needed to have new software installed. In fact, it turned out to be a bit of a bust. Nevertheless, for several years prior, many people were deeply concerned, including my husband and me. We started looking for a secluded, rural community where we thought people stood a better chance in the collapse. Already, of course, there were so many factors that foretold a collapse of our society, including overfishing of the seas, overproduction of agricultural areas, and depletion of aquifers and energy resources.

"The bottom line is that we were convinced that our technology had eclipsed the human ability to maintain it. The collapse may very well have begun last month and is underway as we sit here.

"Listen to me run on. I sound like an old schoolmarm. What herbs did you need, again?"

Sammy asked for blue cohosh. Avalon handed her a pint jar of the bluish-green leaflets. She refused to take any payment, and instead gave Sammy a dozen eggs, kissed her on the cheek, and invited her back, "any time!"

Saturday, September 22

Quint was in the kitchen when Sammy descended the stairs for breakfast. There was a half-full glass of goat's milk at her place. Quint said, "I'm going to take a day off today and get some work done before the barn dance tonight. I'm going to cut some firewood to keep the wood stove in the kitchen going. Would you like to help me?"

"Sure. Do you have a chain saw?" Sammy agreed.

"Yeah, it's twenty years old or more, so it's old school. Perhaps that's a blessing."

Moments later, he said, "Have you heard about the dance tonight at the Daltons?"

Swallowing some milk, Sammy replied, "Emily said something about it a few days ago. I'm surprised people would feel festive enough for dancing."

"It's a tradition around here that we have a dance on the Saturday after the spring and fall equinoxes. So that falls today. People are definitely reeling, if you'll pardon the pun. Everybody feels the need to strive towards some normalcy. I hope you'll come and play your fiddle. The Daltons have a huge barn. If the weather is good, they have it outside; otherwise it's inside the barn."

Sammy finished breakfast and went back upstairs and put on the oldest jeans and T-shirt of Bonnie's she could find. Quint gave her an old flannel shirt of his to wear over top. "I've got two trees in mind," Quint said. "They're both dead already and they're both uphill from the house so we won't have to work so hard carrying the wood." He got a wheelbarrow, two pairs of gloves, and the chain saw from the shed and they trekked uphill to the west. They reached the first tree and Quint sized up his cut. He undercut a V into the trunk, and then cut from the reverse side six inches higher. The tree fell downhill in the direction of the house. He carefully notched several of the larger branches to the 18" lengths to fit the wood stove. Then he began cutting the branches. Sammy thought about hearing protection, but in a perverse way enjoyed the ear-splitting racket of the saw, the first loud mechanical thing she'd heard in weeks.

They worked for several hours together before breaking for lunch. They had a sizeable pile transferred to the house and she was tired. Nevertheless, she went back up the hill with him as he continued until his strength gave out in mid-afternoon. Finally, wiping his brow, he said, "Let's call it a day and get some rest before the dance tonight."

Quint left early to help the Daltons with set-up. Sammy took her violin in its case and her midwife's leather bag to the barn, where she tacked up Jackson. She had rigged up some leather straps she found in the barn such that she could carry her midwife's case and her violin case on either side of the horse like panniers. She rode over to get Jamaal. Sammy peeked into Emily's bedroom and said hello, as Jamaal had told her Emily still wasn't feeling well. Sammy and Jamaal walked together from there to the Daltons, Sammy leading Jackson by the reins.

The usual musicians were in attendance and the disposition seemed good. There were three other people on stage that Sammy had met at the weekly jam sessions. Many of the songs were new to Sammy, so she had to concentrate to keep up. She did a few breaks on her violin and people responded appreciatively. Shane joined them on stage for two pieces, but spent most of his time dancing. Sammy was jealous of one of the prettiest girls who Shane seemed to be flirting with.

They had just finished playing *Ragtime Annie* when DeAngelo Freeman appeared behind the stage. "Sammy, thank goodness you're here! Ebony needs you right away."

"What's wrong?"

"She's having contractions. I went first to Emily's, but she isn't feeling well enough to help. She told me you might be here. She must be really sick if she can't come. Anyway, we need you right away."

"Isn't her due date still several weeks away?"

"Yes, but she thinks this is the time."

Sammy put her violin in the case and pushed it under the chair. Turning to Jamaal, she said, "Will you take this home with you? I'll pick it up tomorrow."

"Sure." Then he nodded to DeAngelo and said, "Good luck, brother!"

Sammy dashed off-stage with DeAngelo two strides in front of her. She mounted Jackson and DeAngelo had evidently borrowed a horse. Together, they cantered towards his home. Sammy was filled with trepidation, wondering if she was ready to provide midwife services if Ebony was truly ready to give birth.

Arriving at their home, Sammy unstrapped her bag and ran inside while DeAngelo secured the horses. Ebony was lying on her bed, in some pain.

Sammy removed her stethoscope and took Ebony's pulse. She palpated Ebony's belly. "How frequent are your contractions?"

"About every half-hour."

"Have they become more frequent?"

"I don't think so."

"You're not dilated. If they aren't becoming more frequent, you may be having false labor contractions. They're called Braxton Hicks. I'll sit with you and we can time them."

The two women sat together for the better part of two hours, timing the contractions which became less intense and less frequent. When they were convinced Ebony would not be giving birth for a few more days, Sammy walked outside. She strapped her bag to Jackson and from the top step of the porch, hoisted herself atop. She began the long walk home, going west where only a tiny sliver of light remained in the sky. A cool wind blew in her face.

As she approached her new home, she could see an oil light burning inside. She had a premonition that something was wrong. She strapped Jackson to the picket fence and ran inside where she saw Jamaal waiting for her.

"I'm sorry. I'm so sorry."

"What's wrong?"

"Your violin. I don't have your violin. Pike gathered me up in conversation after the jam and I forgot about it. I was half-way home when I remembered it. I ran all the way back to the barn. Nobody was around and it was gone."

"I'm sure somebody else picked it up for me. I can't imagine that anybody would steal it."

"I'm just heart-sick. I know what that violin means to you. I have let you down. I am so, so sorry."

"I know it was an honest mistake. I'm sure it will be returned tomorrow," she said, mustering cheerful optimism. "Nobody would steal it, I'm sure."

"You're very sweet." He gave her a hug. "I'll do everything I can to help you find it."

"I am so, so tired. I'm going to bed." An hour later her head hit the pillow, but she couldn't sleep, wracked in grief over her precious lost instrument.

Sunday, September 23

The next morning, Quint rapped on her door waking her from a dream about ice cream. She called him in and told him about the missing violin. "I'm not in the right mood for church today. I am going to stay home."

"We'll pray for you."

Pray that somebody returns my violin, she thought sarcastically.

She dressed, then had a peach and goat's milk for breakfast, and then walked aimlessly around the property. She found a pretty spot on a bluff overlooking the river. It seemed to her that someone had spent time there before, as the grass was tamped down. Perhaps this was where Hattie spent some of her time. She remembered seeing a kite in Bonnie's bedroom and decided this would be a good place to fly it. So she walked back to the house and got it. She launched it into the air, where the breezes held it aloft, seemingly over the shimmering river. She watched an osprey dive into the river and return aloft with a fish in its talons.

It was warm and refreshing in the sun, but when a cloud blocked the sun, a chilling wind brought goosebumps to her arms. A pall of gloom swept over her, and she began to sob. Tears dripped down her cheeks and spilled onto her jeans. The kite dipped and danced. She cried more and more, a river's worth, wishing the liquid would carry her sorrows and trepidations away.

Monday, September 24

Jamaal was at her door early. "Let's go into town and see if we can find your violin. I'm still heart-sick over it." He had hand-written three signs that said: "Lost. Italian violin, lost at Dalton farm, September 21. Any information, See Emily Ayers, Providence. Reward."

They walked together past his house and into town. They went first to the community center and found it still locked. Around the corner, they found Acting Chief Annie Wilkins walking hurriedly out of her office. Jamaal yelled for her first, "Chief Wilkins!"

"What is it?"

"It's my violin," Sammy said. "It's missing."

"So?" said the officer, brusquely.

"I forgot to take it with me," said Jamaal. "It's my fault."

"So what do you want me to do?" the officer said.

"How do police normally find missing things?" Jamaal inquired.

"We investigate the property and talk with anyone who might have been there. But I'm too busy; I have more important things to do than track down your fiddle. People are dying at a frightful pace. There's nothing I can do for you."

"What if it's stolen?" asked Sammy.

"Girl, there's nothing I can do to help you."

"But it's extremely valuable – in fact it's priceless."

The acting chief narrowed her eyes, menacingly. "Look, I'm sorry about your damned fiddle, but you should have been more careful. I gotta go," and she marched away purposefully.

"I'm really sorry," Jamaal echoed again. "I think our best bet is to talk with the people at the dance and see if anyone has seen it. I can't tell you how sorry I am."

Tuesday, September 25

Sammy awoke and decided to return to the Dalton's to see if she could learn anything that might help her find her fiddle. So she tacked up Jackson and rode him. She found Caroline in the garden, picking tomatoes. "Good morning, Caroline! Are you taking the day off from the nursing home?"

"Good morning Sammy! I've got some help this morning but I'll need to go in this afternoon and stay overnight. Have you come to help me can tomatoes today?"

"That's not why I've come, but I'll be happy to help you. It's about my violin." She explained the sequence of events that had transpired two evenings prior, but Caroline had no useful information or advice.

The two picked several bushels of tomatoes and schlepped them back to the house with the help of a plastic wheelbarrow.

Inside the kitchen, the wood stove was already warm with two large pots of water atop it. Caroline explained that one was for the sterilization of the cans, lids and rings, and the other was for loosening the tomato skins. She placed each tomato into the boiling water for 30 to 45 seconds, then removed them and placed them into cold water. Then the skins came off easily. She cut the tomatoes in quarters and cut out the central part around the stem. Then she placed the tomatoes into the sterilized jars and filled them almost to the top with boiling water and a tablespoon of lemon juice. Then she capped them with the lid and the rings and put them back into the large vat of water and left them in the boiling water for 45 minutes before removing the jars with a handy metal jar grabber.

Woody Dalton came inside for lunch to share the meal with his wife before she departed for the nursing home. Sammy joined them for the meal, explaining that she was preparing for a day of fasting for Yom Kippur, the Day of Atonement, which was to begin at sunset. "It is the most important holiday of the year. Jews fast from sundown the prior day until sunset the day of the holiday, which is tomorrow. With all that's gone on, I think the Lord may be having a closer look than usual. So I'm going to try to fast."

She rode Jackson home, un-tacked and brushed him down before turning him out to pasture. Hattie was working in the garden, so Sammy helped for a couple of hours until her strength gave out. Walking inside with two buckets of water, she found Quint home. So she told him about Yom Kippur and mentioned that she'd be fasting. He offered her the best of luck.

She threw more wood on the kitchen stove and heated the water for a bath. She carried the water upstairs to the bathroom. She removed her clothes and did a sponge-bath, using one bucket for the wash water and the other to rinse. It felt good, being clean. She put on a white nightgown that she found in the closet, thinking it to have belonged to one of the twins.

She longed for her violin, and found herself playing the "air-violin," fingering her left hand in vibrato on invisible strings and moving her right hand back and forth holding an invisible bow, silently playing Tchaikovsky's *Serenade Melancolique*. In her mind's eye she saw a grand concert hall and a sea of heads, lightly swaying to the familiar piece. Her fingers moved rapidly and effortlessly, producing sounds that only she herself could hear. Her eyes began to moisten, and they fell closed. A chill swept over her, beginning behind her upper arms and thighs, sweeping across her torso. She played on, seeing the invisible notes in her mind. She finished the piece with tears streaming down her cheeks. She dropped her arms to the side, took a deep breath, and fell into a deep sleep.

Wednesday, September 26

She awoke in a daze, wondering what would be appropriate for the observance. She knew Jews around the world were preparing for, or were already participating in, the rites of the holiday. She pictured black-robed, dreadlocked orthodox Jews praying at the Wailing Wall in Jerusalem, and convinced herself that without the Pulse striking them, their observance would be little different from any before it. She reminded herself that no eating or drinking was allowed. She also remembered that no work was to be done and no make-up or deodorants were allowed, but she had practically stopped using them anyway. Most important, she knew that most of the day was to be spent in the synagogue in prayer. But of course, there was no synagogue. There certainly was no synagogue in Providence – there were only a handful of churches. There was no synagogue in Fries or even Galax. So she found an old blanket and again walked to the banks of the New River, which was the most reverential place she could think of.

She descended steeply through thick woods and jumped a wooden fence. She found a flat spot on what seemed to be a flood-plain of the river, perhaps four feet above it vertically. There was a gentle set of ripples on the water and a small flock of mallard ducks bobbed on the surface. She sat, quietly, and watched whatever movement she could find. Crows cawed from a tree across the river, perhaps a football field length away. Occasionally, a fish jumped from the water. There was nobody in sight, but she could see a cemetery atop the bluff on the other side. There were mostly thick woods on both sides of the river, still mostly green but beginning to turn fall colors.

Her mind replayed many of the scenes of her childhood. She was happy for her childhood and thought it had been good, with many joyous occasions. She recalled some of the Hebrew she'd learned in anticipation of her bat mitzvah and murmured under her breath many of the prayers.

The scene struck her by its beauty, the loving bounty of nature. She removed her sandals and waded into the river up to her knees, feeling its chill on her skin. She stayed in the river until chills overcame her, and she scampered up the bank and returned to the blanket. The air was chilly, but the sun was bright and it reflected off the water in a dazzling shimmer.

She picked up two sticks, each about two feet long, and held them parallel to each other, envisioning them as the scroll handles of the holy Torah. But her eyes saw no parchment, only the river. Its movement and flow transfixed her, and she saw it as a living, breathing thing. It carried water in it, like an artery, carrying the blood of the planet, draining the land and returning the water to the sea. She envisioned her parents and their ice-water deaths in the North Atlantic and concluded that the impact of the airplane hitting the water would have killed them before they even got wet. She cried for them and hoped their souls rested in a heavenly place.

She thought about her transgressions, her trysts with Shane atop her list. She thought of the line, "those who trespass against us," and wondered about whoever had taken her violin. She couldn't imagine what good her violin would do for anyone else. It could never be sold without the buyer wondering how the seller might have obtained it. Would it end up in some second-hand store somewhere, someday? Would anybody else be able to know or appreciate its amazing quality and lineage?

She was surprised to feel elated about being so alone and at one with the earth. She realized that she had never before in her life spent a day totally alone; even the notion had always frightened her. But not on this day. She was terrified, but not frightened – terrified in a good way, emboldened.

Pangs of hunger swept from her gut. She pitched the two sticks into the river, one at a time, and watched them as they swept over the ripples, bobbing and weaving downstream to an unknown future.

She lay on her back on the blanket and let the sunshine warm her face. She fell into a deep sleep and dreamed of flowing liquids, of blood in veins, of water in streams of rain, and of electrons zooming along at the speed of light through endless strands of copper wire.

She awoke hours later, with hunger pangs strong and dizzying. She struggled self-consciously to her feet, thinking that perhaps she was being watched. A kingfisher darted noisily from across the river into a tree behind her and a huge blue heron waded in the shallows. How blissfully unaware were these creatures, she thought, to the turmoil sweeping her world!

The sun still hung stubbornly in the sky as she folded her blanket and walked steeply uphill towards her new home. She was weak with hunger and horribly thirsty, and her tongue sent taste signals to her brain of foods that weren't available to it. She reached the pasture and picked a yellow apple from the tree and gave it to Jackson, where he ate it lustily, oblivious to her hunger pains. "Good boy. You're my Jack-Jack," she said, feeling jealous of his innocence.

Returning to the house, she was surprised to see Hattie sitting on the front porch, knitting a shawl. "Hello Hattie."

The traumatized woman glanced at her briefly while not interrupting a single stitch. Her eyes then returned to their usual vacancy. Sammy sat in a chair beside her, where she had a clear view to the west, letting the sun's rays again bathe her face. The instant its last sliver dropped behind the blue mountains on the horizon, she ran inside and drank a huge glass of water. She ate a raw tomato and two carrots while she boiled water for two potatoes. She ate one herself and put the other on a plate and carried it to where Hattie had been knitting, but had since vanished. Being careful not to overeat, Sammy finished her meal and again washed herself, carrying warm water from the stove to the bathroom. She went upstairs and fell into a restful sleep.

Thursday, September 27

Sammy tacked up Jackson and strapped on her midwife's kit, angry that there was no violin case to counterbalance it, and rode to Carlene Bartlett's General Store in Providence. She carried four jars of canned peaches and six bags of dried apples to barter at the store. She carried a dozen Mason jar lids for currency. Her goal was to return with some tampons and some flour. Both were in short supply, but she was able to procure one box of tampons and a small bag of flour. She also bought a bag of corn meal that someone had traded in the prior day.

Pike was there, buying some canned meat and some potatoes. "How are you holding out, Sammy?"

"I'm fine. Yesterday was Yom Kippur, so I fasted all day. I'm strangely light-headed but re-energized. How are things with you?"

"Keeping the dynamo going at the Fries dam has been problematic. Right now, we're off-line. The exciter has been failing intermittently. Ih think the Pulse damaged the rectifier in it. Each time it fails, it shuts down the dynamo. The older style turbines have small permanent or 'latent' magnetism. They need an external power source to 'excite' the magnets. So it needs an exciter. Yesterday, it failed permanently, so we need a new one. They haven't been made for systems like that for over fifty years. It would be good to have backup rectifiers, too. Ih may be able to get one of the other turbines producing power as well."

"What are you going to do?"

"There are some engineering labs at Virginia Tech where Ih teach. The labs are used to teach the students about practical electricity generation. Ih think there are some old units in a closet. If they'll let me back on campus, Ih might be able to find them and bring them here and retrofit them for our system. Ih've decided to go there tomorrow and see what Ih can find. Ih also want to check on my dog. Ih left him under the care of a neighbor, intending to only be in Galax for a few days."

"If you find the equipment you need, how will you carry it back?"

"Ih talked with Jamaal earlier today; he is going with me. We're going to borrow Emily's horse and wagon. It's about sixty miles from here. Ih figure we can get there in two to three days. If Ih can find my dog, Ih'll bring him back here with us."

"Do you mind if I come, too?"

"It's going to be a long, hard journey. It might be dangerous, too. Are you sure you're up to it?"

"I don't know what I'm up to any more, but I'd still like to go. I'm good with horses and I know Maggie. I can take care of her."

"Do you need to ask Quint if you can go?"

"I'll tell him I'm going, but I don't think I need to ask permission."

"Fine by me. We'll leave Emily's house at 5:00 a.m."

"I don't have a working alarm clock."

"Ih don't either. Get there when you can and whenever we're ready, we'll depart."

Friday, September 28

The next morning, Sammy got out of bed before daybreak. She packed some food, her toothbrush, and a change of clothes, in a knapsack, all by the light of her *Forever-lite*. She decided not to take her midwife's kit, hoping she'd not need it. By the time she reached Emily's, Pike and Jamaal were finishing preparations to the horse and cart, all done by the light of an oil lamp. They had packed some food, some blankets, a tool belt, a Ruger handgun, and a tarp for their camps. They also filled a wooden box with cigarettes to use as currency for trade or safety.

As they departed to the east, a faint glow of the coming day greeted them. The sun crested the horizon as they reached the Fries trailhead of the New River Trail. Pike told them that The New River Trail was Virginia's longest state park, the state's second most visited, prior to the Pulse. It stretched over fifty miles from Pulaski to Fries, with a spur to Galax. The Trail was built on an abandoned railroad grade. He spoke of the history of Fries, retelling much of what Shane had told Sammy already, but added that the railroad link was indispensable to the development of the area. "The river and the cheap power it provided were essential to the operation of the mill in Fries. But the railroad brought raw cotton to it and shipped fabric away, so it was every bit as important." Once the mill closed, there was almost no business for the railroad, so they abandoned the grade. The state bought the right of way and all the bridges, which they converted to a recreational trail. Pike and Jamaal decided that walking the trail as far as Pulaski would be safer and easier on the horse and cart than walking on the paved roads. "I used to come to the trail all the time. I enjoy bicycling and this is a great place to ride. So I'm familiar with it."

The trail was mile-posted, so with Jamaal's pocket watch, they were able to mark their progress, doing about three miles per hour. They stopped at Byllesby Dam where several fishermen were trying to catch something to eat for dinner. Pike nosed around the dam to see the status of the generator there, but apparently everything mechanical had been removed entirely. He found much the same situation at the Buck Dam a couple miles later. Pike explained, "These dams were built about 100 years ago to provide some electricity and some flood control. In the last few decades, electricity from coal became so prevalent that they stopped maintaining these dams entirely. The Fries dam looks like one of the few left that still run, or can be made to run. We'll rue the day we removed the equipment to make power."

Jamaal shrugged, "I suspect folks are ruing the day today."

"True enough!" exclaimed Pike.

They continued through Ivanhoe and into Austinville, where Pike said there had been mining in the early 20th Century. "Lead deposits were found in the 1700s and were mined for decades. There are lots of other minerals here that were mined as well. But the ores aren't particularly rich. When better sources were found, the mines shut down, leaving an environmental mess with all the tailings." Sammy could see on both sides of the trail where expansive fields and piles of unusually colored soil harbored no plants or grasses, starkly contrasting the surrounding verdant fields and forests.

They passed another horse-drawn cart going the other way, and had to squeeze by, as the trail in most places was only wide enough for one cart. The driver and his family looked hungry but generally peaceful. Sammy thought about her grandfather's family perhaps fleeing the Nazis and wondered if their situation had been similar. There was a smell of burning wood and plastic several places along the way. It was eerily hellish.

At several places, they could see where former houses had stood but were now fire residue. Sammy wondered in horror what personal tragedies had befallen them. They rounded a bend to the right and a huge steel beam bridge loomed over the river and trail, held by immense pylons rising from the river and the valley. "That's Interstate 77 up there. Ih'm guessing both of you drove over that bridge last month on your way to Galax." Sammy remembered a bridge over the river, but the enormity never dawned on her the way it did from below. As they approached, they could see that it was in fact two parallel bridges. There were several tractor-trailers sitting immobile on each span, likely exactly where they stopped on that fateful Friday evening.

Just beyond the bridges, there was a stone tower on a bluff to their right. "That's another remnant of ancient engineering," Pike said. "That's called Shot Tower. It was built before the Civil War. It was used to make round bullets, first for the local settlers and then for the Confederate Army. It is 75 feet tall and there is a 75 foot shaft below the base. Lead from Austinville was brought here. It was melted in a kettle at the top of the tower and poured through a sieve that created weighted drops that fell down the tower. As they fell, they became uniformly spherical. When they plunged into a pool of water at the bottom, they solidified." There seemed to be nothing of salvage value, so looters had generally left it alone.

Three miles later, they reached Foster Falls, a recreation site. "Ih thought we might camp here, but we can press on and make a few more miles before sunset." So the trio kept going, passing sporadic settlements and walkers.

Their strength gave out in Allisonia, a tiny community of a dozen or so houses. Pike approached what looked like a former country store and found a family living there. He gave them a carton of cigarettes in exchange for a place to let Maggie graze and a place in the barn to sleep. The lady at the door who looked to be around 35 held a child in her arms. She opened the pack eagerly, stuck it in her mouth and lit it with a kitchen match. She blew the smoke away from the child "I haven't had a cig for a week." She took another deep drag, then coughed and said, "Lord, I miss my smokes." She looked at Jamaal and said to Pike, "I hope I can trust you to leave things as you found them."

"Yes, ma'am."

They entered the barn and found clean, dry hay on which to sleep. Before lying down, Sammy said, "I've been wondering about something."

"What's that?" replied Pike.

"I never heard about Electromagnetic Pulse until last month."

"Not many other people had, either," Pike reassured her.

"Did nobody know what it was or how to prevent it?"

"Lots of scientists knew what it was. There is no way to prevent it. It's like preventing an earthquake or a hurricane. Modern science doesn't know how to prevent these things. But we do know how to mitigate the damage."

"What you mean?" she asked.

"Let's look at Hurricane Katrina that struck the Gulf Coast a few years ago and nearly wiped New Orleans off the map. Hurricane Katrina was a predictable event…"

"Worse than that," said Jamaal. "It was a *predicted* event!"

"True enough, brother Jamaal! Hallelujah! Tell it true! All kidding aside, Jamaal is right. Lots of people predicted that a major hurricane could strike the area and in fact it was inevitable. What caused so much damage was that the levees protecting the city were not sufficient to withstand the huge flow of water and when they failed, water flooded the city."

"So if people knew it was coming, why didn't they do more?" Sammy implored.

"Pike, do you mind if I tackle that one?"

"Not at all."

"Thanks Brother Pike! Okay, let's talk about how things work in this country right now. In corner number one, we have the people. That's you and me and everybody else. In corner number two, we have the government, or in fact several governments: Federal, state, and local. In corner number three, we have the corporations. And in corner number four, we have the natural world. Each has its own characteristics and motivations. Where do you want to start?"

"Let's start with the natural world," said Sammy, thinking about elephants roaming the savannah and wild horses running across the steppes.

"Great! Okay, nature. Nature doesn't give a shit, if you'll pardon my blue language. The universe is populated by intensely inhospitable places and life is thought to be rare because of it. Venus is thought to be as close to hell as imaginable. It's hundreds of degrees hot and covered with caustic gasses. Mars is freezing cold. Other planets have no atmosphere or are freezing or both. Earth is the Goldilocks of planets; it's just right. There may be other Goldilocks planets in other solar systems, but none that we're aware of yet. As far as we know, life only exists on earth."

Pike interjected, "It would be the most important event in history if we ever learned conclusively that life existed anywhere else."

"True. Nevertheless, the earth isn't perfect for life. There are places that are too hot or dry or cold to support much of anything. But the sweet spot is almost universal; there's life just about everywhere on earth, and once it gets going, life adapts adroitly."

Pike chimed in, "And nobody knows where the spark of life came from. Religious people think it came from God. Scientific people think it happened spontaneously. But nobody was around then, so it is a question that will always go unanswered."

Pike stuck a piece of straw in his mouth to chew on, then continued, "Although the earth is a wonderful place for life, it can still throw hurricanes, earthquakes, tornadoes, volcanoes, and all sorts of mischief at us. Some of it is predictable and some not. And some is thrown at us from space. The dinosaurs had a long tenure on earth, something like 160 million years. But when an asteroid struck about 65 million years ago off the north coast of Mexico's Yucatan Peninsula, they were toast. This baby was thought to have unleashed an explosive force 5 million times greater than the Krakatoa volcano. The dust cloud obliterated incoming sunlight for centuries, plunging the earth into an ice age that killed the dinosaurs and along with most of their prey."

"Wow!" Sammy's left eyebrow lifted.

"Wow is right! Serious stuff. If an asteroid like this was coming this way, it would surely obliterate all the humans. Thankfully, impacts this size are exceedingly rare.

"Now then, the Pulse that hit last month was known about in advance, Ih'm sure, by some scientists a few hours before it hit. Did one of them tell our government or our president? If so, could anything be done with only hours notice? Ih'm not sure we'll ever know the real answer. Suppose you were the president and your national security team called you and said, 'We have a potential emergency, an Electromagnetic Pulse that we think is headed to the earth and *may* arrive at a certain time within the next few hours, and *may* strike the United States, or not. And because we haven't acted to protect the grid already, we think you should shut down the entire national grid right away to protect it so that if the Pulse strikes, we can fire it back up right away.' And of course, you know that shutting it off, even for a few hours, will kill hundreds of thousands, perhaps millions of people. What would you do? A better plan would have been to spend some money to better protect the grid to have prevented the widespread damage in the first place."

Sammy said, "You know, Avalon Parker is a friend of mine. She said that her husband hardened their solar electrical system to shield for this."

Pike said, "Avalon. Gorgeous woman. Yes, Ih read that the power grid of the nation could have been protected by the expenditure of as little as $5 per household."

"So why didn't that happen?" Sammy asked, eagerly.

"Jamaal?" Pike asked, passing the expository torch back to the economics professor.

Jamaal resumed, "That brings me in our countdown to corner number three: the corporations. Unlike nature, corporations are a human construct, and therefore are sentient, although not always wise. Corporations see the other groups distinctly, but they also see subsets within the people. They see the people as five groups: shareholders, managers, employees, customers, and everybody else. Their imperative is profit; without it they cannot sustain. So they care about each group, and nature, only insofar as they are necessary to achieve a profit. I'll come back to them in a moment.

"In corner number two, we have governments. Whom the governments serve is in the eye of the beholder, but ostensibly they exist to serve the people. The degree to which they do that is dependent upon the morals, values, and integrity of the elected officials and employees.

"In corner number one, we have us, the people. The people are motivated to live healthy, productive, safe lives and enjoy prosperity and the esteem that comes from others."

"I'm trying to see where you're going with this," Sammy admitted.

"Let's look at the current situation. The electrical grid has been called the largest and most complex structure ever constructed by man. It has proven itself to be extraordinarily reliable. But all engineered things inevitably have problems and none of them lasts forever. The grid has been pieced together over the last several decades from hundreds…"

"Thousands…" interrupted the electrical engineering professor, obviously knowing where the economist was going.

"…Yes, thousands of small, independent electric companies, utilities, and cooperatives. The grid works because one company's electricity, given the same watts, volts, and cycles, is the same as another's. The merging of railroads, for example, wasn't quite as smooth because some locomotives ran on different track widths than others and that needed to be synchronized in order for railroads to merge.

"Now then, the degree to which any particular electrical utility engineered and protected their investments were dictated by their corporate cultures and consciences and the profit imperative. Some, obviously, do a better job than others."

He widened his eyes for emphasis, and then continued. "So, whose job is it to protect the grid? Nature isn't going to protect the grid, because for one, it doesn't give a shit, and two, it is the source of the problem anyway. The people aren't going to protect the grid, because individually they have no structure to do so, although the cost will ultimately be passed to them, as all costs are. So it falls to either the government or the corporations.

"The dynamic looks like this. In this country, we have two competing political parties, the Republicans and the Democrats. What we have now, post Pulse, is yet to be fully known, but that's not the issue for now. Republicans fear that the government has too much control over corporations and those corporations will do the right thing if the government gets out of the way. Democrats are afraid the corporations have too much control over the government and will destroy everything unless the government restrains them."

"Now I see where this is going," said Sammy.

"Tell me, child," Jamaal said, paternally.

"The corporations don't protect the grid because there's no money to be made in it and no return to their owners. And the government won't force them to protect the grid because people think the government has too much power already."

"Wow. Good going!" Jamaal complimented her.

"Yeah, wow," agreed Pike. "So we have an unprecedented national calamity on our hands that could have been drastically mitigated by charging each household $5.00."

"To be fair," Jamaal suggested, "There are lots of other risks out there all the time. We can't protect against all of them."

"Like what?" asked the student amongst professors.

"May Ih?" Pike said, taking the virtual podium. "Most of California, in fact almost all of the populated areas of California, is underlain by unstable geologic plates. So there are always earthquakes happening. Some are insignificant and some are catastrophic. Protecting every building, road, house, and life, can't be done. California is our most populous state. So we as a society decide what risks we're willing to accept.

"Here's another example. There are thousands of pricy homes, piers, and hotels on the Atlantic and Gulf Coasts. From Texas to Maine, these places are in the bull's eye of Atlantic hurricanes. People who own, and in some cases live, in these houses play Russian roulette every year. But people like being near the ocean. Whose job is it to tell them they can't?

"But understand that not making a decision is making a decision, too. Part of the problem is that we can enter a situation with innocence and then learn more about risks but be immobilized by our inability to accept our newfound knowledge about the risk. Hindsight always gives us better answers. So we muddle along, protecting ourselves or not, based upon our perception of the risk."

"You make it sound like corporations are the villains here," Sammy concluded.

"They're only doing what they're supposed to do," said Pike, "and that's to protect their shareholders. They protect their workers or the environment either because not doing so may cost them way more money than doing so or because the government forces them. BP was lax a few years ago in their work in the Gulf of Mexico, allowing the opportunity for the oil spill to happen. In retrospect, Ih'm sure they would have done more to prevent it, but primarily because the clean-up cost way more than the prevention would have cost. They would have needed extraordinarily enlightened leadership to have done it out of the goodness of their hearts."

"My dad works for a corporation."

"That's right!" said Jamaal. "He works for Goldman, doesn't he?"

"Yes."

"Pardon me for being so blunt, my child, but they're the worst of the worst. I've been studying economics for two decades and from what I can tell, they've been behind every meltdown since the Great Depression."

"Really? How?" Sammy asked, defensively.

"They manipulate laws on the creation of money and credit to their benefit. They wield enormous power over the financial system. Do you remember what I talked about at Carlene's store when we set up the scrip system using jar lids?"

"Yes. You said that centuries ago, people only traded in barter or then in some type of scrip. They mined precious metals and minted coins. Now we trade in dollars, or at least we did until the Pulse."

"Good," Jamaal said. "But remember, most of our money not only doesn't have a tangible backing like precious metals, it doesn't really exist in any tangible currency – coins or paper – at all. It is all numbers on computers. So a century ago, the Federal Treasury, which is a part of the Federal Government, gave itself the only national power to create currency, which it did through the Federal mints and printing offices. Now, most of what we think of as money isn't created at all. Now, 'credit' is created. 'Money' is really credit and it is created out of thin air by the Federal Reserve.

"What your dad's company has been doing for decades is manipulating credit and the costs of various investments by buying or selling huge amounts themselves, then profiting on both the rise and the crash. We've seen several market crashes in recent years, the tech stock crash, the gasoline price crash, and the housing crash among others. Each time, Goldman has manipulated prices to their advantage and made a killing."

Sammy reflected, "You know, I've overheard dad talk on the phone with co-workers many times before. Now that I think about it, he's never spoken about the benefit of his clients. It's always about how Goldman can make the most money."

Jamaal said, "Money's right! The average pay for their employees last year was almost $400,000. That's probably as much as fifteen or more of the residents of Providence make combined."

"I suspect my dad isn't an average employee, either," Sammy admitted ruefully. "So if most of the money in the world isn't really money but instead numbers running through computers, and if the Pulse has ruined all of the computers, then what will become of all the money?"

Pike said, "The rest of the world besides the East Coast of the United States is still probably largely functional. But we're now living in a new national economy. You're asking questions – good questions – that Ih suspect nobody really has any answers for. Am Ih right Professor Winston?"

"I surely have no better answer. It's something we can all have nightmares about tonight."

"I've had too many of those lately. I'm going to try to have sweet dreams," Sammy decided. "Goodnight, guys."

"Goodnight, Sammy. It's good having you along."

Saturday, September 29

The trio got an early start the next morning, quickly reaching the long steel bridge over the New River at Hiwassee. The wooden railing was barely two inches wider than the cart, so Pike and Jamaal decided it was necessary to unhitch Maggie and navigate the cart over the bridge themselves. Sammy took Maggie across, and then returned to help the men. On the gentle ascent into Draper, they saw the first bicyclist riding the trail, his panniers looking to be loaded with fruit. In Draper, they left the trail. "We'll be on pavement the rest of the way," said Pike. Green signs said, "Old Wilderness Road," which Pike said was the original settlers' path that brought primarily German and Scots-Irish into the area from Philadelphia from the late 1600s until Revolutionary War days.

They stopped in Newburn where Pike exchanged two cigarette packs to a man sitting on his front porch for some bread and cheese. Across the way to the north they saw where a huge forest fire had consumed much of the southern slope of Draper Mountain. When they asked the man about it, he said a jetliner had crashed there when the Pulse struck. The airliner burst into flames which consumed everything in it, plus the surrounding forest.

They continued into Dublin, passing by several cars disabled on the road. Dublin was the largest town so far. There was evidence of strife all around them. The Wades Grocery Store in town had windows broken out and the shelves were completely looted. Cars in a parking lot were also looted, most with broken windows. Several people eyed the travelers warily as they passed, but nobody threatened them.

Pike had hoped to reach the outskirts of Blacksburg, but their strength and the day's sunlight gave out beyond Fairlawn. In sight of the New River Bridge, they paid a farmer in cigarettes to allow them access to the barn and pasture.

It began to rain heavily and lightning splayed flashes of light across the dark sky. As they were setting up a place to camp in the barn, the farmer invited them inside and gave them a sofa and cushions to sleep on in his living room. The farmer admitted about the cigarettes Pike gave him, "My first wife was a two-pack a day smoker and died at 53 from lung cancer. A person will do just about anything for a smoke if she's addicted. I wouldn't touch these things for anything, but I can use them for trade."

Before falling asleep, Sammy was again curious about the Pulse and asked why it was so damaging.

Pike said, "The grid was a huge antenna for the Pulse. The grid is engineered to be efficient at conducting electricity. When the Pulse hit it, the energy was able to travel on the wires to the place it could do the most damage. That was the transformers. Transformers increase the voltage in order for it to travel long distances through the lines, and then others decrease it so it can be used locally. Many lines carry voltages of 765,000 volts. Volts are like water pressure in a hose. The more pressure, the better the water flows. Amps are units of volume, meaning in our analogy, the amount of water. Volts times amps equal watts. So a transformer can increase the voltage and decrease the amperage with the same watts, then reverse it at the other end so consumers can use it. Nobody has a toaster that can handle 765,000 volts.

"Anyway, the long lines sent the energy of the Pulse to the transformers, which overwhelmed and destroyed them."

Jamaal, this time the student, asked, "Why hasn't this happened before? I'm sure solar flares are common."

Pike pushed his glasses higher on his nose. "Ih wouldn't call them common, but not unheard of, either. Scientists warned us that this year we'd see an increase in solar activity. But apparently nobody in charge was moved to do anything.

"Do you remember the first meeting we had in Fries when Ih talked about prior Pulses? Ih mentioned that there was a strong one in 1859 and a weaker one in 1921, just as the power grid was being developed. The industry has been building a false sense of security and had gotten complacent. Consumers have been stressing the grid with higher loads. It's been good for profit but we've failed to make the safety measures needed to prevent the damage we've now seen. The transformers could have been protected with surge protectors. But we didn't. And now we suffer the consequences.

"Like Jamaal said last night, nature doesn't care. If we don't protect ourselves, we have nobody to blame but ourselves."

Sunday, September 30

In a steady rain, they descended to the highway bridge again over the New River where a man had set up a roadblock. He demanded a pack of cigarettes before he would let them pass. "By what authority do you charge tolls on this public bridge?" Pike demanded.

The man patted his maroon jacket with a "VT" logo, and then opened it to reveal a sawed-off double-barrel shotgun. "By the authority of Bessie, here," he said. Rather than risking an angrier confrontation, Pike handed him the booty. "Next time I see you, it might cost you three packs," the man laughed, rainwater dripping from the brim of his hat. Another bridge, under construction, sat parallel to the first. Cranes and dump trucks stood abandoned as if the workers had simply walked away, which Sammy was sure had been the case.

The tired trio finally reached their immediate destination near Prices Fork at Pike's home off Brooksfield Road. The farmer's market and its extensive garden had been extensively looted. There was a horse carcass lying in the ditch beside the road, partially picked over by scavengers. Pike's house was intact, but the front door was swinging open and there were no animals in sight. Inside, his computer and musical instruments were gone and his television was smashed. The refrigerator was open and there was nothing inside except a box of baking soda. The cupboards were filled with dishes, but the pantry was empty of food. Fighting back tears, he said, "Let's go next door and see if my dog is there."

The three walked 100 yards towards a neighbor's house, but they saw that it was a still-smoldering ruin. Nobody was around. There were a few pumpkins in the garden, but precious little else.

Pike's eyes became misty as Jamaal put his arm on his shoulder. Stoically, Pike said, "Well, we'd best get to the work we came for." They headed to Blacksburg.

The threesome returned to Prices Fork and stopped at Smitty's General Store, where several old men in bib overalls sat outside. Sammy envisioned that these same men were doing much the same thing they'd done before the calamity. Pike recognized one of them. "Wayne, what's happened here?"

"Where ya been, perfesser?"

"Down in Galax. Ih got stuck there when the power failed."

"Oh, it's been plum awful here. Blacksburg was pretty able to keep the peace until a band of hoodlums came up from Roanoke last week. They robbed the whole town. Once the town was empty, folks came out here to find whatever they could. Us locals ain't been too hospitable towards them. Old man Roberts and his boy caught a boy in the chicken coop. They tied him up and marched him here. They strung him up over that tree limb over at the Grange," he pointed across the street. A boy's body was still hanging limp from ropes. Sammy gulped with horror. "Folks are talking like they'll leave him there for a few days until the vultures find them, so as a message to anybody else who has ideas about messing with Prices Fork."

Pike asked about his dog and the people who kept them, but Wayne didn't have any information. One of the other men said he thought there had been a family feud, but nobody knew for sure. Pike's dog was definitely nowhere to be found. Wayne expressed his regrets, saying, "Sad about your dog, perfesser. But these days, folks have bigger fish to fry."

Pike buried his eyes into his hands and Sammy could see him crying. "Let's go," he said.

The troika continued the few miles into Blacksburg, crossing the overpass of highway US-460 and into the University Village shopping area. The shopping center was completely looted and the bakery had been burned almost to the ground. The two-story hotel was guarded by several armed men, but still several windows were broken and glass was everywhere.

They continued towards the main campus, a sprawling collection of Gothic stone buildings. They were met by another armed man, wearing a State Police uniform. Pike explained their business, but they were denied entrance. The Trooper said, "We're not allowed to let anybody on the campus."

"But Ih'm a professor here," Pike insisted.

The Trooper looked at him suspiciously. "I don't care if you're the president of the university. Orders is orders."

As they retreated, Pike said, "No luck here. Ih don't think trying to bribe him would be fruitful, either. Let's get out of here."

They walked towards the Duck Pond and to Smithfield towards the plantation house that was a museum of pioneer life. Several people, refugees from nearby apartment complexes, had taken up residence there. Pike bought safe access to reconnoiter on the property with another package of cigarettes. While Sammy gave Maggie water and left her to graze, Pike quickly shared a plan he'd hatched. "Steam tunnels," he announced.

He explained to his partners that most of the campus was underlain with access utility tunnels. "They were built decades ago to funnel steam from the central power plant to heat all the buildings. Since then, they have been used for water, sewerage, electrical conduit, and all the things the campus buildings need. Almost every large university has a similar system."

"How do you know about them?" Sammy asked.

"The tunnels are the worst kept secret on campus. Every freshman learns about them within the first few weeks of their arrival – at least the men do. Lots of them see exploration of the tunnels as a prank, as a freshman rite of passage. Ih think that's our only way in."

"So we're going to break in?" said Sammy incredulously.

"We're not going to break anything; at least Ih hope we're not. But Ih didn't spend three days walking here to return to Fries with nothing."

So the plan was hatched and the time was set, just after sunset. Jamaal would stay with Maggie some distance from the entrance. Sammy would walk with Pike to the entrance and wait there. Pike would go inside alone. Pike said, "Last night we had a full moon. Tonight the moon will rise about an hour later. It will be bright enough to see someone a hundred yards away. Ih need to get in, get the stuff, get out, and get away, in an hour." The equipment they needed was in DeJarnett Engineering Hall, several hundred yards from Pike's planned entrance near the Duck Pond.

The triumvirate got some rest and ate some of their remaining food in preparation for their planned thievery. As the sun set, they sprang to action. They rode the wagon to within 100 yards of the duck pond. Pike strapped on a tool belt he'd brought and Sammy gave him her trusty *Forever-lite*. They found the entrance within a copse of trees. They encountered their first glitch as they arrived, as the entrance was barely large enough for Pike. Thinking later entrances might be even smaller, Sammy begged Pike to let her go inside as well. So Pike gave Sammy back her flashlight and they entered the dark underground void together.

"Count your steps, Sammy," Pike implored. "Figure 150 steps per hundred yards. We need to go 150 yards to where we hit the main corridor." Sammy went first, her flashlight punching a hole in the darkness. They were in a round tube with a grating holding them 6" from the floor. Pike had to walk in a stoop. They reached the main corridor, with a taller ceiling. Again, there was a grating below but now electrical conduit strung overhead. They turned left and walked another 200 yards. A skunk appeared in the darkness and sent a spray towards them, it falling a few feet short. But the tunnel stunk so badly it burned Sammy's nostrils and brought tears to her eyes. She turned to see Pike crying as well.

Fortuitously, they noticed that the names of the various buildings were now stenciled on the wall. They passed signs for Ellzy Hall, where Architecture was taught, and Caldwell Hall where Chemistry was taught. Finally, they found a stencil marker for DeJarnett Hall, and they turned left into a smaller passageway. They saw several ducts overhead. Pike climbed six steps up the fixed ladder and found a grating which he smashed out with his forearm, but the opening was too small for him to pass through. He descended and said, "Sammy, here's where you become our hero." He gave her detailed directions as to where to go and what to look for. "One of the devices you're looking for weighs perhaps 40 pounds. You'll need to lug it to the duct by yourself and I can carry it out from there. The other one is only about 10 pounds. Can you do that?"

"Looks like I'll have to." He handed her his tool belt and she ascended the ladder, easily slipping through the duct where she stood upright in the pitch-dark hallway.

"Good luck!"

She walked quickly down the corridor and saw several room markers. The one she was looking for was "Electrical Power Lab" which she found with a locked door. She used the screwdriver to pry open the door. There was a metal cage with several pieces of equipment inside. The smaller device, the rectifier, was just as Pike had described it. She quickly carted it back to the waiting accomplice. She got a fuller description about the exciter, and returned to look more carefully. She found it under a cardboard box. She strained to pick it up and then carried it back to the duct. She handed it to Pike. Then she scurried through and they began their escape.

Pike carried the exciter and Sammy carried the smaller regulator, walking ahead. Two rats ran along the grating in front of her and detoured towards the Chemistry building. Sammy recoiled at their sight, picturing a diabolical vision of mega-rats on mysterious chemicals.

Pike and Sammy finally reached the entrance and re-emerged from underground. They walked back to the wagon and joined Jamaal.

"Where the hell do you think you're going?" said a uniformed Virginia Tech policeman who had emerged from the darkness. He shone a dim flashlight towards them. "What have you got there?"

"Oh," said Pike, "we're just borrowing some equipment for an experiment I'm doing. Say, is that you Morris?"

"Who are you?"

"It's your neighbor, Pike McConnell."

"Professor McConnell, what are you doing here?"

Pike explained the situation in Fries and why they had walked all the way there. "Please Morris, this is really important to our community. People are dying and we might be able to save some lives getting the dam working again."

"Maybe, but people are dying here in Blacksburg, too. Won't that thing help here?"

"No. There is no dam here. It's not doing anybody any good now. Let us go save some lives. Ih swear to God, Ih'll bring this back as soon as the power gets restored."

"If it ever does!" the officer said.

"Maybe it won't," said Jamaal, "but if it doesn't, this thing still won't do anybody any good here."

"Well, go on then, get the hell out of here. If anybody finds out I've let you escape, they'll execute me by firing squad." He turned off his light and vanished into the night.

They loaded and secured the devices and immediately began their trip westward back to Fries. As they reached Prices Fork Road, a brilliant near-full moon rose over Paris Mountain to the east.

Part 3: October

Monday, October 1

SAMMY'S EYES AWOKE SCRATCHY and disoriented, as her olfactory processed the familiar and pleasant odor of hay. She got up and looked around. Maggie was in a stall nearby, munching happily on some grain. Maggie unloaded a pile of manure, and Sammy instinctively looked for a mucking rake. Only then did she think to try to place herself, discovering that she was staying in the barn of the farmer where they had stayed the night before. She scooped up the droppings and carried the load to a manure pile outside the barn. She replaced the rake and walked to the farmhouse nearby. She passed Emily's wagon, parked with a canvas drape over what she knew to be the exciter she'd helped steal the day before.

She saw an outhouse and used it before walking inside to find Pike and Jamaal eating eggs and bacon for breakfast. A plump woman with an apron tied around her was working on a woodstove. The farmer who they'd met the day before walked inside. He looked at her and smiled. "Good morning, young lady."

Trying to remember her manners, she said, "I remember you from a couple of days ago, but I don't remember if I ever caught your name. Mine's Sammy – Samantha."

"You've got quite the accent on you, sweetheart," said the man. "I'm Leo Wilkerson and this is my second wife, Cecelia. Cece was helping our daughter in Radford the other day when you came through."

Cecelia said, "I'm sorry I missed you. Getting anything done these days is such a bother."

"Yes, ma'am," said Jamaal.

"Come have a bite to eat, sweetie," said the woman. "Leo's been telling your friend about the happenings here."

"Let me start over," he said. The man named Leo told Pike, Jamaal, and Sammy that he worked at Virginia Tech in the department

218

of Agricultural Extension. He spent most of his time on the road. When the Pulse struck, fortuitously he was at home. As the crisis unfolded, he brought his knowledge closer to home, setting up a co-operative in Dublin similar to Carlene's Store in Providence.

He said there had been a riot in Radford, only a few miles away. Radford was just downstream of the Claytor Lake dam, the largest hydroelectric facility on the entire New River corridor. State police had come to town in an old school bus and had instructed the utility workers to route the power to a nuclear plant in Central Virginia to keep the reactor fuel from melting. Radford had commandeered the power for their city since the Pulse. Some of the technicians refused to cooperate with the police. When the troopers arrested some of them, a melee broke out. Thirty people were killed and another 120 were hurt. Order had been restored, but it was tenuous. "Nobody is safe around here."

So they departed quickly and walked back westward towards Dublin, retracing their previous journey. It rained much of the day. One of the wheels on the wagon was scraping on its axle, generating excess friction and slowing their progress. They joined the New River Trail in Draper and decided to camp nearby, trying to remain out of sight. They draped the canvas tarp from the wagon to a tree, making a lean-to and keeping some of the overnight rain off them. Sammy slept uneasily, worried about being found and hassled.

Tuesday, October 2

The next morning, Sammy, Pike, and Jamaal assessed their situation. It was still raining, but they and their gear had stayed mostly dry overnight. Before taking down the tarpaulin, they ate some food and stashed their blankets in some plastic bags. They continued their journey westward.

Retracing their path, they again had to disconnect the horse and drag their wagon over the trestle bridge at Hiwassee. Because of the problems with the wheel on the wagon, going was slower and they were only able to walk about 15 miles before sunset. Happily, the rain had stopped and the sky became clearer. They camped in a field at the edge of a beautiful, stately forest of hardwood trees near the village of Ivanhoe.

Wednesday, October 3

Knowing that their destination was now only 12 miles further, they were eager to get started. However, they had only gone two miles before the left-rear wheel fell off the wagon. Maggie was spooked and nearly dragged the wagon into a ditch before Sammy, who was driving, was able regain control. Everyone was shaken by the accident and Sammy felt an adrenaline rush.

The three of them worked feverishly to get the wagon back onto the trail. Pike had rigged up a fulcrum beam from a small log he found in the woods to elevate the rear of the wagon to reattach the wheel. The three of them were intently focused on the work when they heard a click behind them that Sammy instantly recognized as cocking of a gun.

"Well, well, well, what have we here?" exclaimed a disheveled, 60-ish man who pointed a pistol at Jamaal. He wore bib overalls, a flannel shirt, and a dirty brown stocking cap. Two other men were standing beside him, one pointing a rifle at Pike and one holding the handle of a handgun still in its holster at his waist. The two other men were younger but equally dirty and untidy. One of them had long, brown hair that had clearly not been washed in weeks. The other had jet black hair and looked Hispanic. Sammy thought he looked familiar but she could not place him.

"What do you want from us?" asked Pike.

"What have you got?" asked the long-haired younger man, sarcastically.

"You need to leave us alone," said Jamaal, in an authoritative voice.

The older one fixed the site of his gun on Jamaal's face and said,

"Shut up, nigger. We are calling the shots here."

The younger man said, "What have you got in the wagon?"

When nobody moved or attempted to answer, he said, "I think I will have a look for myself. Carlos, dammit, pull out your gun and show these people the business end while I check to see what they are carrying." The black haired man did as he was told.

"Let's see here," the long-haired man said, rooting through the luggage on the wagon. "Jackpot! Cigarettes, baby! Lots of cigarettes. Oh, here's a handgun. What is this motor thing?"

"It is part of a dynamo," Pike said. "It is needed in Fries to get electricity flowing again from the dam."

"Well it looks like the good people in Fries are going to need to wait just a bit longer," said the old man. Spittle dripped from the side of his mouth and landed on his beard. He spit a dark wad of juice onto the trail. "And what about you, young lady?" he glowered towards Sammy. The stench of chewing tobacco wafted from his mouth.

"I am just here to help out," Sammy said.

"Well ain't that just righteous of you? And what's with the god-damn Yankee accent?" He reached over and fondled her left breast, from which she recoiled, slapping his hand away.

"Stop that!" she screamed.

"Shut up, girl," he slapped her.

"Leave her alone," yelled Jamaal, lunging at the older man. A bullet flashed in front of his head, fired from the rifle of the man on the wagon, causing Jamaal to quickly recoil. The echo resonated through the valley.

"Back off!" yelled the older man.

The long-haired man, returned to pulling cartons of cigarettes and food from their stash. He shoved them into a knapsack he was carrying.

"What do we do now?" said the quiet, dark-haired, younger man.

The older man, clearly the ringleader, said, "Freddy, pack up the food and cigarettes. Take the gun. I'm going to take this little lady with us. I think she might come in handy," he sneered.

Sammy could see Jamaal seething. She knew he could kill the man with his hands if there weren't guns around. The man pointed his gun directly at Sammy's head and said to Jamaal and Pike, "You two lie on the ground, on your stomach, and put your hands behind your back." Jamaal and Pike did as they were told. The man reached inside his shirt pocket and pulled out several red plastic zip ties. He used one on Jamaal's hands, lashing his wrists together. He crossed Jamaal's legs and he used another zip tie to lash his ankles together. Then he did the same thing to Pike.

He grabbed Sammy and zip tied her hands together behind her back. He took his handkerchief from his back pocket and blindfolded her. "Let's get out of here, fellers."

Sammy felt a hand grab the shirt she was wearing behind her left shoulder and push her forward. They began walking. She could feel the cinders of the trail below her feet. She tried her best to estimate in her mind how much time was elapsing as she walked. For what seemed like 20 or 30 minutes, they remained on the trail, but then she was turned to the right and she felt herself walking sharply downhill through a gully and then back up the other side. Her shoes became wet in the water she could hear trickling beneath her feet. She stumbled and fell, slamming her left cheek against a rock. She screamed with pain. She could feel blood reaching the already malodorous handkerchief. "Damn it, girl. Get up," she heard one of them say, helping her to her feet.

Through her tears, she said, "Listen, I have no idea what you are planning for me, but I know I can't keep up if I can't see where I'm going."

She heard the Hispanic man chuckle. The older man reached behind her head and ripped off his handkerchief. He undid the knot and stuffed it back in his pocket. "Git yourself going, then."

They walked for perhaps an hour beside a gently flowing stream in deep woods. At various times, they appeared to be on an abandoned road grade. At other times, they literally were walking in the stream.

Sammy tried to memorize every aspect of what she saw. The

woods were too dense for her to get a clear view of the sky, but she deduced from the shadows that they were marching westward. She knew that Fries was to the south, meaning to her left. Her cheek continued to throb and drip blood, which she could feel congealing on her face.

Late in the day, the older man said, "I think we better stop here for the night. Let's set up camp."

Sammy took a close look at the surroundings. To her west, where the sun was setting, was a rock outcropping, perhaps 50 yards away. The stream was flowing eastward, back towards the river. There was a steep mountain to the south and a gentler one to the north.

The men sat her on a fallen wall log. Her hands were still tied behind her. The ringleader pulled out some food to eat, some bread, fruit, and carrots. The dark-haired Hispanic man held a carrot in front of her mouth for her to eat it. "Please," she implored, "untie my hands so I can eat."

The older man pulled a switchblade from his pocket and he popped open the blade, twisting it back and forth in front of her. He smiled, showing a mouthful of rotted teeth. "Fine!" He walked behind her and slit the zip tie. He gathered her hands in front of her and using another tie strapped them together again. "That should do for you. Now quit your belly-achin'."

She transferred the bread and carrot to her mouth, both hands moving together. When she was finished, the older man blindfolded her again and tied her feet together at the ankles. She could hear the three of them move somewhat away from her, but the stream was making just enough noise to drown out their conversation. She had nothing to do but sit. Her back began to ache and her cheek still hurt badly.

As she could sense the light fading even through her blindfold, the men returned. The older man said, "Find her a place to bed down."

She said, "I need to pee."

"Dammit!"

"What did you expect?" asked the long-haired man. "Nobody can hold it forever."

"Carlos, take her into the woods and let her pee. Keep your eyes on her."

"I am not going to watch a girl pee." He pulled a small pocket knife from his pocket and slit the zip tie at her feet. He marched with her into the woods. They reached a point out of sight from the others. He said, "Okay girl, do your business." She held up her hands, still tied together, and said, "How am I going to drop my pants with these things on?" She looked at him again and finally recognized him. He had played harmonica at one of the first Fries jam sessions she'd attended.

"I guess you have a point," he said, slitting the tie. "I'm going to sit over there. I am not going to watch but don't try to get away."

She lowered her pants and her panties and she peed. She pulled her pants up, and then she walked towards him. "Okay, I'm done."

He took another zip tie from his pocket and tied her wrists back together, this time in front. He led her back to the camp and sat her down where she had been before. He pushed a pile of leaves together and motioned her to lie down on it. He removed her wet shoes and put them beside her.

"Zip her up good," said the older man.

The younger man held her ankles, and then crossed them. He took another zip tie out of his pocket and looked her in the eye, sympathetically. He zipped the tie, but only around her left ankle rather than both. Realizing the favor he'd done for her, she closed her eyes and tried to get a quick nap. She knew the moon would be rising around 10:00 p.m. and she wanted to escape before then, lest her abductors tried to follow.

Thursday, October 4

Sammy awoke to the thunderous snores of the older man. She grabbed her shoes and she sat upright, and looked around. Between his cacophony and the gurgling of the stream, she prayed she could get away without being heard. She had tried to memorize the area around her, but it was almost completely dark, and as she walked in her socks, a twig snapped. She thought she could see the man named Carlos raise his head slightly.

She began walking away, brushing into a branch that slapped her sore left cheek, and she fought the urge to cry out. She walked about 50 yards and then she stopped and put on her shoes. They were cold and uncomfortable on her feet, but they were better than walking only in her socks.

Although she reckoned her ultimate destination was to the south, she decided it would be deceptive to her captors if they chose to chase her to move north and then west as soon as she could get her bearings. She climbed steadily upward to the woods. She crested a rise, and then descended to the other side where she walked for several hundred yards in a flowing creek, hoping the water would mask her footprints. Eventually, she reached a small clearing and she could see the dim light of the moon rise on the eastern horizon. As she walked across the clearing, the moon rose and her shadow became distinct.

The zip tie was still binding her wrists together. She found a table-size rock with a sharp edge. She began rubbing the zip tie back and forth across it. After several minutes she could feel the plastic band begin to weaken and she yanked her hands free.

The area was deeply wooded, without habitations. When she was convinced that she was not being followed, she took a nap in some tall grass.

She awoke to a rising sun in a sky of brilliant orange and yellow. She came to the edge of a deserted paved highway. She thought first about walking on it and was sure that the highway led to Fries, to her left, south. She walked the highway in that direction for a couple of miles but she began to feel exposed and vulnerable. So she diverted back into the woods on what she thought was a game trail. She stopped beside a clear stream and had some water to drink, but she had no food and she was terribly hungry. She continued onward, generally walking southwesterly. She approached a clearing. An old person was hunched over, tending a garden. Sammy could not tell whether it was a man or a woman. Sammy was afraid to be seen but hunger overwhelmed her fears. She walked into the opening, and called out. "Can you help me please?"

The gardener stood erect and looked at her. "Why yes, young lady. Come hither. What is your name? Why are you here? What happened to your cheek?"

"My name is Ellen," she lied, afraid to reveal too much. "I have lost my way and I have been wandering in the woods."

"Then I will help you," the elderly person said.

Sammy looked closely. The gardener was androgynous, neither man nor woman. Wrinkles covered the old person's face and a mat of white hair rested atop a deeply veined forehead. His or her look was strangely aboriginal, yet kindly and familiar.

"My name is Bailey. I am 104 years old. You don't need to tell me your real name. To me now, you are the girl of the Star." Sammy was flummoxed, as her Star of David necklace pendant was covered by both her shirt and her jacket. "Come inside. You are hungry and I will feed you. Please, come inside."

They walked together over a simple wooden bridge, two yards long, over a bubbling creek. They approached a huge spruce tree, dramatic in how its deep evergreen color contrasted with the changing colors of the nearby hardwood trees. Beside it was a rock sculpted like a chair. Behind the tree was an abode like she'd never seen before. It was seemingly dug into the hillside, with sod arching over the front door and windows, growing grass as surely as the lawn. There was an exposed wooden archway of bent logs. Bailey opened the substantial wooden door, which had a wooden handle but no lock and an Irish Celtic knot medallion, about three inches in diameter, tacked to it. The walls were easily two-feet thick and appeared to be whitewashed cloth over straw bales. The roof was a lattice of sticks that reminded Sammy of a spider web.

Bailey gave Sammy a moist towel and told her to wash off. She could smell fresh eggs, onions, and garlic being cooked. Bailey approached her with a warm, scented washcloth and gently dabbed her swollen cheek. "Lay back, child. I need to wash the dirt out or this will get infected." Sammy felt warm water being poured over her cheek.

Then, Bailey gently rubbed some soap onto it, and then rinsed the soap. "Let's get some food inside of you. Then we will disinfect this wound."

Sammy ate her breakfast as if possessed. She went outside to the outhouse. Inside the outhouse door was tacked a faded poster. It had a picture of an old Indian and under it were the words, "All things are connected. Whatever befalls the earth befalls the sons of the earth. Man did not weave the web of life; he is merely a strand in it. Whatever he does to the web, he does to himself."

Once she was back inside the house, Bailey told her to lie down on the sofa. In a voice that was high and clear but neither masculine or feminine, Bailey began to sing to her,

Go to sleep little child
Go to sleep little child
You and me and the devil is wild
Gonna bring some sleep to the child

Sammy awoke hours later; she could tell from the angle of the afternoon sun. Bailey was gently spreading a paste on Sammy's cheek. "This tincture has an antibiotic in it. It will prevent infection."

When her host was done, Sammy looked about the house. It felt as if a balloon had somehow bubbled under the sod and raised it up and someone had placed the wooden structure under it. Everything was old: the oil lamp, the wind-up phonograph, and the immense wood stove. Herbs hung from strings across the ceiling and dried flower arrangements sat in vases. Arrowheads and Indian pottery dotted the wooden shelves. A colorful feather headdress hung from one wall. It was enchanting.

Bailey gave her a toothbrush, along with clean clothes: woolen pants that fit perfectly and a white canvas shirt. She felt rejuvenated!

Bailey made dinner for the two new friends, serving chicken soup with potatoes, leeks, and barley. It was as delicious as anything Sammy had ever eaten. Sammy had so many questions to ask, but whenever she did, Bailey waived them off. "Eat, rest, and prepare for your journey. You still have many miles to go and there are dangers on the way. I will wake you before daybreak and you will walk south, through the gap of Ewing Mountain and Devils Den. By daybreak you will reach Jones Knob, where the rock outcropping of the old man sits. You will see Stevens Knob in the Iron Mountains, and you will go left around the base. The mountains end there, and you will see your way back to Providence."

Sammy fell back asleep on the couch, wondering how her host knew her destination.

Friday, October 5

Before daybreak, Sammy felt herself being nudged. Bailey said, "It is time for you to depart." The two walked outside where Sammy looked longingly at her host. "I owe you so much!"

"You owe me nothing, child."

"I want so much to repay you."

"Then you will come see me again."

Sammy smiled, and then turned towards the south. She heard her host yell, "Goodbye Samantha!" Seconds later as she reached the edge of the forest, Sammy turned to wave goodbye, but Bailey was nowhere in sight.

She walked the path Bailey had described, first through the woods, then on a mountain trail, then through a huge clearing. The day was spectacularly gorgeous, with a gentle, warm breeze fanning her hair. Leaves on the trees were ablaze with color. She touched her cheek and the soreness was gone. She felt indescribably, inexplicably, giddily happy.

She re-entered the woods and stopped to take a drink from a clear mountain stream. The tiny pool reflected her face and she was swept into hallucinations, seeing her grandfather's face and then Bailey's face, then her own again. She splashed the water against her face and felt new energy sweeping over her. She moved on.

She reached the edge of the woods and a great expanse of landscape spread out before her. She could see a long ribbon of the New River in the distance, with the Blue Ridge Mountains further on, at the far horizon.

Below and to her left, four men on horseback yelled, "There she is!" Pike, Jamaal, and two other men she recognized from Fries, galloped towards her. Jamaal reached her first and almost fell off his horse trying to hug her. "Thank God! Thank God you are safe!"

Words of thanks passed between them as they walked their horses back to Providence. Sammy tried to explain about her experience and about her encounter with Bailey, but whenever she did, it seemed too fanciful and she couldn't tell whether anyone believed her.

Pike and Jamaal told her they were rescued within a couple of hours of her abduction. They were able to continue to Fries to deliver their precious cargo, but filled with regret and guilt, they immediately set out with their little posse to find her. They wandered through the next two nights looking for her.

The other two men left for Fries at the fork of the road in Providence, but Pike and Jamaal escorted her all the way back to Quint and Hattie's house. "We are so sorry, what you went through," Pike said.

Jamaal agreed, "Seeing those thugs drag you away was one of the worst moments of my life."

"Mine, too! I was as scared as I have ever been," Sammy admitted. "Somehow I knew I'd be all right. But I'm glad to be back here. I suppose there is a reason they call this place Providence."

She went inside, but as usual, neither Quint nor Hattie were anywhere to be seen. There was a loaf of bread and some cheese, which she ate with two fresh tomatoes. She went upstairs to her room, and although nightfall was hours away, she fell fast asleep.

Saturday, October 6

Sammy missed Avalon and was eager to share the story of her trip to Blacksburg. So she tacked up Jackson and rode to her friend's house. Avalon was working in her herb room, boiling a decoction.

"Come in, Sammy. How have you been?"

"Oh, my! I have so much to tell you."

The women spoke about all the things that had gone on in the two weeks since they'd seen one another, the theft of the violin, the walk to Blacksburg, and the kidnapping. She mentioned Bailey and asked if Avalon know about the mysterious person.

"There's a persistent rumor about a gnome in the forests north of here. You should take me there sometime."

Sammy felt that her friend was somehow patronizing her, as if Avalon thought this person didn't really exist, but she decided not to push it.

They spent all afternoon together, working with the herbs and in the garden. Avalon went into the chicken coop and emerged with a plump hen. She stuck it headfirst in a funnel, with the neck poking through the downward spout. She grabbed a sharp knife and slit its jugular. Blood drained into a bucket below. The chicken's eyes went pale and blank. Avalon sliced off the bird's head and feet and threw them into a pile nearby.

When their work was done, the woman and the girl walked inside, carrying the chicken, some eggs and vegetables. "Why don't you freshen up yourself?" Avalon suggested, "There is a solar shower in the bathroom and a bathrobe on the door. I don't have a bra but you can wear these panties."

Sammy emerged from the shower and put on the robe that Avalon had given her. She entered the living room to the wonderful smell of chicken soup and fresh vegetables being cooked.

Avalon said, "I have dinner cooking on the stove. Come sit down and let me comb your hair. I think it will feel good for me to comb it for you."

As Avalon swept the comb through her hair, Sammy said, "Last time I was here, you were telling me about the Y2K scare. I am sure you were relieved when nothing really happened."

"Oh no, quite to the contrary. My husband and I were deeply disappointed. We had done extensive amounts of preparation. We had put a garden in place and set up a coop where we could grow chickens. We bought a couple of goats. We bought and installed some solar panels. We were ready.

"I've been here ever since, living exclusively off the grid. I make a little bit of cash selling eggs and wild herbs. And I barter for other things I need.

"As I said, anybody who has given it much thought reaches the same conclusion; the system we have now is not sustainable. I think we talked about this when you and I met. Our society can't endure. We were ready for it to happen and since it was only a matter of time, we wanted it to happen then. But the collapse appears to have been forecast a dozen years too early."

"How could you have been disappointed?" Sammy shrieked unbelievingly. "This is awful!"

"Yes, perhaps for some. But it was inevitable." She stood up and went back to the kitchen and returned with plates of food and a kettle of tea.

Sammy took a sip of her tea. It was neither sweet nor bitter but instead had a caramel-like flavor. It was delicious. They began eating.

Avalon continued her earlier thought, "As I told you, my husband died from pancreatic cancer. It was a horrible experience. He went from being presumably healthy to being dead within six weeks. Since we were living largely in a barter economy, we didn't have health insurance and we didn't have much money. We were able to scrape together enough to have a diagnosis but by the time we got the results, there were no possible positive outcomes. Pancreatic cancer is typically a death sentence. Few people survive it for long.

"One day I made a trip into Fries to sell some eggs and to pick up some coffee, brown sugar, and other foods that we are unable to grow ourselves. He was lying on our sofa, near death. While I was gone, he had mixed a poisonous concoction from our herbs and he was committing suicide. He was still breathing when I found him. He was able to look at me for a moment, long enough to say, 'I love you,' and then he closed his eyes and he passed away.

"He was a special man, filled with curiosity, wonder, and love. I buried him on Easter Sunday in our flower garden. Each spring the emerging flowers bring his spirit into my life."

"Oh, how horrible! I'm sure you were devastated."

"Yes," the older woman said. "It was the worst thing I have ever gone through. But he is gone now and I am still here and my life goes on. All of us who are blessed with long lives will experience the gaining and losing of things and people that are precious to us, but most of them are someday gone. The only thing that we have through our entire lives is ourselves."

The two finished dinner and Sammy washed the dishes while Avalon put the left-over food in the working refrigerator.

When they were done, Sammy said, "I am suddenly feeling a bit drowsy. Do you mind if I lay down?"

"You can recline right here on my sofa if you like. Let me do some massage on your face. I know these past few weeks have been intensely stressful for you. I think a massage might help."

Sammy thought to decline the massage, but having Avalon comb her hair felt good, and the smells of dinner, incense, and massage oil wafted into her nostrils and rendered her powerless. Avalon's fingers massaged her scalp and forehead, brushing gently against her eyebrows and being particularly careful around her bruised cheek. Avalon rested her fingers on Sammy's eyes and gently massaged her eyeballs through her closed eyelids.

Sammy felt Avalon's warm hands on her cheeks, gently smoothing the muscles of her cheekbones. Her hands then went to Sammy's ears and neck. Avalon's hands gently massaged her two vertical ridges on the back of her neck and moved to her shoulders.

The older woman shifted positions and was now sitting beside Sammy. She began massaging Sammy's shoulders and chest. She opened Sammy's bathrobe and moved the Star of David pendant. She worked her way around Sammy's breasts. Sammy was taken aback by the blonde woman's boldness, but she was unable to resist. Avalon began massaging Sammy's rib cage, guiding her fingers gently up and down the gaps between each rib. It felt good, really good. Sammy opened her eyes and stared at the blue irises of her masseuse. Feeling self-conscious, Sammy slurred, "I... I think I should get up," but she completely lacked the strength to do so.

"Just relax, sweet flower. You are carrying way too much stress. Breathe deeply and evenly."

Sammy closed her eyes and took two deep breaths. When she opened her eyes again and looked into Avalon's pupils, she thought she saw in each one a bright red cross. She thought it must be a reflection from something elsewhere in the room but couldn't imagine what it might be. She blinked her eyes and when she reopened them, the red areas were gone. Avalon smiled tenderly. Sammy's eyes fell shut again.

"Relax... Breathe."

Avalon continued massaging, moving to the muscles of Sammy's abdomen. Sammy could feel the pressure increase and decrease as she took each new breath deeply into her lungs. Sammy could feel her head spinning joyously, as if on an amusement park ride, even as her eyes remained closed. The pressure on her gut made her feel as if Avalon's hands had moved inside, massaging her individual internal organs, releasing toxins and becoming rejuvenated.

Then Sammy felt a surprising warmth in the area above her pubic mound. She opened her eyes once again and looked there. She saw a cupped hand of her masseuse resting above her mons. Feeling guilty, she reached down and grabbed Avalon's wrist and slowly pulled her hand away, placing it on her belly. Sammy's little finger rested on smooth skin on the side of Avalon's hand, the place Sammy decided was the scar from the amputated extra digit.

Sammy was surprised, in fact shocked, thinking about what was happening and what Avalon's motivations were. She felt indecisive, as she was the first time with Shane. She steeled herself to protest. Before she moved or said anything, Avalon implored, "Relax. Allow yourself to be taken in by the moment. Allow yourself to find some joy."

Sammy took another deep breath. She convinced herself nobody was being hurt and no harm was being done to anyone. She grabbed Avalon's wrist again. This time she pushed it back to the place from where she had just moved it, except now underneath the thin fabric of her borrowed underwear.

Sammy felt Avalon's fingers massage her labia. Sammy's breathing intensified and the skin on her thighs began to tingle. Her nipples stood erect. As Avalon stroked slowly, Sammy continued to breathe more and more deeply. She felt sweat form above her eyebrows. Her mouth fell open and she moaned and sighed. Avalon's fingers continued to knead and stroke. And then Sammy climaxed with an intensity she had never known was possible.

Sunday, October 7

Sammy awoke from a dream in which she was riding a white horse through a meadow of flowers. She let the smell of tea drift deeply inside her olfactory. She opened her eyes and saw that she was in a strange bedroom and in an unfamiliar bed. She sat upright. She was nude other than the panties that Avalon had loaned her. She got out of bed and put on the cotton robe. She walked into the kitchen where Avalon was preparing eggs, tomatoes, and bread for breakfast.

"Good morning, my little flower!" Avalon exclaimed. "Would you like some tea?"

"Yes, please. But let me use the bathroom first."

"When you're done, I will pour some warm water for you to wash your face."

Sammy was delighted to use indoor plumbing, the fixtures fed with water energized by Avalon's solar panels. Sammy looked through the stained-glass window towards a spectacular morning where a bright sun rose over the hills on the eastern horizon. The trees that covered hillsides and lined the driveway were filled with radiant colors of red, orange, yellow, and emerald. Sammy felt better than she remembered feeling for weeks. She washed her face and brushed her teeth with a toothbrush that Avalon gave her.

"How did you sleep?"

"Wonderful! I don't remember anything that happened since last night. Did we have dinner?"

"Yes, but you seemed a bit dazed through it all." She chuckled, amorously.

"The last thing I remember was being massaged. It felt really good. Did you drug me?" Sammy asked in half-hearted accusation.

A bright smile of shiny white teeth emerged from Avalon face. Then, she giggled. Sammy giggled, too. Then Sammy began laughing a deep, guttural laugh from her belly upwards.

"Well, I can't say anything self-incriminating, now, can I?"

Sammy laughed again, and then blushed. Her eyes shot northward and then returned to the eyes of her host.

Avalon continued, "This is more of an explanation than an excuse, but yesterday was the sixth of the month. As I mentioned, I get a bit crazy on the sixth. You have been through a lot of misery, sadness, and uncertainty. I just thought a bit of ecstasy wouldn't hurt you."

"It didn't!"

Sitting down to breakfast, Sammy told her new friend about her upbringing and the path that led her to Galax and to Fries. They carried on like school girls, until Sammy realized what time it must be.

"Oh my gosh, today is Sunday, isn't it?"

"Yes. Are you due somewhere?"

"Quint insists I attend his church every week."

"That old blowhead! Are you a willing church-goer?"

"I'm always deeply conflicted there. The stuff he spouts is near-nonsense to me. But he's been kind enough to take me in and provide for me. So I feel like I owe him that. When I've skipped church, he's been furious. Once, I thought he was going to murder me."

"If that man ever lays a hand on you, I swear I'll kill him. Don't ever let that self-righteous bastard touch you. There are other people here who can take care of you. In fact, would you like to move in with me?"

"You're very kind to offer and sometime I may take you up on it. But like I said, he and Hattie have been good to provide for me and I feel some responsibility to stay there, at least for now."

"Very well, then you best be going. Let me loan you a dress. I'm sure you've been wearing only dresses you found in his daughter's closet. Let's get you into something a bit more attractive." She walked to her closet and pulled out a bright red dress. "This'll give everybody something to talk about."

Fifteen minutes later, Sammy had saddled and bridled Jackson and was ready to depart. "Thanks for everything. Being with you has been amazing."

"You come back any time. My door is always open."

Sammy threw her leg over Jackson and sat high in the saddle.

"I need to ask you something. Am I a lesbian?"

"Why do you ask?"

"I really liked what happened last night. I keep thinking I should feel guilty, or at least embarrassed. What we did seems really forbidden."

"I don't think you'll read much about it in *Good Housekeeping*," Avalon chuckled. "Seriously, most folks surely consider it taboo."

"But when I've been with boys, it never feels that good. Sometimes it doesn't feel very good at all."

"I'd say 99-percent of the boys – men too – have no idea how to please a woman sexually. Probably 95-percent of them don't care. If you crave muscles and facial hair and penises, go be with a man. But if you want to be satisfied, go be with another girl."

Sammy was thinking about what this meant for her and particularly for her relationship with Shane. Then Avalon spoke again, "As far as sex goes, between two men, it's either 'yes' or an emphatic 'no.' Between two women, it's usually 'maybe.'"

"But I did nothing to satisfy you."

"*Es nada, mi amiga.* Your being here was a gift enough. Having my fingers in your hair, listening to the cry of your orgasm, smelling the scent of your love juices… these are the gifts you've brought me. My sexual satisfaction will come another day."

Sammy looked over the colorful dawn from her high perch on Jackson.

Avalon continued, "You are becoming the woman you will be for the rest of your life. You will experiment with sex and with love; you should experiment. You have been robbed of everybody you ever cared about, cast into an unfamiliar place during a cruel and unforgiving time. But you still have yourself, your life, and your spirit. Let yourself believe that it is okay, even amidst the chaos and sadness, to feel some pleasure, even sexual pleasure."

The blonde woman pulled a blue handle brush through her hair and continued, "Go and find your calling. Rebuild your life around the new things you love and cherish."

Sammy turned her horse away and blew Avalon a kiss. Sammy rode Jackson back to Providence to Quint's church. Walking inside with her crimson dress after the service had begun, she felt like every eye was fixated on her. Quint was visibly peeved by the interruption. Sammy expected she'd get a browbeating later, but she felt giddily emboldened, and she didn't give a damn what Quint thought.

Monday, October 8

When Emily's bell rang in mid-morning, Sammy walked to her house, carrying her midwife's case. Jamaal had hitched Maggie to the newly repaired wagon. The two women drove it to Hilltown, calling on two expectant women: Julie Teel and Allison Perkins. The former was due near the end of November and the latter was due in early November. Then they called on Doris Noson in Stevens Creek, also due near the end of November.

On their way home, Sammy asked her mentor, "Do you pray?"

"No."

"Everybody else around here seems to."

"Most religions share the same goals in worship," Emily asserted. "They express gratitude, ask for help for themselves and others, and seek God. But nobody knows who God is or what God wants. Many Christians think that those who don't pray aren't good Christians. Religious practices are fine, but compliance and adherence to rigid rituals, beliefs, and regulations hamper intellectual growth. The proper reason for ritual is to elevate the spirit."

Emily seemed lost in thought for a moment, but then continued, "I don't want to get religion exactly right. I want to search for answers. Many of my neighbors are suffocated with a stifling case of certitude; they know the answers. That's too tidy for me. I want to go to my grave still searching for them."

Moments later, Emily added, "Before I forget, do you remember the black woman, Ebony Hayes? While you were gone to Blacksburg, I assisted her delivery of a baby girl."

Tuesday, October 9

Sammy was working on the garden on the overcast morning when Marissa arrived. "Hi, Sammy! How are you doing?

"Marissa, it's so good to see you! What a week I've had!" She told her all about the theft of her violin, the walk to and from Blacksburg, and her abduction and escape. She thought for a moment about her tryst with Avalon, but banished the thought from her mind as fast as it arrived.

"What's going on with Hattie?"

"I don't know. I was gone for several days. The only time I saw her was when Quint was yelling at her. I'm afraid he'll someday become abusive."

"He'd better not. I have never threatened anybody, but he'll regret it if he ever lays a hand on her in anger."

The two of them decided to do some laundry, so they set some water on the stove to warm. Sammy reminded Marissa that the weekly jam session in Fries was that night and invited her to go. "Sure! I haven't been in years. I like to sing and I wrote a new song the other day. I could use some fun in my life."

Sammy said, "I need some fun, too. Like I told you, somebody stole my violin. But I'm sure someone will loan me an instrument while they're taking a breather. I may even try to learn to play the banjo!"

They spent much of the afternoon doing the wash. Hattie joined them for some of the work. She had nothing to say when Sammy was around, but when Sammy went outside to drain the water, she could hear Hattie talking with Marissa.

After dinner, Marissa and Sammy walked to Fries, neither carrying an instrument. They stopped at Emily's house where she and Jamaal were playing Scrabble. "You two just go without me," he said.

As they continued on, Sammy asked her friend about her thoughts on the End Times. Marissa said, "I am a Christian woman. I believe in the Lord Jesus Christ. When the End Time comes, I will sit beside my Lord on his throne.

"The apostle John wrote Revelation, the last book in the New Testament of the Bible. In his apocalyptic vision, he sees a Beast emerge from the ocean; the Beast is the Antichrist. It has seven heads and ten horns. Daniel had a similar vision. Each horn is thought to represent a nation. One horn will defeat the others and will set up a one-world government with one ruler. We associate the number 666 as the Number of the Beast.

"Scripture is clear that this one ruler will have absolute power and authority, bestowed by Satan. He will have authority over 'every tribe, people, language, and nation.' Many people conclude that the only way all the other nations will succumb to this power is if they are weakened by famine, plague, or other disaster. Then the people will embrace anyone or anything that will feed them and bring relief.

"This powerful ruler will subdue everyone by tracking them with some sort of satanic mark, like the tattoos the Nazis used on Concentration Camp prisoners. It may be an electronic chip imbedded under the skin on either the forehead or wrist. Those technologies exist today, or did before the Pulse. Without the mark, nobody will be able to conduct commerce, either buy or sell. Without it, you won't be able to buy food to feed yourself. So the urge to succumb will be overwhelming.

"Those left behind will have three choices: bow to the Antichrist, starve, or accept Jesus Christ as their personal Lord and Savior. Those people will be raptured up."

Sammy was incredulous that someone took the rapture seriously.

She asked, "What will happen if a saved person is driving a school bus or piloting an airplane? The occupants will surely die."

"God's judgment will be harsh. I don't think babies will be lost, because they are too young to make an informed decision. But I'm sure there will be collateral damage. The Lord will track the true believers in the Book of Life. Anyone not in it will be surely punished.

"The word 'rapture' never appears in the Bible, but the concept is clear. In the rapture, God removes his believers in order to make way for his righteous judgment to be poured out on earth. God will take both living and dead bodies, giving them all new, glorified bodies. Everyone else will be at the evil mercy of the Antichrist."

"Will the rapture happen all at once?" Sammy asked.

"As I said, it isn't mentioned in the Bible, so nobody knows for sure. That seems most likely. But I can't say."

"Do you think the Pulse has signaled the beginning of the End Times?" Sammy asked.

"I don't know. It's certainly a mess. I don't want to take chances. The reason we Christians are so evangelic is that we want everybody to have eternal life beside the Lord."

Sammy recalled, "Once, some Jehovah Witnesses came to my door. I was bored with practicing my violin and I needed a distraction. So I invited them to sit on our porch and talk with me. They said only 144,000 would be allowed into heaven."

"I don't believe that. I think there is room for everyone in heaven who will accept Christ."

Nearing town, Marissa changed the subject, admitting, "A walk like that would have killed me a couple of months ago. Now I walk from Galax to Providence and practically everywhere I go. I've lost some weight and I feel better and stronger. Having no electricity is a pain in the butt, but it may make me healthier! They say what doesn't kill you makes you stronger. Now I know what they mean."

Sammy clenched her fists and flexed the muscles in her arms. She thought it may have done the same for her.

As they arrived, several people Sammy had gotten to know were delighted to see her. "Your kidnapping is a big story around town," said one of them. "We're so glad you're safe and back with us."

Sammy introduced Marissa to everyone, indicating that she was Quint's sister-in-law. Everyone welcomed her.

Sammy and Marissa sat and listened to several tunes. Sammy remembered a tune that she'd heard when she saw the Harlem Globetrotters play one of their games. Someone told her it was called, *Sweet Georgia Brown*. It brought a smile to her face.

On their way home, Sammy and Marissa spoke about the happiness that music can bring.

Wednesday, October 10

Sammy awoke and decided to call on Professor Dyson at the Nursing Home again. She found the old woman sitting in an upholstered chair in the room where the piano was. "Hello, Professor Dyson."

"Hi, Sammy. It's great to see you again. Did you bring your violin?"

Sammy told her about the theft. The old professor shared her sympathy. Then she said, "I'll play some show tunes and you can sing."

"Sure!" Sammy said. "But there's been something on my mind since last time. You talked about the depletion of the fish in the oceans. Is that unusual?"

"Not at all. We've been depleting lots of things. Here's a for-instance: the Chesapeake Bay is justifiably famous for its oysters. When the settlers arrived, it hosted an abundance that was difficult to fathom. They were huge, too, often three to four times larger than the oysters in England. The habitat was ideal. The depth was mostly shallow and the forests alongside the bay retarded erosion that could damage their gills. Each oyster acts as a tiny pollution treatment plant, filtering organisms and keeping the waters pristine and clear. It was said that a boater could see the bottom of the bay in twenty feet of water. The European settlers began eating the oysters voraciously.

They waded into the water or used rakes from boats. They were mostly eaten in the winter months, supplementing scarcer foods.

"People often thought of the settlers as being hungry or lacking
in food. Surely, poorer people had to be constantly on the lookout
for food, but the continent was amazingly abundant. On the table of
wealthier residents was a variety that would surprise and delight us,
including turkey, ducks, hams, veal, roast beef, apples, peaches, pears,
nuts, figs, raisins, berries, and more.

"Anyway, by the mid 1880s, over 20 million bushels of oysters
were taken annually. The rich flavor made them a worldwide delicacy,
but the shells were in demand as well for mortar and plaster for buildings and roads, for agricultural lime for fertilizer, and grit in chicken
feed. People made fortunes trading oysters and shells. As you can
imagine, the take rapidly exceeded the ability of the resource to regen-
erate. Worse, because the shells were not being returned, new oysters
found a less suitable environment. By the late 1900s, the annual catch
had fallen to 2-percent of its peak.

"Still worse, because the filtering capability of the oysters was
gone, and because of increasing population around the bay, the bay
became increasingly polluted. Where the bay was once dominated by
bottom dwelling species like oysters, today it is dominated by micro-
scopic life suspended in the water. So the clarity is gone. For all in-
tents and purposes, it will never produce oysters as it once did."

Sammy sighed. "What a shame."

The old woman agreed. "This overuse is typical of human behavior. We strip the world of resources until they are depleted. Then
we hope something else will come along to replace it. This can't go
on forever."

Dyson let out with a deep breath, as if to regain her energy, and
said, "Please help me up, dear. My piano beckons."

Thursday, October 11

While eating breakfast, Sammy heard Emily's bell ring. So she finished quickly and tacked up Jackson and strapped on her midwife's kit. She rode over at a trot. It seemed to her that like she and Marissa, Jackson was in better fitness than when she'd arrived, and knew the exercise she was giving him was benefiting his health.

When she arrived, Jamaal met her outside. "I rang the bell, not Emily. I thought perhaps you'd like to go into Fries with me. I need some parts for my radio and I was hoping I could find them at the old TV repair shop."

They walked into town together, talking about their trip back from Blacksburg and her abduction. Sammy tied Jackson to one of the hitching rails that were now in several places around town. They entered the store where an old man wearing a white shirt and bow-tie was inside. Old televisions, radios, computers, and stereos were cluttered everywhere. He explained that his work was practically gone with the limited amount of electricity available, but that several people had traded for old vacuum tubes and wire, presumably for the same reasons as Jamaal.

As they spoke, a boy ran inside and yelled to the old man, "Grampapa, come outside! There looks like there is gonna be a hangin'!"

They all scuttled outside and trotted towards the small parking area across from the community center where the weekly jam sessions were held. A crowd of curious people were gathering near the two flagpoles that still sported the America and Virginia flags. Someone had affixed a metal bar spanning the gap between the poles. A horse-drawn wagon was parked under the bar. Five men stood on the wagon. Sammy looked closely at the bar and there were two wires and one rope hanging from it, tied with nooses. Keene and Carleton were two of the men. Sammy immediately recognized the other three men. They were her erstwhile captors, now bound with their hands behind them. All three were wearing the same filthy clothes that they were wearing when Sammy had escaped. The older man's shirt was torn at the shoulder and was stained red from a significant wound. The Hispanic man had a huge shiner on his left eye that Sammy envisioned he received as his punishment for facilitating her escape. Their feet were tied together with the same type of red zip ties they had used on her.

Keene positioned a wire noose on the older man's neck. As he did, he said in his booming voice, "For skullduggery, thievery, kidnapping…" He moved to the younger long-haired man and reached for the second noose. The man tried to move forward, but with his legs bound, he tumbled off the wagon, cracking his head on the pavement below. "Goddamn it," yelled Keene. "You boys help me get him back up here." Carleton jumped off the wagon and several men rushed forward from the crowd to hoist the man, now limp, back onto the wagon. Carleton lifted himself back on, and then he and Keene elevated the man to a slumped position where they put the noose, its rope now taut, over his neck.

"As I was saying, for thievery, kidnapping, and murder, we find these boys guilty and we're gonna hang 'em."

The Hispanic man lost his bladder, and urine wet his pant legs. Carleton put a wire noose over his head. His eyes drifted to the sky, then to the crowd where he saw Sammy. He fashioned the same sympathetic look that he had on his face when he assisted her escape.

Sammy saw Shane in the crowd and she ran to him. "Make them stop!"

"Why? These men deserve to die."

"Not that man," she pointed.

"I ain't savin' nobody. If you want to save him, you just go right ahead," he sneered.

She hesitated, frozen with trepidation and fear. Nobody in the crowd moved to assist. Shane's mother, the only law there seemed to be around Fries, was nowhere to be seen.

Keene yelled from the wagon, "Let's get this done." He put a paper grocery sack over each man's head. He and Carleton jumped off the wagon. He walked to the horse and walked him forward. As the older man's noose tightened, he shuffled sideways, but soon reached the wagon's end, and he fell. The noose snapped, and his feet dangled mere inches from the ground. The next man, already unconscious if not dead, fell from the wagon. Sammy turned and ran away as she heard the final noose snap.

Sammy sprinted back to where Jackson was waiting. She hugged him and sobbed uncontrollably. Moments later, Jamaal joined her. Handing her his handkerchief, he said, "I've gotten the radio part I need. Let's get out of here." The two friends and her horse walked in the direction of Providence, taking them past where the three men's bodies were still hanging. Pools of excrement and urine fouled the street beneath them.

Jamaal saw Shane talking with some friends. He motioned Shane to speak with him. "Where did they find these guys?" Jamaal asked.

"We found 'em. Keene, Draper, and me, we went huntin' yesterday. We found them a few miles north of here. Once we shot the old man, the other two came peaceful."

"Were you hunting for food or looking for them?"

"Like I said, we went hunting. That's about all I've got to say."

Sammy looked at her recent lover with a mix of astonishment and revulsion. She knew she would never feel any attraction towards him again.

Shane continued, "We figured they needed kilt." He looked at Sammy's bruised cheek and said, "I'm sure you both agree."

Jamaal and Sammy walked away in silence, back towards Providence. Sammy said, "I'm amazed by how quickly law and order seem to have disintegrated."

"I was thinking the same thing myself," Jamaal admitted.

Reaching Emily's house, Jamaal said to Sammy, "Emily and I know your birthday is coming up on Saturday. We'd like to host a party for you. Please invite anyone you like."

Friday, October 12

Sammy worked alone all day, splitting wood and putting up hay. She was exhausted by dinnertime, but before she went upstairs to bed, she left a note on the kitchen table where she was sure Quint and Hattie would see it. "Dear Hattie and Quint, Emily is hosting a birthday party for me tomorrow night. You are both invited. Sammy."

She didn't mention Jamaal at all. She doubted either would come, but she was hopeful.

Saturday, October 13

It was Saturday and her 18th birthday, so Sammy limited her chores and went for a horseback ride on Jackson. She and Jackson walked Lime Kiln Road for two miles, into the Scout Camp. She doubted anybody had been there since the season was likely cut short by the Pulse. Pavement gave way to gravel as she passed several rustic dormitories and a building marked "Mess Hall". She continued to the bank of the River, a river that she'd come to know well. An osprey dove into the water and pulled from it a fish looking almost as large as the bird itself. It flew with great exertion to a branch of a large sycamore tree. The tree's trunk was as white as a sun-bleached skeleton's bones.

She dismounted and walked several hundred yards on the bank. Ahead, she saw two children, fishing. She approached them. "Hi kids! Have you caught anything?"

"Hi lady. We caught two small ones, but they weren't big enough to eat."

"Hey, I caught them!" said the boy, younger than the girl.

"Sorry! I didn't mean nothin' about stealing your thunder."

"My name is Sammy. What's yours?"

The girl said, "My name is Angie Gallimore. I'm ten. This is my pesky brother, Scottie. He's seven."

"Hi," said Scott.

"Where do you live?" Sammy asked them.

"Oh, just up the hill in Providence."

"I'm surprised your mother lets you come here alone."

"Mom don't care. Once she gets a'drinking, she don't care where we go. I'm sure she's sick of havin' us around the house all the time. There ain't been much booze for her to drink lately, but somebody gave her a bottle of whiskey last night," said the girl.

"I never'd a'thought I'd say this," said her brother, "but I miss school. I'm gettin' bored. I miss seein' my friends."

"Where you from?" Angie asked Sammy. "You talk funny."

"New Jersey."

"Why are you here?"

"I was brought here after the Pulse."

"Do you like it here?"

Sammy's mind flooded with emotion and filled with plausible answers to the girl's innocent question. "Yes, I like it here."

"Where's New Jersey?" asked the boy.

"I live near New York City, right across the river."

"There's a river in New York City?"

"Yes. It's called the Hudson. It's a grand river."

"Bigger than this one?"

"Yes. But it's different."

"How?" asked Angie.

"There's development all around it. The water moves, but you can't see it move. There is boat traffic on it, or at least there used to be." She thought about mentioning the airplane that crashed in it a few years earlier, making the pilot a national hero. She thought they'd know about it. But decided against it, thinking they had enough traumas. "It's a wonderful river. People like it."

"I bet nobody likes it as much as the New River," the boy said boastfully. "This is the best river in the world."

Sammy looked upstream where there were a series of small ripples. The yellow, red, and orange trees on the opposite shore reflected brilliantly in the water. "You just may be right about that."

"Do you want to fish?" the boy asked.

"I've never fished before."

"It's easy! Let me show you."

Scotty sat beside her and held the rod in her hand as she cast the hook and bobber into the water. It felt good to have a child's hands on hers.

She left the bobber in the river several moments. It drifted lazily downstream.

"Where's your dad?"

"Nobody knows," said Angie. "He drove a truck. He did deliveries across the country. One day a few years ago, he left and never came back."

"I don't even rightly remember him," Scottie said.

"You know what I remember?" said Angie. "Daddy played a guitar. He had lots of instruments and lots of friends coming over all the time to play music. Once he left, I think mom got rid of all the instruments. I don't know if it was from spite or if she needed the money to buy booze."

"Do you play an instrument?" Sammy asked the older child.

"I would if we had one."

"I would, too!" yelled her brother.

"Do you play an instrument?" Angie asked Sammy.

"Sometimes. I like to play the fiddle. Right now, I don't have one, either."

Sammy cast her hook again. The bobber rested on the surface, then dropped under the water.

"You've got a fish! Tug on your rod!" yelled Angie.

Sammy tugged on the rod and a fish jumped from the water.

"Reel it in!" said Scott.

Sammy reeled in the line and there was a squirming fish on the hook. It was about 14 inches long, mottled green with a lighter underside. "I caught a fish!" she exclaimed. She looked at the children subconsciously and said, "I've never caught a fish before."

They looked at her with a mix of astonishment and regret. "Well," said Scott, "you caught one now. It's big enough to eat. I'll clean it for you." The little boy removed a pocket knife from his jeans and deftly slit the fish's underbelly from the base of the gills to the beginning of the tail. With his diminutive fingers, he rooted out the intestines and other organs. He held it up by sticking his finger from the hole he'd made through the fish's mouth. "Here you go! He's a smallmouth bass. Take him home. He's good eatin'."

She gave him the rod that was still in her hands. "I caught him with your rod. I think he belongs to you."

"Thanks lady."

"Please call me Sammy. I'd better be going. You take care of each other and of your mom."

"We will. I hope we'll see you again."

She mounted Jackson and began the walk back up the hill, wiping tears from her eyes.

Sammy had some cheese and carrots for lunch. She went upstairs and read one of Bonnie's books in bed, falling asleep. When she awoke, she took a sponge bath and washed her hair. She rolled on some deodorant, something she hadn't done for weeks. She had noticed how badly many people smelled from bathing much less frequently than before the Pulse. She wanted to feel clean for her birthday.

She walked to Emily's house. She could smell cookies baking from the kitchen. "They're chocolate chip cookies. One of the women I helped last week gave me a bag of chocolate chips for helping with her delivery. She didn't have much money and I didn't want to accept any payment, but she insisted. When I realized your party was coming up, I accepted them."

Jamaal came inside carrying a load of wood for the stove. Avalon arrived, carrying a vegetable casserole on her bicycle. Woody and Caroline Dalton arrived, having walked there. Pike was walking up the road as Sammy let Woody and Caroline inside.

Dinner was venison steaks, rice, and garden vegetables. Emily explained that she always kept a huge sack of rice in the shed, "Just in case." Much of the dinnertime conversation was about the trip to Blacksburg and the recent hanging. As they were finishing up, there was a knock at the door. When Emily opened it, in walked Marissa and Hattie. Marissa said, "We wanted to be here for you, Sammy." Hattie didn't say anything, but looked at each person for a moment as if she was seeing them all for the first time. "We brought you something," said Marissa.

"Oh," said Emily, "we haven't started giving presents yet. Let's light the candles." She departed into the kitchen and returned with a plate of cookies. One cookie sat alone on a smaller plate with a single small candle on it. Jamaal took a lighter from the mantle and lit it.

Everyone sang,

Happy birthday to you
Happy birthday to you
Happy birthday dear Sammy
Happy birthday to you

Sammy closed her eyes, wished to be going home to New Jersey soon, and opened them again. She emitted a little puff and the candle went out. Everyone cheered. "Okay," said Emily. "Time for presents."

"Us first," said Marissa. She handed Sammy a small box wrapped in a Christmas theme paper and apologized. "It's the only paper I could find."

Sammy unwrapped it and found an antique silver comb. It had a dozen tongs and a small emerald set in the center.

"Please," said Marissa. "Let me put it in your hair." She pulled the comb through Sammy's dark hair four times, and then left it in place. "I found it at one of the antique shops in Galax. The owner was practically giving things away for food."

"It's beautiful!" Emily said.

"You're beautiful!" said Jamaal.

"Thank you, thank you both!"

Avalon handed her a rectangular package that looked too small to contain a book. Sammy unwrapped it and found a box containing a deck of unusual cards. "They're Augury cards," Avalon said. They're a bit like Tarot cards; you can forecast your future. Or you can simply look at them for fun."

Sammy took one from the deck and turned it over. It said, "Growth."

"Thank you!" She leaned to kiss Avalon on her cheek, but Avalon turned a bit and their lips ended together. Everyone except Hattie laughed.

Pike handed her a tiny package wrapped in color newspaper, from the last Sunday comics before the Pulse. She tore it open and inside was a small metal contraption that Sammy didn't recognize. "What's this?"

"It's a Jew's harp. It's a musical instrument. Let me show you how to play it."

He took it from her and held it to his mouth. His upper and lower lips rested over an upper and lower metal frame. He sprung a metal tang and blew through it, producing the first two bars of *When the Saints Go Marching In.*

Sammy laughed. "What did you call it?"

"Some people call it a mouth harp, but everybody Ih know calls it a Jew's harp. As far as Ih know, there is no connection with Jewish people, but Ih still think it sort of fit. And Ih knew you needed a new instrument."

"Thanks! I'll practice for hours!" she replied, feigning sincerity.

"Here's your next one," said Caroline, handing her a small flat rectangular box, wrapped in green paper.

Sammy undid the tape and unwrapped the paper. Inside was a picture frame. It had an ornate, copper-colored frame. Caroline said, "It was my grandmother's. I think her mother bought it at an auction during the Great Depression. It's been sitting in my bureau forever." There was a cardboard backing for it, but no photo or artwork in it.

"Perfect!" yelled Jamaal. "It goes with my present to you. It isn't wrapped." He handed her a leather case. Inside she found what looked like an old camera. It said, "Polaroid Land Company."

"What's this?"

"It's a Polaroid camera!" exclaimed Woody. "Wow!"

"It is a camera from the 1960s," said Jamaal. "They were special in those days because the film developed itself. Before we all had digital cameras, film needed to be developed with special chemicals. Film came on a roll of typically two or three dozen pictures. When a photographer finished a roll, he took it to a camera shop where it was developed and printed onto photo paper. It often took several days. The Polaroid camera's film developed itself, within a minute. I found several boxes of film and a dozen flash bulbs, too. I'll show you how to load it."

He put some film in the camera and a bulb in the socket. Then he pointed it at Sammy. Poof! Sammy was blinded by the light. Jamaal opened a trap-door in the camera base and yanked out a sheet of film paper covered by a black cellophane cover. "We need to wait sixty seconds." He pulled the pocket watch from his pants and began timing. Then he peeled back the cellophane and there was a picture of Sammy with her new comb in her hair.

"Wow! How cool? Where did you get this?" Sammy asked.

"Er, it's actually from Emily, or more precisely from her late husband. I found it in the attic while I was looking for radio parts. I'll be in hock to her for the rest of my life for it, but she let me have it to give to you," he said, sheepishly.

"Thank you both."

Emily said, "I have two presents for you, Sammy. Neither is wrapped. So close your eyes and hold your hand out to your sides with your palm open. I'll be right back with the first one."

Sammy did as she was told. She felt a piece of polished wood reach her palm. "Okay, open your eyes." She looked to her right and in her hand was a deep honey-amber colored violin.

"Oh, my God, *Oh my God!!!*" She hugged it. She held it at arm's length and looked at it again. She hugged it again. "Oh my God!"

"Here," said Emily, handing her a bow. "Why don't you take it for a test drive?"

"Holy shit, Oh my God!" She took the bow and tightened it. She tightened the G string, and then drew her bow across it. She tightened it more. Then the D. Then the A and E.

She held it at arm's length again and said, "Oh, I am so happy to be holding a violin again!" and she broke into tears. Sobbing freely, she drew it to her chin, took a deep breath, and launched lustily into Mozart's *Eine Kleine Nachtmusik*. Tears flowed from her eyes. Then there were more tears, spilling onto the top of the instrument. But she kept playing. Every eye in the room was on her and her amber instrument and she kept playing. She cried and they cried and she kept playing. And when the song was over and she had nothing more to play, the room fell absolutely silent except the ticking of the wall clock.

"Bravo," said Emily, quietly and admiringly. "You're amazing!"

"I can't believe how exceptional you are," Jamaal said.

Pike concurred, "What an outstanding musician!"

She put the instrument down gently beside her and she hugged Emily. "Thank you, thank you, thank you! Where did you get it?"

"It belonged to my husband. He wasn't a great musician, but he appreciated fine music and fine instruments. He bought it thirty years ago in Prague, in the Czech Republic – it was Czechoslovakia in those days. It dates back to the early 1800s. I'm sure it is not as valuable as the instrument you lost, but I know it's very nice. It hasn't been played for over a decade. I'm sure if he had met you, he would want you to have it. So now it's yours."

"Thanks again," Sammy smiled.

Caroline said, "Didn't you say you had a second gift, too?"

"Oh yes, I almost forgot," Emily said. "I won't put you through closing your eyes again, but let me get something else." She walked into the other room and returned with a shiny-rimmed banjo. "Here's something else my husband had that should be yours. Someday when your experience here in Providence is a distant memory, you'll remember bluegrass music and the unholy marriage between the violin and the banjo."

"But I have no idea how to play it. I'm not worthy," Sammy cried.

"Nonsense! I won't hear it."

"We won't either," said Caroline. "You are a master musician and you deserve the finest instruments."

Emily concurred, "When this banjo speaks to you, you will learn to play it. And we know you'll play it well."

She took it from Emily and held it. It was heavy! If her violin had weighed a pound-and-a-half, this instrument weighed fifteen pounds.

"Thank you so much. Thank you all so much. Wow, I can feel it vibrate as I talk."

"Banjos are instruments of slavery and hardship and toil," said Jamaal. "They yearn to speak, to cry, and to sing. May I?"

"Sure," she said, handing it to him.

"I figured we'd be in a classical mood tonight, so I've been practicing something special." He started playing. It was the *Prelude from Violin Partitia #3* and Sammy recognized it. She picked up her new violin and joined him in a duet: Bach for fiddle and banjo. Everyone applauded again, and then he handed it back to her. "Excuse me while I get my own banjo," he said getting up from his chair. "This one is yours now."

They played and sang for hours. Somehow, Hattie slipped away without anyone noticing. Jamaal said, "Before anyone else goes home, let's get some pictures!" They handed the camera around and took turns being the photographer and the photographed. Woody took a group photo with Sammy and her violin, Jamaal and his banjo, Emily, Avalon, Caroline, Marissa, and Pike. Sammy took the backing off the picture frame that Caroline and Woody had given her and put the photo inside. It didn't fit well, with the frame being too large, but she decided it could get properly matted later, someday.

It was late when Marissa and Sammy departed. Before Sammy shut off her *Forever-lite* to go to sleep, she took one more look at her new violin and whispered to herself again, "Oh my God!" banishing the sadness that would come from the notion that this was any lesser of an instrument than her stolen Guarneri. She looked at the photograph of her new friends with sincere and abiding fondness. There was a speck of red in the center of everyone's eyeballs. She couldn't help but notice that the specks in Avalon's eyes were cross-like.

Sunday, October 14

The next morning, Sammy awoke to shouts from the kitchen. She threw on her bathrobe and ran down the stairs to find Quint and Marissa in a verbal fistfight.

"Where were you last night?!" he yelled at her.

"We were at Emily's house. It was Sammy's birthday. You were invited, remember? Where were YOU?"

"None of your damn business. I am the man in this house and I will not be spoken to this way."

Hattie stood in a corner, cowering.

"You knew exactly where we were, or you should have. Sammy

left a note for all of us. She's your guest. Do you think you could have at least been here to wish her a happy birthday?"

"Shut up, woman. I said I won't be spoken to this way in my house. I had business to attend to. It's none of your concern."

"Fine," Marissa yelled back.

"I'm going to church. You are aware that today is Sunday, the day of the Lord, are you not? He awaits me. He awaits you, too, if you can be bothered. Sammy?"

Marissa said with pronounced sarcasm, "Sammy and I are staying right here. We're perfectly capable of being with the Lord without your divine guidance."

He slapped his bible against the table and yelled, "You'll burn in Hell, Marissa Jarrell," and walked towards the front door.

"If you get there first, would you keep the place warm for me?" she retorted, blasphemously.

Hattie ran out the back door, leaving Marissa and Sammy looking at each other. "He is not a good man," Marissa said.

"I've been trying to give him the benefit of the doubt, since he was kind enough to take me in. But I'm starting to think you're right."

"You beware of him, child."

Monday, October 15

Sammy took some of Hattie's cheese to Carlene's store, and then stopped off at Emily and Jamaal's house. Emily was working in the garden. She insisted Sammy go inside to see Jamaal. "He's listening to the radio."

Sammy walked inside and found Jamaal with headphones on. He kept shaking his head, clearly disturbed.

"It's bad, even worse than before. A hurricane swept up the eastern seaboard nine days ago. It stayed largely off-shore off the coast of the Carolinas and Virginia. But it slammed ashore with the eye passing just southwest of New York City, on the Jersey Shore. The spin of hurricanes is counterclockwise, so the winds were awful in the harbor, creating a massive storm surge, almost like a tsunami. The utilities, subways and traffic tunnels are under sea level. Pumps that run on electricity run continuously to keep the water that seeps in from pooling up. The Pulse already crippled the ability to keep the water from accumulating, but the surge swamped everything, as far inland as Wall Street and the old World Trade Center site. Much of the infrastructure of the city is ruined, and without power, there has been almost no effort to restore anything. Many of the buildings are structurally sound, but after the Pulse, there was no cooling, so people literally punched out windows."

Sammy buried her head in her hands.

"I'm so sorry," her friend said.

"What else? Anything worse?"

"There seem to be many mysterious disappearances. People throughout the Pulse-affected area are often just disappearing. Nobody has an explanation."

"I think that's all I can handle. Is there any good news?"

"Yes. Much of the Navy's Atlantic Fleet has returned to the Norfolk Naval Station. The Navy has set up a distribution center there to accept and disseminate relief supplies coming from all over the world – even from our enemies. If I heard it correctly, there was a small shipment from Castro's Cuba and another from Venezuela. There was even a shipment of food from Haiti. Can you imagine, Haiti sending the United States a Care Package? Somebody from San Francisco spoke about a story that has gone viral over what's left of the Internet. A note apparently arrived in Norfolk from a shipment of tropical fruits from Haiti. It was signed by 40 children from a kindergarten class in Port-au-Prince. It said, 'Thank you to the people of the United States of America for what you did when we had our earthquake. We hope this helps.'

"Finland has sent tens of thousands of cellular telephones. Germany has sent hundreds of locomotives and Italy has sent several ships loaded with buses. Word has it that the European Union has agreed on a rescue plan modeled after the Marshall Plan that the United States implemented after World War II to rebuild Europe.

Most people think things will get worse before they get better, but the people of the world are uniting to support us. Maybe some good will come from this tragedy. We can all hope."

Sammy returned to the garden, determined to put the new horrors out of her mind.

Tuesday, October 16

Sammy arrived at the weekly music jam in a buoyant mood, eager to play her new violin. When she took it from the case, several people commented on it and congratulated her. Rhonda, Dowell, and Ortie were talking with some friends when Sammy and Jamaal sat down.

Everyone was playing *Barlow Knife* when Shane walked in and found a chair. He gave her a smile and a nod. Because of his barbaric behavior at the hanging, her feelings for him had soured completely. She barely acknowledged him. They played *Drowsy Maggie* next, letting Sammy take a long break when it came her turn.

Rhonda announced that she had a new song she wanted to sing. Ortie set up to accompany her on his bass. She said, "This one is called, *Rest for the Wicked*. It goes something like this,"

In the bed, I lie with eyes wide open
Thinking over this cold, lonely day
Trying to silence the thoughts and the memories
Trying to drive your vision away
Rest don't come easy for the wicked
Who lied, cheated and lost
I promised I'd give up the whiskey
But now I could use one more shot

Sammy thought Rhonda looked older than her fifteen years, and more worn. Most of the women had lost weight during the ordeal, but Rhonda still looked just as heavy. Sammy wondered if the whisky reference was real, and if Rhonda had become a drinker, at such a young age.

As soon as Rhonda and Ortie finished their song, they summarily left. The group did a couple more songs before breaking up for the night. While Jamaal was talking with someone else, Shane came over and said to Sammy, "Congratulations on your new fiddle. Where'd you get it?"

"Emily gave it to me. It was my birthday on Saturday. I thought you might have come to my party."

"Emily and Jamaal told me about it, but I couldn't make it. I had business to attend to."

"Oh?"

"Mom sent me to Independence to the courthouse with a couple of stragglers caught the other day trying to break into Quint's drug-store. Seems like some of the good townspeople pitched a fit over the hangings last week. So they want accused people to go to the county jail. So mom sent me to Independence to take them to jail. It's a damn long way to Independence and back on a horse-drawn cart. So once I got them to the New River Bridge, I shot them both and threw them over the railing. Damn white trash."

"You WHAT?"

"Are you hard of hearing, girl? We've got to keep the peace around here. Mom don't know yet so I'd appreciate it if you don't say anything to her. Say, how about if I walk you home?"

"Go away and leave me alone," she said to Shane, walking to Jamaal and leading him out the door. Any attraction she had ever felt towards Shane was gone.

Wednesday, October 17

Sammy spent the entire day working around the house. She chopped firewood, cut some hay, and washed clothes. Hattie flitted in and out, helping her with the clothes and hanging them on the clothesline. Sammy was delighted by the corgi, Snoopy, who split his time between the two women. By dinnertime Sammy was exhausted. Per usual, she ate alone.

Thursday, October 18

Sammy awoke and decided it would be fun to select a card from the Augury deck Avalon had given her. The card she chose said, "Leadership."

She had spoken the day before with Emily about visiting Helen Quimby to check on her pregnancy. They rode over in the wagon, drawn by Maggie. Emily had Sammy do the examination first, then she confirmed Sammy's evaluation that all was going well. The due date was November 29. Leaving the Quimby house, Emily said, "Did you hear the second heartbeat?"

"No."

"I did. I think Helen is going to have twins. I thought to mention it, but I decided to keep it a surprise!"

Further on, Sammy spoke to Emily about Revelation, and what she'd heard from Woody, without mentioning him by name. Emily said, "I call it Revelation Fever. It scares the hell out of me."

"What do you mean?"

"My neighbors can't wait for the End Times. These folks would eagerly throw away the Constitution and institute some sort of Law-by-Bible in its place. Jefferson, Madison, Adams… almost all the Founding Fathers were atheist or agnostic, and all of them believed that religion played no part in running a country, or shouldn't. But the religious wackos can't wait for World War III."

"Why?"

"They believe the End Times cannot start during peace time. When Israel was formed, that started the ball rolling. The next step involves the capture of more of the lands of the Bible in Israel's hands. That can't happen without war. So they support any and all wars, even if they have to sacrifice their own children. Christians can't go sit by the throne of Jesus until they're raptured, and they can't be raptured until the beginning of the End Times, and the End Times can't ensue without world war. It's beyond insane."

"I wonder how they're feeling now after the Pulse," Sammy reflected.

"Me, too. I suspect the fundamentalists outside the affected area are looking at it completely different than those here do."

Friday, October 19

Jamaal and Pike came over to help Sammy put up hay for Jackson. They worked for several hours on a cool, crisp morning, but the men were still sweating in wet cotton shirts. Pike's shirt was maroon with an orange VT logo and the words "Hokies on Fire," printed on it. Jamaal's shirt was grey with dark navy blue lettering that said "Hoyas." Nobody knew what either Hoyas or Hokies meant.

The three of them gathered the hay Sammy had cut on Wednesday and raked it over to dry it. Then they all cut as much as their strength would allow.

Caroline came by as they were finishing lunch to pick up some of Hattie's cheese. On her way out, Sammy saw her to the front door and waved goodbye. Twenty minutes later, Pike decided to head home as well.

Moments later, he came running back up the porch yelling madly, "Sammy, Jamaal, come quickly!"

The three ran to the edge of the road. Lying there on the ground were the clothes that Caroline had been wearing and the basket she'd used to carry the cheese. Caroline was nowhere to be seen.

"What the hell?" said Jamaal.

"I don't think I should be thinking what I'm thinking," Pike mumbled.

"Wow. What should we do?" Sammy asked.

"Who knows? People don't just vanish… do they?" Jamaal wondered aloud.

"Is there any law around here?"

"There's Annie Wilkins. She didn't give a damn when my violin was stolen. Do you think she gives a damn when somebody vanishes?"

"I think we should find Woody Dalton first. Then we'll do what he wants us to do."

"I think you're right."

"Sammy," said Pike, "you stay here with the clothes and Jamaal and Ih will look for him."

"What am I supposed to do?"

"How do Ih know? Ih'm an engineering professor. This is beyond my pay grade."

"Mine, too," shrugged Jamaal. "Just don't go vanishing yourself."

The men walked out of sight. Sammy sat on a rock near the road. And sat. And sat. Getting tired of just sitting, she went inside and got her new violin and brought it back, carrying a folding lawn chair from the porch with her. She sat by the fallen clothes. Some of the neighbors happened by and asked what was going on. Sammy thought it must look extraordinarily strange, a girl, sitting on a lawn chair by an unused road, fiddling, in front of a pile of women's clothes and a wicker basket with cheese in it. One woman Sammy had seen before at Quint's church crouched by the clothing and said, "Lord have mercy. She's done been raptured up. She's gone to be with Jesus!" She closed her eyes, gathered her hands together in prayer, and began mumbling. Two other women and a man joined the growing scene and were all praying when Pike and Jamaal returned with Woody.

"I can't believe it," said the new widower. "She's always been devout but I had no idea... It can't be real, can it?"

"I'm thinking somebody should go get the law. I'll head into town and see if I can find Chief Wilkins," said Jamaal. "Sammy, why don't you go inside and get your Polaroid? If this is a crime scene, perhaps somebody should have photos of it."

She went inside and returned with the camera where she took a photo from each angle. Nothing else seemed to be amiss.

Eventually, the crowd of strangers started drifting off, each mumbling incoherently in sobs of grief and disbelief. As darkness approached, Woody decided he needed to go home as well. Sammy and Jamaal stayed behind, wracking their brains as to a plausible explanation of what they'd seen.

Saturday, October 20

The next morning, Sammy heard a knock at the door, but Quint was already there when she reached the bottom of the stairs. Annie Wilkins, wearing her police uniform, said, "I'm here to investigate the rapturin' here yesterday."

Quint turned towards Sammy and said, "You tell her. You were there."

"Yes, ma'am."

"Come outside with me," the officer insisted.

"Yes, ma'am."

Quint followed the women outside past the moped she'd ridden there. It was raining lightly.

"What did you see?" Wilkins asked.

Sammy shrugged, "The deceased, or the presumably deceased, or should I say the raptured woman, Caroline Dalton, left our house just after lunchtime yesterday."

"What was she doing here?"

"She came to pick up some of Hattie's goat cheese for her nursing home. Jamaal Winston, Pike McConnell, and I were here."

"Just you and two men?"

"Ma'am, you need not be thinking what you're thinking. They're my friends."

"I'm a cop. It's my job to be suspicious. Never mind. What did you see?"

"Mrs. Dalton left first. A few minutes later, Pike left too. But within moments he came back yelling for us. So Jamaal and I came out running. What we found is exactly what you see here."

"Nobody has moved anything?"

"No. Well, I took the cheese inside so it wouldn't attract animals.

Otherwise, everything is right where we found it."

The policewoman wrote a few notes on a sheet inside a rectangular box metal clipboard. "Not much to go on or look at. Can you get the clothes back to the raptured woman's husband?"

"Yes, ma'am. Do you need me for anything else?" Sammy asked, helpfully.

"Not now, but I know where to find you if I need you."

"What are you going to do next?" Quint asked.

"What do you want me to do? I don't have any staff. I don't have any investigators. I don't see there's much for me to do."

Handing Wilkins the photos she'd taken, Sammy asked, "You don't really think she's really been raptured up, do you?"

"Like I said, I'm a cop. You're asking the wrong person." She nodded at Quint and said, "You might want to ask him." She walked to the moped and stowed her clipboard. "Ms. Reisinger. Reverend Thompson. Good day." She kicked the starter on the moped and sped away.

Sammy looked at Quint but didn't say anything. It occurred to her that the question he was likely asking himself was not whether the woman had been raptured, but why he hadn't.

"I've got some work to do," he said. "I've got some chores and then I'll need to prepare tomorrow's service." He walked away.

Sammy picked up Caroline's things and carried them inside. She wanted to deliver them to Woody in a vessel more fitting of someone's 'remains' than a shoe box or a grocery bag, but she couldn't think of anything. So she put the clothes themselves in the wicker basket. She picked a fading rose from the garden and put it to her nose and enjoyed its fragrance. She found some wire and wrapped the stem of the rose to the basket's handle and took it inside.

Sunday, October 21

Sammy went to church wearing a black dress of mourning she found in Bonnie's closet. She wore the silver comb Hattie and Marissa had given her. Jamaal, Emily, and Pike attended as well. Woody wore a black suit; it was the first time Sammy had seen him in anything other than bib overalls.

Quint gave a eulogy for Caroline, saying she was now with the Lord. It was a blur to Sammy, as she, like the others, was wracked in grief.

Sammy hadn't noticed that Rhonda and Dowell were not in attendance until Quint mentioned that Ortie had died the prior day when one of his steers trampled him. The funeral would be held in a few days but had not yet been scheduled. People close to Sammy were dying at a terrifying rate.

Quint left for home before Sammy, as she stayed to console Woody and Caroline's other friends. She walked home alone. Approaching the house, she heard Quint inside, yelling. She dashed up the porch stairs and found him berating Hattie in the living room. "Damn, you, woman! Where is the Lord in your life?"

She was holding her arm as if it had been hit. In her other hand, she held her eyeglasses, which had been broken. She said nothing, but she sobbed quietly.

"What's going on here?" Sammy asserted.

"None of your damn business, Jew girl. This is between my wife and me."

"Did you hit Hattie? Did you?" Sammy walked towards him. "I don't care what she did or didn't do to make you so angry, but you will not hit her again!"

"Look at you, Miss Priss!" He grabbed her left arm, squeezing hard.

Wincing, she threw her right arm into his forearm, breaking his grip. "Don't you ever touch me again!"

"This is my house and I am the man here. I will discipline anyone I wish in my house, anytime I wish. If you don't back off, you'll be starving in the woods by nightfall."

Hattie sobbed loudly and ran from the room.

"Listen, Quint," Sammy said assertively. "I appreciate your hospitality, but your aggression is inexcusable. Didn't you preach the gospel of the Lord this morning? Would the Lord approve of your violent behavior?"

An eerie silence engulfed them. His face began to get flush, and a wave of regret seemed to come over him. "I'm going to my room. I need to think." And he walked away.

She ran outside, looking for Hattie, but she was nowhere to be found. A brisk wind struck Sammy in the face and the clouds gathered. She ran through the garden, through Jackson's pasture, and into the barn, looking. It began to rain, with large balls of hail. She finally retreated inside and went to her room, where she picked up her new violin. She played Brahms' *Requiem, 2nd Movement*, letting the rhythm of the music and the pounding of the hailstones on the tin roof soothe her.

Monday, October 22

Sammy had spoken with Jamaal in church about practicing karate. So she rode over and led him outside under the maple tree, which was now fully a brilliant orange. She worked with him through the morning on her positions and her kicks. After they had lunch and some rest, Sammy asked him about the banjo she'd been given. "You said something the other night about the banjo being the instrument of hardship and toil. What did you mean?"

"Ah, Grasshopper let me tell you about your new instrument. The two essential instruments of traditional Appalachian music are the violin and the banjo. Other instruments like guitars, bass fiddles, mandolins, harmonicas, autoharps, and even things like washboards and spoons are nice, but if you have a violin and a banjo you have a band! But the histories of these two instruments couldn't be any more different."

"How so?"

"Your violin has an illustrious heritage. The Greeks and Romans had several stringed instruments like lyres and lutes that can be thought of as the ancestors of the class of hour-glass shaped instruments that comprises the violin, viola, cello, and double bass, which people here call the upright bass. By the time the Middle Ages rolled around, the modern violin emerged. There has been remarkably little variation since. There are violins of different sizes, but the proportions are almost identical."

"When I first started learning to play," she recalled, "my parents wouldn't let me play Grandfather's violin yet. The first one they bought me was smaller."

"That seems appropriate. Your Guarneri was likely played by some of the most accomplished musicians in the world for the two-hundred-plus years since it was made. It gives me goose bumps thinking about where it may have been and who may have played it..."

"And what fabulous musical pieces... It makes me cry," she sighed.

"Me, too. I'm not giving up hope that someday it will find its way back. Anyway, meanwhile, the banjo was travelling a different route. The banjo originated in Africa and was nothing more than a gourd, a skin head stretched over it, a wooden neck, and a single string. When the Europeans began enslaving my people, they let them bring their 'banjers' with them, as they thought the slaves would be more productive if they were allowed some recreation. Many an evening must have been spent outside the slave shacks on the plantations where my people played and danced to the music of their banjos, trying to find some joy in their otherwise interminably hard lives.

"In what must be an irony on top of a paradox on top of an enigma, the banjo was stolen from black people by white people. The whites, of course, considered the blacks to be a substandard race. Yet that didn't keep white people from putting on torn, tattered clothing and soot on their faces and impersonating Negroes in what they called minstrel shows."

When he saw the incredulous look on her face, he said, "That's right, child! White people impersonated black people to entertain white people! A white man from central Virginia, Joel Walker Sweeney, used the banjo in these minstrel shows and helped popularize the instrument for whites. As these shows became more fashionable, fewer and fewer black people wanted to pick up a banjo. Throughout most of the 20th Century, you could find few blacks still playing them."

"How do you know all this stuff?"

"I told you, girl, that I am a student of music. I've been following my grandfather's legacy for years. In a way, you and I are on similar quests, inspired by our grandfathers. Now stop interrupting my lecture. I will entertain questions at the conclusion," he chuckled.

"Yes, Professor Winston," she said, teasing him.

"Now, where was I? Absentminded... Oh yes. In particular banjos migrated from the slaves of the south to the hillbillies of the Appalachian Mountains. There, they mixed with the fiddles that were being brought here by the mostly German, but also Scots-Irish settlers. The people of the mountains were poor, as the land gave them little more than a log or plank cabin, some farm animals, and a garden. Typically, their two most prized possessions were their gun and their banjo or fiddle.

"As the modern age has dawned, the banjo has become more popular and is reaching more affluent musicians. So you will see many now that have mother of pearl inlays, resonator rings, and other variations. In fact, there are banjolins – which are the marriage of the banjo and the mandolin, and the banjolele – the marriage of the banjo and the ukulele. There are four-, five-, and six-string banjos. Banjos are anything but standard.

"Now then, are there any questions, class?"

"No, but my appreciation for the gift Emily gave me is greater. Thank you!" she said, smiling.

"This information will be asked on the final exam," he concluded with a professorial laugh.

Tuesday, October 23

Many of the usual people were at the weekly jam session. Jamaal took his banjo and Sammy decided to take her new banjo, too. She hoped she could practice with it and learn from the other musicians, who had always been helpful. Sure enough, when they played *The Hunters Purse* and she had trouble with one of the transitions, Pike stepped over and showed her the fingering.

Shane arrived late, but contributed on several songs. Rhonda hadn't said a word to Sammy, but she announced that she had written a new song, that she asked to sing, a capella. She announced, "It's called, *Blown Back With The Breeze*."

> *If I was a hawk, I'd flutter my wings*
> *I'd fly so high to the heaven's I would sing*
> *I'd soar across the country, all the way to Eugene*
> *And over Mount Hood, you could hear me sing*
> *Oh, I would roam, I would fly*
> *I would scale the mountain sides*
> *I would drift across the seas*
> *And be blown back with the breeze*
> *If I was a leaf blowing in the wind*
> *I'd be whisked away to Wilburn Ridge*
> *There I'd sit and watch the horizon sun set*
> *See the Blue Ridge skies turn to purple and red*

As they were packing their instruments to depart, Keene brushed by Jamaal and knocked Jamaal's banjo to the floor. The sound resonated through the room and several people winced. Sammy saw Keene snicker, and then keep walking.

"Adults say 'Excuse me' when they make a clumsy mistake," Jamaal said to the big man's back.

"You talking to me, nigger?"

"I was, but my lesson in manners appeared to have fallen on deaf ears. Did you forget your hearing aids?"

Keene turned around, walked back to Jamaal, and pushed him to the floor. "If you know what's good for you, you won't get up."

With that, Jamaal sprung to his feet and glared at his attacker.

Keene continued, "You and the girl here done wore out your

welcome." He lunged at Jamaal again, but this time, Jamaal deflected his attack, grabbed his arm, and somersaulted him to the floor, where he yelped with pain.

Several other men positioned their hands as if boxing and Jamaal and Sammy assumed the "ready" karate position. One man rushed at Jamaal, but was met with a kick to the face, which sent him sprawling.

"Pow!" A shot rang out. Plaster flew from a bullet-hole on the ceiling. Shane drew his gun to his side and said, "Fellers, let's not get too excited. Let's all just go home, shall we?"

Keene, now back on his feet, pointed a finger at Jamaal and said, "Fine. But your days here are numbered, nigger. Same with your little Jew girlfriend." He stormed outside with Draper right behind him.

Outside and on their way back to Providence, Sammy said, "What are you going to do?"

"About what?"

"About Keene and his threat."

"Keene can go to hell. He's just seeing what I'm made of. I won't be intimidated and I'm not going to show the bastard any fear. I can take care of myself. How about you? He threatened you, too."

"I'm a bit freaked out. I've never been threatened before."

Half the disk of the moon overhead lit their way. It was a beautiful night.

"But," she continued, mustering bravery, "if you're not intimidated, I'm not intimidated either."

Wednesday, October 24

Sammy decided to call on Woody to console him over the loss of his wife. So she rode Jackson to his farm. His farmhands told her that he was out somewhere on the land. She spent an hour looking for him, unsuccessfully. Roaming the farmland alone with her horse, she found an abandoned log cabin, nearly collapsed. She wondered how a family had willfully chosen such isolation, a century or more earlier. The scenery was absolutely breathtaking, with rolling blue hills vanishing into the distance to the west.

She eventually rode home, never finding him.

Thursday, October 25

Sammy had just finished eating lunch when she heard Emily's bell ringing. She tidied up and left the jar of apple butter on the table for Hattie, should she come in hungry. She tacked up Jackson and lashed her midwife's kit to the saddle. Then she rode over to Emily's.

Emily was sitting on the front porch waiting for her, wrapped in a blanket, when Sammy arrived. "I'm not feeling well today, dear. Sammy, Mrs. McGuire's husband Steven was here an hour ago. He says she's having contractions every thirty minutes. I've delivered all five of her children and she's always done well. I hate to put this on your shoulders, but I need to you go help her alone."

As Sammy steeled herself for the task to come, Emily gave her instructions. Sammy rode Jackson to a trailer park. It was the same park that Sammy remembered was where Shane and his mother lived. She hoped not to run into him.

She arrived to find Brooke McGuire having regular contractions. She continued to dilate and everything went according to plan. Sammy took a couple of breaks visiting with the other children, ages 3 to 14, in the larger room of the double-wide trailer home. At 5:06 p.m. according to the father's watch, the baby, a girl, was born. Sammy listened to the baby's heartbeat as Emily had always done. All the vital signs were perfect, as was the baby's size and weight. Within minutes, Sammy cut the cord and the baby was suckling at her mother's bosom. Darkness was setting in when she walked outside and secured her bag. She hoisted herself atop Jackson and turned to walk him home.

Just as she passed the trailer next door, she saw a familiar silhouette emerge, back-lit by an oil lamp inside. The male figure descended the steps and began walking towards a bicycle parked on the side of the trailer next to a moped. He turned the bicycle around and was walking it towards the street when he noticed her.

"Quint?"

"Sammy, what are you doing here?"

"I've just helped deliver a baby. What are YOU doing here?"

"None of your damn business. Listen, you will forget you saw me here. You get on home."

She continued to stare at him, processing what she was seeing and what it meant. Then he said, "You won't understand, but I haven't had relations with my wife in two years. Now, get out of here."

Friday, October 26

Sammy spent most of the morning raking hay and putting it up for Jackson. In the afternoon, she rode to Carlene's Country Store and traded some of Hattie's cheese for some pears and corn meal.

Upon her return around dinner time, she found Quint and Hattie in the living room, he actively berating her. The Welsh corgi barked from the corner by the door. Sammy intervened, breaking up their squabble. But as Sammy walked Hattie outside, Hattie sprinted away. Sammy ate alone and went to bed early, tired and stressed.

Saturday, October 27

Sammy was working on the garden on a cool Saturday morning when Marissa arrived, calling for her. Marissa approached and said, "I've just seen Hattie. What went on here yesterday?"

"I'm not sure. When I got back from Carlene's Store, Quint was yelling at her. He was drunk, I'm sure. He beat her up pretty bad. I got them apart, but she ran from me."

"The son of a bitch! What was he so upset about?"

"I really don't know. I was able to break up their fight, because he re-directed his anger towards me. I don't know what he did to her. But he's gotten increasingly violent with both of us."

"Damn it!"

"He's threatening to kick me out. Believe me, I've thought about leaving a million times. Now, though, I feel obligated to be here as much as I can, in case Hattie needs me. Truthfully, I'm not sure what I can do to help her. But I feel I must stay."

Then Sammy told Marissa what she'd seen two nights earlier at the trailer park. Marissa got a pensive look on her face. "I know the man. I know his brother. I know what they're like. I always hoped for Hattie's sake that Quint would be different, but he's not.

"I've always tried to live a good life and see the best in people. I've always tried to do good turns and to contribute when and where I could. I've always believed in Jesus Christ who is my Lord and Savior. I have always cherished the thought of sitting with him in eternal life forever. But that notion is over."

"Over? What do you mean?"

"I'm going to kill Quint. I'm going to kill the son of a bitch before he hurts my sister again or hurts you."

"You're not serious!" Sammy screamed.

"As serious as a heart attack. I just need to figure out how. But within a week, that lying, cheating, abusive scoundrel will be dead; you mark my words."

Sunday, October 28

When Sammy awoke, Marissa was in Ronnie's bed next to her, sitting upright. "Let's go to church together this morning. I'm going to need all the saving I can get."

So they had some breakfast of bread and apple butter with goat's milk to drink, and departed for church. Quint was nowhere to be seen and had apparently left for church early. When they arrived, he was standing outside in his robe, chatting with other parishioners.

Quint presented his sermon in his typical didactic, theatrical way, carefully and dramatically enunciating each syllable of each word. It was about temptation, something that made Sammy giggle. At one point, Marissa nudged her. "I know what I am going to do."

On their walk home, Marissa said, "I am going to poison him."

"Wow. Are you serious?"

"Absolutely. You know an herbalist, don't you?"

"Yes."

"Let's go see her and see what's in her medicine chest. What's her name?"

"Avalon."

"Do you think she'll help us?"

"I don't know. If she did, she'd be an accessory to murder. I know she doesn't care for Quint, either. But I'll ask her."

Monday, October 29

In the morning, Sammy and Marissa took the long walk to Avalon's house. She met them with gracious hospitality. "To what do I owe the honor of your visit?" she asked.

"We're going to kill Quint – I'm going to kill Quint – and I want you to help me," Marissa said succinctly. She told Avalon about Quint's physical abuse towards Hattie and Sammy. Sammy mentioned Quint's presumed affair with Annie Mullins. Marissa and Sammy expressed fears of ongoing violence and infidelity. Avalon said, "Come back tomorrow and I'll have something for you."

Bidding them goodbye, Avalon gave Marissa a little hug, and then while Marissa wasn't looking, she gave Sammy a kiss on the lips. "I'll see you tomorrow."

Tuesday, October 30

As instructed, Sammy rode Jackson to Avalon's house to collect the poison. Avalon said, "This is a reduction of belladonna." She handed Sammy a tiny glass vial closed with a cork. "It is one of the most toxic plants in North America. I've added some seeds of rattle-box for an extra kick. Put a few drops of it in the batter of some pancakes or cookies. Don't even let this stuff touch your skin."

Sammy returned home and did some chores with Marissa. Then after dinner, she rode Jackson into Fries for the weekly jam session. They played *Sally Ann*, *Cotton-Eyed Joe*, and *Tater Patch*. Sammy took a long break on *Orange Blossom Special*, one of everybody's favorite tunes.

Rhonda was in attendance, the first time Sammy had seen her since her father died. Sammy tried to express condolences, but Rhonda brushed her off.

To the crowd, Rhonda said, "I've got another new song to sing for you. It's called *A Lonely Old Man*."

A lonely old man in a dark, dreary room
In a lonely old house filled with sorrow and doom
There's no one around, not a soul can be found
Just a lonely old man in a dark, dreary room
But there's still one friend
That's always been with him
There's still one friend
That brings out the devil in him

Sammy departed, wondering about Rhonda and where she found the inspiration for her song.

Wednesday, October 31

Sammy and Marissa were joined in the garden by Hattie, who seemed to be in unusually good cheer. Sammy wondered if Marissa had said anything to Hattie about the diabolical plot she was in the process of executing. Marissa said to Hattie, "Sammy and I are going into the kitchen to bake some cookies for the children that may trick-or-treat here tonight. Would you like to help us?" Hattie shook her head, no, and vanished into the woods.

"Okay, Sammy," Marissa said. "Let's get to work." They mixed enough batter for two dozen oatmeal cookies from ingredients diminishing in the pantry. They cooked the cookies in the woodstove, leaving batter for two cookies separate. They placed three drops of poison in the batter before spooning it onto a baking pan, reminding themselves repeatedly to be careful with it. As it was coming out of the oven, Marissa said, "I'm going to leave for home tonight. Leave these here at Quint's place at the table. I'm sure he'll be home late and will eat them when he arrives. He should be dead by morning." She put on a yellow jacket with a Wytheville Community College logo, and she departed.

As the sun was nearing the horizon, several children came by to trick-or-treat. Sammy gave each child two cookies, assuring herself that the poisonous pair was safely inside.

Among the trick-or-treaters were two children, a girl and a boy, who arrived together, knocking on the door. She was dressed like a cowgirl, he like a cowboy. The boy was smaller and his ten-gallon hat nearly covered his eyes. A disheveled woman in a kitchen apron stood at the base of the porch stairs, waiting for them. Holding her cloth bag for cookies, the girl said, "Hey, you're the lady with the horse we met at the river. You're the one with the funny accent."

The boy said, "I remember you! Thanks again for giving us the fish."

The mother said, "My children brought home a fish and said a lady had caught it with their gear. Was that you?"

"Yes, ma'am," Sammy said.

"That was mighty generous of you. It was the best meal we ate that week."

"No problem, ma'am. Glad to do it." Sammy introduced herself to the woman, Norma Gallimore.

As she waited for any more trick-or-treaters, Sammy practiced her violin by oil lamp. She heard another knock at the door. Norma Gallimore was there with a frantic expression on her face, her children beside her. "Please come. I think something is wrong."

Sammy followed the woman for several hundred yards southward on Scenic Road. There, on the edge of the road, was a pair of shoes, a yellow jacket and Marissa's book bag. The mother said, "What do you make of this?"

Sammy stood in the dark, transfixed, and searched for words to express her horror and astonishment. "Damn."

The four stood for several moments, in mixed states of befuddlement. Finally, Sammy said, "Please, take the children home. I'll deal with this."

"Thank you."

Sammy stared at the pile for a few moments longer. She brought her hand to her face in sadness and her eyes moistened.

Moments later, Sammy decided that the law enforcement, being what it was – or wasn't – would be of little help to her. She ran back to the house and brought her Polaroid camera and took several snapshots, each of them accompanied by flashbulb lights that seemed like lightning. Then she carried Marissa's things back to the house and hid them in a bureau drawer. She cried herself to sleep.

Part 4: November

Thursday, November 1

SAMMY AWOKE THE NEXT MORNING with a splitting headache, her eyes aching with tears and pain. She shook herself into reality, and replayed in her mind the events of the prior day. What happened to Marissa? Was her fate the same as Caroline's? Where was Quint? Did he take his poison? Was he dead?

She unexpectedly found Hattie sitting in the living room, as if awaiting someone. Sammy wished her good morning, but as usual, Hattie was unresponsive. Entering the kitchen, Sammy saw that the cookies were just where she'd left them, feeling at once relieved that Hattie hadn't eaten them by mistake and consternated that Quint hadn't eaten them either.

She returned from the outhouse and had some cheese and crackers for breakfast, along with a yellow apple. Then, there was a knock at the door. It was Pike.

"Hi," Sammy said eagerly, before seeing the anguish on Pike's face. He entered and saw Hattie.

"Ih'm glad you're both here. Quint is dead. Somebody broke into the pharmacy late yesterday afternoon, apparently looking to steal drugs, and when Quint confronted him, they shot each other. The assailant was recognized as a man from Galax. He's near death himself. Nobody seems interested in treating him or his wounds."

The room was completely silent. Finally Pike said, "Mrs. Thompson, are you okay?"

Hattie's expression remained blank.

Pike looked at Sammy. "Are you?"

Not wishing to betray her prior intentions, she said, "There's been a lot of dying lately."

"Is there anything Ih can do?" Pike asked.

"What's happened with Quint's body?" Sammy inquired.

278

"Mr. Boyd, the undertaker, has it now. Ih suppose there should be a funeral, but since he was the pastor, Ih'm not sure who will organize or officiate. Ih've got to get back to town and work on the power plant."

"Let me talk with Emily and Jamaal and we'll be in touch. I'll see if Hattie will talk with me and let me know her intentions."

Pike departed and Sammy turned to Hattie. "Do you understand what's happened?"

Hattie sat immobile as a tear formed in her left eye and dripped down her cheek. She got up and walked outside. Sammy went into the kitchen where she used a spoon to put the cookies into a plastic bag which she put in her shirt pocket, along with the vial Avalon had given her. She walked outside, crossed the back yard, and approached the barn. She grabbed the metal spade and dug a small hole near the manure pile where she dropped the bag and the vial, and then covered it again.

Sammy rode Jackson to Emily and Jamaal's house, explaining what Pike had told her. They hitched Maggie to the wagon and drove into Fries. They met with Viller Boyd, the undertaker, and arranged to pick up the body the following day. Boyd looked harried. He wore a blood-stained white shirt, and the ring of hair at the base of his skull seemed uncut for months. There would be a simple, wooden casket. Boyd explained that two carpenters were working full-time building them, using primarily wooden slats from the ball-field at the elementary school. He said the ball field was being used as a cemetery, as the town's cemetery was too far away and the ground was too hard to be dug by hand. The ball field's dirt had evidently been placed there five years earlier when the pond behind the dam had been dredged. So it was much easier to dig.

The three of them searched the town for Alice Mullins, the acting police chief, but nobody knew where she was. Someone said she'd been in town earlier and knew Quint was dead, but had left town on other business.

On their way home, Emily said, "I suppose I'll officiate the service this Sunday and will do the graveside service. I'm not sure what

I'll say about the man, because I never cared much for him."

Sammy kept her thoughts to herself, but she wondered how the day would have played out had he returned home the day before and taken her poison as she'd planned.

Jamaal said, "I'll take the wagon back into town to retrieve the body and the casket. I'm sure I can find some folks in Providence to help me unload it and dig the grave in the church cemetery."

Friday, November 2

Emily's bell rang in the early afternoon. Sammy strapped arrived to find Emily waiting for her beside Maggie and the wagon. By late afternoon, they had returned after delivering a baby girl to Allison Perkins in Hilltown.

As they returned to Emily's house, Emily complained about not feeling well. "I'm going to try to get some rest this afternoon and tomorrow so I can hopefully be at Quint's church on Sunday to do the wake."

Saturday, November 3

After doing chores in the morning, Sammy decided to return in the afternoon to Fries to see if there were any personal effects of Quint's still at the pharmacy. After lunch, she saddled Jackson and strapped on her midwife's bag. It was a cool day with lazy, puffy clouds overhead.

She found a woman named Helen Nuckolls staffing the store. Nuckolls told her that she'd worked for Quint briefly years earlier, and that Annie Mullins had asked her to be there temporarily until longer-term plans could be devised.

Angie handed Sammy Quint's spare reading glasses, a silver cup, a pocket knife, and some change. As Sammy was preparing to depart, a man came running into the store, shouting for her.

"Ms. Sammy, Ms. Sammy, please you must help! My wife is going to have the baby!"

"Calm down. I remember when Emily and I called at your house a few weeks ago, but I can't remember your name."

"It's Emilio Vasquez. Please come!" He grabbed her by the sleeve of her sweatshirt and walked her outside. "You must come right away. My wife is in pain and I think she's having problems."

"Let me go and get Emily," Sammy suggested.

Walking towards his moped, Vasquez said, "I already went there. Ms. Emily is very sick. She said she wouldn't be able to come. She wanted you to assist."

"Are you sure your wife is having problems? As I recall, her due date is still a couple of weeks away."

"Yes, please come. She's in a lot of pain."

He turned the key and kicked the kick-starter and the little machine came to life. Sammy untied Jackson's reins and hoisted herself atop him. Vasquez sped northwards on Ivanhoe Road, then turned on Winding Road towards Stevens Creek. Sammy trotted Jackson and occasionally ran him, but she couldn't remember exactly how far away they lived and didn't know how hard she could push Jackson. Every few minutes, Vasquez stopped to wait for her. Each road they took was smaller and more remote than the one before.

Finally, they arrived at the Vasquez house, a tiny wood-frame structure surrounded by forests. He parked the moped and ran to her. "Please hurry."

Sammy grabbed her midwife's bag and trotted inside, leaving Vasquez to tie up Jackson. The expectant mother was in a fetal position on her living room floor, with their three girls playing with dolls near her.

"Hi, Mrs. Vasquez, I'm Sammy Reisinger, Emily Ayres' assistant. Emily is sick today but I'm here to help you. How are you doing?"

The dark-haired Hispanic woman rolled over towards her. "I'm in a lot of pain." She was wearing a loose-fitting yellow T-shirt that said, "*Bebé a bordo*," and navy-blue sweat pants, stretched to the limit.

"Are you having contractions?"

"Yes. I don't know how often."

"Can you get up? Would you like to go to your bedroom?"

"I'll try." Sammy helped her as Emilio walked inside and helped as well.

"Remind me of your name."

"Estella," she said, with a Spanish intonation.

"Okay, Estella, I'll do the best I can."

Emilio and Sammy placed the pregnant woman on her bed. Sammy noticed a large figurine of Jesus of Nazareth tacked to the wall above the bed. Emilio genuflected towards it. Sammy removed the fetoscope from her bag and warmed the sensor in her hand. "I'm going to listen and see how the baby's doing."

She lifted Estella's shirt and placed the diaphragm on her distended belly and began to listen. She couldn't hear any heartbeat. She moved the diaphragm from place to place, but couldn't hear anything except the faint sound of blood movement. She took the diaphragm and placed it between Estella's breasts and listened for her heart, simply to reassure herself that the fetoscope was working. Sure enough, she heard Estella's heart clearly and distinctively, although it was beating rapidly.

"We may have a problem," she said sadly.

"What is it?" asked Emilio.

"I'm not hearing the baby's heartbeat." Sammy felt Estella's belly. It felt full, balloon-like. "I don't feel the baby's body or head distinctly. Roll to your side and let me listen again."

Estella began to moan. "I'm having more contractions."

"Do you remember how long since the last ones?"

"I don't know. When Emilio wasn't here, I was trying to keep track, but the children were fussy and I couldn't concentrate. Owww! Owww!"

"Let me check your cervix." Sammy removed the cloth tape measure from her bag. "Only four centimeters. I'm afraid this is not good."

"What's wrong?" asked Estella.

"I don't know of any other way of saying this. I think your baby is dead," Sammy said sadly.

"¡Dios mío!"

"How will we know?" Estella queried.

"I don't really know," admitted Sammy, now sweating herself. "I've never seen a fetus die in utero." Sammy placed her hands again on Estella's belly.

"Owww! That really hurts!"

"I'm sorry! I don't mean to hurt you, but I'm not sure what's going on. Emily gave me a handbook. Let me let you rest for a moment and I'll see what I can find out." She began thumbing through her book, fruitlessly. She tried to ignore the sobs and heartbroken cries of the couple. One of the children in the living room began screaming. "I'm going to step outside and see about the children." Sammy went into the living room and held the youngest, a girl of about two years. She had on a shirt but no pants or underwear. There was a dark spot on the shag carpeting where one of the girls, likely this one, had urinated. The room smelled awful.

Sammy took the girl in her arms and held her tight. "Settle down, please, oh please." The girl gradually began to calm down and stop crying. Sammy said to all three girls, "Please behave yourselves. Your mother needs you to be good. I need to get back to her and try to help her."

She walked back inside. Estella was crying; Emilio was crying as well. Estella wiped her face with her shirt and said, "We understand that this baby is dead. We mourn for him. I am ready for him to leave my body."

"Estella, I don't mean to scare you, because I really don't know exactly what I'm doing, but I think our problems have only begun."

"What do you mean?" asked Emilio.

"When a baby is being born, the baby does much of the work. Your baby is dead, so he cannot help. Your cervix isn't dilated enough. So the baby is acting like a plug for the blood your body is feeding into the uterine cavity. I need to look at your cervix again." It was still constricted, about five centimeters. "I'm going to try to stretch it." She put her index and ring fingers of both hands together and pushed them inside, then began to spread them.

"Ow!" the woman screamed. "Owww! Please stop."

Sammy persisted.

"Owww! Dear God!"

Sammy removed her fingers and a burst of bloody fluid flowed from the cavity. "What's that?" asked Emilio.

"I think the placenta has been abrupted, meaning it is no longer attached to the uterus wall. Her body is trying to expel the fetus and the placenta. I'm going back in again."

"Owww! My God!"

The children cried from the other room.

Sammy stretched the cervix as much as she could bear, hearing the woman scream. Then she said, "I'm going to let you rest for a moment. Then we have to begin again. I'm going to give you some cotton root bark to help see if we can induce your body into labor." She went into the kitchen and found some water which she poured into a glass. She mixed a few drops of the fluid in her tiny vial in it. She returned and forced Estella to drink half of it. "In ten minutes, I'll need you to drink the rest."

She pulled Emilio aside and said, "Estella's body is trying to feed blood into the placenta. But the placenta has probably detached. So the blood is pooling in the uterine cavity. There is no way to stop the bleeding. She is only 5-6 cm dilated, so the dead fetus can't be expelled. She's losing lots of blood. We've got to get the dead fetus out or she will die."

"What do we do?"

"I don't know. I'm not a surgeon, so I can't simply slit her belly and pull the fetus out like a cesarean section. I'm sure she'd die if I did. So I need to keep stretching her cervix."

She returned to Estella and fed her the remaining cotton root bark solution. She removed her sweatshirt as she explained what she needed to do. "I'm going to keep stretching and you need to keep pushing." They worked for another 45 minutes or so, both sweating profusely in the cool room.

The woman screamed in agony. "*Este dolor me esta matando.*"

Sammy turned to Emilio and asked what she said. "The pain is killing her."

They had made little progress when Sammy noticed that Estella was beginning to go in and out of consciousness. "Work with me, Estella! Don't leave me!"

Estella drifted out of consciousness again. Emilio yelled, "*¡Pelea por tu vida!*"

Sammy became panicky. Indecision wracked her brain as she struggled with what to do. "Keep her talking, Emilio. Keep her awake!"

"Her hands are getting cold. She's shivering," Emilio whispered.

She noticed Estella's lips were turning purple. Sammy realized that Estella was bleeding to death. Sammy had no forceps, but she knew the fetus needed to be extracted. She squeezed her right hand inside Estella's uterus. She felt the fetus' head, but found nothing to grab. She pushed the head back, hoping to extend her hand inside further. Estella awoke from her light-headedness and she screamed. Sammy pulled out her hand, empty. Emilio was wracked with vicarious agony.

"*¡Mi esposa, mi querida esposa!*"

Sammy took a moment to gather her thoughts. Every scenario she could envision had little chance of success. She could do nothing, and Estella would surely die. She could slit her belly and do a C-section, but she had no knowledge of how and few tools to repair the cut. She could slice the inner wall of the birth canal, with likely the same result. But whatever decision she was going to make, she needed to make it quickly!

She reached into her bag and withdrew a sheathed scalpel. "I'm going to slit her birth canal," she told Emilio.

Emilio heard her and recoiled in horror, but Estella didn't. She was unconscious. Sammy made a slit about 1" deep at two o-clock and another at ten o-clock. She reached inside with her right hand and grabbed the dead fetus under its chin, reaching with the fingertips of her index and ring fingers. As gently as she could, she slid her hand and the fetus back through the enlarged canal and into the outside world. Blood spewed everywhere, both from the uterus and the surgical cuts. The fetus was blue and lifeless. It was a boy. She cut its cord and set it at the foot of the bed.

She looked in her bag for a needle and thread to suture the wound. When she looked, Estella's face was ashen and comatose, wide-eyed and frozen in a rictus of distress. Emilio was crying. Sammy reached for Estella's neck to see if should could detect a pulse from the jugular vein. Nothing. She looked at Emilio and said, "She's gone. She's dead. I'm so sorry."

The children walked inside and saw Emilio crying over their dead mother. The two year old saw the blood and the fetus, and screamed. The children ran to their mother and hugged her lifeless body. Emilio said to the corpse, "*Adiós mi amor.*"

"I am sorry, so, so sorry," Sammy said painfully. "I wish I had known what to do. Her death is my fault."

Emilio looked at her not with scorn but with sympathy.

Sammy got up and walked across the room to a small, wooden chair. She sat, surveying the scene of abject misery before her. There were three inconsolable children. There was a new widower, spilling tears over his dead wife. There was the lifeless body of a woman who only an hour before had lived, breathed, and felt pain. The umbilical cord still stretched from her bloody uterus. There was a lifeless fetus, as inert as a child's doll, inhumanly wretched in color, lying at the edge of the bed. Blood was everywhere: on the corpse of Estella, on the dead fetus, and on the sheets. Sammy looked at her hands and they were blood-covered, too, as was her T-shirt. She began to cry as well, joining the chorus of wails.

Time passed; she had no idea how long. She had lost all thought except wretched despair. She got up and found a towel to wipe her face. One of the children had fallen asleep, but otherwise the scene was just as miserable as before. She touched Emilio on the cheek and roused him from his semi-conscious agony. She moved him gently to his chair beside the bed. She took all three children and moved them into his lap. In a small closet in the hallway she found a pillowcase. She took the fetus and wrapped it inside. In the bathroom, Sammy found a washcloth that she used to wipe some of the blood from Estella's corpse. Rigor mortis was setting in, but Sammy moved Estella's legs into a more natural reclining position. She closed Estella's eyes. Then she took a brush from the vanity and brushed Estella's hair. She took the four corners of the bed sheet and wrapped them over the body. She removed the Jesus figurine from the wall and placed it atop the sheet.

"I'm going to sit in the other room," Sammy told Emilio. She took the smallest child, still asleep, from him. She sat on the living room sofa and placed the two-year old in her lap. She stroked the child's jet-black hair.

Her mind flooded with doubt and recrimination. She cursed herself for not being a better student of midwifery, of learning more, faster. She hated what she had seen, what she had done and not done. Why did she live when this good-natured, well-intentioned woman had died? She stroked the child's hair again and again. Then she put the child down and walked back into the bedroom. She picked up her scalpel and turned to walk back into the living room.

"Sammy?"

"Yes, Emilio."

"Thank you for what you did."

"Damn it, Emilio, I killed Estella; I killed your wife."

"No, Sammy, you didn't. You tried to save her. None of us will ever understand why the Lord needed Estella more than He thought we did. She is with Him now. If the Lord didn't need her, He would have let you save her. You did everything you could."

"But I didn't do the *right* thing!" she screamed.

"You did what you thought was best. It wasn't. But you had no options. You are not responsible for her death."

Sammy smiled weakly. "I appreciate your understanding and am so sorry for your loss."

"Thank you. What are you doing with that scalpel?"

She looked at the bloody tool in her hand with a puzzled detachment. She said, "I don't know. I suppose I'm going to clean it and put it away." She looked over her tools that were strewn about. She used the washcloth to wipe the blood from them and she stashed them back in her case.

"I think we should get the body out of here."

"There is a freezer on the back porch. It is empty of food; we ate everything in it after the Pulse. Let's put her body there. Tomorrow I can ride to town and discuss burial with the undertaker."

So with the oldest child helping, they picked up the body, encased by the sheet, and carried it outside. Sammy noticed that evening was coming on and with gathering clouds, it was near dark.

By the light of an oil lamp Emilio had lit, Sammy continued to clean the bedroom while he made dinner for the children. She put her sweatshirt back on. When she could envision no further way to lend comfort or assistance, she said, "Emilio, I must go."

"Yes, I understand. Thank you again for being here and doing your best."

She thought to protest his kind acknowledgement, but her responses all rang hollow in her mind. She put on her sweatshirt and said, "Goodbye."

"Goodbye, Sammy. Please be careful."

She walked outside where she was hit by a blast of cold air. It was pitch dark and raining lightly. She struggled to find Jackson in the dark. She tied her bag onto the back of his saddle with wet straps. She untied the reins and hoisted herself on his back using all the strength she had left. The saddle was wet and it felt cold on her jeans.

She walked him down the driveway which she could barely see, letting him find his best pathway. She turned left on Winding Road, again being startled by how cold it had become. She pulled the hood over her head and stretched the sleeves over her hands. She shivered, feeling the tremble emanate from her upper arms and ripple throughout her torso. It was profoundly dark and she could feel the closeness of the fog. The rain intensified.

The next tremor of shivering was more intense than the first. The rain had picked up and her sweatshirt and jeans became soaked. Water was absorbing into their fabric and it chilled her profoundly.

"Damn, it's cold!" she said to Jackson. She dismounted and took the bag from its straps. She found a towel inside that she wrapped over her shoulders inside her sweatshirt. She took the small cloth tray that she used with the fish-scale to weigh newborns and put it under her hood like a bonnet. She found two plastic bags and she stuffed them inside her pants and positioned them atop her cold thighs. She took out her *Forever-lite* flashlight, but fumbled it in her fingers and dropped it in the mud. When she bent to pick it up, a cold stream of water ran down her chest.

She thought about what Jamaal had said, that rain was colder than snow and how quickly exposure could kill someone. She shook violently. While trying to re-attach her bag, she realized that her fingers were losing circulation and her fingertips were numb. She winced, thinking about the cold dead fingers of Estella's corpse. She walked in front of Jackson and wrapped her hands around his ample head. She squeezed him and stammered, "I'm in trouble, Jack-Jack. Please help me." She let go and he nutated his head, knowingly.

She looked around but her vision was vacant. She could see no lights anywhere and the sky was featureless. Outer space would have given no fewer points of reference or security.

Somehow, she found a stump in the darkness and managed to mount him again. "Please take me home, boy." The massive, wet gelding walked forward.

She shivered violently again. Her breathing was rapid and shallow and she couldn't control it. Her jaw lay open and her head shook violently. She kicked his side, urging him to trot, thinking it would build some heat. But she almost fell from him, her hands too cold to manipulate the reins. Water trickled over her shoulders and onto her breasts and down the spine of her back. She could see nothing, not even her horse's head. She fumbled for the flashlight and somehow pressed the switch to turn on the beam, but it illuminated only mist in the enveloping cloud.

Her eyes fell shut, then open again, then shut.

She saw a rainbow. Bluebird.

A burning house. House.

A tree. Big tree. With a swing.

Red crosses in white eyes.

Crucifix. Jesus. Manger. Swaddling clothes. Baby Jesus.

Notes, musical notes. And scales. Mozart.

Shofar wailing.

Devil, fiery hell. Burning.

Jackson stopped abruptly and she almost fell off, shaking her hallucinations. "Holy crap, it's cold! Shit!" The great beast stopped moving. She kicked him again. He stood, immobile. She tried to kick him again, but her legs would not respond. He still hesitated. Then he turned completely around and began walking again. The reins fell from her hands.

Treble clef. Clef.

Dead fetus. Dead fetuses. Bloody.

Placenta.

The torah. Reading the holy torah.

Beethoven sonata.

Airplane crash.

Icebergs and polar bears, whales, narwhals.

Cold. David, Star. Oh, cold!

Machine guns blazing.

Crucifix.

Mysteriously, inexplicably, she began to feel warm. She whipped back the hood of her sweatshirt and threw off the cloth tray. Rainwater streamed down her face and neck, flooding her torso. But it didn't feel cold any more. It didn't feel anything.

666. The Beast.

Aurora borealis.

Holocaust, gas chambers, bayoneted babies. Hitler.

Shema Yisrael Adonai eloheinu Adonai ehad.

A small branch of a low-hanging tree swept across her arm, startling her and causing her to nearly fall. She was jolted to reality, but reality gave her nothing but cold, dark and wet. A light flickered in the distance, but she was unable to respond to it.

Snow on rooftops.

Santa.

May the words of my mouth…

World Trade Center towers, aflame.

Airplanes, engines failing, crashing.

A barely audible, tinkling sound struck her eardrums. Then she heard a dog bark. Then the tinkling became louder. Jackson stopped walking. More barking. Sammy willed her eyes open and shut, shattering the phantasm. A light appeared before her. She looked to see what appeared to be a door, opening. A figure dressed in a white robe materialized. The figure vanished but the light in the doorway remained. The dog barked. Her eyes fell shut again.

Then she felt a hand grab her left wrist. "Sammy!" a familiar female voice rang out. "What in the Devil's name are you doing out in this mess?" The hand pulled her from the saddle and she fell onto the shoulders of the figure in white. "Oh, Jesus, you are like an icicle! Talk to me, girl, RIGHT NOW!"

"I." Sammy recognized it was Avalon's voice.

"Damn!" Avalon exclaimed. "Your skin is so cold!"

Sammy felt herself being carried on Avalon's shoulders.

"I've got the sauna going. I was just on my way there myself." The woman opened the door to the sauna. The blast of warmth hit Sammy in the face and shook her awake.

"Here. Sit here," Avalon said. "Let me get you out of these clothes." She peeled off Sammy's sweatshirt, t-shirt and bra, and pitched them into a pile. Then she removed Sammy's sneakers and socks, wringing them out. She made Sammy stand and she wrestled her cold jeans to the floor. "You sit here for a minute."

Three candles flickered on a shelf above and the red glow of the fire radiated from the glass door of the woodstove. Avalon said, "I'm going out to secure Jackson. I'll be back soon."

The open door sent in another blast of cool air. Soon the sauna had re-warmed. Sammy began shivering all over again, violently enough to almost throw her from the bench. Within moments, her toes and fingertips were still numb, but her body felt warm, almost hot. It was luxurious, heavenly, almost sacred. The door opened again and with it came a blast of cold air and Avalon. "Hey, girl! I see you've decided to rejoin the living. I've brought you some water to drink."

"Oh, Avalon. Thank you, thank you. Oh, God, I love you." She got up and hugged her rescuer, oblivious to her own near-nudity. "You've saved my life!" She took a sip from the plastic glass. "I've never been so cold!"

"Just doin' my job, ma'am. Let's get good and hot. I've been cold all day. It's great to be in this sauna. I thought I'd be here alone, but it is nice having you with me."

Sammy sat down again, rested her head against the wooden wall, and cried, the emotion of the day washing over her. She cried a river, bawling like a child.

When time passed and Sammy opened her eyes again, the older woman was naked, reclining with her eyes closed. She was glistening red in the heat and dim light. Sammy was transfixed by her image. She had a goddess' form, with a thin, muscled torso, well-proportioned breasts, angelic face, wide shoulders, and shapely legs. Beads of sweat clung to her perfect skin. The only sign of her age was crows-feet wrinkles beside her eyes. The candle-light danced on her form seductively. Avalon opened her eyes and said to Sammy, "You look like you've never seen a naked woman."

Sammy's mind drifted to the bloated, pained form of Estella, writhing in excruciating agony just before she died, mere hours earlier. "I'm sorry; I didn't mean to stare. I'm just amazed. You're absolutely beautiful!"

"Good genes, wholesome food, plenty of exercise, and righteous living," Avalon laughed at her own joke. "Okay, maybe three out of four. Thanks, though. Say, are you hungry?"

"I feel like I haven't eaten since the dawn of time. I'm famished."

"Are you warm enough?"

"I almost wish you'd serve me in here. The heat is nearly suffocating; it's burning my nostrils." She forced a wry smile. "Two hours ago, I never thought I'd ever be warm again. But yes, I'm ready to go inside and eat."

Sammy put back on the robe that Avalon had given her, along with a pair of plastic sandals. Avalon led her to the shower where she washed off the sweat. Avalon showered after her. There was some beef stew already cooking on the stove. Avalon opened a bottle of red wine, "from my special stash," and the two discussed Sammy's travails.

"I've never had anybody die in front of me. It was awful, worse than awful. It was absolutely hellish."

Avalon listened attentively and supportively. Her final thoughts were, "Don't blame yourself. I'm sure there was nothing you could have done to save her."

Adjourning to the living room, Avalon brought a steaming pot of tea. Putting her nose to the cup, Sammy recognized the warm smell of caramel. While waiting for the brown liquid to cool, they discussed Quint's death, and the fact that their poison went unused. "I'm sure there will be some sort of wake for him tomorrow at the church. Given that I was actively plotting to kill him myself, I'm not sure it is kosher for me to attend."

"You're welcome to stay up here with me if you wish."

"I'd better get home first thing and see how Hattie is doing."

"Whatever you're comfortable with."

Sammy took a sip of her tea. "I've had this tea before. It brings back warm, wet memories."

Avalon laughed, guiltily. "I swear I'm on best behavior from now on."

Sammy smiled, feeling a libidinous tingling in her breasts.

The women sat up for an hour more, Avalon massaging Sammy's fingers and toes, sore from the cold, and discussing the news Sammy had heard in town and the hangings there. Finally, Sammy took a huge yawn. Avalon said, "You've had quite a day. Why don't you get some sleep?"

Sammy used the bathroom again and re-entered the living room where Avalon had spread the tools and accessories from Sammy's midwife's kit on the rug to dry. She had put a clean sheet and a pillow on the sofa.

"Goodnight, my sweet flower. Happy dreams."

"Happy dreams to you, too. Thanks again for what you did for me tonight. I will never forget it."

She walked towards Sammy and engulfed her in an embrace. Then she kissed her, meshing lips. Then, holding her at arm's length, said, "If you should be so moved, the door to my bedroom will be open." Avalon winked, smiled, and then departed to her room.

Sunday, November 4

Day broke to a clearing sky, bright and brisk. Sammy went outside before Avalon awoke to check on Jackson. She found him in a small paddock where he had been fed and watered. "Good boy, Jack-Jack!" she hugged him.

Avalon, still dressed in her robe, came outside to join them. "How's your big guy doing?"

"No worse for the wear, it seems. I almost froze to death but he was unfazed, his same old horse hyper-space self." She gave him a clump of grass from outside the paddock which he chomped loudly. Green drool dripped from his mouth.

Walking back inside with Avalon, Sammy said, "You know, what Jackson did last night was pretty amazing."

"How so?"

"I know horses. His instinct would have told him to go where he felt safe and secure, which would have been Quint and Hattie's place. But I never would have made it that far. I would have died from exposure. Instead of going where he would be safe, he took me where I would be warm, safe, and secure."

"We don't get to ask him why, do we?"

"All I can think to do is hug him, thank him, and love him."

Avalon loaned Sammy some clean, dry clothes to wear. The two friends finished breakfast of canned peaches, cheese, and bread, and Sammy prepared to depart. She put all her midwife's tools back into a still wet leather case. They walked outside toward the horse.

Avalon said, "You know, what you said about Jackson's selfless-ness got me thinking. An old lover of mine used to say, 'There are two types of problems in this world: your problems and somebody else's problems.' Emilio and Estella had a problem yesterday and you made it your problem. You didn't have to. You had no obligation to them. You could have walked away, and by doing so saved yourself hours of agony, grief, and the real risk of your own death. Did you ever at any point yesterday consider walking away from their problem?"

Sammy thought about it, but before she could answer, Avalon answered her own question. "No. No you didn't. You absolutely didn't think about it, not for an instant. You put their problem on your shoulders and you carried it, unfailingly, unselfishly, and unflinchingly. You were unsuccessful in your efforts, but you can never be blamed for trying. Lesser people, of whom the world has plenty, would have sprinted away."

"Thanks. That makes me feel better."

"You think I'm done. I'm not. The people of the Appalachians have suffered generations of indignities from the outside world and in some especially tragic cases from each other. People here have endured trial after trial, tribulation after tribulation. These are strong people. The situation we're in now is worse than ever before, but to many people here, it is just more of the same.

"You are not here because you want to be, but instead by catastrophic circumstance. You could have caved. You could have made a lifestyle of self-pity and loathing. But you didn't. Instead, you have taken it upon yourself to make this place better: more compassionate and more civilized. I bow to you, for you represent the best humanity has to offer."

"Thanks again. I don't know what to say."

"Don't say anything. Just keep doing what your heart tells you, always. When the world reaches a new normal and you seek a new path for yourself, always remember to keep doing what your heart tells you. Do that and you will never have a regret in your life."

"Thanks again."

"Come back and see me any time. My door is always open."

"Sometimes I worry about you up here alone," Sammy admitted.

"I'm fine; there's nothing to worry about. The coyotes leave us alone because they're frightfully afraid of Barkus. And the people leave us alone because they think I'm the Devil, or at least his friend."

"I think you're an angel."

"I think you're an angel, too."

Sammy saddled up Jackson and rode away, back to Providence. The day was stunningly clear. Although the leaves had all fallen from the trees, the landscape was delightful in primarily brown earth-tones. It amazed her how quickly nature had taken her from near death to the height of elation.

Reaching her destination, Sammy untacked Jackson and left him to roam in his pasture, feeding him one of the last remaining apples still on the tree. She carried her kit inside and was surprised to find Hattie sitting alone in the living room, dressed in black. "Good morning, Hattie." The woman said nothing. "Do you know that Quint is dead?" The woman nodded slightly. "Do you want to go to the church?"

"No."

"That's fine. Neither do I," Sammy admitted, mildly surprised that the habitually mute woman expressed herself verbally, albeit with a single word.

Nothing.

"Are you okay?" Sammy asked.

Nothing.

"Have you had anything to eat?" Sammy asked her near-mute hostess. "Okay, let's just sit here together for a while."

Sammy and Hattie sat quietly for some time. Finally, Sammy went to her and stood by her side. She stroked her hair, that hadn't been combed. "I feel your pain."

Sammy went upstairs and got the violin Emily had given her and she took it to the front porch. She gently lifted it from the leather case and removed the bow. She tightened the bow and drew it across the strings. She twisted the tuning pegs to tune it. Then she played *Meditation from Thais*, the saddest tune she knew.

Monday, November 5

Sammy awoke to the distant sound of the clanging of Emily's bell. She saddled up Jackson, strapped on the now-dry midwife's kit, and trotted over. Jamaal had hitched Maggie to the wagon, and the two women rode together to Stevens Creek to call on Julie Shelor who was due at the end of the month. As they got underway, Sammy told Emily about her experience with Estella and Emilio.

Emily said that by the prior day, she had begun to start feeling better and she had attended the church service and wake, officiated by Carlene. Sammy asked if Chief Wilkins and Shane were in attendance, and Emily responded affirmatively. She said, "Shane asked me about you. Not having any idea what you went through, I assumed you were fine. Do you have something going on with him?"

"I liked him when I met him, but not so much now. Now I avoid him."

Julie was fine, having no problems or complications. Emily assured her that her delivery would still be a few weeks away.

On the way home, they discussed Estella and her fetus' death in more detail. "Here's what it sounds like to me must have happened," Emily offered. "It is usually impossible to know why a fetus dies. But when it does, the woman is in real trouble, although she seldom knows it. Prior to the Pulse, a woman would go to a hospital where once the fetus was determined to be dead, an obstetrics surgeon would remove the fetus surgically. The mother would be stitched up and within a few days would be fine. But in earlier eras, many mothers died the same way Estella died yesterday."

"What should I have done?"

"I think you assessed the situation pretty well, that your options were few and all were bad. Your only other real option was to slit her belly and remove the dead fetus, but even an experienced surgeon would have faced substantial problems with infection and excessive bleeding if this was done outside a hospital. I think Estella was doomed before you even arrived."

"I'm not sure how I should feel about that. I felt really helpless,"

Sammy admitted.

"I'm sure you did. Anybody would have. But the lesson here is to keep your chin up and your head held high. Resolve yourself to learning more, being better skilled at everything you do, and moving on. Above all, don't beat yourself up. If you blame yourself, it will impede your progress and you will do a worse job the next time."

"I'm sure you're right."

"Medicine is an inexact science," the midwife said. "Nature is the best healer and a midwife's job is usually comforting the mother and letting nature take its course. Sometimes nature is cruel and things go to hell. Before modern medicine, thousands, maybe millions of mothers worldwide died in childbirth. It's tragic, but it's life. We all must go on."

Tuesday, November 6

Sammy spent the morning with her chores, but was looking forward to relaxing and playing her new violin again at that evening's jam session. Jamaal had told her the day before that he wanted to stay with Emily. So Sammy strapped her midwife's kit – desperately hoping she wouldn't need it – and her violin case to the back of Jackson's saddle and trotted most of the way into Fries.

Many of the regular people were there. Several were talking about Quint's tragic death and expressed their sympathies to her. One of them asked Sammy about her welfare without him. "It will be tough for Hattie and me, but life is tough for everybody these days." One woman she had seen before said, "I heard about what you did for Mr. and Mrs. Vasquez. It's tragic about what happened. Don't hold yourself to blame, girl."

Rhonda was particularly standoffish, making Sammy wonder again what she may have done to have earned her quondam friend's scorn. Sammy thought to confront her, then just dropped it.

Shane was there. He smiled at her several times. At one point, she felt that he was sizing her up lustily.

They played *Woodchopper's Reel*, *Tobin's Jig*, and *Sally Ann*. The mood was decidedly more somber than usual, owing Sammy thought to the death of Quint. The night was milder than the evening she'd been caught in the rain, but she still decided to leave before the session was over.

She was strapping her violin case to Jackson's saddle when Shane appeared, carrying his banjo case. "You're leaving early tonight. What's wrong?"

"Nothing really. I'm just tired and I'm ready to go home." She stood on a railing and hoisted herself atop her steed.

"Listen, I'll walk you home."

"No thank you. I'll be fine."

"No, I insist," he said, grabbing Jackson's reins near his bit.

"Let go of him, please."

Shane pretended not to hear her. He turned the horse and began walking towards Providence, leading Jackson.

Soon, they were beyond the edge of town. She insisted, "Please let go of us. I don't want you with me."

Again, he held firm and kept walking. A mile passed and she decided to take more drastic action. She removed her left foot from the stirrup and kicked Shane hard in the shoulder, simultaneously yanking on the reins to try to free them from him. Jackson skittered sideways and reacted angrily, but Shane never loosened his grip.

"Damn it, girl. Don't you do that again or I'll make you sorry."

"Let us go!"

"I'll let you go when I'm good and ready, and not before. So shut yourself up."

They continued in silence, uninterrupted only by the hooting of an owl. Her mind reeled, pondering her new horror, thinking about her karate training, and searching for a way to wrest the power of the situation from him. After the long walk back at the barn, Shane placed his banjo case on the ground, and in the same instant grabbed Sammy's pants just above the small of her back and yanked her off, throwing her to the dirt.

"Now then…" he said.

"Get the hell out of here, you asshole!" she screamed.

He unzipped his jacket and threw it towards his banjo case. "Don't be so disrespectful. Is that any way to talk? Southern girls don't talk to their boyfriends that way."

"You're not my boyfriend…"

He began unbuttoning his shirt.

"… and I am not having sex with you again."

He scrunched his eyebrows and said, "I don't recall asking, now did I?"

She decided she would fight for her life before she would succumb to him again. She assumed her "ready" karate position.

"Well look at you, now," he said condescendingly.

She lunged forward with her left foot, and then kicked him hard with her right, connecting to his ribcage and sending him spiraling to the ground.

"Damn, Jew girl! Where'd you learn that?"

She held her "ready" position and prepared to strike again.

"So you're going to be feisty tonight! Suit yourself," picking himself up. "If you hit me again, it's going to get really bad for you."

Karate: power. Samurai: weapon! She looked behind her and there was just enough light to see the metal spade that was often left leaning against the barn. She picked it up and ran at him, swinging it hard at his head. He lifted his forearm and the blade smacked it, but with the other hand he managed to grab it and he yanked it hard, sending her sprawling. He was holding the spade now and she had no defense.

"Goddamn it, you Jew whore! I'm done playing around."

Jackson snorted from behind Shane, and Shane reflexively swung the spade into the horse's shoulder, hitting the great beast hard. Sammy yelped, agonized over seeing her horse attacked and sensing that he would flee. Instead, the horse didn't flinch or back an inch.

Jackson glared at his attacker looking to Sammy as if he was accepting of what he must do. He snorted hard. His eyes glistened in the dim light. Jackson walked slowly towards Sammy's attacker, herding Shane towards the wall of the barn. Jackson bobbed his head up and down, and then snorted again as if sizing him up. Then he rose onto his hind feet, standing majestically, mythically grand, looking double his normal size, rippling with sinew and athleticism.

Shane instinctively held the shovel horizontally in front of his body, using it for a shield. But it was a futile act.

The great beast walked one step forward on its hind legs. It swung its left fore-hoof once, landing just above the bridge of Shane's nose, shattering his skull like a ball-peen hammer striking a wine goblet. The silence was broken with a sound like a huge, cracked eggshell. The 185-pound man crumpled like a leaf and smacked the ground.

Jackson dropped back on all four hooves and backed a few feet away. Then he walked towards Sammy who was still lying on the ground, and nuzzled her cheek.

For a moment, she shook violently, involuntarily, too afraid to stand. Then she petted her horse on the nose. "Oh, my, Jack-Jack," she murmured silently. She rose to her feet and walked to her erstwhile lover for a closer look. His arm was twisted at an odd angle behind him and his right cheek was planted against the dirt. Sammy turned his head towards her and she could see that his skull above his forehead was indented by an inch or more, and had the imprint of Jackson's horseshoe on it. She thought to look for a pulse on the jugular, but understood immediately that it was pointless. Nevertheless, she grabbed his neck with both hands and squeezed with all her might. "You fucker!"

She gradually loosened her grip, deciding that inflicting pain on a corpse was futile, other than to soothe her anger and rage. She dropped her hands and stood over him. She walked to Jackson and gave him a hug. She realized he had saved her life again, the second time within a week. From her experience around horses, she knew they instinctively ran from trouble. And yet Jackson didn't, defying equine instinct again.

Now what? she wondered. She drug Shane's body towards the barn, not really knowing what to do with it. It was too heavy for her to move for more than a few feet. What to do?

She saw that Jackson's wound from Shane's attack was minor. She mounted Jackson and galloped to Emily's house, where an oil lamp still glowed inside. When she knocked, Jamaal met her at the door. "Please, you must come with me. I have a problem and need your help."

"I'm not feeling well; neither is Emily. What is it?"

"It's important. Please!"

Sensing her urgency, he said, "Okay, let me get my coat."

He hoisted himself onto the saddle behind her and they rode back to the barn where everything was exactly as she'd left it. She told him what had happened and how Jackson had saved her again. "What do you think we should do?"

He looked over the scene. In near darkness, he saw the banjo case, the jacket, and the stiff. "I've got an idea."

The two of them stripped the body naked. Then they drug it towards the side of the barn close to the manure pile. Jamaal retrieved the spade Shane had used last to strike Jackson and began digging a cavity in the pile. They placed Shane's cadaver in the cavity and covered it with horse shit. Jamaal said, grabbing Shane's clothing and banjo case, "Let's go for a little walk."

Sammy untacked Jackson and set him loose in his pasture. Then Jamaal and Sammy walked back towards town, carrying Shane's things. At one point, they thought they saw someone coming so they dove into the underbrush. But it was two deer. They emerged, covered in mud and briers. Finally, Jamaal said, "This looks like a good place to be raptured, doesn't it?"

"Yes," Sammy concurred.

Jamaal placed Shane's two shoes on the ground, parallel to one another with one slightly forward, facing Fries. He stuffed the lower part of the socks into the shoes as if a body had simply vanished from within them, and then draped the pants, underpants, t-shirt, and jacket over them. He dropped the banjo case from chest high, hoping to break it convincingly. "Let's git!"

They walked rapidly back to Providence. Jamaal walked Sammy all the way back to the edge of her yard and then left for Emily's. Sammy ran to the barn where she retrieved her violin case and midwife's kit, then walked towards the back door of the house. She had the sense that she was being watched, that perhaps Hattie was some-where close by.

Wednesday, November 7

Sammy awoke, still apprehensive about the prior evening's events. She decided to continue with her life as if nothing had happened and hope for the best.

She walked to Woody's farm because days earlier, she had prom-ised him she would help take one of his steers to Carlene's Store for butchery. She wasn't excited about watching the process, but felt that if she was going to consume the beef, she should be prepared to help produce it. Along the way, she again was overwhelmed with dread about what had happened the day before and whether there would be repercussions.

Woody had chosen a black and white steer of about 900 pounds. He tied a halter around its neck and the man, woman, and animal marched back towards Providence. Woody said, "Nobody likes the killing part. It's bad enough taking a life, any life. But it's where the food comes from. I don't take pride in that part. I take pride in grow-ing them well."

They arrived at the store where Carlene had set up a butcher-ing area. There was a thick horizontal pole, suspended about 12 feet from the ground, upon which a block-and-tackle hoist was attached. "Once we get the steer here, we work as quickly as we can. We work especially quickly with pigs. Swine are intelligent and they sense what's going on. Beef, sheep, and fowl are more submissive, almost as if they understand that you have taken care of them as they've grown and now it is time for them to take care of you."

He led the steer near the pole and without saying anything to Sammy or warning her about what was to happen, he produced a 22-gauge rifle and shot the animal in the forehead. The animal im-mediately fell to the ground. Two other men and Carlene gathered spontaneously and as Woody tied a rope to the dead steer's left hind leg, they pulled the rope lifting the steer. Woody put on a plastic apron and grabbed a knife from a nearby holder above a table, sharpening the knife as he approached the animal. He placed a plastic trash bin underneath and then slit the animal's jugular vein, spilling the blood into it. "I think it is important to bleed out the animal within one minute," he told her.

Woody used his knife again to slit the carcass' gut. The viscera fell into another bucket, some on its own and some with additional slitting. The heart, stomach, and intestinal track were huge. Sammy was revolted, but determined to watch the entire process. Woody continued to talk as he worked, "I'm glad you're watching the butcher of a steer rather than a pig. For one thing, beef is Kosher and swine isn't. But for the other thing, more than any other animal, swine resembles humans.

"Please grab a knife," he asked her.

Sammy did what she was told. She joined the others as they began the process of stripping the skin from the carcass, using the knives to assist. Meanwhile, using a large knife, Woody had severed the head and pulled it away. Soon, a single, large skin fell to the ground. "There are two significant moments in this process. First is when the animal is killed. The second is when it is skinned. This completes the process of turning an animal into food. From here, it's just separating the cuts.

"We need to work quickly. Before the Pulse, we would chill the carcass for several hours to impede the formation of bacteria. We still butcher only on cooler days, but now we rely on speed. This carcass needs to be cut in a few hours and eaten within a couple of days."

Woody and one of the other men tied the carcass' other leg to the horizontal pole, separating the two legs. Then one of the men used a huge saw to separate the carcass into two halves. It was hard work and he sweated profusely.

"Nice looking carcass," said Carlene.

Everybody then began slicing off huge chunks of meat, some weighing fifty pounds or more. They carried the meat to the table where further, finer cutting was done, disposing of much of the fat and bones.

"What do you do with the left-overs?" Sammy asked.

"About 60-percent of the live weight of the animal is converted into food. The other stuff, like the head, horns, blood, lower legs, bones, and organs, are all used in some way or another. There's a guy named Arnie who takes the heads and uses them as bait to shoot coyotes. He feeds the coyote meat to his pigs and is probably doing the sheep farmers a favor by decreasing the population. Most of the other stuff is used as fertilizer."

Sammy returned home late in the day with a package of meat for dinner, proud of the work she'd done and the new knowledge she'd accumulated.

Thursday, November 8

Sammy had gone into Providence to the General Store to trade some cheese and Mason jar lids, and to see if Carlene had any cooking oil to sell. As she emerged from the store, she saw Fries' police chief, Annie Wilkins, arrive on her moped. Sammy was strapping her package to Jackson's saddle as the woman approached her. Wilkins was only an inch taller than Sammy, but outweighed her by thirty pounds with another several pounds of police gear. "Ms. Reisinger, I'd like to have a word with you."

"Yes, ma'am."

"I'm not going to mince words with you, young lady. Where's my boy?"

"Oh, Shane? I haven't seen him for a couple of days," she said honestly. "Is he all right?"

"Don't mess with me or you'll be sorry. You know he's not all right. Where is he?"

"I don't know."

"Listen, several people saw him leave with you from the music jam in Fries night before last. You won't deny that."

"No, ma'am. He left with me. He walked me most of the way home, gentlemanly. Then he left and I assume he walked home from there. Did he not arrive?" she asked innocently.

"No, he didn't arrive. His banjo and his clothes were found yesterday laying on the road. I suspect you know how that happened."

"No, ma'am," she lied. "I don't."

"I think you do. Why don't you tell me?"

"I already told you what I know. I hope you find him."

"Fine. But if you're lying, I'll be on you like white on rice."

The Chief got on her moped and sped away.

Carlene Bartlett descended the stairs of her store and approached Sammy. "I didn't see much of that, but it didn't seem too congenial."

"It was friendly enough," she lied again. "She seems to have misplaced her son and just wondered if I'd seen him."

Friday, November 9

Sammy awoke feeling woozy and collapsed to the floor as soon as she tried to stand up. She shook off her dizziness and stood again. Her head throbbed and her throat was raw. She had to pee, so she tried to stand again, this time successfully, holding onto the bed's footboard. She struggled into her robe and she walked downstairs, collecting her outdoor sandals on her way to the outhouse. Back inside, she found a glass of goat's milk in the kitchen which she drank. She also filled another glass with water and took it upstairs, stopping to rest on every third step.

She plopped herself back into bed. She found herself shivering and sweating at the same time. Her muscles ached throughout her body. She fell back asleep.

She had many dreams, mostly of people yelling at her. She dreamed that Emily's bell was ringing over and over again.

At one point, she awoke to see Avalon spooning syrup into her mouth. She heard Avalon say something like "One hundred and five," and felt her place a cold washcloth on her forehead. Later, she thought she sensed Hattie standing beside the bed.

The sun was low in her window when Avalon returned. Sammy

had Avalon's help getting down the stairs and to the outhouse again. She felt nauseous reaching the top of the stairs, but Avalon produced a bowl to catch her vomit. The taste it left in her mouth was painful and Avalon gave her an herbal leaf to chew on.

Saturday, November 10

The next day produced more of the same. Sammy felt awful, weak and feverish. She alternatively wrapped her covers tightly and then threw them off. Extracting a thin mercury thermometer from under her tongue, Avalon said, "Your fever is still high." Sammy sat up long enough to eat a noodle broth that Avalon spooned into her mouth.

"What's the matter with me? I feel like I've been dumped into a landfill."

"You have the flu. There are a lot of people who are sick right now. I think you probably contracted it from Emily and Jamaal who have both been sick, although you seem to have gotten the worst of it. Keep resting. It will pass, I hope."

Sunday, November 11

After her morning constitutional, she returned to bed feeling slightly better than the two prior days. A knock at her door produced Jamaal. "How are you feeling, my girl?"

"Like slippery cow shit," she joked.

"At least your sense of humor is back," he hugged her.

"Just."

"I felt like crap earlier in the week, but my fever wasn't as high as yours. Emily and I were both stricken," Jamaal admitted.

"How long have I been sick?" she slurred.

"A couple of days. It looks like you're on the mend. Several people in town have died from the flu this week."

"You're kidding! From the flu?"

"Sure enough! The flu used to be a major killer. Did you know that an epidemic struck world-wide in 1918 at the close of the First World War and killed more people than had died in the War?"

"No, I didn't. I'm glad you didn't tell me yesterday!"

"It was really a pandemic, striking people throughout the world. It took eighteen months to run its course and a quarter of the world's population had it at one time or another. It killed over fifty-million people. It killed people by causing their immune system to overreact, ravaging their bodies."

"Is this one as deadly?"

"Nobody knows yet. Without the communication we used to have, we're not sure how widespread it is. The bad news is that our medical systems have been crippled. The good news is that people aren't traveling like they did before the crash. Three months ago someone could catch a disease in Africa and spread it to Europe where it could spread to Asia and the Americas before the carriers even knew they were sick."

She laughed, "At least you won't catch anything from me; you already had it!"

"True, true. What else is going on?"

"You know Keene and his nephew Draper who picked a fight with us the other week at the music jam in Fries? I was in town yester-day and they tried to provoke another fistfight with me. White trash!"

"What are you going to do?"

"Nothing. Watch my back, but nothing. I can take care of myself."

"They seem like they really want you gone. Perhaps me, too."

"They're just blowing smoke. I won't be intimidated."

"Please be careful," she begged.

"You, too."

"I will. Oh, did I tell you that Shane's mother suspects me of his death?"

"I'm not surprised." He poured her some water. "Everybody saw you leave town with him. What did you tell her?"

"I told her that he followed me most of the way home and then he left."

"Did she believe you?"

"No, I don't think so," she offered, taking a sip.

"Did she ask about me?"

"No, as far as I know she doesn't suspect you at all."

"Okay, good. If she asks me anything, I will tell her that I was home all evening with Emily."

"Will Emily vouch for you?"

"She wasn't feeling well and was asleep when you came. So I don't think she knew I was gone."

"Okay, let's stick with that story."

"Listen, girl, I'd best be going. I hope you feel better." He kissed her on her forehead and then departed.

Monday, November 12

Sammy felt much better the next day, so when she heard Emily's bell ring around lunchtime, she tacked up Jackson and rode over. They went to Brooke and Steven McGuire where they added a fifth child, a girl, to their growing family. Everything went well. Sammy was still weak, so she watched Emily work.

Sammy was home by dinnertime where she ate alone. There were chicken pieces on the stove that she assumed Hattie had cooked. She ate that with some carrots and turnips. Much to her surprise, she found that she'd developed a taste for turnips. She amused herself with the image of a post-Pulse McDonald's serving McTurnip burgers.

After dinner, she practiced her violin in the living room by the light of an oil lamp. As she was wrapping up, she saw a bright light in the distance outside the window. She slid on her shoes and grabbed her coat and sprinted outside. It was clearly the light of something burning. She ran all the way to Emily and Jamaal's house. By the time she arrived, it was fully engulfed in flames. Tongues of fire shot through the broken windows around the metal bars. The heat was too intense for her or any of the other bystanders to even approach it. The house would be a total loss, surely. But what about Emily and Jamaal? She fell to her knees and sobbed.

Time passed and the flames began to subside. She forced herself to look at what once was a home. She asked the people nearby if they'd seen Emily or Jamaal escape, but nobody had seen either of them.

Arson? Accident? Sammy wondered what had happened and how it had started. It began to rain, with drops sizzling on the fire. Sammy was forced to return home, making the long, sad walk. She felt that someone had ripped out her gut.

Tuesday, November 13

Sammy was drawn back to the grisly scene the next morning. Woody Dalton was picking through the rubble along with several other men. Some wood was still smoldering, but the rain had dampened what the fire hadn't consumed. The metal items from the house were clearly visible, things like the woodstove, the bars from the windows, and the plumbing. Otherwise, there was nothing but charred rubble. At least that was all Sammy could see from the sidewalk.

Woody walked towards her, brushing his hands on his Carhartt bib overalls. He said, "I'm really sorry about what happened here. I know Emily and Jamaal were your friends."

"I've been crying all night."

"Something strange, though. Did anyone else live here?"

"No. What did you find?"

"There are three skeletons in the rubble. You can tell the sex of a skeleton by the shape of the head and the pelvis. A male's pelvis is generally narrower and has a sharper pelvic angle and a smaller pelvic outlet. The male's head is generally larger than the female and has a large brow ridge and a squarer chin. We found one skeleton that was from a short female; we're sure it is Emily's. Then we found two male skeletons. We assume one is Jamaal's. But we don't know whose the other is. Do you have any ideas?"

"No."

"I suppose that dental records are a thing of the past. One of the guys has gone into town to see if Chief Wilkins and Viller Boyd, the undertaker, can come have a look. The Chief will probably just make a record of it and go on to the next one. I don't see any reason to take the skeletons into Fries. I'll bury them this afternoon in Emily's family cemetery."

"Do you know how the fire started?"

"There's no way to tell without more equipment than we have now. It's a puzzle, though."

"What's that?"

"The fire was intense and it seems to have spread rapidly. Still, we found the skeletons together in the main room and I can't imagine why they didn't just open the door and escape."

Sammy took Maggie, Emily's horse, back to Hattie's place and left her in a pasture near Jackson's.

Sammy forced herself to go to Fries that evening for the weekly jam session. It was poorly attended. She overheard some of the men talking about Shane, wondering what had happened to him. They never looked her way or seemed to suspect her.

Wednesday, November 14

Sammy collected the bell from Emily's house. The wooden pole it had been on was 15-feet from the house, but the flames were so intense that the wood had become charred. She left the pole standing but stood on Jackson's saddle and with two adjustable wrenches removed the bell. She took it to the Providence General Store where she asked Carlene Bartlett if she could have it re-attached. "Will you be my dispatcher? If someone needs me, they can come here and ring for me. I'll come as quickly as I can."

"Yes, I'll be happy to do that for you. Are you going to keep delivering babies?"

"That's what Emily would want. I honor her friendship and sacrifice. I'll do the best I can."

Thursday, November 15

As Sammy was leaving the Providence General Store after trading some goat cheese, the police chief rode into the lot on her moped, in almost a déjà vu moment for Sammy, replicating the previous week's encounter. "Chief Wilkins."

"Sammy, you're a liar."

"I beg your pardon," Sammy said, taken aback.

"You know his clothes and banjo were found on the road."

"Yes, ma'am, you told me that yourself. I suppose he got raptured up like Mrs. Dalton and Hattie's sister Marissa."

"He didn't get raptured up! He didn't give a shit about Jesus Fucking Christ!" She lunged at Sammy, grabbing her jacket collar with both hands. "Where is he?!"

Sammy placed the first and ring fingers of her right hand together and shot them hard to the throat of the policewoman. Wilkins recoiled in pain, gasping for breath, clearly surprised by the ferocity of Sammy's counterattack. "Back off!" Sammy yelled. "Don't you ever touch me again! Your boy is not my problem; he's probably burning in hell. You need to leave me alone. I know all about you, about you and Quint. If the people of Fries find out about your affair, you'll be ruined. You just get on your scooter and head back to town."

The new police chief pointed her finger at Sammy while clutching her throat with her other hand. She yelled, "I'm on you now. I won't let go. You hear me?"

"Don't threaten me," Sammy yelled defiantly. "Get back on your broom and fly away."

As Sammy watched the moped depart, the skin prickled all over her body.

Friday, November 16

Sammy tacked up Jackson and attached her midwife's bag as always, and then returned to Carlene's General Store in order to assist Woody butchering another steer. It was a cool, foggy day. The carcass was hanging from a winch behind the store and she was cutting meat on a nearby table when she was surprised to see Dowell, Rhonda's brother, come running up. "Ms. Sammy, please come quick. Rh-Rhonda needs you."

"What's wrong?"

"I donna know. It's her belly."

"Okay, let me wash my hands and we can go. Carlene, I'll see you later."

The boy was mentally deficient, but he was in excellent physical condition. He ran most of the way to their house, while Sammy rode Jackson alongside him. She offered him a ride, but he seemed intimidated by the horse. When they arrived, Sammy saw the same immobile hound dog she'd remembered the evening of the Pulse.

Dowell and Sammy entered the living room of the double-wide house trailer. It was filthy, with papers, rubbish, and clothing strewn about.

Rhonda was reclining on the sofa, looking sweaty, as if she'd just returned from a run, which Sammy knew she didn't do. Sammy spoke first. "Your brother says you need me?"

"You're the damn midwife, aren't you?"

"You're pregnant?" Sammy asked incredulously.

"No shit, Sherlock."

Sammy did a double-take. "You never said anything about it, smartass."

"I didn't figure it out myself until a week ago. I've been missing periods for months, but I never gave it much thought. Last week, I felt some kicking. Then what was I supposed to do?"

"When are you due?"

"How the hell am I supposed to know? All I knows is that I'm having contractions. And I think I'm beginning to open up."

"When did you have sex? And who did you have sex with?"

"I had sex last spring for the first time. Maybe a couple of times since."

"You're only fifteen. Who did you have sex with?"

"I'm sixteen. And it's none of your damn business; what does it matter? Owww!"

"Well, if you want my help, you'd best act like it. I need to examine you."

"You think I'm going to let you stare at my crotch?"

"Unless you expect this baby to emerge from somewhere else, that'd be the idea."

"Owww!"

"Do you want me here or not?"

"Owww. I guess so."

"Then take your pants off and lift your shirt up." Sammy removed the fetoscope from her bag and placed the sensor in her hands to warm it. Then she placed it on Rhonda's belly. While listening, the smell of the room reached her olfactory. It smelled musty and stale, as if it hadn't been cleaned for awhile. "The baby's heart sounds good." She took out her tape measure and said, "You're about six centimeters dilated."

The boy sat quietly across the room as if perplexed about the part he was to play.

"Can you give me something for the pain?" the girl asked.

"Let's get you through a couple more contractions and see how you do. I don't like to give medications unless they're absolutely necessary. Do you feel like you can make it to your bedroom? I think things may go better in there."

"Let me see," Rhonda said. She stood up and with Sammy and Dowell beside her, walked into the bedroom that she evidently shared with him, at least until their father had died. There were clothes strewn everywhere. Rhonda reclined on her bed which was unmade with dirty sheets.

The curtains were mostly drawn and with the overcast sky, it was dark in the room. Sammy removed the *Forever-lite* from her kit and strapped it to her forehead and took another look. The cervix was still dilating normally and Sammy could see the baby's head. It appeared to have wisps of reddish hair.

Sammy sat back and contemplated the new information. As she did, her light shined on a pile of clothes in the corner where a familiar, red, reflective light shown back at her. Thunderbolts of insight fired in her head. "Whose baby is this?" she asked again.

"None of your business."

"It's Shane's baby."

"Fuck you."

"It's Shane's baby! And that's my violin." She walked over, unearthed her violin case, and brought it back to the bed. "You stole my violin."

"I hate you."

With more incredulity, "You stole my violin! You BITCH!"

"Damn right! I wanted to punish you. You have everything! You are rich, pretty, and smart. And you stole Shane from me."

"What?!? I didn't steal anybody from anybody. It's Shane's baby. Nine months. When was it, spring break?"

"Yeah, he came back on spring break and we had sex. A couple of times."

"You were only fifteen!"

"So what? He told me he loved me."

"And you believed him? He told you he loved you so he could get into your pants. Months later, when he showed an interest in me, you got jealous and stole my violin. Do you know what this violin means to me?"

"I don't give a rat's ass what your goddamn fiddle means to you."

"Fine. Then you can go straight to hell. Have your goddamn baby by yourself." She got up and threw her flashlight and fetoscope back in her kit. She grabbed the straps of the kit and the violin case and walked out, slamming the front door.

She strapped both to Jackson and she mounted him. She turned south towards the New River, fuming. She could feel her pulse rate accelerating and her temples throbbing with each heartbeat. "Bitch!"

Arriving at the riverbank, she stopped and dismounted, unstrapping the violin case from the saddle. She sat on a log on a grassy flat. The overcast sky opened at various times, allowing beams of light to hit the water. She unzipped the long zipper and removed the precious, priceless Guarneri, the link to her beloved Grandfather who adored her, deeply and unconditionally. She put it to her lips and kissed it. She tuned it and began to draw long strokes with the bow.

An osprey dove into the river and emerged with a fish. The osprey carried it to the branch of a nearby tree.

Her mind raced through the ages, through her own life, her graduation, her Bat Mitzvah, the downing of the Trade Center towers, the childhood memories of her first horse. She thought of her Grandfather and his stories of symphonies and struggles and the Holocaust. Of World War I and the flu pandemic. Of Amati and Stradivarius, and old man Guarneri, working amidst wood chips and glue smells in medieval Italy. Of Jesus and the Jews and the crucifixion. Of pre-history and Cro-Magnons and dinosaurs. And she thought of the river in front of her, flowing eternally to the sea, carrying the blood of the body of planet earth in the endless cycle of water. She picked up her violin again and she played song after song, whatever came into her head. She played and played, making up pieces as she went. The sun broke through the clouds and sent a beam glistening off the river and onto her face.

She looked at her precious violin, carefully studying the familiar grains and colors of the wood. She marveled at its lightweight, timeless beauty and its magical, mythical tone.

A murder of crows cawed loudly from a tree just upstream from her. She put the chinrest to her chin again and played *Sunrise Sunset*, the wedding song from *Fiddler on the Roof*. The crows fell silent, as if in reverence. The entire world stood still, except the river, the majestic New River, which flowed eternally, forever and ever, as it always had.

She finished the song. She closed her eyes and took a deep breath. She realized she was still mad as hell, but she felt an overwhelming sense of responsibility. She tenderly placed her Guarneri and the bow back into the case and zipped it up. She stood up and carried it back to Jackson, who was munching some grass nearby. She strapped it to his saddle, mounted him, and said, "Let's go, Jack-Jack," and rode him back to Rhonda's house.

She carried her kit back inside, entering without knocking. She found Rhonda in the same place she'd left her, except she was in considerably more pain. Not greeting her with either scorn or congeniality, Sammy said brusquely, "Let's see how you're doing."

Rhonda was similarly unexpressive towards Sammy, but spread her legs as instructed.

"You're thirteen centimeters. It won't be long now."

"I'm in a lot of pain."

Deal with it, Sammy felt like shouting. Instead, she said, "Okay, let me give you some Lobelia." Sammy walked into the kitchen with her vial of St. Johns wort and placed 20 drops in the only glass of water she could find, which had obviously been used before. She returned with it to Rhonda, who drank lustily.

Neither girl said much as the delivery progressed. However, Sammy detected that Rhonda was bleeding internally as Estella Vasquez had done, which was the reason for Rhonda's excessive discomfort. Sammy's enmity for Rhonda was still weighing on her, but she surely didn't want her to die as Vasquez had, and the baby certainly deserved its chance in life.

The baby emerged smoothly, face towards Rhonda's anus, and the shoulders slid out properly as well, but its delivery was accompanied with a significant amount of blood, which turned the bed cherry. It was a girl. She had wispy, crimson hair. Life came to her quickly, and she began breathing normally. Sammy held her to her ear so she could hear the newborn's heart song, like the flutter of a butterfly's wing. Sammy wrapped it in the cleanest towel she could find and placed it on Rhonda's chest. However, Sammy could see that Rhonda was going in and out of consciousness. Her lips were purple and her hands and feet were cold. She was clearly in shock.

Sammy elevated Rhonda's feet and fed her more water with 50 drops of angelica and 50 drops of blue cohosh mixed in. Then she palpated Rhonda's belly and the placenta emerged. Sammy cut the umbilical cord two inches from the baby's belly and tied the end with a rubber band.

The baby began to cry with hunger, but Rhonda wasn't feeding it. Sammy asked Dowell if they had any milk, but there was none. She considered her options and decided to return home to fetch some goat's milk. "Dowell," she said to the boy, "I need your help. Your sister needs your help." She explained the situation and left the comatose mother and the hungry infant in the care of the mentally deficient boy. She hopped on Jackson and galloped home, retrieving a bottle of goat's milk. She also brought a rubber dishwashing glove in which she had poked a pin-hole in the thumb and boiled for a few moments on the stove to sterilize.

Over an hour had passed by the time she returned, finding the scene much the same as when she'd left it. She poured a small quantity of milk into the glove and let the baby feed. The baby opened crystalline azure eyes and looked at Sammy's, longingly. Sammy held the baby to her ear again. She was enchanted.

Sammy stayed well into the evening, fixing herself and Dowell some of the last food they had around and feeding goat's milk to the baby. Rhonda was still asleep most of the time, and she complained about dizziness the two times she got up. Sammy and Dowell helped her outside to and from the outhouse, where she complained vociferously about being cold.

Sammy knew the three Shelors wouldn't be self-sufficient, yet she had no way to transport them. On the way home, she hatched a plan to transfer them the next day to Hattie's house.

Saturday, November 17

Sammy rode Jackson back to Rhonda's house in the morning and fed the baby again. The baby was soiled and crying. The trailer was freezing cold. Sammy had brought some cloth diapers she found in the linen closet at Hattie's house that she thought had probably been there for twenty years. Sammy made a fire in the small pot-bellied stove in the living room and warmed some water to wash the baby. Then she fed the baby goat's milk from the glove. Still, Rhonda was unable to eat and the boy was hungry.

Once the trailer had warmed, she rode Jackson to Woody's house and asked his help. He instructed one of his farmhands to saddle up two horses. Sammy rode back to Hattie's place and put a halter on Maggie, which she led back to Emily's house, where she rendezvoused with Woody and his helper. They hitched Maggie to Emily's wagon. From there, the farmhand drove the wagon back to Hattie's house where they retrieved some blankets and an inflatable pad.

Finally arriving at Rhonda's trailer, they packed several belongings in the wagon for Rhonda, Dowell, and the baby. The men carried Rhonda outside and placed her on the back of the wagon. Sammy held the baby in her arms, and the boy sat in the back with his sister. The procession drove back to Hattie's house. Sammy found Hattie in the kitchen where she explained the situation. "Rhonda and her baby and brother need to be with us for awhile until they can take care of themselves." Hattie nodded her understanding and went to her own bedroom to prepare it for the new arrivals. Dowell would sleep in Hattie's dead son's room. Hattie would sleep on the twin bed beside Sammy's. It took some time to get everyone situated. Woody sent his helper back to the farm to get some work done. Sammy put extra wood in the stove to have the house a few degrees warmer than usual. She fed the baby again and then set her down for a nap in a bureau drawer in Hattie's room.

Hattie flitted about but didn't seem perturbed by the new living arrangement. She returned to the house with some fresh goat's milk. Once everyone was settled and napping, Sammy availed herself of a nap as well. When she awoke, she pulled her Guarneri from the cases, ecstatic to have it back, and played several lullabies.

Sunday, November 18

The baby kept Sammy jumping most of the night. She completely forgot it was Sunday and was only reminded when Pike stopped by for a visit. He had heard that Sammy had taken in Rhonda and her family and asked if he could help with anything.

Pike spoke about the progress he and some others were making downtown with the dam and electrifying the town. During the course of their conversation, Sammy said, "Pike, when I went to Woody's house yesterday, he had an old farm tractor working. I got to thinking about why some machinery works and some doesn't."

Pike reminded her, "We talked about that when we went to Blacksburg. The old stuff works because the Pulse basically blasted anything with microprocessors in it," the professor explained again. "New cars, for example, have electronic ignitions. So they were crippled."

"Is it possible that a car could be shielded?"

"What do you mean?"

"Hattie's Subaru has been sitting for two years in the metal Quonset hut they use as a garage. There are lightning rods on the top."

"Ih think Ih know where you're going with this."

"If the juice from the Pulse struck the rods, could it have been grounded to the earth, thereby bypassing the car?"

"It's possible. By now, the gasoline in it would be degraded and some of the lines and orifices might be plugged. And Ih'm sure the battery is dead. But Ih've got some starting fluid in the garage and there's a battery we've been using downtown at the dam. Tell you what... If Ih can take Emily's horse and wagon, Ih'll retrieve them tomorrow and we'll see if we can get the car started."

Monday, November 19

Pike returned with the battery and starting fluid, carrying them in an old grocery store cart. He removed the old battery and installed the charged one. Sammy opened the driver's door and the interior lights came on.

"Do you have the key?"

"It's still in the ignition. I don't think Quint or Hattie ever took it inside."

"Turn it one click," he instructed. "Let's see what happens."

"The dashboard lights are on."

He removed the air filter and shot some starting fluid into the manifold. "Give it a go!"

She turned the key and the engine began spinning.

"Pump the accelerator once or twice."

The engine caught, and sent a plume of black smoke out the exhaust pipe. "Yes!" they yelled in unison.

"Let's let it run for a few minutes," Pike said. "In fact, let's take it for a ride." He got in beside her and clicked his seat belt, more out of habit than anything else. She put it in Reverse and backed it to where she could turn it forward out the driveway. Putting it in Drive, she inched towards the street. The car sputtered and coughed on bad gas, but it ran! She and he squealed with glee over their newfound sense of motoring freedom.

"Let's not get too carried away," he said, tempering their enthusiasm. "We still need to get some fresh gasoline in it. The convenience store in town got a small shipment a couple of weeks ago. Chief Wilkins has been allocating it as she deems appropriate, given the need. If you want to use the car during your house calls, you'll need to ask her if your work is considered vital."

"Ah, we're not the best of friends."

"No worries. Ih'll do it for you. Ih'll drive it to town right now and ask her. Ih won't let her say 'no.'"

Two hours later, Pike returned with the Subaru, full of fuel. Sammy gave him a big hug. "Thanks for everything you've done for me."

"Thanks for what you've done for this community. We are forever in your debt."

"As I am in yours!"

Tuesday, November 20

Sammy awoke before dawn, hearing the ringing of the bell at

the Providence General Store. She dressed quickly but couldn't resist pulling a card from the Augury deck. It said, "Infinite Abundance."

She grabbed her kit and drove Hattie's car there. She found 9-year old Sam Quimby there, having run nearly three miles from Stevens Creek. She put the boy in the passenger seat of the car and they drove back to his home together. Helen was lying in bed, clearly in the midst of contractions. Her belly was huge. There was an old wind-up mantle clock sitting on the bureau. "Have you been watching your contractions?"

"Yes. Every fifteen minutes."

"How do you feel?" taking the fetoscope from her kit.

"Ready. Eager. Fearful. I'm so glad you're here. I wish Ronnie was here, too."

"Everything is going to be fine. I hear two heartbeats. I think you're going to have twins."

The pregnant woman smiled broadly.

Within an hour, first a baby girl and then a baby boy slid outside the birth canal and were resting with umbilical cords still attached at their mother's chest. Helen expelled twin placentas. Sammy clipped the cords and weighed the babies. The girl was six pounds five ounces and the boy was six pounds two ounces. Sammy held them one at a time to her ears, listening to the flutter of their hearts.

Sammy tidied her equipment and made sure everything was fine. She was gone within two hours of the deliveries, awash with the joy of successful newborns.

Wednesday, November 21

Sammy drove Hattie's car south towards the river, then west to Carsonville where she called on Angela Noson. Everything appeared to be going well. The mother-to-be didn't know who the father was, but she was in the care of her mother and aunt, and appeared to be in good cheer. "I expect it will be a couple more weeks. Let me know if things start cooking sooner," Sammy told her.

As she walked back to the car, her eye was drawn to the heavens where she saw something that made her heart race. It was a thin, straight, white line, being drawn as she watched. It was a contrail, the stream of a jetliner whose silver form she could make out. Thirty thousand feet above her, somebody was flying! What did it mean?

Before bed, she pulled a card from the Augury deck. It said, "Appreciation."

Thursday, November 22

Sammy awoke early on this national day of Thanksgiving, eager for the activities ahead. She had decided that to give thanks to her friends, she would make dinner. She had invited Pike, Woody, Carlene, and Avalon, to join Hattie, Rhonda, Dowell, and the unnamed newborn baby to be her guests at Hattie's house. And she'd invited Angie and Scottie, the two children she'd met at the river and again at Halloween, along with their mother, Norma.

Sammy had driven to Avalon's house the day before to get two freshly killed chickens. Hattie had made some white cheese the day before. She busied herself making a vegetable stew with potatoes, carrots, onions, radishes, leeks and turnips. The kitchen smelled wonderful!

Sammy fed the baby goat's milk from the glove. Sammy touched her nose and she smiled. Sammy brought their noses together and smiled at the newborn girl, maternally.

Sammy spent the rest of the day preparing. She took the best china and silverware from the cabinet, along with two candle holders. Setting the table, she bristled with excitement.

She gave herself a sponge bath and washed her hair, using water heated on the stove. She put on some eyeliner and perfume, the first time she'd done so in weeks.

She fed the baby, which she'd taken to calling "Boopser," for no reason she could think of. Woody arrived, carrying two bottles of wine. Others arrived one at a time, each bringing something to share.

In spite of the travails of recent weeks, everyone seemed buoyant. Sammy told everyone about the contrail she'd seen the day before. "Better times are ahead!" she said, eating a chicken wing.

As they finished eating, Pike said, "When Ih was growing up, my family always gave thanks on this day, person by person. Can we do that here?"

All heads nodded in acknowledgment. Sammy acknowledged his idea, "You start us off, Pike."

"Great! Ih'm thankful that the dam is working in Fries and that a few people over there are able to have light on their meal tonight. We can only generate enough power for a few essential utilities in town, but Ih hope it's a start."

Woody said, "I lost my precious Caroline. But I'm thankful she's in heaven sitting beside her Lord and Savior, Jesus Christ. When I'm done with the work He sent me here to do, I hope to join her again."

"I'm thankful for all this food!" exclaimed Dowell, eagerly.

Everyone clapped.

Carlene the storekeeper said, "I'm thankful that my customers are helping me through this difficult time. The day the world crashed, my vendors stopped bringing me things to sell, but my customers have kept coming back. Their generosity amazes me."

Avalon said, "I am thankful for another year of blessed life here in Southwest Virginia, the most beautiful place on earth, with all of you, the finest, most honorable, and caring people on earth."

The baby began to whimper, so Sammy got up and picked her up, returning with her to the table.

"…and the most bighearted," said Norma, the children's mom. "Without you and all our neighbors, we surely would have starved by now. We're thankful to you all."

"I'm thankful for my new baby," Rhonda said weakly. "She almost did me in!"

"How about you, Sammy?" Scottie yelled.

Looking over the gathering of new friends gathered before her, Sammy's mind flooded with images, of the Galax stage, the theft of her Guarneri, the Tech steam tunnels, Bailey, the death of Estella

Vasquez, the recovery of her Guarneri, and the birth of Boopser. She looked at the baby, cooing in her arms. "I'm thankful..." she began. She choked back some tears. "I'm so sorry that Jamaal and Emily are no longer with us, but I'm thankful..."

And then, as she fumbled for an answer, their universe instantly went bright! The chandelier's lights burned brightly, just as they had burned the night the Pulse had struck. Everyone at the table seemed stunned, astonished at the intensity of the artificial light. A CD player in the kitchen crackled to life, playing *America the Beautiful.* "Oh my God!" Sammy shouted.

"The power has been restored," said Pike. "The grid is alive again."

"It's over! Our long nightmare is over," yelled Carlene.

Everyone jumped up and started hugging each other. Sammy almost dropped baby Boopser twice. Avalon filled everyone's glass again and said, "I propose a toast. To the indomitable will of the human spirit."

"Cheers!"

"Bravo!"

Pike and Avalon cleared the table and washed dishes, now using running water from the kitchen faucet. The electric water heater had no hot water, but they used water heated from the wood stove. Meanwhile, Sammy got her Guarneri and tuned it up. She played *Embryonic Journey* solo, which everyone complimented. Soon Pike accompanied her on his banjo and they did the *Maple Leaf Rag, The Entertainer, Pine Apple Rag, Black Mountain Rag,* and every other rag they could think of.

Everyone except Norma and her children stayed well into the night and Sammy was exhausted by the time her guests began to filter out the front door, where it was raining steadily. Sammy offered to drive Avalon home, but she declined. "I'm well dressed for the night. You take care of the baby."

Friday, November 23

Sammy awoke with a hangover. It had been a long time since she'd had more than a sip of wine. She woke up and took care of Rhonda, her brother, and the baby. She realized that as the day after Thanksgiving, it would still be a work holiday, but she didn't quite understand what a "work holiday" meant any more.

Feeding the baby in the living room, she pulled the lamp cord over and over, on and off, almost giddy with the instantaneous light it provided, wondering how she'd ever taken such a simple thing for granted.

And then she heard the faint sound of Emily's bell. So she put the baby on the floor on a blanket and told Dowell to find Hattie if the baby needed any help. She grabbed her midwife's bag, and flew out the door, returning hours later after another successful delivery.

Saturday, November 24

Sammy drove the car into Fries to see if the sole convenience store had any gasoline so she could continue to service her clients. She parked near the pump but didn't have any money to pay for gas and didn't know the new protocol. She decided to try to find Pike to ask him.

No sooner than she had gone looking, she saw him sprinting towards her.

"Pike, I'm glad you're here. I need some gasoline…"

"Forget the gasoline. Ih want to show you something. Come quickly please."

They ran to a building where he kept his radio and electronic equipment. He picked up a headset and said into it, "Are you still there? Okay. Hold for just a moment."

"Sammy, put these on," he gave her the headset. "I want you to say, 'Hello.'"

"Hello, this is Sammy."

"Sammy?" she heard a familiar voice say.

"Yes."

"It's me. It's your mom."

"Oh my God! Oh my God, *oh my God*! Mom! Oh, my God, is it really you?"

"It's really me Samantha. Is it really you?"

"It's me mom. I can't believe this. Oh my God! I thought you were dead. Where are you?"

"We're in New Jersey, honey. We were in Paris the night of the Pulse and there was a huge thunderstorm over De Gaulle airport. So our flight was cancelled. We've been in Paris since then until three weeks ago. We finally got a flight back across the ocean to Denver. Then we basically hitchhiked back to New Jersey. Our house in Alpine has been looted, so we went to the cottage in Sussex. It is fine."

"How did you find me?"

"We didn't find you. You found us. Your friend Pike apparently was on the radio all night last night, tracking us down. He has some ham radio friends in Alpine that followed referral after referral until he found us here. We're over at the Piasecki's house right now, on Mr. Piasecki's radio."

Sammy turned and smiled at her friend Pike, who was beaming with excitement for her through damp, tired eyes.

"Now that we know you are safe and where you are, we'll make plans to get there as soon as we can to pick you up. Are you okay?"

Sammy's mind again raced through the events since August. She fought off emotion and said, "Yes, mom. I've been fine. Everyone here has taken care of me."

"Your dad wants to say hello."

"Okay."

"Hi, sweetheart," Ira Reisinger said.

"Hi, dad."

"We are so relieved you are okay. You can't believe the carnage up here. Looters came flooding out of the city and ransacked everything in Alpine. I'm almost glad we weren't home. Have you been cared for?"

"Yes, at times better and at times worse. It's been crazy."

"How's your Guarneri?"

"It's fine. I think it likes Bluegrass music," she laughed. She knew intuitively not to mention the theft.

"All our cars are ruined, except my old '72 Mustang seems to work. I'll need to arrange some things before we can drive it there; it hasn't been on the road for awhile. Put me back on with your friend Pike so we can arrange to let you know when we can come."

"Dad, I love you. Tell mom I love her, too."

"We love you, too, Samantha."

She gave the headset back to Pike. He said, "Tell Mr. Piasecki Ih'll be back online on Monday at 800 hours." Then he flipped three switches and the dials went dim.

Sammy gave him a huge hug. "Thank you, thank you, thank you!"

"Just doin' my job, ma'am. Ih am so happy for you Sammy."

They walked back to the store where Sammy had left Hattie's car. Pike walked inside and when he returned, had her pull next to the pump. He pumped exactly 10 gallons into the car. "What do I owe the store?" she asked.

"It's all taken care of."

Sammy drove home in a blur, giddy with excitement and enthusiasm. She parked the car, eager to run inside and proclaim her great news to Hattie, Rhonda, Dowell, and baby Boopser. She got half-way up the stairs and then she froze. What would they make of her good news? Would they share her enthusiasm?

She ran back to her car and turned the key. She drove back into Providence, then turned on Spring Valley Road, and then drove to Avalon's house. She knocked lightly at the door and then let herself inside, where she found the woman knitting by her stove.

"Come in my precious flower. I'm making a hat for Rhonda's baby."

"I have some news today."

"You're going home."

"Yes! How did you know?"

"Devil's intuition. What's the story?"

"Now that the power is back on, Pike was able to contact my

folks. I was sure they were dead, but he didn't give up." She explained their prolonged stay in Paris and their eventual return to the states.

"I'm really happy for you, my precious flower. I'll miss you."

Sammy was suddenly shocked, oblivious to the notion that she'd be leaving this friend behind. "I'm so embarrassed. I was so excited about my own situation, I forgot about you and everyone here."

"We'll be okay. Please, revel in your joy." She gave Sammy a big hug. "Have you told Hattie?"

"No. I'm afraid to."

"Tomorrow, why don't you go to church and tell everyone. Then you can go back to Hattie's and tell her. I'll go to church to support you."

Sunday, November 25

Sammy fed the baby, and then fed herself and Dowell. She helped Rhonda to the bathroom – indoors! – which now had hot running water. She drew a bath for Rhonda and helped her in and out, letting her bathe in privacy. Finally, she dressed the baby in a dress she found on one of Ronnie's dolls. She put on the red dress that Avalon gave her. Then she drove Dowell and the baby to church.

Carlene had fully taken over officiating duties since Quint's death. As she led the congregation in recitation of the Lord's Prayer, Sammy saw Avalon enter the room and sit by herself on the back pew. Carlene selected *Guide Me, O Thou Great Jehovah* for the congregation to sing. Then she said, "Sammy, would you please come forward? You all know Sammy by now. She's been with us since the Pulse, staying at Preacher Quint and Hattie's place. She has some news for us."

Sammy reached the pulpit and looked over the congregation, faces she now recognized. "First, I want you all to meet baby Shelor. Rhonda Shelor gave birth to this special baby girl on November 16th. Rhonda has had a case of anemia since the baby was born, so she hasn't given the baby a name yet. I've been calling her Boopser. I don't know why."

Everyone laughed.

"Please come up here, Dowell. This is the happy uncle."

Dowell approached Sammy and said, "Hello everybody!"

"Everyone please welcome baby Shelor to our congregation," said Carlene. "Sammy, you have other news for us, don't you?"

"Yes. As you all know, I've been here since the Pulse. My parents were in Europe the week I was in Galax. They were scheduled to be on an airplane nearing New York when the Pulse struck. So I assumed they were dead."

The congregation was whisper silent in anticipation.

"Pike McConnell has been working with the ham radio in Fries. Yesterday, he put me on the radio and I spoke with my mother!"

The crowd erupted with excitement.

"Wonderful!"

"Congratulations!"

"So," she continued, "My parents will be coming soon to pick me up. I'm going home!"

The silence returned. She waited for a moment, not knowing what to expect. Then she and Dowell started to walk back to their pews.

"We're happy for you, Sammy," said Carlene.

"That's wonderful, Sammy."

"We'll miss you."

"We wish you all the happiness in the world."

Monday, November 26

Sammy drove Hattie's Subaru to town and met with Pike again. He reached Sarah on the radio and handed the headset to Sammy.

"Hi, mom."

"Hi, sweetheart. I can't get over hearing your voice again. I'm dying to see you."

"When can you come down?" Sammy begged.

"Your daddy has gotten the car running. He's trying to line up some resources along the way so we can be sure of having enough gas to make the trip and get home, too."

"I'm so excited about seeing you!"

"Me, too, honey."

"When do you think it will be?"

"Only a few more days. We'll let you know."

Tuesday, November 27

With the arrival of her parents and her ultimate departure loom-
ing, Sammy began to take stock of those in the community that she
wanted to give her final regards. One was the centenarian, Bailey, who
had sheltered her weeks earlier after her kidnapping. So she tacked up
Jackson, packed a lunch, and strapped on her violin case and an extra
jacket. She set Jackson on a path northward. It was a crisp late fall
day, with a touch of frost across the fields of grass. Jackson felt light-
footed to Sammy, and eager for the day's adventure. He was more
graceful, athletic, and beautiful to her than ever before. As he exerted,
shots of mist flew from his nostrils.

She retraced her path carefully. She went around to the right of
the base of Stevens Knob in the Iron Mountains. She saw the outcropping of the old man on Jones Knob. Then she passed through
the gap of Ewing Mountain and Devils Den. She reached a familiar
meadow, where she found the huge, dramatic spruce tree that contrasted even more with the stark, treeless hardwoods around. But her
eyes deceived her. Strangely, there was no garden. There was a bubbling creek, but no little bridge over it. There was no sign of human
activity at all.

She stood still for several moments, mystified. She dismounted
and led Jackson to where she was sure the house had been, but there
was no sign of it whatsoever. Her mind reeled with implications.
Where did her rescuer go? Where was the house? How could everything have disappeared?

She unstrapped her violin case. She took a long leap over the
bubbling creek, and then wandered around the tree where she found

a rock sculpted like a chair. She sat on it and withdrew her Guarneri. She tuned it and began playing *Ashoken Farewell,* one of the most mournful tunes she knew. She looked to the sky on a cool, cloudless day and counted four distinct vapor trails in the heavens above.

Something sparkling and metallic on the ground caught her eye. She walked several feet away and found, partially hidden by the soil, a medallion. She picked it up and brushed off the dirt. It appeared to have been buried for decades. A Celtic knot was engraved on it.

She returned to her seat and played for an hour or so, stopping to munch on her food. She drank from the little stream of water, marveling at its clarity and coolness. Then she packed her instrument away, along with the medallion. She mounted her steed and rode back to Providence.

Putting Jackson's saddle and bridle away, she noticed some books, partially covered by a saddle pad. She removed the pad and took a closer look. There were six books, all on the subject of midwifery. They had Emily's name written longhand on the inside covers. Clearly, Emily had left them for her before the fire, but she was flummoxed to have not noticed them before. She carried them to the house.

Once inside, she found a note on the dining room table. It said, "Sammy, I heard from your parents. They expect to drive down on Friday and will take you home on Saturday. I gave them directions to Hattie's house. Love, Pike."

Wednesday, November 28

Sammy heard the bell ring before dawn. She drove to the General Store where she found Julie Teel's husband Don who had apparently walked there. He said his wife was having contractions. Sammy put him in the passenger seat of the car and drove him home. Within three hours, Julie had given birth to their second son.

Sammy packed up her gear and drove to see Mrs. Minnick in Hilltown and Regina Noson in Riverside. Both seemed ready to pop. Sammy examined each before confessing that she was only a day from departure from Providence with her parents. Each confession was met with sadness and apprehension.

"Who will help me deliver my baby?"

"How will I get help if I need it? Who will be here for me?"

With each admonition, Sammy spoke as reassuringly as possible. "With the power back on, surely the hospital in Galax will re-open soon. You'll find someone to take you there. I'm sure whoever was the OBGYN there will be available again."

On her way back to Hattie's house, she was wracked in grief and guilt. She decided to call on Professor Dyson at the Providence Nursing Home, seeking her solace. She carried her Guarneri inside.

She spoke briefly with Martha Allen who, with her son Frank, had been running the center for Woody since Caroline's disappearance. "We're hanging in there. It's a blessing to have power again."

Sammy found Margaret Dyson playing her piano.

"Hello little lady. Where have you been? I've missed you."

"It's good to see you again. I brought my violin. May I play with you? What are you playing today?"

"I've been in a Rodgers and Hammerstein mood. Do you know *Oh What a Beautiful Mornin*? Help me with it."

Dyson's thin, bony fingers moved deftly across the blacks and whites. She wore wool gloves with the fingers cut off. It was cold in the room. But she sang and played eagerly.

The lights were on, but there had been no delivery of heating oil, so the furnace still wasn't operational. Frank was installing a woodstove that Sammy recognized as coming from Emily's house. The wood covering of the handles had burned off, but it looked otherwise to be in good shape. Mist rose from Dr. Dyson's mouth as she sang.

"Do you know this one, child?" She sang and played *Some enchanted evening*.

Sammy played a solo. The old woman was clearly delighted. When the music was over, Sammy said, "I've really enjoyed our conversations." She struggled with telling her elderly friend about her impending departure.

"The pleasure has all been mine, my dear. It's an occupational hazard of people my age that our friends keep dying. We don't have many chances to make new ones. Getting to talk with you and play with you has been a blessing for me." She became wistful for a moment and said, "I'm a teacher. I've been talking about the environment and sustainability to hundreds, perhaps thousands of students and friends over the years. It hasn't made a difference. The world's biological systems are in worse shape now than when I started.

"Listen to me run on. Say, do you know this one? Louis Armstrong made it famous. Sing with me." She began singing,

I see trees of green... red roses too

Sammy joined in, singing in harmony, boisterously. As they concluded, looking at each other as they sang,

It's a wonderful world...,

Dyson smiled expansively.

"Bravo, Dr. Dyson!" Sammy clapped.

"Bravo to you, too, Sammy. This nursing home is my last stop in life. Playing this piano and meeting people like you is all I have left. When I can't play this piano any more, it's time for me to go. Say, would you please get me some water?"

"Sure."

Sammy walked to the kitchen where fresh, clear water poured from the tap into the clean glass in her hand. When she returned, Dr. Dyson was still on her piano bench, sitting quietly. Dyson said, "Would you help me up, please? I'd like to go sit on that upholstered chair. I'm feeling a might trifling."

Sammy took the woman's hand and held her upright. She was bony thin and her hand felt like ice. After she sat in the chair, Sammy didn't let go of her hand. "Thanks. You know, when I can't play this piano any more, it's time for me to go."

Then she closed her eyes, her head slumped to her left, and she passed away.

Sammy's eyes misted and she sniffled. "Frank, would you please help me?"

The black man came over and instantly knew Dr. Dyson had died. He went to another room and retrieved the stretcher that he'd used for way too many corpses. He put Dyson's dead body on it. "I'll dig another grave this evenin'. We'll bury her in the morning."

Sammy put her Guarneri away and drove home.

Thursday, November 29

It was the morning of the day her parents were scheduled to arrive and Sammy was a knot of anticipation. Would they arrive before dark? Would they be any worse for wear? What would they think of Hattie and Providence and her friends? She had put a sign at the General Store inviting everyone to meet her parents and celebrate their reunion. "Please come to Hattie Thompson's house at 7:00 p.m. tonight to wish me a happy return home to New Jersey. Everyone is invited. Samantha Reisinger"

Knowing she would never ride Jackson again, she saddled up and rode him south to the river where she'd caught the bass weeks earlier. Two old cars passed her, surprising her at how fast they moved.

She sat by the river. As with a prior visit, she was joined by Angie and Scottie.

"Miss Sammy, why don't you see if you can catch another fish?" Scottie said.

"Where was my lucky spot?"

"Right over there!"

So Sammy cast her bait into the river. Moments later when the sinker bobbed, she yanked the rod and a fish sprang from the green water. This time, the hook failed to grab and the fish sailed through the air and fell back into the river.

"Say, kids," Sammy announced, "did you hear that I'm going home tomorrow to New Jersey?"

"Why?" Angie asked, plaintively.

"Because it is my home. I miss my parents and my horse. My parents are coming for me. They'll be here tonight. Please come over and meet them. Bring your mother with you."

"But why are you going home?" Scottie pleaded.

"Just because," she said, not knowing how to fully explain her reasons.

"I don't know where New Jersey is or what it looks like," Angie said innocently, "I'm sure it's nice if you live there. But heaven itself couldn't be any prettier than here."

Sammy looked at the rays of sunshine bouncing off the rippling waters. She pulled a handkerchief from her pocket and buried her tears in it, hoping the children wouldn't notice.

Sammy rode Jackson back to Hattie's house and untacked him. She lingered by his pasture longer than usual, soaking in her last few hours with him. She embarrassed herself thinking that he was cognizant of her impending departure. He acted like his normal equine self, but somehow she was convinced he knew.

She went inside and packed her belongings. She took a long shower, basking in the pleasure of ample, running, hot water. She noticed that Hattie had made a big pot of vegetable stew. She was setting the table when she heard a horn sound outside. She ran through the front door and flew down six stairs and straight into the arms of her Dad who was emerging from the driver's seat of the Mustang. Before she could let go, her mother walked around and joined them in a family hug. "I love you mom! I love you Dad! I am so glad to see you."

"We love you, too, sweetheart! For awhile, we thought we'd never see you again."

"Brrrr, it's cold out here," Sammy shivered. "Let's go in."

"Are your hosts here?" Ira asked, ascending the stairs.

"There's a lot I haven't told you. The man of the house, Quint, was killed a few weeks ago by a robber trying to steal drugs from his store. Hattie is here somewhere. She hasn't been around much since I arrived. She and Quint lost all their children to tragic accidents before I arrived. So Hattie has been living a secluded life ever since. Now she's lost Quint, too. Oh, and her sister died too, last month, and they were really close."

"What a shame," said her mother. "I wish I could have helped her. I'm sure she has a form of PTSD."

"But we do have two new people here, three actually. A friend

I met at the Fiddlers Convention in August is here. She's just had a baby. She lost a lot of blood and has been weak since, but she's here now, along with the baby and her brother, who's mildly retarded. His name is Dowell."

They went inside and looked around. "This is where I've been living since August," Sammy said. "It's started to feel like home."

Dowell approached them and held out his hand. "My name is Dowell. Rhonda is my sister."

Sammy picked up the baby from her basket where she was playing with some wooden thread bobbins. "This is the baby. Her mother has been too weak to name her yet. I've been calling her Boopser. I have no idea why. Here, mom. Hold her for me while I heat up some goat's milk." Sammy kissed the baby and gave her to her mother.

"Anyway," Sammy continued, "let's eat. I invited some people over later to meet you. I told them to come after supper, around 7:00 p.m. Of course, even when the clocks worked around here, folks tell me they never paid too much attention to them." The grandfather clock began playing the Westminster chime and then sounded six gongs. Sammy ladled some milk into the plastic glove and gave it to her mother to feed the baby.

Her parents, Ira and Sarah, told Sammy about being in Paris for three months, trying daily to re-establish communication with her and arrange a flight back to the States. They asked Sammy over and over about her experiences in Providence, but she shrugged them off, explaining there would be plenty of time later to fill them in.

Spooning some soup from the pot to three bowls, her father said, "We're pretty tired, Sammy. We were able to find a motel in Galax to spend the night. So I don't think we'll stay long after dinner. You'll come with us, won't you?"

"If it's okay with you, dad, I'd like to spend my last night here."

Sammy was slurping the last liquid from the bowl when the doorbell rang. It was Angie, Scottie, and their mom, Norma. Sammy introduced everyone. Norma said, "I'm sorry we've come so early, but I'm trying to get the kids in bed at a reasonable hour. Now that the TV is on, they're wanting to stay up later and later. We went months without it and now I'm thinkin' I may just throw it away. It turns my kids into zombies. We were happier without it."

Angie and Scottie told Ira and Sarah about Sammy's amazing fishing prowess. As they were preparing to leave, the doorbell rang again. Woody appeared at the door, carrying a paper package.

"You have other guests," Norma said, "we gotta go." She gave Sammy a hug and said, "We wish you all the best. Everyone here in Providence adores you. Please come back and see us someday." Then the two kids hugged Sammy as well. Scottie said, "Goodbye Sammy. We'll miss you. Goodbye Sammy's dad and mommy, too." Everyone laughed.

"Oh, please wait just a moment," Sammy said to Norma, as an idea struck her brain. "I have something for the kids. Don't leave!"

She bolted from the room and ran upstairs, two steps at a time. She grabbed the cases for the violin and the banjo that Emily had given her and ran downstairs with them. She motioned to Angie and said, "Here's something for you." Sammy opened the case and handed her Emily's violin. "I want you to have this. It's yours to keep forever. It is a fine instrument and it has been played by some wonderful musicians."

"It's mine?" the girl said, wide-eyed.

"Yes, but it comes with two conditions. You must learn to play it. And you must never sell it. When you are no longer able to play it, you must give it away to someone special."

"I promise. I will."

"Scottie?"

"Yes?" he stepped forward.

"This banjo is for you. It comes with the same two conditions. I know you're young, but do you think you can handle it?"

"I promise, too. When you come back someday, you can hear me play it. I'm gonna get really good at it, I swear I am!"

"I know you will," Sammy agreed.

"You will come back someday, won't you?" He looked at her longingly, then at her parents, waiting for some sign of approval. Ira clenched his jaw and Sarah raised her hands to her cheek.

"Yes," Sammy affirmed. "I will. If you promise to practice every day, I promise to come back and hear how good you've gotten."

The Gallimores exchanged hugs with Sammy again and headed to the door. Sammy gave a stern look to Norma and said admonishingly, "If I ever come back, those instruments better be in the hands of those kids." Norma nodded.

Rhonda entered the room as Sammy introduced her parents to Woody. To her surprise, Hattie walked in as well. Sammy began her introductions over again, leaving nobody out. Woody handed the package to Sammy and said, "Here are some steaks. I suppose you won't be around to eat them, but I'm sure Hattie and Rhonda need some food."

The doorbell rang again and in came Pike. Carlene followed him, entering as he moved to close the door.

Sammy made introductions still again, especially recognizin Pike's contributions to the community and his efforts to link her with her parents. She gave him a big hug and kissed him on the cheek. Sarah also hugged him for his relentless determination to find them.

Everyone began chatting in smaller groups, with Sammy watching the scene from an uneasy detachment. Feeling a sense of anticipation she couldn't understand, she walked outside to the front porch. A full moon hung overhead and it illuminated the yard almost to the point of giving it color. She looked in the distance and there were several artificial lights burning. She envisioned happy families with each one, all looking to rebuild their lives in the reemerging reality. Then she saw a bouncing light approach and Avalon stepped off her bicycle and parked it against the fence. She ascended the stairs, looking more goddess-like than Sammy had ever seen her. Without speaking, the two women embraced, Avalon thrusting her tongue inside Sammy's mouth and wrapping it across her teeth.

"I'm so glad you're here. We must go inside," the younger woman said. "If Dad sees me doing this, he'll pee in his pants."

The introductions began again. Sammy said, "Avalon saved my life one night. I almost froze to death, but she was there for me." She didn't think her parents really understood the gravity of her situation.

Almost as quickly as her friends trickled in, they began trickling out. Pike said, "I'll be back to say goodbye again in the morning."

"Please be here by 7:30 a.m.," her dad said, "as we want to get an early start. It's a long drive and we still don't know what we'll encounter."

"I'll be here, too," said Avalon.

"Goodnight, everybody!"

"Goodnight!"

Sammy shut the door on her friends and parents, and returned to find Hattie had disappeared, Rhonda had retreated to her bedroom, and the baby and Dowell were still where she'd left them. "Dowell, please get ready for bed," she told the boy.

She picked up the baby and changed the diaper, using some old towels she'd found and washed. She fed her more goat's milk, laughing and cooing at each other. "I love you, Boopser,"

"Cooo"

She put the baby into her basket and another log on the fire. She went upstairs, turning on and off lights as she went, thinking about what a luxury it was to have instant light. She used the toilet and fell asleep, exhausted.

Friday, November 30

Sammy awoke before daybreak to the sound of the baby crying. She noticed as she awoke that Hattie had spent the night in the twin bed beside her.

Sammy fed the baby and was relaxing in the living room when Dowell came in. She said, "Do you understand that I am leaving today?"

"When will you be back?" the boy asked, averting his eyes.

"I don't know."

"Where are you going?" the boy asked.

"I'm going home."

"This is your home," he said, confidently.

Sammy was speechless. She had no idea what to say.

"This is your home. When will you be back?" he said again.

"Soon, I hope."

Sammy handed the boy his niece. "Please hold her for me. I need to bring my stuff downstairs."

Sammy ran up the stairs and used the bathroom, brushing her teeth and hair. She took everything back into the bedroom where she packed her final items into her travel case. She took it downstairs to the porch along with the case containing her precious Guarneri. She opened her midwife's case and withdrew her *Forever-lite* and stashed it in her travel case. She put the stack of Emily's books on midwifery in a cloth bag.

As she opened the front door, she saw the Mustang pulling into the driveway. She noticed Avalon standing by her bicycle which was in exactly the place it was the night before, making Sammy wonder if Avalon had ever gone home at all. She greeted her friend and then said, "Thanks for being here again. I was just looking at my midwife's case. I have no idea what to do with it. Do you think I should take it home?"

"Do you think you'll use it again?"

"I don't know. I'm conflicted. I want my life to return to normal, but I'm not sure what that means any more."

"Do you want to do midwifery again?"

"The burden of responsibility scares me to death. But then again, somehow I can't imagine not holding newborn babies in my hands."

"Why don't you leave it with me? I'll hold onto it for a few months. If you want it back, let me know. Otherwise, I'll make sure it gets into good hands, the hands of someone who will use it."

"Thanks." Sammy handed it to her friend, but then equivocated. "Let me get something from inside." She opened it and withdrew her fetoscope. "I'm going to take this with me as a sentimental reminder of my time here in Providence."

"Good choice. Good decision."

Moments later, Pike arrived on foot.

Her dad ascended the stairs and grabbed Sammy's belongings and stuffed them into the car's tiny trunk and back seat. Dowell had carried the baby outside and Hattie and Rhonda appeared as well. Pike, Avalon, Hattie, Rhonda, Dowell, the baby, and Ira and Sarah Reisinger stood in a circle looking at Sammy. Nobody moved in the silent, anticipative moment. The sun had poked over the horizon and long shadows formed across the matted grass, covered with a sheen of frost.

"Well, Sammy," said Ira.

"Well, I guess I should say goodbye. I feel like Dorothy saying goodbye to her friends in Oz. I feel like if I click my heels together three times, I'll be back in Kansas, or in this case, New Jersey."

Everyone laughed.

She gave Rhonda a perfunctory hug. "Take care of the baby. Best of luck to you."

"I will. Listen, I'm sorry about what I did. I was wrong about you. I appreciate what you've done for me."

"I hope you make some good decisions with your life," Sammy admonished. "You have a baby now and she needs you."

Rhonda nodded her head and smiled.

Sammy turned to Pike and gave him a bigger hug. "Thank you so, so much."

"You're welcome. Ih'm glad this story has a happy ending. What you've done for this community overwhelms my little favor to you. Ih hope you'll come back sometime. Everyone here loves you."

"Thanks.

"Avalon?"

"My precious flower."

"How can I ever repay you?"

They hugged tightly.

"You already have, a thousand times over."

"I love you."

"I love you, too. My door is always open," she winked. She took a step back. Sammy noticed that Pike had put his arm behind her back. Sammy felt profoundly happy for both of them.

Sammy turned to Hattie who was quietly sobbing. A tear dripped from her eye and onto her cheek. "Hattie, I'm so sorry for everything that has happened to you." She didn't know whether to hug her or extend her handshake. She realized she had never touched her host.

"Sammy," the woman's voice said, quivering. "Please don't go."

"Oh, Hattie. I must go. Please tell me you'll be fine." She could barely believe the bereaved woman had spoken. She reached forward and kissed her on the cheek.

Sammy shook Dowell by the shoulders and said, "You've grown a lot since I met you. Take care of your sister and your new niece," thinking Dowell and the niece would surely become best of friends. "Let me hold the baby one last time." She took the baby from him and cradled her in her arms. The baby swung her arms and giggled. Sammy saw bright blue eyes open wide. The baby grinned broadly. Sammy lifted the baby's face toward her own and kissed it once, twice, three times. Then she hugged her tightly. Then she raised the infant and held her close to her ear. Even through the baby's wrap, Sammy could hear the butterfly flutter of her heartbeat. The baby squealed in glee. Sammy gave the baby back to Dowell. She walked past her parents and said, "Okay," and squeezed into the rear seat of the car, not looking back. She burst into tears.

She heard the car start and the crunch of tires on gravel. In her next moment of awareness, she looked from the window and saw green Interstate highway signs. They stopped somewhere in Maryland for lunch, but the conversation was a blur. Her dad said something about the backwardness of the people they'd left earlier in the day. Sammy dismissed it as coming from someone who had been living in luxury in Paris for months while her friends were toiling under catastrophe. She decided her best option was to keep them talking and not offer too many details on her experience.

Her mother said, "I remember like it was yesterday. We were at De Gaulle airport, awaiting loading. The woman at the desk spoke in French, but we all got the gist of it. The thunderstorms in the area were intense, with lots of hail and lightning. We would need to wait. I called you to let you know, but you didn't answer. Perhaps you were playing music. Instead of leaving a message, I figured I'd call back as soon as we knew definitively when we were leaving. The storms persisted and it was late when we were told all outbound flights had been cancelled. When I tried to call you, nothing worked. Then we heard the news about the Pulse on the French TV. They didn't have many details, but they said the entire East Coast of America had been impacted. They had on various scientists and experts, explaining what the Pulse was and what it meant, but the impact wasn't clear until the next day when we were told that no airplanes could fly there."

Ira said, "We were desperate to get home and start looking for you, but it took three months until we could get a flight across the Atlantic. They flew us to Denver, which had only been impacted mildly."

Sarah said, "Then we caught a series of diesel buses back to the east coast. Most of the unaffected buses were west of Denver when the Pulse struck. Buses run on diesel so there are no spark plugs or ignition, which apparently made them more resilient to the Pulse and more easily retrofitted.

"Anyway," her mom continued, "we finally made it home. But the house was a wreck. It had been ransacked – the whole neighborhood had been looted by gangs of people fleeing New York City. The pool was filthy with scum in it."

"I heard about that," said Sammy. "One of my friends pieced together a radio, and he heard the news. How bad was it?"

"Bad," said her dad. "Really bad. All of New York's utilities are underground, and most of the tunnels have been flooded. They're ruined. The city is a wasteland of filth and devastation."

"How about Wall Street?"

"The financial industry doesn't really exist any more, at least not here on the East Coast. The West Coast exchanges still function, but I've not been able to determine what's going on with Goldman. As far as I know, I'm unemployed."

While this information was settling in Sammy's mind, her mother continued.

"So we were able to gather a few belongings and make our way to the house in Sussex. That's where we were when your friend Pike found us. The lights came back on the day before Thanksgiving, but the phones don't work."

"I was able to purchase some gold coins in France," said her dad. "Even at the unaffected airports, there hasn't been much going on in the way of airport security. I've been using them to trade for various things."

"Don't you have some money stored up somewhere?" Sammy asked innocently.

"As far as I can tell, our portfolio doesn't exist any more. It is all ones and zeros on a computer screen, and now the computers don't work. So does the 'money' really exist any more?"

Sammy told them about the General Store and the scrip system of canning jar lids. She talked about the nursing home and the dead residents. Sarah said, "We heard on the radio yesterday that twenty- to twenty-five percent of the entire population of the Eastern United States has died since the Pulse. Maybe more; certainly more in the cities. We didn't stay in Alpine long, but I'm sure many of our neighbors were lost."

For the first time in months, Sammy thought about her erstwhile chaperone. "How's Ella? Have you seen her?"

"We have no idea," said Ira. "We haven't contacted her. It's all too depressing."

"At least we have you here with us, Samantha," said Sarah. "We need to count our blessings. Lots of other people aren't so lucky."

They walked outside to the car to continue their journey. It was bitterly cold, with strong winds but fortunately no snow. Sammy snuggled into the tiny rear seat, feeling cocooned, but safe in her parents' warm presence. She slept most of the rest of the way. It was dark when they arrived. The vacation home had electric baseboard heat, so her parents were able to warm it comfortably.

All they had for dinner was bread and some cheese that Hattie had given them. Sarah said, "I'll go into the village tomorrow and see what food there is around."

Sammy fell blissfully asleep, cuddling Ralph, the stuffed Panda bear that always waited for her at their second home.

Part 5: December

Saturday, December 1

SAMMY AWOKE WITH BRIGHT SUN shining on her eyes from her easterly bedroom window. "What day is today?" she yelled to her mother as she dressed herself. She had showered and had luxuriated in what seemed to be an endless supply of hot water.

"I think it is Saturday," Sarah replied. "I've lost track of time."

"Me, too. Where's dad?"

"He went into the village to see what's going on."

Sammy walked into the dining room, pulling on a clean blue T-shirt.

"Look at you!" said her mom. "Look at your muscles!"

Sammy flexed her arms over her head. "Yeah, I guess that's what hard living will do. Oh, mom," she ran over and hugged her. "You won't believe what I've been through." She told her mother everything she could remember, from the walk to Blacksburg, the kidnapping, the hangings, and the deaths of Caroline, Marissa, Quint, and Shane. And she told her about Jamaal and Emily and the horrific fire that took their lives. "You're lucky you were in France."

"Your dad and I knew that. But we never considered staying. We love Paris, but it isn't home. And we were desperate to find you. Have some breakfast and then let's go have a look at your horse."

"How is Wilbur?"

"She's lost a lot of weight. Our caretakers fed her some hay every week or two, but everybody here has had their hands full, just like where you were in Virginia. Apparently some people tried to steal her. But somehow she's okay."

The mother and daughter went outside and found Wilbur grazing peacefully in her pasture. She was a much smaller horse than Jackson, only thirteen hands. She came trotting over when she saw Sammy. Sammy embraced her, thinking to herself how Wilbur almost seemed like a toy, a miniature, compared to the mighty, regal Jackson. That Jackson had saved her life, not once but twice, seemed surreal in the presence of this diminutive, placid animal that had been hers since the first riding lesson days. She thought of Jackson longingly and she missed him.

Ira returned in the afternoon with a piece of beef and some carrots. He said, "The grocery store is open again, but food is being rationed. They are only getting one small shipment each day. It's like a goddamn third-world country around here." Sammy's mind pictured the brutal hanging in Fries and knew what was now happening in New Jersey couldn't be any worse.

Sunday, December 2

There was a small Jewish worship center in Sussex, given the preponderance of second homes there and the extraordinary wealth of the Jewish community in the New York area. Sammy and her parents drove there for a morning service. Ira let Sammy drive his prized Mustang.

Inside the hall, which seated about twenty, were some people they recognized and many they didn't. There was a rabbi who had fled with some friends from his congregation in the Bronx. He described the scene a week after the Pulse, when rampaging bands of people marauded through the streets. "It was like my grandmother described when the Nazis came to Rotterdam." He said the gangs weren't pursuing Jews specifically, but attacked and looted at random. Fires burned uncontrollably for days on end. As much as 70-percent of the city's population was killed or exiled. The new arrivals put tremendous strain on the neighboring towns, where people were already close to starving. He encouraged other people to tell their stories, thinking it would be cathartic.

One woman said she was a nurse in an emergency room at a hospital in Staten Island. When the pulse struck, she was assisting in surgery. Everyone thought the backup unit would come on and supply power for a few days, but it never did, because the controls were destroyed. The patient, undergoing a kidney transplant, died on the operating room table, as did the donor.

One man said he was an undertaker near Columbia Presbyterian Medical Center on the upper West Side of Manhattan. His studio quickly was overwhelmed by the flood of incoming fatalities. They had no caskets and quickly ran out of embalming fluids. The refrigerated vaults were useless, other than for simply parking the stiffs until they could be removed and dumped in mass graves in Fort Washington Park alongside the Hudson.

Sammy's mind flew again through her experiences. But she felt uncomfortable speaking about them to these, primarily unknown people. In spite of the awful things she'd seen, her mind continued to focus on the grace and generosity she'd experienced. It seemed to her that her parents were surprised by the intensity of the hellish mess that most of the East Coast had become while they were stuck in Europe.

On the way out, her mom was talking with a friend, so she waited in the car with her dad. He said, "One day this week, I'm going back to Alpine. The house is pretty much destroyed, but if you come with me we may find some of your things still in it." She agreed to.

When her mother returned to the car, she said, "My friend Mrs. Silvers died on Saturday. There will be a service in the Presbyterian Church. We all need to go."

Monday, December 3

Sammy awoke, finding herself inexplicably drawn to the church for the service. She didn't know Mrs. Silvers well, other than knowing she and her mom played bridge together often.

An hour before the service, Sammy told her father that she wanted to try to contact Pike and let him know she'd arrived home safely. They went to the Piasecki's house together and Ira asked his friend if he could connect with Pike. Sammy learned that the Piasecki's home was in New Rochelle, in Westchester County just north of New York City. They were able to escape to their second home in Sussex days after the Pulse with their sixteen-year-old son and eleven-year-old daughter. Mr. Piasecki was a retired Special Operations Army commander, which Sammy thought may have had something to do with his interest in radios.

The three of them entered the den and Mr. Piasecki began working the dials of the radio. Soon, he said into the microphone, "Hello, Pike McConnell? Yes, this is Frank Piasecki. I have someone here who wants to speak with you." He handed the headset to Sammy.

"Hi Pike," she said hopefully. "Yes, it's me, Sammy. How are you doing? Oh, good! How's Rhonda's baby? Good! Has she given it a name yet? Oh's that's wonderful." She smiled broadly.

"Yes, the drive went well. I'm happy to be home. Yes. Yes, they're fine.

"I don't know yet. Yes. Okay, I will. Please tell everyone I said hello. Pike, I really appreciate what you did for me. Oh, thanks. Okay, bye!"

Walking to the wake, Ira asked Sammy what Pike had to say. She replied, "Everyone is doing fine. The baby is growing."

"You thanked Pike for something," Ira said.

She replied, "He said everyone misses me and appreciates what I did for the community." She didn't mention he'd also said everyone loves her.

Mr. and Mrs. Piasecki accompanied Sammy and Ira to the church. Sammy's mother met them there. The main sanctuary was gorgeous, with soaring exposed wood beams overhead and immense stained glass panels on three sides. It wasn't large by city standards, but it held around 120 seats. Sammy sat through it with an unimpassioned stoicism, lost in thought.

Then she hatched a plan.

After the ceremony, she approached the Reverend Mathew Bender, asking his permission, which he readily granted. By that evening, she was busy at work on the dining room table, hand lettering posters on any paper she could find.

Benefit Concert, an evening with Vivaldi
Samantha Reisinger
Playing her 1740 Guarneri Violin
January 1, 7:30 p.m.
Sussex Presbyterian Church
Clove Avenue
Have food? Bring some.
Need food? Take some.

As she wished her parents a good night, her dad said, "I heard you ask Pike on the radio if they had named the baby. What did he say?"

"He said Rhonda decided to name her 'Emily.'"

"That's a beautiful name," Sarah said.

Tuesday, December 4

Sammy awoke with an irrepressible eagerness. She saddled up Wilbur and rode to town with fifteen hand-written posters and a box of thumb tacks. She posted them in every store that would let her.

She returned home and untacked Wilbur. She had some fresh bread that her mom found at the store the day before which was wonderful, plus some cheddar cheese that a local farm had made; it was good but not as good as Hattie's.

Then she opened the cabinet in the living room where she'd been throwing sheet music for years and she withdrew the sheets titled *Le quattro stagioni*, The Four Seasons, composed by Antonio Vivaldi in 1723. She decided she would play *Summer* first. In the third of its three movements, it evokes a thunderstorm, which she felt was symbolic of the Pulse. Then she would play *Winter*, representing the plunge into the dark period that symbolized the months of darkness and increasing cold that she and everyone who would be attending had experienced. Then she would play *Spring*, representing the emerging optimism of the return to normalcy.

She looked over the extensive pages and began to read and feel the music that would emanate from the notes. The intensity of feeling she knew the great composer's works would elicit pleased her. She took out her Guarneri, tightened her bow, and began tuning. Then she took her first furtive steps towards learning the pieces.

Wednesday, December 5

Sammy spent the morning riding Wilbur and trying to resuscitate the horse's fitness and old dressage skills. She had lunch and then returned to her room and began practicing her newly chosen musical selections. Eventually, she was overcome with tension and she took a nap, only to return to her work when she awoke. Before she knew it, dinner had come and gone.

Thursday, December 6

"Sammy, let's go," said her father. She had just taken a shower and her dad was eager to get underway on their planned journey to their home in Alpine. This time, he drove the Mustang, filled with gasoline for the first time since they'd gotten back from Providence. Her father's driving had less than its usual precision and Sammy noticed a slight smell of alcohol on him.

The drive typically took 90 minutes, but this time it was much longer, with her dad stopping several times to survey the damage, particularly as they left the mountainous area at Bloomingdale and entered the Jersey Plains. North Paramus was the worst hit, with burned homes and cars everywhere. The Franklin Lakes Plaza's storefronts had no unbroken window panes.

The mansions of Alpine were blissfully shielded from the view of the road, although Sammy imagined the destruction behind the screens was horrific. As her father turned into their driveway her gut wrapped in knots, fearing what the next few moments might portend.

There was trash across the yard and three of the big trees in the yard had been chopped down, apparently for firewood. Sammy guessed that some refugees had helped themselves to the place, breaking down the door and taking up residence. Evidence of occupancy was everywhere, from the piles of trash left in the kitchen to the carcass of what appeared to be a dog in the dining room. A closet in the hallway smelled of urine. The stench was awful. The pool in back was green with algae and was littered with trash. Sammy went to her room and found clothes strewn about and her jewelry gone. Her bed had soiled linens where someone, obviously dirty, had slept. She found a few clothes left in her bureau and closet. When she found the deep violet dress she'd last worn for a friend's wedding, she knew it was time for her to leave. She found her father in the basement. The immense combination lock on his scotch cellar had thwarted any thieves and he was eagerly packing booze into boxes to carry back to Sussex in the Mustang.

Sammy went back upstairs and found a few framed photographs and albums that she thought her mother might want. Then they packed the trunk and rear seat of the Mustang tightly with scotch.

As they were leaving, Sammy said, "Dad, would you mind driving down by the River?"

"Whatever for?"

"I'm not sure. I just want to see the Hudson."

"I don't think it will be pretty, but sure."

He drove to the Alpine Yacht Club's pier, where 55 boats were normally moored. There appeared to have been only five or six, with several more swamped or overturned. A colony of black-faced gulls fought for a morsel of food. A dead man's body rested on the shore, partially submerged. There was no boat traffic on the river.

"Thanks dad. I've had enough."

Friday, December 7

Sammy awoke and after eating some fresh bread and eggs, got to work practicing her music. Other than taking a ride on Wilbur in the late morning, she stayed focused on her music all day. It snowed lightly outside and the snow was beautiful resting on the trees.

Saturday, December 8

When her mom called her to dinner, Sammy immediately noticed that a menorah sat in the center of the table, with two candles, one at an end and the other in the middle of the nine-slot candelabra. "Mom, it's Hanukkah!"

"Yes, baby. It starts tonight."

"I hadn't given it any thought. I barely know what day it is."

"What day is it?" her mom quizzed.

"Ah, Thursday?" Sammy guessed.

"No, baby. It's Saturday. You've had your head buried in your music ever since you got home. Do you think you might want to take a break, perhaps get a life?"

"No. Not right now. I don't know why, but right now, I don't want a life. I want to be with Vivaldi and my Guarneri. I feel like I'm wearing down the wood on its neck, I'm playing so much."

"Well, don't kill yourself."

Sammy said the blessing over the candles as she lit them, using a kitchen match to light the shamus and using it to light the other one, "*Baruch atah Adonai, Eloheinu Melech Ha-Olam, asher kiddeshanu b'mitzvotav, vitzivanu, lehadlik ner shel Hanukkah.* Blessed art Thou, Lord our God, Ruler of the universe, who has sanctified us with His commandments, and has commanded us to kindle the lights of Hanukkah."

Sunday, December 9

Sammy's day was much the same as the previous. She spent the morning riding Wilbur and the afternoon and evening practicing her violin.

Her mother had placed three candles in the menorah for this, the second day. She asked Sammy to recite the prayer.

"I have a present for you," her dad said, handing her a small paper sack. She opened it and found a set of strings for her violin. "I thought you might need these someday."

"Thank you, dad."

She practiced for two more hours before her eyesight began to fade. Giving her father a goodnight kiss, she saw a glass of scotch on the rocks next to him and an empty bottle. He slurred his speech when he said goodnight.

Monday, December 10

Rather than riding Wilbur this morning, she decided to go on a run. She had tried out for the cross country team as a sophomore at Alpine School but was cut from the team. Still, she enjoyed running and hadn't done so since before the Pulse. She ran to Nepaulin Lake but was disappointed to find that almost the entire shoreline was privately owned and fenced off. So she ran the roads, which still had little traffic. She noticed that the highway to Hamburg had several old buses running. There were signs of neglect and abuse throughout the neighborhoods, but nothing like the mess in Alpine. Returning home, she ate lunch and returned to her music.

At dinner that night, she lit the candles again, this time there were four of them. She asked her father about the buses. He had heard that decisions had been made to try to resuscitate public transportation first, before attempting to retrofit any private automobiles with updated ignition systems. Many old buses, some that had been mothballed for years, had been pressed into service. There were also many rail lines emanating from the New York area prior to the Pulse. Old locomotives and passenger cars were being used on infrequent, typically unscheduled trips around northeastern New Jersey, but none were able to cross the Hudson because the tunnels were swamped.

Her father stumbled as he left the table and smacked his head against the china cabinet. As Sammy wiped away the blood, she smelled alcohol on his breath. "Dad, you've been drinking!"

"What of it?"

"Ira!" yelled her mother.

"Don't either of you tell me what to do. What else am I going to do every day?"

"Please, dad, don't become a drunk," Sammy scolded.

Tuesday, December 11

Sammy rode Wilbur again in the morning. But otherwise, it was the same routine all day with her violin. Her mom did talk her into helping with laundry and cleaning the house. They lit five candles on this the fourth night.

After dinner, Sammy was thinking about Avalon and decided to write her a letter. She grabbed a pen and paper, thinking to herself that she hadn't actually written a letter in longhand since she was a child.

Dear Avalon,

I am home now, safe and sound. I really miss you and everyone in Providence. Our second home here in Sussex is familiar but unfamiliar at the same time. I feel disoriented and out of place.

I have decided to play a recital at a church here in town. It will be on New Year's Day. I am going to play Vivaldi. I don't know what the future will bring after that.

She thought about saying "I'll see you soon," but it sounded contrived. She didn't know what else to say.

Please tell everybody hello for me.

Love, Sammy

Wednesday, December 12

Making a decision to alternate days of running and riding, this was a run day. So Sammy set off for another trip around Nepaulin Lake, then westward to Plumbsock and back, which took her two hours. Then it was back to her violin. She chided herself when she became angered by the interruption of a broken string.

She was lighting the candles and in the middle of the blessing when there was a knock at the door.

"I'll see who it is," said Ira, leaving from the table.

Sammy had finished lighting the candles but had discontinued the prayer, waiting for her father's return, when he re-entered and said, "Sammy, there's a man at the door who asked to see you. It's a black man."

Clueless, Sammy exited the dining room and re-opened the front door her dad had shut. "Jamaal! Jamaal! Oh my god! It's you!" She wrapped her arms around him, and then held him at arm's length, looking at him with astonishment.

"May I come in? Gosh, Sammy, you look like you've seen a ghost. I thought ghosts were white," he chuckled.

"Who is it, Sammy?" her mother yelled from the dining room.

"Please come in," Sammy said, giving him another hug. "You're here! You're not dead."

"Alive and well. I'm alive, anyway," he said.

Sarah Reisinger entered the room followed by her husband. "Sammy?"

"Mom, this is Jamaal Winston, er, Professor Jamaal Winston. Dad."

"At your service, ma'am. Sir," Jamaal said respectively.

"Jamaal was the man stuck with me in Providence. He was killed in a fire. At least I thought he was killed in a fire," Sammy said, breathlessly.

"Well, Professor Winston, you don't look dead to me," said Sarah. "But I'll bet you're hungry."

"Yes, ma'am," he smiled.

"Well," Sarah said, "we're just sitting down to eat. Ira, would you please grab another chair. Sammy, please set a place setting for your friend. Come on, let's go to the table."

"I can't believe this," Sammy kept repeating. She hugged him again. "What happened?"

Instead of telling her about his last days in Providence, as they ate he talked about the past few weeks. He hitchhiked south to Montgomery, Alabama, to try unsuccessfully to find his wife. Then he went to Auburn to see some of his professors from college. "But I knew if the lights ever came back on, I needed to find you again and tell you what happened to me and Emily. I'm so tired now. Can I tell you in the morning?"

"Where are you staying Professor Winston?" asked Sarah.

"Please, it is Jamaal. I'm not sure where I'm staying. I'm pretty much homeless right now. My backpack and my banjo are about it."

Ira looked at him menacingly and ahemed.

Sarah brushed off her husband's impoliteness. "Then you'll stay here with us. You're a friend of Sammy's so our house is your house."

"That's very kind of you, Mrs. Reisinger."

"Sarah. Please call me Sarah."

"Sarah, then. Thanks, and I'll take you up on that." Turning to Ira, he said, "And I promise not to overstay my welcome, sir."

Sarah rose and collected several plates from the table. "Sammy has been practicing some classical music. She's going to do a recital. Sammy, why don't you two go into the sunroom and you can show Jamaal what you've been working on? Ira and I will clean the table."

So Jamaal got his pack and his banjo from the living room and the two old friends went into the sunroom. Jamaal played only one song until he tired, but Sammy played for him until he fell asleep on the chair. "Jamaal, mom has made your bed in the guest room. Come, get some sleep." Showing him his room, towels, and bed, Sammy said, "I'm so glad you're alive. I'm so glad you're here."

"Me, too," he added.

Thursday, December 13

The next morning, Sammy broke from her routine to catch up

with her friend. They had breakfast together, and then went for a walk in the woods off Sherman Ridge Road, where a mere dusting of snow remained. "So what happened?" Sammy insisted.

"It's a long, complicated story. There's still a lot of it that I don't know and have just pieced together from what I saw and heard. Here goes.

"You remember Keene and Draper, the two men who were hassling me... really hassling both of us? After that little round of fisticuffs we had, they made a couple of threats. But I blew them off. I never figured they'd do anything crazy.

"The night of the fire, Emily asked me to go into the cave to get some herbs for her midwifery kit. I took my flashlight – it was after dinner and was dark anyway. I got inside and was fumbling around trying to find my way. Near where she stored her herbs, I found my banjo with its case and a small knapsack with some of my clothes and some food in it. On top of it was this note."

He dug a folded piece of paper from his pocket and handed it to Sammy. She unfolded it and read it aloud.

"Jamaal, You are not welcome in my house any longer. Please do not return. Emily."

"Wow," Sammy said. "I thought you two got along."

"We did! I always thought very highly of her. And I was sure she thought highly of me, too. So needless to say, I was pretty upset. I thought about it for awhile, there in the cold dark cave. I wondered if I had done something wrong. I couldn't reconcile it in my mind. Why would she send me to retrieve something and then tell me not to come back? It made no sense.

"So I decided I would return right away and apologize if necessary. I was within 200 yards of the house when through a window I saw a flame erupt in the living room. I took a few steps towards it. Then I figured something awful was happening inside and any attempts at doing something heroic would be fruitless. I knew it was best for me to vamoose."

"What do you think happened?"

"Most of this is conjecture. I think Emily got wind of the fact that these guys were coming for me. And she knew when. I think she lured them inside the house, perhaps telling them I was upstairs. Then she bolted the doors with the three of them inside and probably threw the oil lamp against the wall of books, splashing oil against flammable material."

"But she was inside, too!"

"True! I think she sacrificed herself to save me. Her health was declining rapidly. The cancer was beginning to kill her. She probably only had a few more weeks to live. I've often pictured in my mind the scene of these men running down the stairs after not finding me and instead finding that little grey-haired lady standing before a burning conflagration with a self-satisfied grin on her face, knowing she'd hornswoggled them."

"What did you do then?"

"Do you remember the people we met, Ebony and DeAngelo? I walked to their house and they hid me out for a couple of weeks until I decided to make my way to Montgomery. DeAngelo said he'd heard in Providence about the fire and everybody thought Emily and I had died in it. So it accomplished exactly what she had intended."

"Wow."

"Wow is right."

"You know," it occurred to Sammy, "I'll bet that was why she gave me those instruments when she did. Oh, do you know what else? A few days after the power came back on, I found several books about midwifery that had belonged to Emily. They were in Jackson's barn. I'm sure she left them there for me, knowing what she was about to do."

"Emily was a saint. She did so much for me..."

"...And for all the women of Providence, me included," Sammy concurred.

It began to snow lightly. Sammy tightened her jacket.

"Say, I've got a story to tell you, too." She told him about Bailey and about her unsuccessful search for the cabin in the days before her departure. "What do you make of that?"

"I have no idea. That is a puzzle we may never solve. I'll tell you one thing, though. The disaster sure brought out the best and worst in people."

"True enough!"

They returned to the house and had some lunch. The two of them jammed all afternoon. When he got tired, she continued playing, alternating between the bluegrass music she'd learned in Fries and the Vivaldi in front of her.

Sammy, Jamaal, and Sammy's folks lit seven candles that night. After dinner, Sammy and Jamaal played some show tunes, and on *Getting to Know You* from *The King and I*, Sarah sang all the lyrics she knew. Jamaal applauded heartily.

Before they said goodnight, Jamaal announced, "I'll be leaving tomorrow. Thank you all for your hospitality."

"Please don't run off," Sarah said.

"I've got some things I need to do down in Georgetown. I told you when I arrived that I wouldn't overstay my welcome."

Saying goodnight at his door, Jamaal asked Sammy, "Whatever happened to Emily's banjo and violin?"

She told him about recovering her Guarneri from Rhonda and the birth of Rhonda's baby. She continued, "I met two children at the edge of the New River back in September. When I got my Guarneri back, I didn't really feel like the instruments were mine to keep. Like rivers, instruments like that have much longer lives than people. It was great that Emily gave them to me. But I thought they belonged near that river, that old New River, in Providence. When I gave them away, it brought tears to my eyes to think those kids would someday be passing them on to their kids and theirs to theirs. I think I did the right thing; I hope so."

Jamaal smiled and began to hum, then to sing, "*Will the circle, be unbroken, by and by Lord, by and by.*" He kissed her on the cheek and went into his room, skipping merrily and singing, "*There's a better, home awaiting…*"

Friday, December 14

Jamaal prepared his satchel and banjo case for departure. Sammy walked with him to the end of the sidewalk. "How will you get to DC?"

"I'm not sure. I'll walk into town. Then I'll see about buses. If I can get to Newark, I think train service is improving every day."

"When will I see you again?"

"I'm going back south to continue to look for my wife. But you'll see me again. I promise."

"I will count my days," she smiled.

"Ah, the poetry of youth. You take care. I'll miss you."

"Likewise."

She walked with him to the edge of her yard and gave him a long-heart-felt hug. He backed one step away, put his hand to his heart, and then walked towards town.

Sammy waved at his vanishing figure, and then walked inside and returned to her work.

Saturday, December 15

Sammy spent the day playing her Guarneri with a singular focus. Her mom interrupted her around 2:00 p.m. to insist she get some food and some exercise. So she ate some lunch and took a walk around the neighborhood. There were some kids kicking a soccer ball around a street nearby, but the school's field, like so many others, had become a graveyard.

Sammy returned home and buried her eyes again in her music.

Sunday, December 16

Sammy awoke and opened the blinds to her window, and outside snow was falling gently. There appeared to be about two inches of accumulation. It had covered the pine trees in the yard and it was beautiful. She skipped her run, but instead did an indoor aerobic workout listening to classical music on the old transistor radio. During an afternoon break from practicing, she walked outside and caught snowflakes on her tongue like she'd done as a child. She thought about Jamaal and wondered if he was safe and warm. She thought about Jackson, and whether it was snowing in Providence, with flakes landing on his back. She thought about Pike, Woody, Carlene, and the Gallimore kids. And she thought about Avalon, perhaps donning her robe for the sauna, and she felt libidinous.

She passed several people also walking, and noted that many were smiling, something too rare during the blackout. Then it was back to her practice.

Monday, December 17

It snowed all day long, and the accumulation reached a foot. Sammy shoveled the sidewalk, convincing herself that her dad wouldn't do it. She felt stronger than she ever felt.

Back inside, she turned her music stand to the window, playing *Spring* over and over.

That evening, she got out her pen and paper and wrote another letter.

Dear Hattie, Rhonda, Dowell, and baby Emily,

I hope you are all doing well. I am home now practicing for a recital I am doing on New Years Day.

Hattie, I appreciate what you and Quint did to sustain me during the difficult time.

Rhonda, I'm sorry things became so strained between us. I hope all is forgiven and you have a happy, successful life.

Dowell, I know you are doing a good job of being the man of the house.

Baby Emily, I love you dearly.

I hope everyone has a nice Christmas.

So long,

Sammy

She addressed an envelope and took it to the mailbox, not knowing if there would be any restored mail service, but feeling good about writing anyway.

Thursday, December 20

Three days passed, each of them a carbon-copy of the days before, with running and horseback riding her only breaks from hours before her music stand. She practiced diligently, with the structured process she'd learned. She identified the difficult bars, determined why they were difficult, learned to play them, and then put them into the context of the overall piece.

When her arms were too tired to hold her bow, she still studied the sheet music looking for clues inside the notes as to the intentions of the composer. She wanted to ensure that her performance was better than good. She wanted to be *outstanding*. She wanted a performance that nobody in attendance would ever forget.

Friday, December 21

During breakfast, Sammy noticed on the calendar on the kitchen wall that it was December 21, the shortest day of the year and the first day of winter. She felt happy, thinking that a number of corners had turned since Thanksgiving. The sun would be returning now with each day longer than the prior.

Before practicing her music, she penned another letter.

Dear Avalon,

I think of you often and fondly. I am practicing diligently for my recital. Did I tell you I'm playing Vivaldi? I have made myself stay focused on this event. I think it is a technique to keep me from thinking about the future.

As bad as things were in Providence in the aftermath of the Pulse, this area suffered even worse. I'm glad I wasn't here.

My head is a mess. I learned so much about life and love in Providence. But I still don't know what it all means and where I am supposed to go with my life.

I love Hattie and I love Pike for what he did for me, and I love baby Emily. I love you, too, but I don't understand how.

I hope you have a Merry Christmas. I will be thinking about you.

Hugs,

Sammy

Saturday, December 22

"Sammy, you have a guest," said Sarah, leading a red-haired woman into the sunroom where Sammy held her violin by her chin.

"Ella!"

"Hi, Sammy. It's so good to see you! I've been worried sick about you."

"You, too. How have you been doing?" She gave her erstwhile chaperone a big hug. "Wow! I can feel how you've been doing. When are you due?"

"I'm due April 14th. I was at home with my fiancé when the Pulse hit. Like everybody else, we figured it was just a short power failure. Nothing else to do with the electricity out. You know…"

"Yes, I suspect we'll see a mini-baby-boom in the April time frame. Congratulations!"

Sammy could see Ella's jaw clench and face begin to quiver. Then Ella described her own personal nightmare scenario. Her mother, whose broken hip was Ella's reason for returning home, died a few weeks later due to complications. Ella and her fiancé were married in late September, but three weeks later, a band of thugs from the city rampaged through Alpine. Archie was never seen again. Ella took refuge in a convent affiliated with her church. She said, choking back tears, "I'm going to have to raise this baby myself."

Sammy hugged her, thinking about the horrors she'd seen. Then Ella continued, "The worst thing that happened to the community was the mass suicide. Did anyone tell you about it?"

"No. What happened?"

"About forty kids from The Hudson School took poison together about ten days after the Pulse. Many of them had left notes for their parents saying they understood their future was ruined and their present wasn't worth living. When they were discovered, they were lying in a large circle, dead. Of all the awful things, it was the most horrible." Sammy recoiled in thought, understanding that the dead would surely have included many of her classmates.

When it came to Sammy's turn, she tried to stay upbeat about her situation in Providence, working with Emily, learning midwifery, and knowing Jamaal, Pike, Caroline, Woody, and the others. She never mentioned the rape attempt, the kidnapping, or the hangings she'd witnessed. Or Avalon. She mentioned her special relationship with Jackson and that he'd saved her life twice, although she didn't go into details.

The two women chatted for nearly an hour when Ella decided to take her leave. Parting, she said, "I'm so relieved to know you're okay. I have felt guilty since the moment the Pulse struck and I knew you were stranded."

"You shouldn't have! You did nothing wrong. It was a horrible thing to go through, but it was no worse for me than anyone else. I think I've grown a lot. I certainly feel that I matured a lot."

"I understand you're doing a recital."

"Yes, I hope you can come."

"I'll see. Getting around is still problematic. But if I can find a ride, I will try to come."

"Goodbye."

"Bye."

Before returning to her music, Sammy picked a card from her Augury deck. It said, "Hearts Desires."

Sunday, December 23

For the first time since her practices began, she allowed her mother to sit and listen. Her mother was predictably complimentary, but Sammy heard the flaws and wasn't satisfied. Her practices continued.

Monday, December 24

On the days went. Her father reminded her it was Christmas Eve, but she was unmoved. She continued to work on her music, over and over again, breaking only for an afternoon run. That evening, she was rummaging through her things and came upon *Heart and Hands*, the midwifery book that Emily had given her. As she began thumbing through it, her mind swept back through all the deliveries she'd seen and assisted, both successful and unsuccessful, in Providence.

Tuesday, December 25

Sammy and her parents were invited to Christmas dinner with the Piaseckis.

Dinner was a nice, simple meal of beef and potatoes. Other food items were still scarce. The Piaseckis asked Sammy about her concert and invited her to play her violin, but she'd left it behind at home. She didn't feel ready to perform, so she used that as her excuse.

As the Reisingers departed for home, her father stumbled on the porch stairs and fell, landing on his face. He had a nasty gash across the bridge of his nose. Sammy and Mr. Piasecki helped him to his feet. Mrs. Piasecki produced a handkerchief to catch the blood dripping onto and staining the snow. Rather than walk back inside, Sammy and Sarah took him home. Bandaging him, Sammy again smelled alcohol on his breath.

Wednesday, December 26

Sammy was surprised the next morning to find Mrs. Piasecki at her doorstep. "How's your father?"

"He's okay. Thanks for checking on him. You're very kind."

"Listen, Sammy, I've got something to ask you. Earlier in my life, I was a pretty fair pianist. I know the recital you're doing is a special thing for you, but if you'd like an accompanist, I'd be happy to practice with you and share the stage."

"Yes, Mrs. Piasecki. I think that would be very nice. I've been a bit fanatic with my practicing lately. It would be good to have some company."

"Great! If we can start tomorrow, please come to my house. You're violin is easier to transport that my piano. I promise not to steal your thunder. It's your event."

Thursday, December 27

Sarah came into Sammy's room with a smile in her face and a letter in her hand. She said, "You have something here from one of your friends in Providence."

Sammy opened the letter excitedly. It was postmarked December 11, so it had taken over two weeks to get there. Sammy read it aloud to her mother.

My dear Sammy,

I hope this letter finds you safe and sound and happy to be home with your parents. The weather has been frightfully cold this week and we have new snow on the ground almost every day. I've been using the sauna often.

Sammy blushed after reading that aloud, wondering how much she'd told her mother about her closeness with Avalon and the night she almost froze to death.

I try to see Hattie, Rhonda, Dowell and the baby every few days. Hattie seems happier than I've seen her in years. Our community has suffered so much and it's great to see happy eyes again. Jackson seems lonely; there's nobody to ride him. I'm not sure he'd let anybody else ride him except you.

Everyone misses you terribly, but nobody more than me. We count the days until we see you again.

Much love,

Avalon

"That's very nice," said her mother, smiling.

Sammy ran to her and hugged her mother with all her might as her tears flowed.

Sunday, December 30

The final days of the year came and went and the year came to a close. Sammy spent three hours each morning practicing with Mrs. Piasecki. Then she returned home to practice more alone.

Monday, December 31

Sammy awoke and took one long look at every note and every bar of her music. She knew and was confident in her heart and mind that she was prepared as never before to perform flawlessly. She was ready. She took a long walk around Sussex and made a point to speak with everyone she met.

"Good luck to you tomorrow, Sammy!"

"I'm looking forward to your concert, Sammy. You'll be great!"

"Thanks for doing this concert for us, Samantha!"

Part 6: January

Tuesday, January 1

SAMMY VISUALIZED SNOW as she stirred with the beginnings of awakening in her warm bed. Sure enough, when Sammy opened her eyes and gazed outside, two inches of pristine white blanketed the ground. On this, her special day, municipal snow removal seemed to be a relic of pre-Pulse. But she decided to go for a short run to clear her mind and pump her circulatory system in preparation for the evening's work.

Again, several neighbors wished her good luck.

Upon her return home, she sat by the fire in the woodstove. As she rested, in her mind's eye she pictured each bow-stroke and fingering movement. She smiled with the self-satisfied feeling that she was ready to do her best.

She ate some lunch with her father, who seemed lethargic and cranky. Still, she admonished him to be on time that evening. She would go alone ahead of time to prepare.

She set aside two satchels, one with her dress and shoes for the evening and the other her red case containing her Guarneri. Then she took a long nap.

Her alarm buzzed at 4:00 p.m. She took a shower and dressed in wool pants, a flannel shirt, and riding boots. She pulled a card from the Augury deck. It said, "Timing."

She carried her violin case and her satchel containing her dress, makeup, and musical scores to the barn. She tacked up Wilbur and strapped the violin and satchel to her saddle. She hopped aboard and rode him into town in the snow, where she roped him to a metal railing fence around the church.

She went inside and spoke with Reverend Bender. He told her to make herself at home, and showed her where she could change into her dress. "I'm going home for an hour to have something to eat and

372

get my wife. We'll be back around 7:00 p.m."

Sammy dabbed on some makeup and donned her dress. She looked at herself in the mirror, and caught the glint of light reflecting from her Star of David necklace. She affixed her earrings. Then she carried her violin case to the pulpit, set three steps above the congregation floor.

Mrs. Piasecki arrived and Sammy helped her arrange her piano and the sheets of music. Reverend Bender had placed a microphone on stage for her. She turned on the sound system and then the mic. She tried the lights to make sure there would be sufficient illumination of Mrs. Piasecki's sheet music.

Sammy withdrew her precious Guarneri from the case. Lacking the electronic tuner that was ruined by the Pulse, she tuned it to the piano. She tightened her bow and made several long strokes with it. Then she and Mrs. Piasecki played the first two dozen bars to the first selection, Summer.

"Nice," said a woman who had walked in with three children, without Sammy's notice.

"Thank you. We're just warming up."

"It sounds great. I'm so excited about hearing live music again. I promise to keep my kids on their best behavior."

The kids looked to be perhaps nine, twelve, and fifteen. Sammy spoke to the youngest, a girl. "Have you ever heard a violin concert?"

"No ma'am."

"It will be long. Try not to think about the music itself. Try to think about where the music takes your mind."

"We're excited," the mother said. "Thanks for doing this. I hope my children become inspired by your music."

"Thanks for coming. You're very kind."

Other people began arriving, chatting with one another. Two black couples entered together. Sammy heard one man say he'd never been in this church before. An Asian man and a Caucasian woman arrived, holding hands. Sammy felt pleased in bringing people together.

Reverend Bender arrived with his wife. "Need any help?"

"No thanks. I think we're good to go. Oh, could we set up a card table in case anyone brings food?"

"Sure. I'll get one for the lobby."

Sammy went to the bathroom for the final time pre-show. She returned to the lobby and it was buzzing with activity. Mrs. Piasecki was visiting with friends of hers. Several bags of donated food had already been placed on the table. Sammy tried to greet each person individually to thank them for coming. All she heard back was, "Thank you so much for doing this for our community!"

Then, by premonition, she was pulled outside the front door. As she stood in the swirling snow, she saw a special visitor.

"Jamaal, my friend. Welcome."

"Samantha! You look stunning." He put down his belongings and gave her a big hug.

"Thank you so much for coming. I am so happy you are here."

"I wouldn't miss this for the world," he beamed.

"How did you get here?"

"Hitchhiked. Have you ever hitchhiked in a snowstorm?"

"Well again, I'm glad you're here. I dreamed you'd be here," she said, smiling. "I see you brought your banjo."

"Yup! I don't leave home without it."

"Come in please. Reverend Bender's wife Cindy will take your coat. Come help me greet my guests."

"Where are your parents?" he asked.

"I don't know. They should be here any minute."

"I'd like to sit with them when they arrive. I'll keep my eyes open for them."

Sammy visited with several more people as they arrived. The table rapidly filled with food. When the wall clock showed 7:20 p.m., Sammy and Mrs. Piasecki took their leave and went back to Reverend Bender's office, accompanied by him. He said, "I'll be happy to introduce you tonight."

"That would be great," Sammy said.

"Is there anything special you'd like me to say?"

"No, thanks. Just tell them who I am and thank Mrs. Piasecki for accompanying me. I'll introduce my pieces."

He left for a moment. As he re-entered the room, he said, "Are you ready?"

"Yes. Let's go."

Reverend Bender, Sammy, and Mrs. Piasecki walked on stage together. The audience applauded graciously. The Reverend Bender spoke into the microphone, "Good evening, ladies and gentlemen. Welcome to our church, those of you who attend here regularly and those here for the first time. Our doors are open to you regardless of your faith. Please come back any time.

"Tonight we have a special guest. Samantha Reisinger is here to perform three classical violin pieces for us tonight. She will be accompanied by our own congregation member Julia Piasecki. Please help me welcome Sammy."

The audience applauded again.

"Before I turn over the event to her, I would be remiss if I didn't mention that this event is entirely of Sammy's volition and initiative. Last year was the saddest, most difficult of most of our lives. With the New Year we symbolically celebrate a new beginning. Sammy's selfless act of making this happen is exemplary of the human spirit that I hope will permeate the New Year and the rest of our lives. When she is done, please thank her for her magnanimous gesture to our community. Sammy."

The audience applauded quietly. She adjusted the mic to her shorter stance.

"Good evening everyone. Thank you Reverend Bender for your kind introduction. Thank you Mrs. Piasecki for assisting me. And thank you all for coming.

"My name is Samantha Reisinger. From the day after the Pulse hit, until a month ago, I was a guest in the home of strangers in a small town in Southwest Virginia. I am alive this evening and in a position to play some of the most amazing music ever written on one of the most incredible instruments ever made due to the kindness of people who had no stake in my life except pure human kindness. And my musicianship, I think, is better because of my stay there.

"Five parts have come together tonight; the music, the instrument, the hall, the musicians, and the audience, to provide what I hope for you will be a special event. I already know it will be for me. You honor me by your presence. I hope I perform in a way befitting that honor.

"I have chosen three of the Vivaldi Concertos from what are collectively called *The Four Seasons*, to play for you tonight. These will be thematic to the tragedy we've endured. The first I will play is *Summer*. The third movement is a Presto, which is thought to evoke a thunderstorm. In fact, it is often called 'the storm' movement. It will represent that awful evening last August when the Pulse struck.

"The second I will play is *Winter*. I am skipping *Autumn*, symbolic of the plunge into the cold darkness that the months of September, October, and November represented.

"I will finish by playing *Spring*, which conveys a light, energetic, and optimistic mood which conforms to the emerging new era and the New Year. I hope this piece will be cathartic, helping us all wipe away the pain and suffering we've endured.

"Then I have an unannounced special encore piece, should I have earned your approval.

"We'll get started now. Thanks again for bringing the food that's in the back. Please take anything home you need for your family or friends. If there is anything left, Reverend Bender said he'd deliver it to the food bank. Thank you again for coming."

Sammy made a final adjustment of the microphone to her violin's position. She looked to Mrs. Piasecki who nodded her approval. The lights dimmed in the audience area. She looked over the audience again, but couldn't find her parents. Jamaal was there on the second row. He flashed a thumbs-up and smiled at her. The room was almost full. She placed a handkerchief across the chin rest and tucked the Guarneri under her chin. She took a deep breath, and then she began.

The first few bars came and were gone. She focused tightly on fingering her vibratos and maintaining proper pressure on her bow. The piece quickly passed, as she concentrated heavily on the minute placement of her left fingers on the strings. She felt peaceful, confident, and *Mushin no shin*: in the moment. During the third movement, the Presto, she felt a tear forming in her eye thinking about the ferocity of the Pulse.

At the piece's conclusion, she bowed as the audience applauded politely. "Thank you," she said into the microphone. She held her hand towards Mrs. Piasecki, who stood and bowed. The audience applauded her as well.

She took a sip of water from the glass Reverend Bender had left her. She closed her eyes and took a few deep breaths, preparing herself for the somber mood of the next piece.

Then she began again.

The second Concerto, *Winter*, was colored with icy high notes, with her left, fingering hand working well towards the body of the instrument and with some plucking, rather than bowing, of the strings. She bobbed and swayed with the music, heightening the intonation. It was difficult to see the audience with most of the lights directed towards her. But as she concluded, the audience reaction was somber, yet appreciative and respectful.

She launched into the *Spring* concerto with eagerness and enthusiasm. Her mind twirled around the impressive chapel and she saw angels singing and swirling. Because she was Jewish, the religious overtures weren't hers, but she felt their spirit nonetheless. She looked into the audience where Jamaal sat. With the dim light, she could barely make him out. But she smiled in his direction anyway. Then she saw an old man beside him, who looked kindly and familiar. She continued on, trying unsuccessfully to banish stray thoughts. A flood of impressions swept through her mind, dominated by her image of the New River, its flowing, gurgling waters, glistening in the morning sun. She felt newborn babies by her ear and heard the butterfly flutter of their heartbeats. She saw Jackson running, prancing through his pasture, free and grand. Her mind reached a strange detachment from the moment, as if her Guarneri had come to life, singing its vibrant song, as if it was the musician and she the instrument, it moving her fingers and bow spontaneously. She felt light-headed and buoyant, exuberant.

And then, the universe went dark. And the sound system failed.

The audience emitted a collective groan.

But her music continued. As if by the invisible hand of a great cosmic force, Vivaldi's brilliance still echoed through the sanctuary, silencing the audience. She saw in her mind's eye the notes emblazoned on a virtual screen before her. She kept playing. Her Guarneri kept playing, on and on. Bolder and louder! It was pitch-black in the cavernous room, but her Guarneri began radiating an eerie luminescence, as did her bow. The sound became grander and fuller, as if her Guarneri was rebelling, refusing to be silenced, insisting that it be heard, whether amplified or not. The angels danced from the panels of glass and began emanating their own colorful glow. The sound grew and grew, resonating every synapse in her body. She was sure the audience felt the same energy. The skin on her arms prickled and she felt adrenaline coursing through her veins. She was singularly focused, energized!

The last four bars came clearly into her mind and the piece neared its end. As quickly as they had gone off, the pulpit lights went on again. But the sound system still stayed off. Her room was purely sound, musicians, instruments, and audience.

And then, the music ended. There was a pregnant silence, and then the applause was vociferous, rapturous and thunderous. She was elated, ecstatic. Her eyes were moist. She brushed her handkerchief across her face, and then with Mrs. Piasecki took a deep bow.

"Bravo!" someone shouted.

"Thank you! Thank you! Thank you!" she bowed again. She directed the joy towards Mrs. Piasecki, rewarding her contribution.

"Hurrah!"

"Bravo!" Everyone stood and clapped.

"More!"

She bowed a third time.

"Encore!"

"Encore!"

"Thank you all so much," she yelled, her voice now unamplified. "Thank you so much for coming. Thank you."

"Encore!"

"Oh yes, I offered the possibility of an encore. For this number, I have a special guest in the audience who I'd like to accompany me. Could we please have the house lights on?"

The room was swept in artificial light. Mrs. Piasecki walked from her piano offstage and Sammy nodded thanks to her.

She pointed at her friend and said, "Jamaal Winston, would you please come on stage? Bring your banjo."

The older man was no longer next to Jamaal. But Jamaal got up and walked to the back of the chapel where he'd left his things. He removed his banjo and walked forward towards her. On his way, she said, "As I mentioned, I was marooned in a tiny community in Southwest Virginia during the blackout. The place was called Providence. As I have had this month to reflect, I have concluded it is no coincidence that I was placed there. Providence means the care, control, or guardianship of a deity. It was my destiny to be there and to receive the graces of that community. One of those graces was their music. It was primal, primitive, and imbued with the essences of life."

Jamaal wrapped the strap of his banjo over his head.

Sammy continued, "One of the people who kept me alive and sane was this kind gentleman before you."

Jamaal tuned his banjo and said to the audience, "Ladies and gentlemen, it is one of the greatest honors of my life to share the stage for just this brief moment with this incredible musician and wonderful human being. It may be true that Providence, Virginia, sustained Samantha Reisinger. But it is a hundred times truer that Samantha Reisinger sustained Providence, Virginia."

Sammy smiled warmly at her friend.

"We have a little tune to play for you," Sammy said. "It isn't classical. It wasn't written by Mozart or Beethoven or Bach. Perhaps nobody knows who wrote it. It is a simple tune, in the genre called Bluegrass, and it speaks of the pain and travails of the ages. It is called *Durang's Hornpipe*. Jamaal and I last played this tune on stage at the world's preeminent gathering of Bluegrass musicians in Galax, Virginia, the night the Pulse struck. I think it is fitting that in playing it again, we bookend that horrible time and prepare ourselves for a new beginning. We hope it will serve as a new beginning for you, too."

Jamaal added, "It was named for John Durang, who was reputedly George Washington's favorite performer, the first notable professional dancer born in America. Before we begin," he added, "this is not sit-in-your-chair music. This is stand-on-your-feet-and-clap music. There will be no more decorum here!" Everyone laughed.

Then she looked at him and nodded.

He began playing his banjo. She joined him, just as she'd done in Galax. The music built together and she couldn't suppress a wide grin growing on her face. The audience rose from their chairs and began clapping in time. He began smiling, too. As the song came to its close, everyone yelped and clapped harder.

"Thank you!"

"Thank you everyone," Jamaal echoed.

"Thank you for coming." The two musicians bowed graciously to the audience, then hugged each other.

Sammy placed her Guarneri in its case and with Jamaal walked towards the audience. She shook several hands and thanked as many people personally as she could. Everyone thanked her for putting the event together and spoke about how the joy they felt was palpable.

Gradually the audience filtered out. Sammy wiped down her violin and told Jamaal she'd change into her flannel shirt and wool pants. She rolled up her dress and put it in a bag, then emerged to find him ready to go.

"Did you see my parents?"

"No," he said sadly, knowing they'd missed a special moment.

"I don't think they were here at all," she said with resignation.

"I'm very sorry, Sammy. I hope they're okay. I know how much it meant to you to have them here."

"It's okay. We've all had lots of disappointments lately. I hope they're okay, too."

Sammy invited her friend to stay at the house, which she was sure he would accept. At his insistence, she rode Wilbur while he walked alongside, slowly. He talked non-stop about the concert, how magnificent and inspired was her musicianship and how rapt the audience was.

Nearing home, her curiosity overcame her. "Did you notice the older man sitting next to you?"

"Yes, he looked like he was 90 or older. He had a very kindly face and a familiar, pleasant manner. I don't exactly know when he arrived. One moment during your second piece, he was just there. During the gap before your final piece, I said, 'Good evening,' to him. He smiled at me and patted my hand, paternally. He said, 'It is a wonderful evening for me, the best night of my life.' Then you started playing again.

"In the middle of your final piece, *Spring*, he patted me on the hand again. I looked towards him. He was smiling, in fact beaming! He pointed a finger toward you and he nodded. And he said something too faint for me to hear. But I could easily tell what he was saying."

"What was it?"

"He said, 'That's my girl!' I figured he may have known you. He looked so proud. I nodded back, feeling the same pride. Do you know him?"

Choking back tears, Sammy said, "Yes, I think so. He's an old friend."

"Strangest thing, though," Jamaal continued. "When the lights went out, I know he was there beside me. But when the lights came back on, he was gone. How could a man that old slip away in the dark over a row of people without causing a stir? It was as if he wasn't real, as if I had envisaged him. He vanished like an apparition. I still can't quite get over it. What do you make of it?"

They reached her home and she dismounted Wilbur. "Well," she began, wondering what to say next. But before she could answer, a car she didn't recognize turned in the driveway. Her mother and father emerged, he with a sling around his neck.

"Ira, you go inside," Sarah told her spouse. "I'll be in in a minute."

Then to Sammy she said, "I am so sorry, Sammy. Your father drove the car into a ditch on the way to your concert. He was drunk. We spent the evening at the clinic downtown. Hi Jamaal. Thank you for being here. How did the concert go?"

"It was superb, Sarah! Your daughter was magnificent. She is a gift from heaven."

"Sammy, I am sorry. I am furious with your father. He may regret he didn't kill himself when he hears the tongue-lashing he's going to get from me in the morning. Come in, you two. I'm sure you're tired."

The trio went inside and prepared for bed. Sarah was correct; Sammy was tired. She kissed her mom and her friend on the cheek and fell fast asleep.

Wednesday, January 2

Sometime before dawn, she found Jamaal dressed and sitting beside her on her bed. "Sammy, my sweet child, I must go."

"Why so soon? Where are you going?"

"I appreciate having this place to stay overnight, but this is not my house. I don't want to be here when your dad gets that tongue-lashing your mom talked about. I suspect this is not your house anymore either. But you go back to sleep. There is still weariness in your eyes."

"Where are you going?" she asked again.

"Back south. I'm still holding hope that I can find my wife, although her trail seems to have turned cold. You never gave up hope your parents were alive and I'm not giving up, either. And I hear echoes of my grandfather Hurt back in Mississippi. The area he was from was one of the poorest in America. They may not have noticed we had a blackout," he laughed.

"When will I see you again?"

"I'm not sure. But you will. I found you here and I will find you again. You have a full life ahead of you. Go live it. You will always be in my heart."

He kissed her forehead and was gone.

Hours later, the sunlight hit her bedroom curtains as she still dozed. She heard her parents yelling at each other in the kitchen, but she stayed in bed. When she finally got up to have some breakfast, she passed her father. He said simply, "I'm sorry."

She smiled and walked back to her room where she put on running shoes and tights, a shirt and a jacket. She went into the snow and ran. The running was slow due to the wet, slippery conditions. But she ran the longest run in her life. Her mind felt clear and refreshed.

Upon her return, she found her parents in their living room, reading. "Mom, Dad, I have something to tell you. I'm leaving in the morning."

"What?" said her dad, incredulously. "Where are you going?"

"I'm going to Winston-Salem. I'm going to school."

She saw her parents looking at each other, not knowing what to say. Then her dad said, "We haven't even heard if there will be anything going on."

"I'm going anyway," Sammy said assertively. "If there is nothing going on, I'll help make something go on."

"Are you sure you're doing the right thing?" her mom asked.

"I don't know. But I need to follow my heart. My heart isn't here in New Jersey."

Again, her parents looked at each other, seemingly realizing that dissuading her would be futile.

Sammy broke the silence and said, "Is there bus service from here to Newark?"

"I think so, baby. I'll check it for you," her mom said.

Thursday, January 3

The next day, she packed her things. She filled her soft suitcase with six shirts, four shorts, two long pairs of pants, two belts, two pair of shoes, and a heavy jacket. She had a toothbrush, hairbrush, makeup, and some jewelry. She packed her *Forever-lite* forehead flashlight. She packed the photo of her grandfather and the photo Woody had taken of her with Jamaal, Emily, Avalon, Caroline, Marissa, and Pike at her birthday party. She packed *Heart and Hands*, the book Emily had given her.

And she had her Guarneri inside its case. Before packing her Augury cards, she drew one from the deck. It said, "You're on the right path."

She kissed her dad on the cheek and said, "Please, dad, stay off the bottle."

"I'll try. Good luck honey. Let us hear from you."

"I will."

Then her mother drove her to town to the bus stop. Her mother handed her six small gold pieces. "Put these in your pocket. I hope they come in handy when you need them."

"Bye, mom. I love you."

"Love you too, sweetheart."

The bus took her to the Newark train station, which was buzzing with activity. The train system had been the first transportation system to revive after the blackout ended. The railroad companies had worked cooperatively to transfer working locomotives from the West Coast to the East, and broken locomotives to the West for refurbishing. Passenger cars had been carried from overseas and from all over the continent to carry the huge demand of passengers. Sammy changed trains in Philadelphia. The itinerary said, "Harrisburg, Hagerstown, Martinsburg, Winchester, Harrisonburg, Staunton, Roanoke, Wytheville, Bristol, Knoxville." The further south she went, the less snow there was.

Friday, January 4

The train rumbled overnight and Sammy slept intermittently in her seat. Her mind was conflicted but strangely elated. She was uncertain what the future would bring, but was optimistic about it nonetheless.

It was daybreak when it stopped in Roanoke. Sammy stayed on board until Wytheville, where she debarked for a local bus with the itinerary of "Galax, Mt. Airy, Winston-Salem, Greensboro, Raleigh."

The bus was an old diesel, looking like a relic of the 1960s. As Sammy stood in line to board, the driver, a good-natured black woman in a grey uniform punched the ticket of each passenger and announced destinations.

"Mt. Airy. Good morning, ma'am."

"Raleigh. That's my home. Welcome aboard, sir."

"Greensboro. Good morning sir."

The driver took Sammy's ticket from her and said, "Good morning sweetie. Winston-Salem. Welcome aboard." She punched it, and then handed it back. Sammy thanked her, and then sat alone on the second row.

The bus backtracked to the northeast to Fort Chiswell, and then turned due south. It rumbled over the huge Interstate 77 Bridge crossing high above the New River and the trail Sammy had walked three months earlier on her walk with Jamaal and Pike to Blacksburg. The driver left the Interstate in Galax and drove a half-mile away to a strip mall that served as a bus stop.

Several people sat on outside benches. One was a mother with two children, wrapped in jackets. An older man looked up and Sammy caught his eye. He had a kindly face and seemed familiar.

The driver yelled to her passengers, "Ladies and Gentlemen, please take a bathroom break if you need to. We depart in five minutes."

Sammy looked at the man through her frosted window. Not understanding her own motivations, she picked up her travel bag and her violin case, and got off the bus. She felt compelled to sit by him, but as she reached the bottom step of the bus, she realized he had vanished. She walked to the bench and sat where she'd seen him sitting. A bright winter sun shone on her cheeks, warming them. She lost herself in thoughts unexplainable.

A few minutes later, the driver ascended the three stairs to her bus and then yelled, "All aboard." The door closed on the bus.

Then the door opened again. The driver descended the stairs and walked towards Sammy. "Sweetie, I've got a schedule to keep. Are you getting back on board?"

Sammy looked up at her and smiled.